ALSO BY SAMANTHA YOUNG

THERE WITH YOU

AN ADAIR FAMILY NOVEL

SAMANTHA YOUNG

There With You

An Adair Family Novel
Book Two

By Samantha Young
Copyright © 2021 Samantha Young

Drip Drop Teardrop, a novella

Titles Co-written with Kristen Callihan

Outmatched

Titles Written Under S. Young

True Immortality Series:
War of hearts
Kiss of Vengeance
Kiss of Eternity: A True Immortality Short Story
Bound by Forever

Fear of Fire and Shadow

War of the Covens Trilogy:

Hunted
Destined
Ascended

ABOUT THE AUTHOR

Samantha Young is a *New York Times*, *USA Today* and *Wall Street Journal* bestselling author from Stirlingshire, Scotland. She's been nominated for the Goodreads Choice Award for Best Author and Best Romance for her international bestseller *On Dublin Street*. *On Dublin Street* is Samantha's first adult contemporary romance series and has sold in 31 countries.

Visit Samantha Young online at
http://authorsamanthayoung.com
Instagram @AuthorSamanthaYoung
Facebook http://www.facebook.com/authorsamanthayoung

ACKNOWLEDGMENTS

Living in Ardnoch with the Adair siblings continues to be a beautiful escape from a difficult year, and I hope it provides a wonderful escape for my readers too.

For the most part, writing is a solitary endeavor, but publishing most certainly is not. I have to thank my wonderful editor Jennifer Sommersby Young for always, *always* being there to help make me a better writer and storyteller.

Thank you to Julie Deaton for jumping on to proofread *There With You* in the final hours! I appreciate it so much and thank you for catching those sneaky Britishisms that creep into my American characters' dialogue now and then.

And thank you to my bestie and PA extraordinaire Ashleen Walker for handling all the little things and supporting me through everything. I appreciate you so much. Love you lots!

I want to say a huge thank you to Catherine Cowles, who not only let me to ramble on and on about Regan and Thane's story for weeks, lol, but was also so generous with her time as to read an early copy of their romance. You are an amazing light of support and kindness in the book community (and beyond!), Catherine, and I'm so very grateful for your friendship!

The life of a writer doesn't stop with the book. Our job expands beyond the written word to marketing, advertising, graphic design, social media management, and more. Help from those in the know goes a long way. A huge thank-you to Nina Grinstead at Valentine PR for your encouragement, support, insight and advice. You're a star!

Thank you to every single blogger, Instagrammer, and book lover who has helped spread the word about my books. You all are appreciated so much! On that note, a massive thank-you to the fantastic readers in my private Facebook group, Sam's Clan McBookish. You're truly special and the loveliest readers a girl could ask for! Your continued and ceaseless support is awe-inspiring and I'm so grateful for you all.

A massive thank-you to Hang Le for once again creating a stunning cover that establishes the perfect visual atmosphere for this story and this series. You amaze me!

As always, thank you to my agent Lauren Abramo for making it possible for readers all over the world to find my words. You're phenomenal, and I'm so lucky to have you!

A huge thank-you to my family and friends for always supporting and encouraging me, and for listening to me talk, sometimes in circles, about the worlds I live in.

Finally, to you, thank you for reading. It means the everything to me.

1

REGAN

The Scottish countryside was pretty epic, a contrasting yet perfect combo of lush and rugged, bright grass greens, muddy browns, and ambers. Smooth, rolling hills and then startling peaks and troughs. But I remained untouched by its heroic scenery as the cab drove through the Highlands from Inverness-shire to Sutherland. To Ardnoch Estate. I could see it with my eyes, but I couldn't feel it with my heart. I couldn't feel anything past the nervous churning in my gut.

My decision to flee Boston for Scotland only hit me as the flight from London descended toward Inverness. The Highland airport couldn't have been in a more picturesque spot, sitting near the banks of a lake, or a loch as they call it in Scotland. The water was surrounded by the hills that immediately came to mind when anyone said the words Scottish Highlands.

Yet I'd wanted to vomit as soon as the wheels juddered on impact with the runway.

Knee bouncing as I watched the time on my phone tick

by, I tried to regulate my breathing. The winding roads were not helping my nervous nausea.

"How much farther?" I asked the driver. Again.

He stared at me in the rearview mirror. "We're only about ten minutes away fe Ardnoch." His brow furrowed. "Ye sure they'll let ye in? A long way ta come ta be turned away."

This would be the third time he'd asked. And for a reason. Our destination was Ardnoch Castle and Estate, an exclusive members-only club for the film and TV industry's elite. To join, potential members had to pay an extortionate fee on top of annual dues. Its owner was an ex-Hollywood action star, the Scottish actor Lachlan Adair. The estate once belonged to his family, and he'd turned it into a prestigious members-only club.

And I knew all that because he's dating my big sister.

"I'm sure."

The thought of Robyn made those butterflies in my belly swarm. I couldn't wait to see her, and yet I dreaded it. I'd made so many mistakes, and I didn't know how to fix them.

I'd never been good at admitting when I was wrong or knowing how to turn things around. Robyn had always been my guide. Not anymore.

A horrible ache flamed in my chest, joining the butterflies.

"I've never had a fare wantin' ta go ta Ardnoch. Aye, ma wife will find this aw a bit interesting, I'll tell ya that. She's fascinated by aw yone celebrity stuff, ye ken. Makes me take day trips yone way ta see if she can catch a wee glimpse of a famous person. Or Adair himself. We're fe Macduff, nor-east of here, an' we moved ta the Sneck—that's Inverness, ye ken—a few years back ta be nearer ta the bairns and the granbairns, but sometimes I think ta maself the wife moved us here ta be nearer ta Ardnoch." He chuckled, completely oblivious that I couldn't understand a damn thing he was saying. Did everyone in Scotland speak like this? If so, I was screwed.

"'Tis a good thing ye arrived on such an auspicious day. Ta see the Highlands in aw its beauty. But be prepared, it can be a right dreich place and summer will be fast endin'. I hope ye packed mare than yer dookers? Ye got yer ganzies and yer wellyboots wi' ye? 'Cause it'll turn from right mochie ta right oorlich faster than ye can blink."

It sounded like there was a question in there. "Yeah?" I answered.

"Aye, aye, that's good. A well-prepared lass, that's what I like ta see." He peered at me in the rearview. "Ye sure ye're awright? Yer lookin' a wee bit peelie-wally back there?"

I understood half of that. "I'm okay."

It wasn't a complete lie. Part of me was shit-scared to see Robyn again, but I was so relieved to be out of Boston and heading to one of the most heavily secured estates on the planet. Especially since one of their former members went all stalker/murderer on Lachlan and my sister.

The thought made me flinch. I couldn't face the idea of something happening to her. Which was why our relationship was in the mess it was in.

My visit to see Robyn was so past overdue. There was no excuse for it.

Robyn, my big sister, my hero, the love of my freaking life, probably hated me.

What did I do?

How did I approach her?

With my usual easy-breezy Regan way?

Or did I get down on my knees and beg her to forgive me?

I winced just thinking about the latter. I wasn't a "get down on my knees and beg for forgiveness" type. And yet, no one deserved an apology more than Robyn. She'd been through the toughest eighteen months of her life. And where was I?

Hiding.

Like a coward.

Biting my lip against the fresh tears pricking my eyes, I stared unseeing into the woodlands as we passed. There was never a better time for me to put my acting skills to good use.

"Almost there," the driver announced, and I heard his turn signal moments before we turned right down a short gravel drive. A vast brick wall and massive wrought iron gate abruptly blocked our way.

"What now?" I asked.

"Dinna ken." He craned his neck around to look at me. "De ye have the number of someone inside?"

I did. I had Robyn's international number, but I'd never used it. And I was kind of hoping there would be a run-up to seeing her. Maybe it would be Uncle Mac who came to the gates.

The thought of Uncle Mac caused some confliction. Part of me was excited to see Robyn's birth father, but another part still hated him for how much his abandonment had hurt her.

Robyn and I are half sisters. My dad is Seth Penhaligon, a Boston detective. Robyn's dad, Mac, is Scottish and met our mom, Stacey, when he came to the States to live with a relative. He lied about his age (he was only sixteen!) and got our college-age mom pregnant with Robyn. They split soon after, and Mac introduced Mom to my dad. By then, Mac was a cop, along with Dad, though Mac eventually left the police force and got into private security.

I'd adored Uncle Mac. He was this big, handsome Scot who told the most amazing stories. When I was around eight and Robyn was twelve, he took a job as part of the young

Hollywood actor Lachlan Adair's private security team. Other than a visit when Robyn was fourteen, she never saw Mac again.

Until almost six months ago, when she'd come to Scotland to hash things out with him. Mac was now head of security at Ardnoch Estate.

And boy, Robyn had gotten a lot more than she'd bargained for.

Self-reproach was a knife across my gut.

"Well?" the cabbie asked.

"Uh …" I glanced down at my phone. Well, damn. I'd thought there would be a security booth with a guard in it at the gate. Before I could launch into a feeble explanation about why I didn't want to call the one person who could grant me access, the driver said, "Someone's comin'."

I glanced up and saw a black Range Rover coming down the gravel drive surrounded by dark woodland on either side. The vehicle stopped and a man got out. He was stylish for a security guard, wearing black suit pants and a beautifully tailored black shirt, along with very cool sunglasses. I noted a wired earpiece in his left ear.

"That's yer cue," said the driver.

Taking a deep breath, I got out of the cab, my stiletto heels wobbling on the gravel. Straightening my shoulders and pasting on a bright smile, I sashayed toward the gate, ignoring the slip of my heels.

"This is private property. I'm going to have to ask you to leave," the man behind the gate said in a softer Scottish brogue that I could actually understand.

"I don't think so, handsome." I grinned, wrapping a hand around a bar of the gate. "I'm here to see my sister."

His expression (what I could see of it behind the glasses) didn't change. "And who might that be?"

"Your boss's babe."

"Elaborate."

Despite my nervousness, my smile was genuine. This guy was a hoot. "I'm Regan Penhaligon. Robyn's sister."

I thought I detected a slight change in his demeanor, but I wasn't sure. "Do you have identification?"

"Uh, I have my passport."

"I'll need to see it."

"Wow, you guys really do take your security seriously, huh?" *Works for me*, I thought, as I wandered back to the cab and pulled open the back passenger door.

"Everythin' awright?" the cabbie asked as I rifled through my large purse for my passport.

"Terminator over there just wants identification."

The cabbie chuckled as I found the passport.

I wanted to race across the gravel driveway. Now that I was this close to seeing my sister, I wanted it over with. I needed to know if she hated me or if we could get past this. However, my pride forced me to act cool and casual as I walked to the gate.

"Here you go." I passed the passport through the decorative bars.

Security Guy took it and flipped it open. After a quick scan, he said, "One moment, please."

Pressed against the gate, I watched as he stalked to his SUV, leaned in, and spoke in an inaudible murmur, to whom I didn't know. But seconds later, he returned. "I'll need you and the driver to hand over any recording devices—mobile phone, cameras, etc."

"Are you serious?"

His answer was a stony nothing.

He was serious.

With a sigh, I handed over my cell and then went to tell the cabbie the news. My driver seemed completely unperturbed about handing over his phone.

"You're not annoyed?" I asked quietly through his window.

"Och, no. They could have just had ye switch vehicles. This means I'm driving ye in. Not many folks get ta drive onta Ardnoch Estate. Wait till ma wife hears aboot this."

"Okay, great!"

Glad he was chipper about the whole thing, I took his phone to Security Guy, who confiscated it and instructed, "Tell your driver the gates will open momentarily. He will follow my vehicle and not deviate. We'll escort him back to the gate once we've delivered you to your sister and he'll get his phone back then."

His militant attitude amused me so much it almost distracted me from Robyn. "Okay, Sarge." I returned to the cab. After I got in, I relayed the info and we waited. First the Range Rover did a tight U-turn, and then the gates opened.

Those anxious butterflies came back with a vengeance while my cabbie hooted, "My Carolann will no' believe this. Pity they took ma phone. Wid have loved some pictures."

I couldn't answer.

I pressed my forehead to the window as the cab drove slowly up a gravel drive through thick woodlands. Sunbeams cut through the trees, casting rays across the vehicles' path. And it seemed awhile before we were driving out of them into bright sunshine that illuminated manicured lawns. Miles of them. Flat near the building in the distance, but increasingly rolling farther away. Little flags on the distant lawns suggested it was a golf course.

The gravel drive led toward the immense building up ahead.

Not just any building.

A castle.

My sister's boyfriend owned a freaking castle.

With turrets and everything.

"Holy shit," I whispered as we drew nearer. The castle was six stories tall and who knew how old. It was like Downton Abbey, but bigger. The thought of Downton Abbey reminded me of bingeing the show with Robyn. An ache flared in my chest, along with another flurry of nerves in my belly. Eyeing the parapets and the St. Andrew's Cross flag that fluttered in the breeze, I took in a deep breath.

It was then I spotted the people standing outside the majestic building awaiting our arrival.

Waiting for me.

The cab pulled up, and I focused on no one but my sister.

Robyn.

She stood huddled into a man's side, her eyes on my cab. Dressed in workout gear, little makeup, and hair scraped back into a ponytail.

And she'd never looked more beautiful.

Memories flooded me and I wanted to launch myself out of the vehicle and into her arms and have her take care of everything.

Yet I knew it couldn't be that way anymore.

Instead, I forced a smile, threw open the passenger door, and stepped out. Hand to my hip, I cocked it, pushing my grin so my dimples appeared. "Hey, sis." I winked at her. "Did you miss me?"

2

REGAN

....

T he way Robyn stared blankly at me, I realized I'd made a fundamental error in my greeting.

I knew my sister better than I knew anyone.

Hurt hid behind her obvious anger.

Ignoring the two men at her side, my smile faltered, and I stepped toward her.

"*I missed you*," I confessed.

Robyn pulled out of the very recognizable Lachlan Adair's embrace and crossed her arms defensively as she neared me. "Funny, it hasn't seemed that way for the past eighteen months. Not after I got shot, not after Dad got stabbed, or after Lucy Wainwright tried to murder Lachlan and me."

Holding back a flinch, I swallowed hard. My sister was a cop who got shot in the line of duty. That moment was the beginning of my life spiraling out of control. Robyn quit, opened a photography business, and around a year after she was shot, she traveled to Scotland to find some closure with her father, Mac Galbraith. Mom and Dad said her relationship with Mac was in a good place, despite Robyn falling in love with his boss and best friend Lachlan Adair.

As for Lucy Wainwright, she was an Oscar-winning actor who had been a member of the club and a good friend of Lachlan's. However, according to my mom's retelling, she wanted more than friendship from him and when she couldn't have it, she started leaving threatening messages around the estate. Things escalated when the estate mechanic joined her in the misdeeds. The mechanic stabbed Mac, attacked Robyn, ran her off the road, and then helped Lucy kidnap Lachlan. Robyn was the one who found Lachlan, and with help from a local farmer, they both escaped unscathed. The mechanic didn't. Lucy killed him right before she tried to kill my sister. Now the actor was facing trial, which meant my sister was also facing said trial as a witness.

There was no excuse for my absence from Robyn's life through all that.

Not a good one, anyway.

Robyn was the brave one. I was the coward.

"I'm here now." I put my arms around her and squeezed.

Closing my eyes against the burn of tears, I realized my sister had changed her perfume. For years, she'd worn the same scent. I'd even bought her a bottle at the airport. But she smelled different.

And she felt different.

She was hard and unyielding in my arms.

Once upon a time, there was nothing better than a Robyn hug.

Realizing she wasn't going to return my embrace, my heart crumpled and I pulled away. But then she made an aggravated sound in the back of her throat seconds before her arms closed around me.

Tears stung my nose as I pressed my cheek to her

shoulder and clung to her. She held me so tight I could barely breathe, but I didn't care.

"I could kill you," she whispered hoarsely.

Hearing the pain in her voice, my eyes flew open and caught in Lachlan's cool, azure gaze. His eyes narrowed, his expression softening from hard to thoughtful at whatever he saw on my face. Disconcerted, I pulled out of Robyn's embrace and slapped her arm playfully. "But what a dull place the world would be if you did."

My sister studied me with those penetrating, ever-changing eyes of hers. I'd always been jealous of the eyes she'd inherited from Mac. While we shared the same large, oval shape, Robyn's were technically hazel, but they changed color depending on her mood or the surrounding colors. Mine were an ordinary chestnut brown.

"Eh, hate ta interrupt, but the meter is still tickin', ya ken," the cab driver called behind me.

"Pardon?" I wrinkled my nose in confusion.

"The. Meter. Is. Tickin'. Ya. Ken," he repeated like I was deaf.

To be fair, saying it slower and louder meant I picked up the word *meter* and deduced what he was saying from that. "Damn. Okay." I flicked Robyn a look. "Let me just pay this guy." I lowered my voice. "He's been talking about some random guy called Ken the entire ride up here like I'm supposed to know who that is."

Mirth suddenly brightened Robyn's eyes, and she made a choking sound.

"What?"

She swallowed another snort of laughter and replied, her voice trembling with amusement. "He's saying 'you know.' 'Ken' means 'know' in Scots."

I laughed loudly at my mistake, and we shared a grin.

11

Then something like mistrust entered my sister's expression, and the light moment dissipated as quickly as it happened.

"Jock will take care of your fare." Lachlan approached and nodded beyond me. I turned to see Sarge (a.k.a. Jock) leaning in to pay the driver; a guy dressed in a modern version of livery retrieved my suitcase from the trunk. This place really was like Downton Abbey, or at least one of the estates described in my beloved racy historical romances.

"My purse is on the back seat," I said, but the guy was already pulling it out of the cab for me. "Thank you!" I waved at the driver, who gave me a big smile.

"So," Robyn said, "you could have just returned my phone calls. You didn't need to come all the way to Scotland."

"Of course, I did. I wanted to make sure you were okay. And to see what the allure was." I covered my hurt at her defection from Boston. Did she even think about me when she decided to move to an entirely different continent?

I winced at my selfishness. Robyn didn't owe me anything.

Lachlan, whose face I'd seen a million times in film, was obviously a pivotal part of the appeal. A good few inches over six feet tall, broad shouldered, clothes that showcased the body of an action star, sandy-blond hair, unshaven cheeks, and rugged features. The man was a blaze.

Then my eyes met Uncle Mac's.

I tensed.

He was ... not at all what I'd expected. Younger looking than I'd anticipated. But then, he was only in his mid-forties. Even then, he didn't look his age. The same height as Lachlan, Mac was just as broad shouldered, possibly even more muscular in his tight black T-shirt that showed off all that power. His dark hair was speckled with salt and pepper, and he wore it longish so it curled around his nape. Also like Lachlan, he had that designer stubble thing going on.

He was a dead ringer for that guy out of *True Blood* and *Magic Mike*, and he didn't look any older than Lachlan.

I couldn't call him Uncle Mac anymore. It was too weird. "Jesus, Mac, it's been an age and yet you've stopped aging, apparently." I eyed him thoughtfully. "I suppose if Robyn forgives you, I guess I should, huh?"

Mac studied me. "It's been a long time, Regan. We've been worried about you."

My smile strained. "Worried about moi? Why ever for? I'm fabulous." I spun on my heels and gestured up to the castle. "And clearly so is Robyn." I glanced over my shoulder at my sister. "A boyfriend with a castle. Nice."

"Fiancé," Robyn corrected, lifting her left hand.

A diamond winked blindingly in the sunlight.

It knocked the breath right out of me.

Robyn was engaged.

She was *marrying* Lachlan Adair.

My sister was engaged and I hadn't known about it?

She was never coming back to Boston.

I wanted to scream at her. I wanted to tell Lachlan to go screw himself. Why couldn't he have married one of the millions of other women who must have thrown themselves at him over the years?

But I knew why.

There was no one like Robyn.

She was special.

And the bastard had snapped her up and stolen her away.

Lachlan's gaze was sharp, probing. Quickly banking my ire toward him, I shrugged and threw my hands in the air, my voice a little too high-pitched as I cried, "Well, this calls for champagne!"

My sister had been wrong when she talked me out of running away to New York to become a thespian. I'd have made a damn good actor.

Instead of champagne, Robyn and Lachlan bundled me into another Range Rover with my luggage and informed me I'd be staying with them at Lachlan's home. This unwelcome news had concerned me, but I'd covered it, pretending not to be perturbed. I'd stupidly assumed that Lachlan's home was on Ardnoch Estate.

Under heavy security.

It wasn't.

They didn't even provide me with a tour of the place before they escorted me off the damn grounds.

Standing at the edge of Lachlan Adair's backyard—a grassy cliff that jutted over the sea—I experienced an emotion that shamed me.

Jealousy.

A bracing, cool evening wind pushed at my body, whipping dangerously at the short hemline of my dress. I didn't care. Who was here to see me flash them? My sister's fiancé's home felt like it was on the edge of nowhere. If it weren't for the identical house next door, it would feel like I was on some alien, lonesome part of the planet.

My sister's fiancé.

That painful lump in my throat returned.

Fighting back tears that made me feel small and childish, I couldn't rid myself of the image of Robyn cuddling Lachlan as I sat in the back of the SUV waiting. He'd bent his forehead to hers, murmuring something. It was clear he was asking if she was okay.

I didn't know what she'd replied, but I could guess it

wasn't good. They'd shared a lingering kiss filled with so much emotion I had to look away. It seemed intrusive to watch.

Never mind the surreal surroundings I found myself in; what was discombobulating was seeing Robyn with Lachlan. I'd never seen her so into a guy before. Like … staring at him as if he were her universe, and vice versa.

I pushed down my envy.

Not because she'd found that—I wanted that for Robyn. I wanted her to have the most fulfilled, amazing life anyone could ever wish for. Yet in finding it, I was losing her even more than I already had.

Fiancé.

"So when did you get engaged?" I asked when they got into the vehicle.

"I just proposed," Lachlan replied.

That made me feel somewhat better. I'd thought maybe she'd told Mom and Dad that she didn't want me to know just yet. And the thought of her keeping something so huge from me hurt.

Which was completely hypocritical since I'd been keeping stuff from her for over a year.

Still. Robyn was getting married.

And to Lachlan Adair, of all people.

Knowing how much Robyn used to resent Lachlan—considering she'd thought he was complicit in Mac's abandonment of her—it was a shock when our parents told me she was in a relationship with him and staying in Scotland.

She and I were the estranged ones now.

How life had flipped, huh?

"Who are *you*?"

I startled.

Following the young, high-toned voice, I turned to my right.

Lachlan's yard and his neighbor's weren't separated by a fence. I'd thought it odd. His beautiful, contemporary, clearly architect-designed house was perched over the water in a little place Lachlan called Caelmore, just outside the village of Ardnoch.

Needing a breather, not wanting my sister to see past my devil-may-care attitude, I'd abandoned my luggage in the luxurious guest room Lachlan had shown me to, kicked off my shoes, and strode out via the wall-to-wall bifold doors at the back of the open-plan living space. They led onto a deck with steps that took me to grass that stretched onward to the cliff's edge.

A security fence sat along the cliff's edge. Staring at the two small children who gawked at me in curiosity, I guessed the fence was for their safety. They both had dark hair and wore the same light blue sweaters with an embroidered logo on the chest. The girl wore a blue-and-black-plaid skirt, while the boy wore black pants. School uniforms.

"Hey." I grinned as I walked toward them. "I'm Regan."

The little boy stood straighter, puffing out his chest as he grabbed onto the smaller girl's hand. "We're not supposed to talk to strangers." He spoke in a lovely, anglicized accent, his Scottish brogue pushing through here and there, particularly prominent in his hard *t*'s.

I nodded, trying not to laugh. "That's a good rule. But you asked me a question first."

The boy looked down at the girl in irritation. "That was Eilidh's fault." He pronounced her name *Ay-Lay*. "You know better, Eilidh."

Eilidh wasn't paying attention. She was staring at my feet. "Where are your shoes?"

I curled my toes into the cool grass and gestured to the house. "I left them inside."

The boy frowned. "You know Uncle Lachlan and Aunt Robyn?"

It was a gut punch.

"Aunt Robyn?" I whispered.

The boy nodded. "She's going to be Uncle Lachlan's wife, so we're allowed to call her Aunt Robyn now."

Tightness crawled across my chest. "You live next door?"

His eyes narrowed in suspicion. "I'm not sure I should answer that. You're still a stranger."

If I wasn't currently suffering from debilitating jealousy and hurt that my sister had gone and created a whole new life that didn't involve me, I might have laughed.

"Eilidh, Lewis," a deep, masculine voice called, drawing our attention. A tall man with broad shoulders and an unkempt appearance strode toward us. His eyes were on me as he stopped behind the children, his hands protectively on their shoulders. "Who do we have here?"

I strode forward and his gaze lowered down my legs to my bare feet. I could have sworn his lips twitched, but it was hard to tell because a thick brown beard surrounded his mouth.

"Hey." I held out my hand to him. "I'm Regan Penhaligon."

His blue-gray eyes narrowed slightly, and then his hand was in mine. He gave me a strong, firm shake, and I felt the rasp of the calluses on his palm as he released me. "You're Robyn's sister."

"Yeah." *And you are?*

"I'm Lachlan's brother, Thane. These are my children, Eilidh and Lewis. We live next door. Robyn didn't say you were coming."

I smiled, shrugging my shoulders and replying breezily, "I surprised her."

His eyes turned a cool blue. "I see."

And I got the impression he did see.

Shame made my skin hot.

I wasn't stupid. It wasn't just Robyn who was acting weird and cold with me. Mac and Lachlan had been equally cool. I knew I deserved it, but it was still horrible. Obviously, Robyn had told Lachlan and Mac I'd flaked on her, and it seemed Lachlan had spread the word to his family members.

"Yeah. Isn't it great?" I grinned falsely. "I've never been to Scotland before. Fantastic houses, by the way."

"Dad designed them," Lewis piped up. "He's an archi ... archi*tect*, and I'm going to be one too."

Wow.

I stared at Thane, seeing him in a new light. Honestly, he gave off a kind of lumberjack vibe. Thick, sandy-blond hair, a beard that was more brown than blond and in desperate need of a trim, and not exactly country-chic attire. His cable-knit sweater had seen better days, his jeans were so faded it was a wonder they weren't falling apart, and he wore a pair of muddy hiking boots.

His appearance did not say extraordinarily talented architect.

Then again, I should know all about not judging a book by its cover.

"That's amazing," I said, genuine. "Really, the houses are beautiful." The two plots were almost identical except each had a second, differently sized building made of the same materials. The one on Thane's plot was a little larger, like a guest house.

Uncertainty glimmered in his eyes. "Thank you."

"Daddy, can I take off my shoes too?" Eilidh suddenly asked.

I smiled. "It feels pretty nice."

"You'll catch a cold." Thane shook his head. "Anyway, it's teatime." He turned his son and daughter toward the house.

I was curious about their mom, my eyes moving to their home, wondering if she was inside waiting for them.

"Thane!" Lachlan's voice carried loudly across the yards.

"Uncle Lachlan!" Eilidh shot past me like a little bullet.

I turned to watch Lachlan hurry down the steps of the decking to catch his niece in his arms. The wind stole their exchange from my ears. But whatever was said, it made Eilidh erupt into infectious giggles as he settled her on his hip and walked toward us. He grinned and suddenly I saw an image of him from a movie, wearing that same boyish, wicked smile. Not only was I again reminded that my sister's fiancé was famous, but seeing him interact with his niece took him up a few million notches on the hotness scale.

"You've met Regan, then?" he asked Thane.

The brothers stood next to each other, and I saw the resemblance. Lachlan was a few inches taller than Thane, his eyes a little bluer, but they both shared the same rugged, Scandinavian handsomeness that made me wonder if there wasn't a little Viking mixed up in their Scottish blood.

They exchanged a wordless conversation, but I was more perceptive than people thought. They weren't happy with my arrival. I could see it in Lachlan's clenched jaw and Thane's suspicious expression.

Pretending I couldn't give a shit, I grinned at Eilidh. She seemed happy to be in her uncle's arms, but she was staring at me with big, beautiful blue-gray eyes. Her gaze dropped to my cheek, and she lifted a small hand as if to touch me.

"Why do your cheeks do that when you smile?" she asked.

"Do what?" I teased, knowing exactly what she was talking about. I'd inherited my father's dimples.

"That!" She giggled, pointing at my left cheek.

"They're dimples, Eilidh," Thane answered.

"But why?"

Perhaps being in Scotland, surrounded by lilting Scottish

accents, I was reminded of a story Mac once told to explain my dimples. "Fairies gave them to me. You see, when they wander out of Faerie and into our world, they don't want humans to know what they are, and having fairy dust on them would be a big giveaway. So they made these little pockets in my cheeks so they can hide their fairy dust in them."

"Really?" Eilidh was wide-eyed.

I nodded.

"Uh-uh," Lewis disputed. "Fairies aren't real."

"Yeah, they are!" Eilidh disagreed vehemently. "Uncle Mac says so!"

I tried not to be annoyed by the realization that after Mac had left Robyn to rot in Boston, he'd made an entirely new life for himself in Scotland where these little kids called him *uncle*. "It was Mac who told me about my dimples and the fairy dust." My smile wavered just as I met Lachlan's gaze, and something sharpened in his.

I glanced away but found myself snared in the curiosity that lit Thane's eyes.

"You know, I'm a little hungry." I backed toward the house.

"That's why I came out." Lachlan turned to Thane. "Robyn's ordered enough takeaway to feed an army. Do you and the kids want to join us? She ordered everything from Chinese to chicken nuggets."

"Chicken nuggets!" Eilidh yelled with more enthusiasm than I'd felt for anything in years. Lachlan winced, even as his shoulders shook with amusement.

His brother's eyes flicked to me. "Are you sure?"

"Yeah, definitely. The kids are a nice distraction for Robyn."

From me?

Ouch.

"I'm not sure."

"Please, Dad." Lewis tugged on his sweater.

"Chicken"—Eilidh's voice deepened hilariously, her eyes taking on a wild madness as she stared at her father—"nuuuggeeets."

We all laughed and for a moment, it broke the tension.

Maybe the kids *were* an excellent distraction.

3

REGAN

S o was *Thane's wife not in the picture?* I wondered as everyone put together plates of food at the nearby kitchen island before settling at the large dining table. There had been no mention of asking a wife to join us for dinner, so I assumed Thane was divorced. He didn't wear a wedding ring.

Watching Eilidh point out to her dad what she wanted on her plate, I piped up, "Why don't you make a chicken nugget mash bowl?"

Eilidh stared at me with round eyes, her expression intrigued. "What's that?"

I looked at Thane. "May I?"

He nodded and stepped away from the island. "Have at it."

"So." I grinned at Eilidh as I got up from my seat and went to her. "I can pretty much make chicken nuggets into twenty different meals."

"It's true," Robyn agreed, and my heart lightened at her nostalgic smile. "Regan was the neighborhood babysitter, and then she was a nanny during the summers for a few years. She got creative recreating takeout food."

From the age of thirteen, I babysat the neighborhood kids. It was how I made a little extra cash throughout high school. I liked kids. They were sweet and funny and guileless. Because of that, I'd started taking on summer nanny positions for families during their school breaks. I worked as a nanny every summer from eighteen to twenty-two.

"Surprising," Lachlan murmured. "The nanny part, that is."

His insinuation made me defensive. "Why?"

He seemed unperturbed by the slight bite in my tone. "You just don't seem like the responsible type."

"Lachlan," Robyn warned.

I didn't want her sticking up for me when she was the reason he thought I was a useless flake. "I see my sister has been filling your head with the crap our parents filled her head with."

Lachlan raised an eyebrow while Robyn stiffened in her seat. She opened her mouth to answer, but I looked away and smiled down at Thane's daughter and teased, "Okay, so don't freak out, but I'm gonna cut up the nuggets."

Eilidh's eyes got bigger, but she nodded with trust.

Grinning through the tension emanating from the adults in the room, I quickly set to work scooping some mashed potatoes from the takeout container into a bowl. I then arranged the chicken nuggets around the edges of the mash. There wasn't any gravy, but there was ketchup. I shook the bottle at her. "You like?"

She nodded as she threw her arms out wide. "This much."

Chuckling, I drizzled the ketchup over the mash and chicken nuggets and carried it to the table for her. "Enjoy."

She dove in that bowl with so much delight, a person might think I'd given her a golden crown. Thane gave me a nod of thanks and took a seat to eat his dinner.

I sat next to Lewis, across from Robyn, and said, "Next time, I'll show you how to do chicken nugget nachos."

"I'd like that too," Lewis said.

"Yeah?"

He nodded and took a bite out of a burger. Robyn really had ordered everything she could think of.

"What else can you make?" Lewis asked around a mouthful.

"Please swallow before you talk," Thane admonished in a tone that suggested he'd said the same thing a million times before.

"Anything a six-year-old would want to eat, Regan can do it," my sister answered for me.

"Actually, my cooking skills have progressed a little since high school. I took a few cooking classes when I was in Europe and Asia."

"Cooking classes in Europe and Asia." Robyn whistled. "How very cultured of you."

Thankfully, Eilidh spoke up so I could avoid my sister's passive-aggressive comment. "This. Is. SO. GOOD." She banged her fork on the table in emphasis.

"Yeah? Can I have a bite?"

She nodded enthusiastically and pushed the bowl across the table toward me. I took a scoopful of ketchup-soaked nuggets and mash on my fork. Chewing it, I nodded, my eyes dramatic and round. When I swallowed, I agreed, "So. Good."

Her answering grin was the cutest thing I'd ever seen, her little face lighting up. When she spoke again, it was with kid randomness. "I love your nail varnish. Will you paint my nails?"

"I don't know. That's up to your dad."

Thane shook his head. "You're too young for nail varnish."

"But, Daddy!"

24

Sensing a tantrum on the horizon, I intervened, "Nail polish is for when you're older. But I could braid your hair. Have you ever worn a fishtail braid?"

"What's a braid?"

I raised an eyebrow. Did her mom not braid her hair?

"It's a pleat," Thane answered.

Her expression cleared, and I realized we'd hit on a cultural misunderstanding. Scots called braids *pleats*, just like they called polish *varnish* and *ken* was know. I filed that away. "I can pleat your hair later. A fishtail is such a cute look."

"It doesn't sound cute." She wrinkled her nose, making me laugh.

"Don't think of it as a fishtail ... think of it more like a mermaid tail."

"I love mermaids!" Eilidh gasped, her eyes round with excitement.

Oh my God, she was so cute I could die.

"Lucy," she panted around her food, "Lucy tried to pleat my hair once, but she said it was too curly."

Before I could say that I'd have no problem mastering her wild curls, a thick tension fell over the table.

Then I realized why.

Lucy.

Did she mean Lucy Wainwright?

Shit.

And why was a starlet offering to braid Eilidh's hair and not her mother?

"Dad said we're not allowed to talk about Lucy, Eilidh. You're so stupid," Lewis snapped, his cheeks reddening with frustration.

Eilidh's face crumpled.

"Lewis, I didn't say that, and don't speak to your sister that way." Thane glared angrily at his son.

Lewis looked like someone had slapped him. "But you said—"

"You misunderstood me." Thane sighed wearily. "The point is, you never speak to each other like that. Okay?"

Seeing tears brighten in Eilidh's face, I hurried to distract her. "I can pleat your hair for school tomorrow."

Her eyes widened. "Really?"

I nodded, smiling.

"Tomorrow is Saturday," Lewis reminded me sullenly, his eyes to his food.

His dad watched him with a pained, worried expression. Jeez. What was going on here?

"Right. Well, I can pleat Eilidh's hair anytime."

"Tomorrow?" She bounced impatiently in her seat. "I want a mermaid's tail!"

"Sure. It's a plan," I promised, and then nudged Lewis's elbow. "So school, huh? What grade are you in?"

He looked up at me, his cheeks still red from his dad's earlier admonishment. "Grade?"

"Primary class," Robyn offered.

"I just started primary three."

I didn't know what that meant. "Just started?"

"School just started back this week," Thane replied.

"Oh, right. So ... primary three. That makes you ... eight, nine?" I guessed by his height.

His eyes lit up. "Seven."

"You're tall for seven. Must get that from your dad and uncle, huh?"

Lewis looked pleased and nodded.

Grinning, I turned to Eilidh. "And what primary class are you in?"

"Five!" She splayed the fingers of her right hand.

Her brother giggled. "Not age, Eils. *Class.* She's in primary one. It was her *first*-ever week at school."

"Wow. Big week for you then?"

She nodded rapidly around a mouthful.

Seriously. So freaking cute.

"She got Ms. Hansen, and she's the best teacher." Lewis grimaced. "I got Mrs. Welsh."

"You don't like Mrs. Welsh?"

He wrinkled his nose. "She's grumpy and doesn't like the boys and she picks on you if you don't know the answer to something. And she smells."

Thane sighed heavily. Looking at him, I could tell he wanted to reprimand Lewis for insulting his teacher, but after the moment they just had, he was probably reluctant to pile it on.

"Does she really smell, or are you just saying that because you don't like her?"

He thought about this. "Well, Connor said she smells."

"Who's Connor?"

"One of my friends."

"So ... because Connor said Mrs. Welsh smells, you all say it now?"

He nodded.

"Is it true?"

He shrugged. "Not really. But the other stuff is."

"Okay. Well, it sucks that Mrs. Welsh is impatient and grumpy, but we shouldn't really say mean stuff about people if it's not true, right?"

Lewis considered this. "So I should stop saying she smells?"

"Yeah. It would be the right thing to do. The kind thing."

"But I can say she's mean? Because that's true."

Trying not to laugh, I replied diplomatically, "That's fine if it's true, and it's always good to be honest, especially if someone is picking on you, no matter what age they are. But I always say it's best to fight unkindness with kindness. So anytime you come across someone in life who isn't very nice to you, it does no good to come down to their level and be unkind in return. And sometimes, when you're kind to someone who hasn't been kind to you, you change their attitude, and they stop being mean to you. Yeah?"

I was shocked by how attentive this seven-year-old boy was, but Lewis was hanging on to my every word and seemed to process it. Finally, he nodded and said, "Okay."

It was only then that I realized the table was quiet. Looking up, I found my three adult companions staring at me: Thane in gratitude, Lachlan in surprise, and my sister with an expression that veered between pride and melancholy.

The melancholy gutted me.

"Finished!" Eilidh yelled, breaking the moment. She had ketchup all over her cheeks.

I grinned, grateful for the cutie. "Did you eat any of it or just get it all over your face?"

Joy glittered in her eyes, and she slapped her little hands down on the table and cackled. Her loud, hilarious giggling was so infectious, she made us all burst into laughter.

It was a pity her magic didn't last.

~

A while later, Thane and his cute kids left with the promise that I'd pop by in the morning to braid Eilidh's hair. Jet lag had hit me, and Robyn sensed I was fading.

"Let me help with the dishes," I offered for the thousandth time as she and Lachlan tidied up.

"We have a dishwasher," Robyn repeated. "You look exhausted. Go to bed."

My eyelids *were* drooping, so I followed her order and

stumbled upstairs. I barely remembered changing into pjs and getting into bed.

It would be hours later when an electronic sound filtered into my unconsciousness, and I forced open my heavy eyes, blinking against the light flooding into the room. It took me a minute to remember where I was.

Groaning as soft daylight illuminated the bedroom, I rolled over in the super comfortable guest bed and fumbled for my phone on the side table. The screen lit up—six o'clock in the morning.

The blackout blinds were on an automatic timer.

For six o'clock in the morning.

"We'll need to do something about that," I muttered grumpily as I shoved myself into a sitting position. It was then I registered the email notification banner on my phone.

All I saw was the word *Austin* and a wave of nausea rose in my gut.

No, no, how could he have this email?

Fingers shaking, I clicked on it, relief washing through me when I realized it was just stupid spam for a discount on a hike-and-bike trail tour in Austin, Texas.

"Fuck," I muttered, cradling my head in my hands. It had been five months since my last email from Austin, when I'd finally stopped letting him control my life with his harassment and deleted my email and social media accounts, changed my cell number, and pretended he'd never existed.

It was his last email that had finally awakened my fighting spirit. His words were so unhinged, they were seared on my memory.

Beautiful, I can't sleep again. How many hours of sleep have I lost over you? You owe me those hours. Hours I should have been inside you, watching you come, making those sweet noises you make as you're reaching for it. I want to punish you so badly for making me feel this way. It's your fault I'm so fucked up. You made

*me love you. You're making me chase you. But when I find you,
when we find each other, you'll see what I see. That we're meant to
be together. I would never hurt you. Anything I say or do is to keep
you safe with me.*

I can't wait to make love to you.

*But first, you'll get the punishment fuck you think you escaped.
I've been imagining it over and over in my head. I want it to hurt
so you can feel my pain. God, it makes me so hard just thinking
about it.*

You see what you do to me?

I love you. I love you so much, Regan. You'll see it too. Soon.

All my love,

Austin

Remembering that morning in my motel room in California when I'd opened that email, my nausea intensified. At the time I'd thrown my phone across the bed, hurried to the bathroom, slammed up the toilet seat, fallen to my knees, and gagged.

Nothing came up.

I'd dry heaved over it for what seemed like ages. Shuddering, tears had rolled down my cheeks, and I'd swiped angrily at them.

Just remembering that morning still made me furious and sick to my stomach.

I'd leaned against the dirty tile wall and hugged my body, trying to hold in the sobs that wanted to break free.

I'd never hated anyone before.

Not until Austin.

I hadn't known a person could so entirely derail a life. That their harassment could take over everything. Shape your decisions. That was when I'd decided enough was enough. I returned to Boston. I thought he was out of my life.

Then he came back.

Scotland and Robyn were a fresh start, though. I left that shit behind in Boston.

I stumbled into the swank adjoining bathroom (all marble tile and fancy fixtures), and then slowly returned to the bedroom. The view outside distracted me from dark thoughts of the past.

"Holy..." I walked to the floor-to-ceiling windows that overlooked the sea. Yesterday had been a bright, sunny day. The morning was a little gray, a mist hanging over the water. But it took nothing away from its beauty. If I were a painter, I'd sit at that window all day putting color to canvas.

Unfortunately, my painting phase had lasted exactly three days before I realized I had zero talent and I was trying to force the interest.

Movement outside caught my attention, and I saw my sister in her workout gear walking toward the house from the west. Perhaps from the beach? It wouldn't surprise me if she'd been up at dawn running along the seafront. Probably because of me. Robyn was a runner because it helped her center her thoughts.

Thinking of my strong sister, I glanced back at the phone on the bed.

When she was fifteen, a date sexually assaulted Robyn.

She didn't let him win. Didn't let him make her feel weak. Instead, she empowered herself.

Robyn trained in mixed martial arts.

I'd never been interested in sports. I liked yoga and Pilates, but that was as far as I'd ever taken enforced physical activity. To be honest, I'd rather be running around, staying active in a natural, day-to-day manner.

However, eight months ago I'd begun to understand Robyn's need to be able to defend herself.

~

"Morning," I called gaily as I strolled into the kitchen.

I'd showered and dressed, hoping to catch my sister and her fiancé before they left the house.

Thankfully, they were both sitting at the island sipping coffee.

"Morning." Robyn moved to slip off a stool. "Let me get you a coffee."

"I can do that." I waved her away as I maneuvered around the fancy kitchen. "I thought you might train me in MMA."

The silence at my back made me turn around.

Robyn gaped over the brim of her coffee mug while Lachlan watched her closely.

"What?" I asked a little defensively, afraid she was already suspicious about my motives.

"You want to learn MMA?"

"Yeah." I shrugged like it was no big deal.

"You hate martial arts. And sports in general."

"Well," I said, leaning against the counter, "I thought it would be a nice thing for us to do together, to spend time together."

"That's the only reason?" My big sister frowned, her expression concerned.

I veered just close enough to the truth that it would stall the questions. "While I was in Asia, I got cornered by this guy. If it hadn't been for this other guy showing up, I'd hate to think what might have happened. And then seeing you reminded me you're a badass. Just got me thinking that I should learn to defend myself."

Robyn was already making her way to me. "Are you okay? Are you sure it wasn't worse than what you're saying?"

I reached for her, squeezing her hand while I smiled. "You're such a worrier. It was just as I said."

She studied me. "Something is off. I can tell."

I released her hand. "Things are just weird between us,

that's all. I'm trying to move us past it. I thought spending time together would help."

Suddenly, a coolness entered Robyn's eyes, and she crossed her arms. "How long are you planning to stay?"

"As long as I'm legally allowed, I guess." I glanced at Lachlan. "If that's okay?"

He looked at Robyn. "As long as it's okay with your sister, it's okay with me."

Before Robyn could respond, I hurried to say, "I'm going to get a job while I'm here, find somewhere to rent, so I'm not in your hair and, like, mooching off you and your boyfriend."

"Fiancé." She scowled. "And you wouldn't be mooching. I want you here." *Where I can keep an eye on you*, she didn't say.

"Then I'll pay rent. Once I find a job. Know where I might get one?" I queried. I wouldn't lie, I was kind of hoping Lachlan might offer up a server gig at the estate. Or anything, really.

Instead, he said, "I'll ask around the village."

Did he really not have an available position?

Or did he not want me working at his elite estate?

If it was the latter, which I suspected it was, it meant he didn't trust me.

Great.

I really had my work cut out for me.

4
THANE

As he followed Gordanna Redburn through the bifold doors at the back of the house and onto the decking, Thane wondered who was interviewing who here.

"The children being abed at this hour will not do," she commented as she walked down the steps into the back garden. "We'll keep school hours at the weekends too."

"I don't need you at the weekend." *Or at all.* He glowered at her back.

The young woman was buttoned up so tight, it was difficult to believe she was only twenty-three. And it wasn't her conservative clothing or the prim bun she wore; it was her pinched mouth and militant demeanor.

Thane groaned inwardly in despair. Gordanna had come all the way from Cornwall for this interview. She was the tenth person he'd interviewed for the job of live-in nanny housekeeper, and she was the tenth person he was going to have to reject. It was incredibly difficult to find someone who wanted to live in such a remote part of Scotland, and Thane was quickly losing the luxury of being picky.

He'd never considered Caelmore that remote, considering Ardnoch was right next door and was a famous village. But to those used to large towns and cities, the Highlands were somewhere you visited for the scenic beauty, not a place most would consider settling down. Most people needed to be near large hospitals, vet services, shops, restaurants, and convenient amenities, not to mention excellent Wi-Fi and phone signals. Those weren't bad here; they just weren't the best.

Living somewhere that required patience and effort in exchange for the stunning surroundings? That compromise wasn't for everyone.

Including decent nanny housekeepers. This one hadn't referred to Eilidh and Lewis by anything but "the children" since her arrival.

Thane was screwed.

"But … I thought this was a live-in position?" Gordanna frowned at him.

"Yes, it is." The guest annex was perfect for whomever got the position because it even had its own kitchenette. "But I don't work at the weekends and would like to spend all that time with Eilidh and Lewis, which means you'd have your weekends to yourself."

Her perturbed expression was almost comical. Apparently, it had never occurred to Gordanna Redburn to have a social life.

She harrumphed and turned on her heel again, marching toward the cliff's edge. "This fence will never do!" she called over her shoulder to be heard against the wind. His agitation grew. Already this interview was taking twice as long as he'd hoped, and he'd told her taxi driver to wait on her. The meter was ticking—the meter he was paying for.

"Excuse me?" he said as he neared. "What about the fence?"

Gordanna scowled at him as she gestured at his safety

fence. "It's ridiculous to have something so flimsy as a guard between young children and a cliff's edge."

Thane narrowed his eyes at her scolding tone. How dare a young woman barely out of school reprimand his parental skills? "I'm an architect, Ms. Redburn. Trust me when I say this is a sufficient safety fence."

From the moment she'd arrived, she'd picked apart his house, ordering all the changes that would need to be made to make it safe for the children who had lived in it their whole lives without it ever harming them.

"He's right, you know," a familiar voice said.

Both he and the annoying candidate turned to see Regan Penhaligon standing on Lachlan's lawn. The American and her attractive dimples had appeared as if out of nowhere. "About the fence being safe," Regan continued. "I tried to throw myself over it last night, and it morphed into a Transformer that saved me and then offered a therapy session."

Trying not to laugh at her utter weirdness, Thane chanced a glance at Gordanna. She looked far from amused as she ran her eyes over Regan and raised an eyebrow. Regan wore a dress much like the one she'd worn yesterday. Conservative neckline. Not very conservative hemline.

Just like yesterday, she was barefoot, her toenails painted a bold red.

Regan's amusement fled at Gordanna's perusal, and she crossed her arms and glowered at the young woman as if to say, "Problem?"

"You are?" Gordanna asked, as if she had the right to know.

"Thane's going to be my sister's brother-in-law."

"And do you have a name?"

Good Christ, this woman was a trip.

"Regan. Yours?"

"I'm Gordanna Redburn." She held out a hand to Regan. "I'm the children's nanny housekeeper."

Uh, what? Thane turned to her, clearing his throat as he prepared for the coming awkwardness. "Ms. Redburn, there seems to be a misunderstanding. This is just an interview."

She dropped her hand before Regan could take it. "I assumed since I'd traveled all the way from Tintagel that this was all just a formality."

"No. It's an interview. And I paid for your travel expenses and accommodation."

She drew herself up straight. "Mr. Adair, I assure you, you will not find a better candidate than me to look after the children."

"Eilidh and Lewis," he said, his irritation building. "My children are called Eilidh and Lewis. Not 'the children.' And I'm afraid I haven't made a decision yet regarding the position."

Understanding what that meant, she sniffed haughtily. "Well, thank you for wasting my time. I'll see myself out, and I'll invoice you for the taxi fare!"

Before Thane could say anything else, the woman marched down the side of the house.

"What on earth did I just walk in on?"

The wind blew Regan's copper-red hair off her face, revealing her elegant bone structure. While Thane could absolutely see what Lachlan found attractive in Robyn, his soon-to-be sister-in-law wasn't a classic beauty. Her half sister, however, was. She had high apple cheekbones, those disarming dimples, warm, oval-shaped, chestnut-brown eyes surrounded by thick, dark lashes, and lips that were neither too thin nor too full. A resemblance existed between the sisters, but where Robyn's nose was a little long, Regan's was dainty.

Overall, the younger sister had the style of someone who

cared about her appearance. Robyn didn't and somehow was more attractive for it. Lachlan's fiancée had a certain charisma that was far more appealing than any physical perfection could ever be.

"Well?" Regan pushed.

Thane scratched his beard and sighed. "I've been working as a freelance architect, but the jobs just aren't coming in. To run a business, you need time to advertise it, and I don't have time, what with juggling full-time childcare. So I've had to return to my job with a firm in Inverness. Between the commute and the work, I'm looking to hire a live-in nanny housekeeper. We had one when Eilidh was little, but she left for a position in the States."

"And fence lady was the best you could get?" Regan screwed up her face.

Irritated by her blasé attitude, he bit out, "You try finding a nanny who will leave their life behind to live in the Highlands."

Her eyes grew round. "I'm sorry. I didn't mean to be flippant. But honestly, I only met her for five seconds, and she's not good enough for Eilidh and Lewis."

Remembering how well Regan had gotten along with his children, a smile prodded his lips. "No, she isn't." He looked beyond her to his brother's house. "Where are Robyn and Lachlan?"

Regan shrugged and stared out at the water, not meeting his gaze. "They went out."

"Without you?"

She shrugged again. "They had stuff to do." Finally, she looked at him, grinning as if she hadn't a care in the world. But he saw shadows in the back of her eyes. "I turned up out of the blue. They had plans."

Something was going on with Robyn's sister. He couldn't imagine Robyn hadn't noticed it herself. Behind the smiles and carefree attitude was sadness and something else. Desperation?

Remembering the last redhead with shadows in her eyes who got past his defenses, Thane promptly ignored his growing curiosity. "Right. I better get back inside. Eilidh and Lewis will wake any second." He took a step toward the house as he realized, "You're up early."

"Jet lag. And stupid automatic blinds in the guest room."

He chuckled. "Ah. I see. Well. I better go."

"Wait." She stepped toward him, her short dress fluttering a little dangerously in the breeze. "I was actually coming over because I promised Eilidh I'd braid her hair."

"Right." He remembered. Part of him wasn't too sure about Regan spending time with his children. But last night she'd been brilliant with them, while he was constantly doing and saying the wrong things. It was the first time in weeks both Eilidh and Lewis had laughed that much. Well, not Eilidh. His Eilidh-Bug found many reasons to giggle. But Lewis, his serious wee man, had been too broody for a little boy since Lucy. Thane had a terrible feeling he'd bungled that entire conversation.

"Eilidh's not even up yet."

"Then maybe I can come over to talk with you."

He raised an eyebrow. "Regarding?"

She grinned. "The genius plan that just occurred to me."

He waited.

Regan threw out her arms as if to say, "Voila" and continued, "Meet your new nanny housekeeper."

Confused, he shook his head. "What?"

"I'm staying here for the six months I'm legally allowed, and I need a job. Like Robbie said, I am amazing with kids and have lots of experience as a nanny. And I know I don't look like it, but I can clean, I can cook, I can do laundry. Six months gives you plenty of time to find a perfect and permanent nanny housekeeper."

Thrown by the offer, Thane tried to think of a polite way to say "no way in hell."

"Regan … I just don't think it would be a good idea to hire a family member. And for all intents and purposes, that's what you are now."

There. That was diplomatic. And reasonable.

Her face fell. "Oh."

Guilt suffused him, which irritated him. "I'll keep an ear out about other jobs that might work for you, though."

"Right."

"So … I'll see you later, then."

"But what about Eilidh?"

He sighed. "Some other time."

"But I promised her today." Regan crossed her arms again and tilted her chin stubbornly. "I don't know about you, but I don't break my promises."

"That's not what I've heard."

He cursed himself as soon as the words slipped out.

Regan stepped back as if he'd punched her in the gut.

The remorse he'd experienced earlier was nothing compared to now. "Regan—"

She held up a hand, cutting him off. "I have no idea what my sister has told you about me. And I don't care. I love her dearly. In fact, she's the person I love most in this world."

He heard the sincerity in her words, but it confused him, considering she'd abandoned Robyn when she needed her little sister the most.

"But Robbie and I are different people, and with a little distance, I realized our parents kind of turned us into exaggerated versions of who we really are. I think that made her see me in a way that wasn't reality. I've got this wild reputation that I don't deserve, like I'm not someone a person can count on. But I am."

He gave her a flat smile. "Regan ... when you don't answer your sister's calls or emails after someone almost *murders* her —twice—that is the very definition of someone a person *cannot* count on."

Tears brightened her pretty eyes, but Thane refused to be moved by them. He'd fallen for pretty, false tears before. A redhead who liked to play the victim.

However, Regan swallowed hard, blinked rapidly to push back the tears, and threw her shoulders back. "Yeah, I guess that's true. I've made a lot of mistakes when it comes to Robyn, but I'm here to do better. To be better for her. And I don't need anyone to believe that. Words are just words. My actions will speak for themselves." Her eyes narrowed. "So this is me. I don't break my promises. And I promised a sweet little girl I'd braid her hair today."

Feeling his resolve crumble, Thane grumbled and gestured toward the house. "Come on in."

The woman beamed those bloody dimples at him as she sashayed past. "You've got coffee, right?"

"Yes." He followed her inside. "Would you like a pastry with that, madam?"

Ignoring his sarcasm, she replied with annoying perkiness, "Sure!" and then side-eyed him as they walked into the house. "You weren't kidding about pastries, right? Because you got my hopes up to here." She raised her arm past her head.

Trying not to laugh at her playfulness, Thane assured her, "Not kidding. I bought them to prepare for Ms. Redburn's early visit. Apparently, however, 'pastries are an unhealthy breakfast temptation to have around children.'"

Regan snorted. "What an uptight bore. I'm a way better

candidate than she is." She winked at him. Actually winked at him.

Refusing to be charmed by Robyn's sister, he set about heating the coffee and setting a plate out for her to choose from the array of pastries. Turning to look at Regan, he watched as she moved around, taking in the place. It was the same layout as Lachlan's, but his late wife, Fran, had chosen a more traditional shaker-style kitchen.

As if the thought of Fran had conjured her presence, Regan caught sight of the wall that led toward the front entrance—the wall with all their family photographs.

He stilled as she walked over and studied the images.

Knowing it was coming, he braced himself as she turned to ask in a soft, gentle tone, "Where's their mom?"

The hollowness that always followed a mention or thought of Fran opened in his chest as he crossed the room to stand with Regan. He brushed a thumb over one of the framed photographs.

Him and Fran on their wedding day.

"Francine died," he replied. "Two months after Eilidh was born."

"I'm so sorry." He felt her hand on his shoulder, the gentle squeeze of comfort.

Shrugging off her touch, he marched back into the kitchen. "How do you take your coffee?"

Silence followed his question, but to his relief, it was soon followed by, "Milk, two sugars."

He raised an eyebrow, grateful for the change of subject. She returned to the island, her expression a little wary. "Two sugars?"

Regan gave him a half-hearted smile. "Sweet tooth."

"Dad?"

Lewis stood at the bottom of the staircase in his Marvel

pajamas, rubbing sleep from his eyes as he stared curiously at Regan.

"Hey, bud." Thane strolled over to his son to give him a morning kiss on his head. "Your sister still sleeping?"

Lewis nodded, his focus on Regan.

"Morning." She gave him a little wave.

In answer, Lewis surprised Thane by walking over to climb a little sluggishly onto the stool beside her. Unlike Eilidh, who woke up bright and bubbly, Lewis was like his old man and needed time to wake up. He rarely talked until he'd eaten breakfast.

"Hi," he said to Regan. "You came."

"I promised I would."

"Eils will be glad." Lewis yawned and then asked randomly, "Have you seen the Red Sox play?"

His son liked American baseball. Watching their interaction in curiosity, Thane pushed Regan's coffee and a plate for her pastry toward her, took her thanks, and got Lewis's breakfast together. All the while, he listened to the two of them chat about baseball. Regan's dad was into baseball, so she'd gone to games when she was younger, but she admitted she wasn't one for sports. Though, she announced proudly, Robyn was going to teach her MMA.

Even when Thane had put a bowl of cereal and juice in front of his son, Lewis didn't take his eyes off Regan. She chatted animatedly with him about the small baseball team his friends had formed, and he noted how relaxed Lewis was.

Lewis wasn't even three years old when his mum died. Like his father and his uncle Lachlan, he was serious by nature. He was also protective of his family and sister, and shy of strangers. He'd never really taken to anyone outside the family, including Robyn and Lucy, the way Eilidh had.

But there he was smiling and giggling at Regan's story about a time in high school when she was supposed to be guarding home plate and someone walked by with a hot dog, and she was so busy trying to persuade them that the hot dog should be hers that she let someone slide into home.

"Did you get the hot dog?" Lewis asked.

Regan grinned mischievously. "Best hot dog ever."

So focused on how his son interacted with this woman, this near stranger, he didn't hear Eilidh come down the stairs.

"Regan!" his daughter squealed, and he turned to watch her almost trip off the last step in her excitement to get to Robyn's sister.

Regan hopped off her stool to catch Eilidh as she flew at her. Despite her slender build, she hauled Eilidh into her arms with ease, beaming at her. "Hey, superstar."

Eilidh clasped Regan's face in the palm of her hands and said with an almost grown-up tenderness, "You came!"

And just like that, Thane saw the genuine fondness soften Regan's expression. "I keep my promises."

Fuck.

Thane couldn't possibly be considering accepting Regan's proposal.

It was preposterous. His kids hadn't even known the woman for twenty-four hours. And yet, they'd bonded with her faster than he'd seen them take to anyone.

Moreover, he'd liked how she'd handled Lewis at dinner. What she'd said about kindness and the way she'd defused the tension at the table. She had a knack for knowing just the right thing to say to the children to settle them.

Lachlan would be against it.

So would Robyn.

Or would they?

Regan had worked as a professional nanny, so clearly, other parents had trusted her with their kids.

And Thane was in a real bind.

He started work on Monday, and he still had no nanny.

What was he even thinking?

No.

He hadn't been entirely lying when he said that hiring family wasn't always a good idea. Besides, Robyn might not want Regan around for the next six months.

No.

Regan was out of the question. He'd just have to come up with something else. And fast.

5

REGAN

Blisters chafed in gnawing pain at the back of my heels and along my toes as I finally turned down the narrow country road that led to the impressive contemporary homes in the distance. I could hear the sea and smell the salt in the air.

The distance from Ardnoch village to Caelmore didn't seem like much when I was in the car. It's why I'd insisted, after Robyn dropped me off this morning, that I could walk back. She'd offered a pair of her hiking boots, but I'd refused because she wore a size bigger than me, and I thought that would be worse. I was wrong. Thinking of the hiking boots I'd left back in Boston, along with half of my belongings, I whimpered as I limped along the private, packed-dirt road.

"Screw it." I kicked off my heels and sighed in relief as my swollen, hot feet met cool earth.

Bending to collect the Mary Janes I'd assumed would be better than the stilettos I'd brought, I cursed my love of heels and dresses. In my rush to leave, I'd stupidly left all my back-packing gear behind. A cheap flight meant the inability to take luggage over a certain weight. I'd brought a tiny suitcase, and there was not a pair of sneakers or flats to be found in it. If I was going to stay, that would have to change.

Though, it was doubtful I could stay if I didn't find a job soon. I'd spent all morning and part of the afternoon charming every shop, café, and restaurant owner in the village.

Ardnoch was the quaintest place I'd ever been.

A main square with a large parking lot for visitors was central to Ardnoch. I'd discovered on my employment quest that the shops, restaurants, hotels, and bed-and-breakfasts were scattered throughout the village on cute row streets.

The historical architecture and design was amazing. Prior to coming here, I'd stalked Robyn's Instagram for her new photos, so I'd seen Ardnoch through her lens. But seeing it in real life was even better. I knew from my sister's photo captions that all the buildings here predated the mid-twentieth century, and dominating it all, near the Gloaming—the town's biggest hotel, right on the square—was a medieval cathedral. The main thoroughfare of Ardnoch was called Castle Street. Guessing it was so named since it was the road that led out of the village toward Ardnoch Castle and Estate.

Castle Street was an avenue of identical nineteenth-century terraced houses with dormer windows. A lot of the homes had been converted into boutiques, cafés, and inns. Off Castle Street were identical row streets with fewer converted businesses. Still, I left no stone unturned and walked the four-block radius before it became apparent the rest of the buildings were residential.

No one was hiring.

It was the end of the summer, and soon they would let go the temporary staff they'd hired for the tourist season. How could an entire village not need new employees? No servers, no shop assistants, no cleaners, nothing!

And after the increasingly awkward and tension-filled

interactions with Robyn over the weekend, there was no other option but to get a job and move out of Lachlan's house. I knew she wanted me to stay, but I didn't think it was a good idea.

Lachlan was a quiet one. I still hadn't figured him out. All I knew so far was that he watched over Robyn like a man ready to take a bullet for her. With me, he was a different kind of watchful. Sometimes, it was like he saw too much.

Like how much of a coward I was.

I still couldn't bring myself to broach the subject of me disappearing on Robyn. At least now she was talking to me. What if she really hated me after I explained what had been going on in my head? She might think it was as pathetic an excuse as I did.

She'd see once and for all how codependent I was.

How not brave I was.

It wasn't easy being a coward and even more difficult when your big sister was fearless.

Except she seemed to tiptoe around the elephant in the room as much as I did. That realization made me even more nervous. But at least it was all a giant distraction from the bastard who'd plagued my life for eight months.

The thought juddered through me, and I immediately threw it out.

The sound of an engine at my back helped with the disposal of bad thoughts, and I glanced over my shoulder to see a green Defender moving slowly toward me. Wondering who it could be, I stepped into the grass at the side of the road and leaned as far back as I could to allow the vehicle to pass. Instead, it slowed, a blond woman at the wheel.

She rolled to a stop and I heard, "Regan!" from the back seat.

Eilidh pushed her face between the blond woman's seat

and the empty passenger seat. Lewis's head hovered above hers.

"Hey, guys." I grinned. "How's it going?"

"I got Best Drawing today!" Eilidh beamed.

I leaned against the passenger door. "Great job! I'm not surprised. Superstars tend to win a lot." She giggled at my wink, and I turned to Lewis. "Hey, buddy. How are you?"

He shrugged but gave me a small smile before he gestured to the woman at the wheel. "This is Aunt Arrochar."

The sole Adair sister. I'd been curious to meet her after hearing Robyn speak so fondly of her.

"Hey, I'm Robbie's sister, Regan."

Arrochar leaned over and popped open the door. "Get in."

"Thanks." I hopped in and noted her gaze on my feet. "Wrong shoe choice. I walked from the village."

She raised light blond eyebrows above striking, pale-blue eyes. "If you intend to stay here, we'll need to get you proper walking boots." She stuck out a slim hand. "Like Lewis said, I'm Arrochar. Lachlan and Thane's sister. It's nice to meet you, Regan."

I shook her hand and felt a tap on my shoulder. Eilidh grinned cheekily at me.

"I told my friends about the fairy dust in your cheeks. Anna says her big sister Rosie has the same ones in her cheeks, but no one told her about the fairy dust. She can't wait to tell Rosie."

I chuckled. "I'm sure it will come as a surprise to her."

"Eilidh, sit back, sweetie, we're not home yet," Arrochar ordered quietly. Her niece did as she was told.

"Where's Thane?" I asked the aunt. From first impressions, we couldn't be more unalike. Her platinum-blond hair was so much lighter than the sandy color of her siblings that I'd guess it was dyed. It was the only thing about her that suggested appearance was important. I'd dressed in an impractical short dress in the mod silhouette I favored, my makeup and hair done. Arrochar had her long hair pulled back into a messy ponytail. As far as I could see, she wore only mascara, and her clothes were definitely utilitarian. Jeans, lightweight blue-plaid shirt with a white T-shirt beneath, and Converse.

And yet the ordinary clothes did nothing to distract from her striking features. She wasn't classically pretty; she was something more. I wasn't sure if it was her eye color or the way she held herself or what ... but Arrochar Adair was an unusual kind of beautiful.

If she sensed my perusal, she ignored it as she responded to my question about Thane. "Inverness at his new job. He can't find a nanny, so I offered to take a few days off work to look after the kids so he can find someone. Pronto."

I frowned. He'd made his sister take time off work when he had a perfectly responsible adult with a lot of time on her hands around to help? Not wanting to utter my irritation in front of the kids, I pressed my lips tight.

Arrochar spoke as we pulled into Thane's driveway. "You're not at all what I expected."

"Because I'm not Lara Croft's younger replica?"

She snorted and threw me an appreciative grin. "Pretty much."

I rolled my eyes but chuckled as I eased out of the Defender, grateful Thane's driveway was paved and not gravel.

"Can Regan come play with me, Aunt Arro?" Eilidh asked around the other side of the vehicle as they got out.

"I'm sure Regan has plans."

"I really don't." I walked around the SUV to join the threesome. "If I'm not intruding, that is."

"Not at all," Arrochar assured. "But"—she gave Lewis a pointed look—"you *will* do your homework first." She turned to me. "Eilidh doesn't get homework. They've introduced a new style of teaching since I was a bairn and primary one is a lot like nursery now. I don't get it. *I* could handle homework when I was five."

I didn't have time to offer an opinion about how not all kids were at the same stage developmentally at five because Eilidh rushed to me and grabbed my hand.

"Come on, Regan." She tugged me forward, overjoyed to have me there.

A tender ache echoed in my chest as I let her lead me toward the house. Catching Arrochar's curious look, I saw a hint of bemusement in her expression.

Lewis waited for us at the house, and as Arrochar let us in, he said, "I told Connor we should stop saying Mrs. Welsh smells when it isn't true."

I tried not to raise an eyebrow. "And what did Connor say?"

He wrinkled his nose. "He called me the teacher's pet."

Oh, shit.

"But then Mrs. Welsh was mean to him for no reason. She made him read out a chapter of the book we're reading, and he isn't so fast and she kept being mean and telling him to read faster. And I told her she was being mean to him. So me and Connor are okay now."

I met Arrochar's gaze, and she said, "Tell her what happened next, Lewis."

Frustration crossed his face. "We both got sent to Mrs. Cooley's office."

At my questioning look, Arrochar supplied, "The head teacher."

"What? What for?"

"For being disrespectful," she replied as she guided the kids to the kitchen. "You can grab a snack before you start your homework."

"Surely that's not fair if the boys weren't in the wrong," I said quietly as Lewis and Eilidh hurried ahead into the kitchen.

Their aunt turned to me. "It isn't fair. Mrs. Welsh spoke to both me and Connor's mum first without explaining the situation. The kids told us exactly what happened once we came out of the classroom, and Connor's mum lost her shit," she whispered, her eyes sparking with anger. "She's filing a complaint with the head teacher. But in the heat of the argument, Lewis called Mrs. Welsh names, and that's not on, so Thane will need to have a chat with him."

It didn't sit right with me that he should be vilified in this scenario, but he also shouldn't call his teacher names. "Rock, meet hard place," I muttered under my breath.

"Exactly."

"Aunt Arro, I can't reach the peanut butter!" Eilidh yelled from the kitchen.

We caught up with the kids to help them. For two strangers, we fell into a companionable sync as we prepared a light snack for Eilidh and Lewis and settled them at the dining table. Afterward, Arrochar gave me some salve and Band-Aids for my battered feet.

"So." Arrochar smiled curiously as we sat beside each other at the island with coffees. "What brings you to Ardnoch?"

Right to it, huh? I smirked. "My sister."

"Aye, that visit is long overdue."

I raised an eyebrow at her directness, and she shrugged. "Sorry. None of my business. But you should know I'm not just Lachlan's sister. I've become very fond of Robyn."

The warning made me bristle. "Well, I'm more than fond of Robbie. I love her more than I love anything."

"Does *she* know that?"

I jerked back like she'd slapped me.

Arrochar winced. "Regan, I'm sor—"

"Regan! Can you help me with my homework?" Eilidh yelled across the large living space.

Her aunt sighed. "You don't have homework, Eils. You just want Regan's attention."

Eilidh's answer was to scrunch up her face and growl in a deep voice, "Spoilsport."

I looked away so she couldn't see me laugh.

"Don't give me the monster voice, Eilidh Francine Adair. Why don't you finish the new drawing you started in class? It's my turn to chat with Regan. You'll get yours later."

That seemed to settle her.

"Monster voice?" I asked quietly.

Arrochar snorted, her pale eyes sparkling with amusement. "About a year ago she started saying stuff in a deep voice that cracks us up. We call it her monster voice, but we do not know where she picked it up. It's just intrinsically Eilidh. She's a bit weird, which means she fits in perfectly with the rest of us Adairs."

"She's adorable." I watched her and Lewis, heads bent over their work. "They both are."

"My brother is doing a fantastic job," Arrochar said, pride in her voice.

Thinking of Thane and his dead wife, sadness filled my tone. "I can't imagine having to raise two kids after losing the love of my life."

"It was difficult." Arrochar turned to me, keeping her voice low so the kids couldn't hear. "He was still with a company in Inverness back then, so he hired a nanny. She was around until Eilidh turned two and Thane decided to go freelance. He's juggled work and raising them for the past three years, but it's been a struggle. I know it wasn't a straightforward decision for him to return to working with a company. He doesn't like the idea of his children being raised by a nanny. It was never what he and Fran intended."

"Was Fran a stay-at-home mom?"

"She was a maths teacher. She was from the Borders originally. They met at university, and she loved Thane enough to follow him back to the Highlands. Luckily, she got a job at the local high school. I'm sure Lachlan had something to do with that. My eldest brother isn't above nepotism." She smiled fondly and then shadows entered her eyes. "Thane and Fran were the happiest people I knew. They designed this house together. Lewis was born just as the construction was completed. Fran had barely returned from maternity leave when she fell pregnant with Eilidh, and she decided to quit her job. Be a full-time mum. Thane would never have asked it of her, but I know he was relieved there would always be someone around. We didn't have that, you see," she said so softly, it was almost a whisper. "Our mum died after giving birth to me. Thane was six years old. Our dad kind of checked out for a while. Lachlan and Thane practically raised me. Anyway." She shook her head. "Thane wanted something different for Eilidh and Lewis."

My heart broke for them all, realizing life had repeated itself. "I'm so sorry."

She shrugged. "What can you do? It is what it is."

"Can I ask … how Fran died?"

Arrochar winced but before she could respond, Lewis called over suspiciously, "What are you guys whispering about?"

We tensed for a second, then I grinned at him. "*Girl* stuff."

He wrinkled his nose and turned back to his homework like I suspected he might.

Arrochar chuckled. "You're good with them."

"I used to nanny. During summers at college."

"Really?" Her eyes lit up. "I don't suppose you're looking for a job, are you?"

"I've spent all afternoon looking for a job."

"Huh. Does Thane know you nanny?"

"Yup." I raised an eyebrow. "But I think my sister might have filled his head with the notion that I'm irresponsible."

"Are you?"

I studied the way she studied me and decided I liked Arrochar Adair. There was no judgment in her expression, even though I was sure she'd been told just as much about me as Thane had. She was blunt and direct, but I appreciated that. And it seemed to me she was the kind of person who liked to make up her own mind about people, which I respected.

"No. Fundamentally, no." I shook my head. "I have been impulsive in the past, but I'm not sure irresponsibility always goes hand in hand with that trait. Besides, believe me when I say something recently cured me of my impulsivity. And yeah, I haven't been there for Robyn when I should have been. I have an excuse. It isn't a great one ... but I'd hate to think that one mistake will be held against me for the rest of my life."

Arrochar considered this. "You should talk to Mac. I think he, more than anyone, will understand whatever it is you're going through when it comes to Robyn."

Anger flushed through me. "I haven't been there for my sister these past eighteen months. That's not the same as a father abandoning his child."

"Mac didn't abandon her," Arrochar bit back. "It's more complicated than that, something you'd know if you'd been around for Robyn to tell you."

I stifled the urge to argue. Instead, I wondered at her vehement defense of Mac. "There seems to be a lot I don't know," I eventually replied.

The stiffness eased from her shoulders. "Sorry for snapping. I just ... I'm protective of Mac. What happened with Robyn ... it was a pain he carried for a long time. Finally, things are good between them. I don't want anyone to upset that."

"I'm not here to tear shreds out of Mac," I assured her, though I was curious to discover what had gone down between him and my sister. "I'm here to put things right with Robyn. And to do that, I need to stick around—to stick around, I need a job."

"Aunt Arro, is it my turn yet?" Eilidh called over, cutting through the intensity of the moment.

Thankfully.

Arrochar rolled her eyes. "Your presence is required."

Laughing, I hopped off the stool to give Eilidh my time.

~

While Arro prepared dinner, I hung out with Eilidh on the couch. An animation was on the TV, but Eilidh was too busy playing with my hair and chatting about her friends to pay attention. The only time she did was when a character started singing a song and she stopped to sing along with them.

Arro and I cheered and clapped after every one of her renditions.

Lewis was allowed to play video games, preapproved by his father, for one hour before dinner each day, so he'd disappeared into his bedroom to do that while we girls hung out downstairs.

I was pretty sure my hair was a ratty bird's nest from Eilidh's ministrations, but it made her happy, so I wasn't going to be precious about it.

She was in the middle of asking me if she could call me

"Ree-Ree" when the sound of the front door slamming jolted her attention from me. "Daddy!" she squealed and took off out of the room.

"How's my wee Eilidh-Bug?" he replied moments later in that deep, gravelly voice.

The tenderness in his voice was a beautiful thing to hear.

Eilidh's answering chatter was so fast I couldn't make it out, even as Thane strode into the open-plan room with his daughter settled on his hip. He stared down into her face with such love, I vowed in that very moment to find a guy who would look at our kids just like that.

"Is that right?" he murmured in response to whatever she'd said.

"And Ree-Ree let me play with her hair for ages!"

Apparently, I was Ree-Ree now, permission granted or not.

Arrochar and I shared an amused look.

"Ree-Ree?" Thane frowned and then glanced into the room. He stiffened when he saw me. "Regan?"

"Hey." I waved, knowing I probably looked like a lunatic because of whatever Eilidh had done to my hair.

"Hi," Arrochar said, drawing his attention. "Dinner is almost ready. I picked up Regan on her way back from the village. The kids asked her to hang out with us."

"Right, right." He nodded, his eyes coming back to me. "Are you staying for dinner?"

There wasn't exactly a welcoming tone to his question. "No. I should get back. Robyn will wonder where I am." I hoped. She hadn't texted me all day.

"But." Arrochar strode toward her brother and tugged Eilidh out of his arms and into hers. "Regan would like to discuss something with you in private."

I would? I frowned at her.

She made a face and then mouthed, "Nanny."

Right.

Usually I wouldn't badger someone about a job he clearly didn't want to give to me, but I was running out of options. And honestly, the idea of some Gordanna Redburn nanny looking after Eilidh and Lewis pissed me off. At least with me they'd be safe, cared for, and having fun.

"Right." I jumped to my feet, stalking toward their father. "Yeah, can we talk?"

His eyebrows were still puckered, but he nodded and gestured for me to follow him. He led me to a room off the entrance that I hadn't been in before.

The small space overlooked the fields beyond the driveway. It held a desk with a smart desktop computer, neatly piled papers, bookshelves filled with folders, and walls with framed house plans. His office.

He closed the door and turned to me. Without Eilidh in his arms, I finally noticed his attire. Instead of the rugged sweater and jeans I'd only ever seen him in, he wore a dark gray shirt, open at the collar, with a pair of black suit pants. He had not, however, trimmed his beard or his hair, and the overall look was incongruously appealing.

"Well?" Thane said.

I placed my hands on my hips and gave him what I hoped was a charming smile. "You need a nanny. And I need a job."

He opened his mouth to speak, but I cut him off. "I've spent all day looking." I stuck out one of my bare, sore feet. Thane looked at it in consternation. "I cut my feet walking all over the village and back in search of a crappy job. And all the while, here in this gorgeous house, are two amazing kids who get along with me, and they need a nanny."

Their father's eyes traveled back up my body from my feet to my face. "Regan—"

"Before you say no again, let me email you my references. I am an exceptional nanny with impressive experience. I used to nanny for the mayor of Providence and his wife."

Thane drew in a breath. "Regan—"

"Lewis actually talks to me, and Arro says that's unusual for him. And I'm pretty sure Eilidh and I are twins born nineteen years apart. Though"—I gestured to whatever was happening with my hair—"I need to give her some styling lessons for sure."

His lips twitched. "Regan—"

"I would never do anything to hurt them," I said in all seriousness. "They need someone. You need help. I'm offering it, and you can trust that the offer comes from a good place."

"Not an entirely altruistic place, though."

I shrugged. "I've never lied about needing a job. But this wouldn't feel like a job. Except for the cooking and cleaning part, of course. But the kid part, no. They're wonderful kids."

"On their good days."

"All kids have ups and downs. I know it's difficult." I took a step toward him and hated how he seemed to tense warily. "I nannied for this one little boy whose parents treated him as if he were a social accessory. Trotted him out to display to their friends and then had the nanny trot him back out of sight again when he wasn't required. Which was most of the time. I've never met a child with bigger trust issues, and being a nanny to a kid who doesn't trust you or anyone is one of the most difficult things I've ever had to do. Almost as difficult as stemming the urge to berate his parents for neglect … but that's another story.

"My point is … Eilidh and Lewis are loved, and it shows. They're good kids who will have tantrums on days they're tired or hungry or frustrated and not sure why. That's kids. I know that. I'm prepared for it. Besides, Robyn is their aunt now. If you want reassurance I'll take this job seriously, you have it, because I won't do anything else to hurt my sister or the people she cares about. I'm a much better solution to your problem than some nanny who's only here to cash her paycheck."

Thane studied me so long after my little speech, I squirmed.

Finally, he replied, "First, let me talk to Robyn. I don't know what's going on between you two, but if offering you a job is a problem for her, then I can't do it."

As much as I understood and was grateful he was looking out for Robyn, I couldn't help but experience a niggle of hurt at the very idea my sister would stand in my way. I didn't let it show. Instead, I nodded. "I get it."

His expression softened. "Good. Now I'm sure your sister is looking for you." His eyes flickered to my hair, his mirth obvious. "And you best sort that," he said, gesturing to my head, "before it stays like that permanently."

I patted my head, suddenly dreading looking in a mirror.

REGAN

Perhaps today was the wrong day to start MMA training with my sister. As we stood in the studio on the Ardnoch Estate grounds with Robyn's friend Eredine, I attempted to act normal. Like I wasn't still reeling from the conversation I'd overheard last night.

The previous evening, I'd been in my room reading a romantic suspense e-book when I heard the murmur of a familiar voice downstairs. My room was off the stairwell, and I could hear anyone who came into the house.

At the sound of Thane's voice, my curiosity piqued, so I snuck out of my room and stood at the top of the stairs to eavesdrop. Not very mature of me, I know, but I hoped that he'd come over to ask Robyn about the job. They disappeared into the kitchen, and I tiptoed downstairs to listen out of sight. I had to strain to hear as they spoke in low tones.

When Thane finished explaining my proposition to Robyn and Lachlan, I waited tensely for my sister's reaction.

Finally, she replied, "What is it you're asking me?"

"Two things, really. If you think it's wise to hire Regan to look after Eilidh and Lewis, and if so, would it be an issue for you? I don't want to make any problems for you, Robyn. For all I know, you want Regan on a flight back to the States."

I sucked in a breath at the thought, squeezing my eyes closed.

Please don't hurt me, please don't hurt me.

"I don't want that," Robyn replied wearily.

I relaxed, tears burning my eyes.

"I prefer her here where I can keep an eye on her."

Like I wasn't a twenty-five-year-old woman but a wild sixteen-year-old up to no good?

Jeez, my sister really was living in the past.

Your fault, a sneering voice said in my head.

Yup, I knew that too.

"Do you think I'd be insane to hire her? I'm really in a jam here."

Insane?

A little melodramatic.

Stung, I crossed my arms over my chest. This was what happened when you eavesdropped.

"Of course not," Robyn replied, and she sounded a little defensive.

I smirked. *Thank you, sis.*

"Are you sure?" Lachlan asked. "This is my nephew and niece we're talking about, Robyn."

I scowled. I *knew* he didn't like me.

"I know that. And I know how much they mean to you. I love them too. I would never suggest putting them in harm's way. And while Regan has acted impulsive and irresponsible in many situations in her life—"

Say what?

"She's like a whole other person with kids. I always thought she should go into teaching."

She did? She thought I could do that?

"But anyway, Regan is only ever irresponsible with herself."

"Really, because I thought abandoning you after you got shot and then ignoring your calls after Lucy tried to murder you was pretty irresponsible." Lachlan's voice was hard.

I flinched, remorse an ugly sensation.

"I can't explain that." I barely heard my sister's response.

There was a moment of silence and then Thane cleared his throat. "So … your opinion is that she's responsible with children?"

"Absolutely. She's never lost a job, nanny or otherwise. And she didn't just do it for the money. She enjoys taking care of kids. And you saw her with Eilidh and Lewis the other night. Kids love her. She's great with them. If you want to hire her, do it. But keep looking for someone else, Thane. I don't know this version of Regan as well as I used to know her. This version of her is unpredictable. Selfish and unkind in a way she never was before. So she might decide next week to pack her bags and leave."

The tears in my eyes slipped free.

It was an awful thing to hear the person you loved most call you selfish and unkind.

"Maybe I shouldn't hire her." Thane sighed heavily. "I don't want someone selfish and unkind looking after my kids."

To my shock, it was Lachlan who spoke up. "I can't believe I'm saying this, but … for someone apparently so selfish and unkind, she taught Lewis a lesson about kindness without preaching at him. She sensed the tension Lucy's name caused with the children at the table and defused it in seconds. She was naturally aware of their emotions throughout dinner and steered the conversation around them. I thought she showed intuitiveness and caring toward them that frankly shocked me.

63

"And while I know you're not ready to hear this, Braveheart, there is something going on with that woman. Mac thinks so too. She's not telling you something. Mac thinks it could be why she's been avoiding you for so long."

Damn. I gaped down the hallway toward the sound of my sister's fiancé's voice. Mac (and Lachlan!) saw too much.

After a moment, Robyn said, "Calling her unkind was wrong. I'm frustrated with her for acting like everything is all fine and dandy between us, and it came from that. It's not true. Regan is not an unkind person. She never has been. Inconsiderate is a better word for her. And Lachlan's right. There's something going on, and I won't find out what that is if she doesn't stick around. While her having a great-paying job she enjoys would help in that matter, I don't want you to feel obligated to hire her when it involves Eilidh and Lewis."

"We're talking in circles now," Thane huffed, a tinge of amusement in his voice. "Robyn, I'm in desperate need of a nanny housekeeper. Arrochar is watching the children tomorrow, but she has to return to work on Thursday."

"I told you I'd take the kids to school and pick them up," Lachlan offered.

"I can do the same. We'll take turns," Robyn added.

"And I appreciate it. But we can't go on like that, never knowing until the last minute who can watch them and when. I need a nanny and someone to take care of the house. Regan emailed over a very impressive set of references. So … should I hire her or not?"

I waited with bated breath.

Robyn replied, "Do it. She'll take good care of them. But like I said … don't stop looking for someone more permanent."

After that, I'd hurried quietly upstairs and tried not to let their words repeat over and over in my head.

That morning, Robyn drove us to Ardnoch to meet with

the yoga and Pilates instructor, Eredine Willows, who was training in MMA with Robyn too.

"Do I get a tour of the castle and estate at some point?" I asked as Robyn swung her car by what she called "the mews." Turned out it was just an old-fashioned term for garage.

"Lachlan is pretty stringent about stuff like that. His members pay big bucks for complete privacy."

"Didn't he let you roam the estate?"

"I was investigating a crime." Her tone brokered no further argument, and I shut up. "*And* he wanted in my pants." She shot me a smirk.

I chuckled, but it still bugged me to be treated like I was untrustworthy. While I had shown a lack of consideration for my sister these past eighteen months, I'd done nothing in my twenty-five years on the planet to suggest I was the kind of person who couldn't be trusted to walk around a private estate without pissing off its inhabitants.

As we walked down the gravel driveway, past the impressive castle, I caught no glimpses of a famous person. I caught no glimpse of anyone. Robyn ushered us down a path that led away from the castle. Soon, however, a small loch edged with modern cabins appeared, and I forgot my annoyance.

The cabins were compact and clad in silvered wooden larch. Each had a floor-to-ceiling glass window that looked out over the loch. The flowered shrubbery and small trees that grew around the loch reflected in the water so it was more green than blue.

"This is so pretty."

Robyn grinned. "Great place for yoga, right?"

Definitely. "So is your new backyard, though."

My sister chuckled because it was true and then knocked on the door to the first and largest cabin.

"Come in!" a feminine, American-accented voice called.

We stepped into a large, rectangular room with mirrors

along the wall opposite the door. The wall to our left was made entirely of glass, revealing a spectacular and tranquil view over the loch. Mats and other equipment were stored on the back wall to our right on floor-to-ceiling shelving.

Standing in the middle of the room, hands on hips and a small smile on her face, was Eredine Willows.

Even though Robyn and I were fairly tall, Eredine was taller. I guessed at least five ten. She was stunning with dark brown curls I watched her pile into a large topknot. With smooth, golden-brown skin and hazel eyes so light they almost looked green, I guessed her to be around my age, but I wasn't sure.

Robyn had given me a quick catch-up in the car. She knew little about Eredine's past, but she knew that the young woman was good friends with Lucy Wainwright and had taken her betrayal hard. I was strictly not to mention the Oscar-winning actor who was currently in jail, awaiting trial for almost killing my sister.

The thought made me flinch as Robyn and Eredine chatted while setting up the wrestling mat. When Mom and Dad told me about Robyn and Lucy—when I saw the news splashed across tabloids—I'd felt distant from it as much as the thought of it horrified me. Now, being here, seeing my sister alive but how affected she and her friends were by Lucy's homicidal behavior, a simmering rage burned in my gut.

They better put that woman away for life, or I might be tempted to kill her myself.

"So, Regan, what is it you do?" Eredine asked with a friendly smile as she straightened from helping Robyn.

"She's a vagabond," Robyn answered with a slight bite to her tone.

I glowered at my sister before smoothing my expression

into bland politeness. "I'm a nanny, though without a position at the moment."

"So that's your profession now?" Robyn raised an eyebrow.

Trying not to let her goad me, I shrugged. "Well, it's the job I've been employed in the most."

She snorted, giving me a dirty look.

"It is," I insisted. "Why are you being such a bitch?"

Eredine sucked in a breath.

Robyn narrowed her eyes. "In front of Eredine, really?"

"You started it with the tone."

"I didn't say anything."

"You're being passive-aggressive, and it's not like you."

"I guess we're both acting unlike ourselves, then."

"Is this how it's going to be the entire time I'm here?" I huffed, crossing my arms as I noted Eredine sneak toward the exit. I didn't blame her. We'd just invaded her space and immediately started arguing. I couldn't even be embarrassed about it, I was so mad.

And I wasn't the only one.

Robyn's face turned red. My sister was a slow burn. She rarely lost her shit, but when she did, it was explosive.

She detonated. "You left me six weeks after I got shot, and I barely heard from you again in over a year!"

I flinched at her shriek. It was filled with so much pain and anger, emotions she'd clearly buried deep because I had never seen my sister look so unraveled. Not even after she got shot.

And I'd done that to her.

A sob burst up from my gut, and I covered my mouth as it tried to escape.

The door closed softly behind Eredine.

"Don't." Robyn pointed a finger at me, tears blurring her

vision. "Don't you cry when you're the one who wronged me."

I nodded, covering my face with my hands as I sobbed in a choked voice. "I know."

Yet as much as I tried, I couldn't hold back eighteen months' worth of tears. Instead, I stumbled back, hitting the wall as my legs gave out and I slid to the floor. "I'm sorry," I managed before I hid my face in my knees and cried. Robyn wasn't the only one who'd bottled everything up. Easy-breezy Regan had fled the building.

Hyperaware of my sister's movements, she slid down the wall, her shoulder touching mine as she settled beside me.

"Talk to me," she whispered hoarsely. "I was always the one you talked to. I don't understand what changed."

Hearing her voice break forced me to pull myself together. I lifted my head out of my knees and swiped at my face, seeing the black mascara streaks across my fingers and not giving a shit. Meeting Robyn's teary gaze, I repeated, "I'm so sorry."

"I appreciate the apology." She tucked a strand of loose hair behind my ear, a gesture that was so heartbreakingly familiar, I struggled to hold back more tears. It had been so long since Robyn had been willingly affectionate with me. And it was all my fault. "But I want to know why. It's never made sense to me, Ree. One minute we were as close as two sisters could be, and the next you were halfway around the world avoiding my calls. For eighteen months."

I took a shuddering breath. "Have you ever done something? Something you regretted, but fear kept you stuck in the same cycle of repetition that you just didn't know how to break?"

Robyn narrowed her eyes as she contemplated me.

I gave her a sad smirk. "No. You'd never let that happen. You're not a coward, like me."

"Don't say that."

"It's the truth." I shrugged angrily and looked out the window, not wanting to see her expression as I finally explained myself. "You know when we were kids, I never thought it was weird that when I got hurt or upset, you were the person I wanted, not Mom or Dad. I wanted to spend all my time with you. As we got older, I realized other kids needed their parents more than their siblings. Not me." I shook my head, smirking through watery tears. "I was the weirdo who depended on my big sister like everyone else depended on their mom and dad."

I heard Robyn's breathing change and turned to see the tears brighten her eyes.

That set me off again, so I looked away. "You know I love Mom and Dad. I'm not saying I don't ... but I needed you in a way I didn't need them. Adored you. You were as much my hero as Dad was. Maybe more. Everything was always bright and shiny in my world as long as I had you." Remembering the phone call from my dad, the one where he told me Robyn was in critical condition after being shot three times in the chest, I shuddered. I'd never experienced terror like it. Even after what I'd been through since, nothing had come close to the fear that paralyzed me when I thought Robyn might die.

"When you got shot ... I ... I saw you hooked up to those machines, tubes coming out of you, breathing for you, and the doctors said you'd died on the table and you might not wake up ..." I met her anguished gaze. "Something switched off inside me. Like my mind couldn't cope with the fear or something ... I don't know." Shame swamped me. "I realized, I guess, that so much of my happiness depended on your existence. It freaked me out. I ... I don't know how to explain it. It just sounds pathetic and cowardly."

"It's not." Robyn tugged my hand into hers and clasped it, her expression pleading. "Keep talking to me."

"I needed to know I could survive alone," I admitted hollowly. "That my happiness wasn't dependent on you or other people. Even when you woke up and it was clear you were going to be fine, the fear didn't go away. I thought for sure you would go back to the job, and I'd have this constant terror of something else happening to you hovering over me. So ... I ran."

"You went on the backpacking trip we'd planned together."

I winced at her wounded tone. "Yes. Not to hurt you intentionally. It's just that I met a bunch of people through this online group, and they were leaving so I decided to ... run away. I had the inheritance from Dad's mom." I referred to the $5000 my grandmother had put in a bank account for me when I was born. I'd always planned to use it on my backpacking trip with Robyn. "It was enough to ..." Self-recrimination oozed from every part of me. "Run away. Something you would never do."

She frowned but nodded for me to continue.

"I realized within weeks of leaving how selfish I was being, and I hated myself for leaving you, for thinking only of myself. I can never take that back, but I want you to know that I am fully aware of how selfish that was."

Robyn squeezed my hand in answer.

"I didn't know how to return to you," I practically pleaded with her now. "I was paralyzed by my bad choices, wondering how you'd ever forgive me ... and the time just kept stretching on and it got harder and harder to come back. I was so goddamn scared that I'd damaged us irrevocably."

The truth, the whole truth, hovered on the tip of my tongue, but I couldn't quite admit just how badly I'd screwed up. "While on the trip, one of the guys ... we slept together, and he got really clingy and obsessive. He's one reason I didn't come back because I was trying to put some distance between him and me. Eventually, I returned to Boston once I could face you, but you'd left for Scotland. And I was not in a good place. I started seeing Maddox, a guy who was not good for me—but I ended it," I assured her. "And I was finally getting up the courage to face what I'd done to us. I'd booked a flight to Scotland."

Her eyes widened. "When?"

"Before Lucy. The day before my flight, Mom called to tell me what happened. And I'm ashamed to admit, I spiraled again." Suddenly, I did something I thought I'd never do; I turned to sit on my knees in front of my big sister and took both her hands in mine. "Please forgive me for being a quitter, a coward, selfish, inconsiderate, and unkind to you." I pulled her closer. "I know it might not mean anything to you, but everything you've ever thought of me, I've thought a million things worse. I've hated who I've been this past year and a half, but I'm here to prove that's not who I really am. I can be better. I *am* better. I know I am. Tell me you can forgive me. I'm not asking for it right away, but tell me you can at least try … because if you can't, I can't be here, Robyn. I don't want to hate myself anymore. If I stay here with you hating me, I'm afraid I'll never stop hating myself too."

My sister pulled her hands from mine, but to my utter relief, it was only to enfold them in hers and squeeze them so hard it almost hurt. Her expression was fierce, her changeable eyes flashing an intense green. "You are my sister. I can be mad at you. I can have times when I don't understand you. But I could never hate you. I love you. And I forgive you."

A sob of pure gratitude broke free. Robyn hauled me into her arms. Burrowing into her, I rested my head on her shoulder, my arm tight around her waist, and cried.

She hushed me, rubbing a soothing hand up and down my arm. I felt like a little girl again. "You were right," she said. "The other day when you mentioned how I was perpetuating the narrative Mom and Seth created for us—mostly Mom—you were right. I've thought a lot about it over the past weekend, with input from Lachlan, who is never without an opinion." Her tone was dry. "And he helped me see that until the shooting, I'd unfairly labeled you because of Mom. He helped me realize that the things you got up to as a teenager were no more or no less than what most teens get up to. Our parents constantly compared you to me, and that's not fair because I am, and have always been, boring and responsible."

"You could never be boring." I pulled out of her embrace. "But you're right. Mom *and* Dad made it out as if I was some wild child. What did I ever do that other kids didn't? The only real thing I ever did wrong was not knowing what I wanted to do with my life and abandoning you when you needed me." I winced. "Sounds pretty bad when you say it out loud."

Robyn huffed a small laugh.

"Sorry."

She shook her head, her smile wavering. "Something you mentioned—this guy, this obsessive one. Did he hurt you? Is that why you want to learn self-defense?"

Attempting not to stiffen at the mention of Austin, I lowered my eyes. "He scared me, he didn't physically hurt me. But yeah, he's the inspiration for the training."

"Is he still a problem?"

There was a chance he wanted to be, but I was in Scotland now, and there was no way he could get to me here. For a start, he didn't know where I'd gone. "No," I said, more out of wishful thinking than wanting to lie to her. So, okay, I didn't want my big sister thinking I couldn't handle myself or that I was a big screwup too.

"You're sure?"

I nodded. "The training is just so I know how to defend myself. I should have learned long ago."

"Physical activity isn't really your thing."

I wiggled my eyebrows. "Depends on the activity."

"Stop!" She laughed, pushing me away.

And just like that, we felt like Robbie and Ree again.

"I love you," I said.

Her expression softened. "I love you, too, kid."

Just like that, a weight lifted from my chest.

~

"So you were keeping it from me deliberately?" I whispered in pretend aggravation and not-so-pretend awe as Robyn led me into the foyer of Ardnoch Castle. I wasn't sure you could call it a mere foyer.

"No, not deliberately." Robyn made a face. "I just had to make sure I had my Regan back. I wasn't kidding. It's important to Lachlan that as few nonmembers have access to the estate as possible."

When she'd said she'd give me the tour I'd been hankering after, I quickly fixed my makeup in case we met anyone famous. There was no hiding my bloodshot eyes, but I was too happy Robyn had forgiven me to fuss about it.

I nodded, my attention dancing from one thing to the next. "Holy cow."

"Right?" I could hear my sister's smile in that one word.

The huge entrance had polished parquet flooring that made the space seem like it went on forever. The décor was very Scottish and traditional, but amped up a million knots on the luxury meter. A grand staircase descended before us, fitted with a red-and-gray tartan wool runner. It led to a landing where three floor-to-ceiling stained glass windows spilled a kaleido-

73

scope of light down it. Then the staircase branched off at either side, twin staircases ascending to the floor above, which I could partially see from the galleried balconies at either end of the reception hall. There was a huge hearth on the wall adjacent to the entrance and opposite the staircase, but no fire burned within. I'd love to see it all lit up during the winter months.

Opposite the fire sat two matching suede-and-fabric buttoned sofas with a coffee table in between. More light spilled into the hall from large openings that led to other rooms on this floor. There was a chatter of voices beyond them, and I eyed the doorways in curiosity.

"Members' lounge rooms," Robyn offered. "We'll avoid those because it's brunch and they'll be busy."

Damn. I was not above wanting to see a celebrity!

As usual, my sister read me and laughed. "You'll spot someone famous at some point. And doesn't Lachlan count, anyway?"

"Sure." I shrugged. "But it's amazing how quickly he just became the guy who's marrying my sister. And calls her 'Braveheart.' Aww, don't think I didn't notice that. It's adorable."

"Shut up." She mock scowled and gestured for me to follow her. She led me down a doorway next to the arches, through a wide, exquisitely decorated corridor. "The first room I'm showing you is the room I know you'll love the most."

We stopped at a large, solid wooden door that was propped open. Robyn peeked her head in and turned to me with a relaxed smile. "It's empty."

Since I was already looking beyond her and could see into the room, I almost bulldozed her to get inside. I grinned at the sound of my sister's laughter.

Wall-to-wall, dark oak bookshelves, a large, open fireplace, comfortable armchairs, footstools, and sofas made up the library.

A castle library.

I was in heaven.

Floor-to-ceiling windows on either side of the fireplace let light in so it didn't seem too dark. The plethora of table lamps aided in chasing off the gloom too. Luxurious velvet curtains at the windows pooled on the wooden floors, most of which were covered in Aubusson carpets.

And the bookshelves were filled top to bottom with books.

Ladders on rails allowed readers to climb to the top rows to select their reading material.

"It's happening." I raised my arms dramatically as I spun in the room. "I'm finally Belle."

Robyn chuckled. "I knew you'd love this."

While my big sister wasn't much of a reader, I had gotten the bookworm gene from Mom. When I wasn't kissing boys under the bleachers in high school, someone could usually find me there curled up with a good book.

"Can I live here forever?" I climbed a ladder to the top, spread out one arm, and began singing the song "Little Town" from Disney's *Beauty and the Beast*.

My sister veered between hysterical laughter and trying to shush me. Unfortunately, the harder she laughed, the louder I sang.

Then my eyes moved from her and caught sight of her fiancé leaning against the library doorway, his arms crossed over his chest and his eyes locked on Robyn. He wore an expression so fierce with love, it made me want to cry big, fat happy tears for her.

Instead, I abruptly cut off with an "Oops!"

Robyn stopped laughing and looked to the doorway. She

gave her fiancé an apologetic look. "I'm sorry. Were we being too loud?"

He pushed up off the jamb with a grin and jerked a thumb toward me. "I could hear Disney Princess all the way to my stage office."

I hung on the ladder, suddenly not seeing the funny in it anymore. I didn't want to get Robyn into trouble. "I'm sorry. My fault."

As he slid an arm around Robyn, cuddling her into his side, Lachlan looked up at me and shook his head with a small smile. "It's fine. You have a lovely voice."

I beamed. "Why, thank you." Relieved he was cool with my antics, I turned back to the shelves to caress the row of classics before me.

"Ree loves your library. I told you she would."

"The song and the way she's making love to the shelves gives her away."

I lifted my cheek from the wood. "Hmm?" I turned on the ladder and clutched at my chest dramatically. "Can you fall in love at first sight?"

"I'm starting to see what you mean about her." I heard him say.

That drew my attention. "What does that mean?"

As I climbed down the ladder, Robyn said, "I told Lachlan you could charm the pants off a Russian dictator. I blame the dimples."

At her fond teasing, a rush of warmth filled my chest and I jumped off the last rung to face her with a big grin. "What, these?" I pointed to my dimples. "It is not my fault fairies put fairy dust pockets in my cheeks."

Her eyes widened. "You remember that?"

I shrugged. "Of course."

Robyn turned to Lachlan. "Is Dad here?"

He shook his head. "Mac's at home, getting ready for his flight."

"Oh, shit, yeah. I said I'd stop by before he goes." Robyn looked at me. "Dad's got a meeting with a guy in California about some new security tech for the estate. I want to say goodbye before he leaves. Is that okay?"

"Oh, you should do that alone." I didn't want to intrude on their farewell, especially since I felt weird about Mac.

"I can give Regan a tour of the rest of the estate and make sure she gets home okay."

Robyn frowned at me. "I don't know. Would that be okay?"

Realizing her anxiety came from the fact that we'd just found some clarity with one another, I waved away her concerns. "I'll be fine. I'll see you at home."

"Okay. Thanks." She turned into Lachlan, reaching up to clasp his face in her hands. "Thank you. And … things are good now," she said meaningfully.

"Yeah?"

Robyn nodded. "Yeah."

I chuckled. "You are as subtle as an elephant at a mouse party. Robbie and I had a good chat. We cleared the air. Apologies were made. Begging was exacted on knees. And voilà! We're loved up again."

The couple stared at each other for a beat, then Robyn said dryly, "And now she's back to being a facetious pain in my ass."

Rolling my eyes at Lachlan's answering grin, I walked away to study more of the library's collection while Robyn and her fiancé moved toward the door. I tried to ignore the sound of kissing, which was easy when I spotted a copy of *Gulliver's Travels*. It was a favorite of mine, a satirical adventure that was so much more than any movie adaptation had ever made it out to be. Many of the classics bored me to tears. But not *Gulliver's Travels*.

The leather-bound book looked old and a little fragile. Handling it with care, I opened it to the copyright page and nearly dropped the thing in heart failure.

"Is this a first edition?" I practically shrieked, holding the book away from me as I turned to see my sister and Lachlan frowning. "*Gulliver's Travels*."

Lachlan's expression cleared. "Aye. It was my great-grandfather's."

"Shouldn't this be protected in bubble wrap and locked in a safe somewhere?"

He grinned. "Where no one can enjoy it?"

"It's a first edition. This is the Hope Diamond of books."

Lachlan chuckled. "Not quite. It's not worth what you think it is."

"But it's worth more than a hundred dollars, right?"

"A fair bit more, yes."

"And you just have it sitting on a shelf where any Neanderthal can pick it up?"

My soon-to-be brother-in-law seemed to find my horror hilarious. "I assure you my guests know how to treat rare books, Regan."

I harrumphed, gently putting the book back on its shelf.

"*Gulliver's Travels* is one of Regan's favorites," Robyn offered.

"Is that so? You can borrow it if you like."

I stepped away from the bookshelf, my eyes round with terror. "And accidentally lose it or spill coffee on its pages? No thanks."

My sister, lips pursed with amusement, stepped out into the hall. "I need to go. I'll see you both back at the house."

Lachlan reached for her again, like he couldn't help

himself, and pressed another quick kiss to her lips before he finally released her.

Once she'd departed, he turned to me.

I grinned at him. "You may be keeping my sister in Scotland, an entire ocean away from Boston, but ... I've reluctantly decided to like you."

He raised an eyebrow. "Lucky me."

At that, I grinned harder.

Footsteps rushing back down the corridor distracted us. Robyn was suddenly there, hurrying over to me as she held out her phone. "It's Thane. I told him he needs to be quick."

Pulse racing with anticipation, I took my sister's cell and answered cheerily, "Hello, Mr. Adair!"

There was silence and then the sound of choked laughter before his deep voice rumbled through the phone. "You can call me Thane."

"Oh, I know. I was just being professional since I'm pretty sure you're about to offer me a job."

I ignored my sister's exasperated look and smirked.

"I could change my mind," Thane teased.

"I don't think you will. And I accept."

He chuckled. "Good. I'll send over a contract. You start tomorrow bright and early at 6:30 a.m. That work?"

"Perfect!" Grateful, I dropped my teasing and said, "I really appreciate this, Thane."

"No problem."

He hung up, and I handed the phone back to Robyn. "I got the job!"

7

REGAN

My excitement over getting the job waned as I began to worry I was acting irresponsibly toward Thane and his kids. So desperate for Robyn not to think I was an impulsive failure, I'd kept the truth from her. And the problem was, I needed her advice.

Staring at my packed luggage at the end of the fabulous bed in the fabulous guest suite I missed already, I shook off my nerves and wandered downstairs. Robyn had returned home two minutes ago and called up to tell me she'd brought takeout.

I walked into the main living space and found Robyn at the island with the Chinese food laid out for us.

"Hey, thanks," I said as I slowly approached, not feeling very hungry.

"I promise this is the last of the takeout for now. I just need to go grocery shopping, and I didn't want to cook."

"I could have cooked."

"Like I said, there's very little in the house. Sit, sit, eat."

I took the stool next to her and stared at the food.

"You okay?"

Turning to my sister, I shook my head. Exhaling nervously, I replied, "I wasn't honest with you earlier, and now I'm not sure taking this job with Thane is a good idea."

Robyn stopped eating and turned toward me on her stool. "*Okay?*"

"I guess ... I *am* sure that it's okay to take the job, but I want to be *certain* sure, and I trust your judgment."

My sister waited patiently for me to continue.

"The thing is ... the guy who got clingy and obsessive ..."

Her eyes narrowed. "Yeah?"

"It was ... it was worse than I let on."

"How much worse?" I could hear the "somebody's gonna die" tone in my sister's voice and while it comforted me, it also made me ashamed. She already had so much on her plate with the upcoming Lucy Wainwright trial, I didn't want to add to it. Yet I needed her advice. Selfish, selfish, selfish.

"I'm awful." I slumped wearily. "You have all this shit going on with Lucy. You don't need to know this."

"Lucy's trial won't be until next year. We're not postponing life for a year. Now you have me worried, so tell me what's going on," she demanded. "And for the record, I don't care how much shit is going on in my life. If my sister is in trouble or someone has hurt her, I want to be the first to know about it from now on. Do we understand each other?"

Usually when Robyn used her cop voice, as I called it, I teased her. However, this was definitely not a time for teasing. I heaved a sigh. "I want you to know before I tell you all this that it was the kick up the ass I needed, and I am done making impulsive decisions."

Seeing her patience fade, I hurried on. "I was in Ho Chi Minh City last New Year's Eve. With the group I'd met through social media."

"I remember." She glared at the reminder I'd taken our trip without her.

"I'm sorry," I whispered.

Robyn suddenly shook her head. "No, I'm sorry. You've apologized. I'm letting it go. It's just a damn trip."

I looked away, because we both knew it was more than that. "We were three months in Europe first. All of us spent the two months after that working in Mykonos to save up enough cash to get to Asia. I bartended at a nightclub. Not exactly the stuff backpacking dreams are made of," I said wryly. "Anyway, minus two of the girls we originally set out with, we finally got to Thailand in November, and between learning our lesson in Europe and Southeast Asia being a little cheaper, we thought we could do three months there. I experienced things I never thought I would." I smiled, a little proud of myself, despite the circumstances.

Robyn's eyes warmed. "Like what?"

"A jungle trek in Cambodia." I grinned at her surprised face. "I know, right? My legs looked so toned that entire trip."

She laughed. "I bet."

"Anyway." I shrugged. "The whole time … like the eight months we'd all been traveling together, this one friend, Austin, had made it clear he wanted more with me. Not in a creepy or clingy way. Not then." No, the fucker had totally blindsided me. "But he wasn't my type. There was zero chemistry there."

"So what happened?"

"Like I told you earlier, I regretted leaving you for months and felt stuck. Christmas came and went without you. Then it was New Year's, and I was depressed as hell. I missed you, I missed Mom and Dad, and Boston in the winter … and I was lonely." I reluctantly met her gaze. "I was lonely, I was drunk, and I was impulsive."

"You slept with Austin," she surmised, no judgment in her voice or expression.

I nodded, my pulse increasing as I remembered the

following days. "The next morning he acted like we were together-together. At first, I didn't know what to say because I felt so bad about it, and then when I told him it was just a one-night stand, it was like he couldn't hear it. A few nights later ..." My heart raced at the memories. "We were all out for the night at a party. I decided not to drink. Like my instincts were subconsciously warning me to keep my faculties intact. The party was at this apartment near where we were staying in District 3. Austin kept getting in my face, and I finally lost it and yelled at him to leave me alone.

"One of the other guys, Liam, had enough and told Austin to back off, or he'd make him back off. And Liam offered to walk me back to my room. Nothing happened. Liam was with Desi, one of the other girls, and was just being a good guy. He said Austin was a good guy, too, and he just had a crush, but he'd talk to him, and it would all be okay. However, I was barely in my room five minutes when Austin picked the lock and broke in."

Fear glittered in Robyn's eyes, and I hurried to assure her. "He didn't hurt me. He just ... wouldn't let me out of the room. Kept trying to convince me we were meant to be together and how he'd kill himself if I didn't feel the same."

"Son of a bitch," Robyn whispered.

"I knew it was manipulation. I was finally seeing who he really was." Anger warred with the terror he'd awakened. "But I was so scared," I admitted, "I didn't know how he far he'd take it."

"How far did he take it?"

"I was sharing a room with Desi's best friend, Kylie. When she couldn't get in, Liam showed up and demanded Austin open the door. Austin did and pretended like it was all good, like he hadn't kept me trapped in there with him all night, refusing to let me out. Everyone tried to brush it off as harmless, so I packed my stuff and used what money I had left to get a ticket home. Except the cheapest flight I could get was to California. So I stayed there for a few months, working a couple of server jobs in San Diego. I was afraid to come home to you, like I said, but I felt stupid for sleeping with him. And ... he had my email and was on all my social media accounts."

"He harassed you?"

I nodded. "I blocked him on social media, but it was like a car crash. His emails kept coming in, and it was like I *had* to read them. I couldn't look away. I think I didn't delete my email for so long because I hoped that eventually, the emails would stop and I'd know he'd gotten bored. His emails were much of the same as what he'd said in that hotel room in Vietnam. But one day in April, I got an email that made me sick to my stomach."

"What was in it?"

I stared unseeing at the takeout cartons. "It was sexual. He threatened to rape me."

Robyn sucked in a breath, and I finally looked at her.

"That's when I got angry. I decided enough was enough. I deleted my email account and packed up my stuff and called Dad to see if he could help me pay for a ticket to come home. Something I still owe him." I sighed heavily, beyond irritated with myself.

"And when you got home, I wasn't there."

At the self-admonishing note in my sister's voice, I glared at her. "Don't do that. I'm the one who abandoned you, not the other way."

"But I didn't know you were going through this. That some asshole has been harassing you. Stalking you."

I flinched at the word *stalking* considering what it meant to her. "Not stalking. Ish. Not like ... not like Lucy. When I got back to Boston, my head was still up my ass and I got a job at a bar where I met Maddox. You know, the hot, dangerous type." I looked away, not wanting to think about my stupidity with that guy. "He was an asshole, but he was a tough son of a bitch and I guess, moronically, I thought he would make me safe. Eventually, I pulled my head *out* of my ass, dumped him, got a job at a coffee place and a server gig at night. Anyway, I was gaining the courage to fix things between you and me."

"But then all the stuff with Lucy happened."

"Yeah. When Mom called to say you were home … that same day … Austin found me in Boston."

"What?" She narrowed her eyes.

I gave her a sad smile. "I was planning on stopping by Mom and Dad's after work, but Austin walked into the coffee shop that afternoon." Indignation churned in my gut. "He played it as if nothing had happened, like we were just two friends meeting again after an absence. I was stunned. I didn't know what to do. All I knew was that I didn't want you to know how much I'd messed up."

"Regan …" She reached for my hand. "I'm sorry if I made you feel you were letting me down."

I shrugged. "You didn't. I was just always comparing myself to you and constantly coming up short."

"Don't. That's not fair to either of us."

I nodded, emotion thickening in my throat.

"What happened?"

"It was weird … he'd come into the coffee place, twice a week, same time each visit. But there was nothing more to it. He didn't threaten or badger me. It weirded me out, but it went on like that for months, nothing happening, before I got on that flight to Scotland."

Robyn pushed her half-eaten and now cold Chinese away. "Nothing at all?"

"Nothing."

"Damn."

"Damn? Isn't it a good thing?"

"Yeah and no." She got up off her stool, running a hand through her hair as she stared pensively across the large room. "It doesn't fit the usual pattern. Normally these things escalate."

"Maybe he got counseling?"

"Yeah, but if he got help, he shouldn't have been coming into the coffee shop twice a week."

"Maybe he liked the coffee."

My sister side-eyed me.

I sighed. "I know, it's weird."

"Is this why you don't think you should take the job?"

I nodded. "Is it responsible for me to become involved in Thane and the children's lives when I have this hanging over me?"

Robyn considered this for what seemed forever and then exhaled slowly. "Let me call Autry first and get him to do a background check on this guy. See where he is and what he's up to. I doubt we've got a problem here, but I think we should still leave a statement with Autry."

Autry was Robyn's close friend and ex-beat partner back in Boston. He worked as a beat cop at the same precinct as my dad. I worried my lip with my teeth before admitting. "I didn't want Dad to know."

"Seth would not blame you for this. He, more than anyone, knows how these kinds of people work. You are not to blame."

And there it was. The thing I couldn't admit to my sister.

That somehow this *was* all my fault.

～

"I just hung up with Autry and ..." Robyn's voice trailed

off as she marched into my room and noted my luggage. She glared at it. "What is that?"

"First, what did Autry say?"

Robyn glowered at me. "Luggage?"

"Autry?" I insisted.

She gave in first. "First, this guy has a record of harassment. Two women. He slept with them and started stalking them."

"Wonderful." I slumped on my bed.

"Good news … he's never taken it further than stalking and has desisted once the police got involved. So Autry is going to stop by his apartment and give him a warning. Seth doesn't need to know about it. Autry is still going to monitor Austin's movements. With behavior like that, we're never completely out of the woods, but I'm confident he won't follow you to Scotland. He probably doesn't even know you're here."

Relief crashed through me in a flood. "I'm so stupid for not telling you sooner." It was like she'd lifted this weight from my shoulders.

"Oh, sweetie." My sister sat down on the bed beside me. "It's okay. You can have a fresh start here. And I think the job with Eilidh and Lewis will take your mind off things. They're good kids."

I nodded, sniffling. I'd been nothing but a watering can since arriving in Scotland.

Eventually, I pulled away, gave her a grateful smile, and got up to check my makeup. Touching it up, I caught sight of Robyn in the reflection, glaring at my luggage again.

"Wanna explain this?"

"I'm packed just in case you advised me I could take the job." I turned to her.

"But you just got here."

"And I'm not going anywhere. It's just next door."

A blank mask fell over Robyn's face. "Fine."

It wasn't fine. It was far from fine, and suddenly guilt squashed my elation over the Austin news. "Thane told you it was a live-in job, right?"

She frowned. "He never mentioned that."

"He has a guest house for the nanny."

"Right. I forgot. I just thought with him being next door, you wouldn't need to move out."

"It gives us all space." I gestured around the room. "You and Lachlan don't want me hanging around all the time when you just got engaged." I raised an eyebrow. "You were loud last night."

Her lips parted in dismay, and I knew if my sister could blush, she'd be a tomato.

Worried she assumed I didn't want to live with her, I smothered my laughter and rushed to say, "It's not that I don't want to live with you. I just thought for three adults, this was a better plan. And I'm right next door, which is kind of perfect. I'll spend all my free time with you. When you're not busy, that is, and we'll catch up on everything. I promise. Please don't take this the wrong way."

At my worried expression, Robyn relaxed. "Sorry. I'm not trying to smother you. Or make you feel guilty for wanting space. You're right about everything. Especially if I'm so loud." She raised an eyebrow.

"Hey, *he's* loud too. Very loud. Good job." I winked lasciviously at her.

"Shut up." My sister then continued like I hadn't spoken. "I just ... you just got here, you know. And you've been through a lot, and I want you to feel safe. Besides, I thought you'd be living here while you were working."

I pulled her to her feet and into a tight hug, relieved when she embraced me in return. "You are going to see so much of me, you'll be sick of me. Besides"—I reluctantly retreated —"you're still going to teach me MMA, right?"

Her expression turned determined. "You bet your ass. You're going to learn to defend yourself so the next time some asshole tries to trap you in a room, you can turn his balls to mincemeat."

"You are scary sometimes. Speaking of, you'll owe me a dollar for every time you bruise me during our sessions."

Robyn made a face. "But you bruise like a peach."

"I *do* bruise like a peach."

She smiled but there was still a glimmer of sadness in her eyes. "I've missed you a lot."

Emotion burned in my throat, but I grinned my way through it. "Right back at you. And I'll be a hop, skip, and a jump from your doorstep."

"I can't believe you're giving up this very large guest room for Thane's little guest ... *box*."

Thinking of the huge walk-in shower, the hotel-quality bed, and the phenomenal view from my window, I couldn't believe it either. Robyn laughed at the face I made. "You can still back out, you know."

"Nah, Eilidh and Lewis are great. You're right. I need this. I can't imagine finding a better job." Thane had emailed the contract, and whoa, the pay was good!

"You say that now before you've had to clean toilets."

And that was why the pay was good.

"Party pooper."

Robyn's lips twitched.

"Pun not intended! Aargh. I'm leaving now."

Despite not wanting me to leave, Robyn helped me downstairs with my luggage. I trundled my suitcase toward the front door.

"Have you told Mom and Seth you're staying here for months?" Robyn asked.

Something in her tone made my spine straighten. I turned to her as I opened the door. "Yeah. I called Dad while you were on the phone with Autry."

She tried to hide her surprise, but I still saw it.

I sighed. "I know I don't want Dad to know about Austin … but everything else … I meant it when I said I was turning over a new leaf. I want to keep the people I love close, even if we're not physically close. No more shutting anyone out, including Mom and Dad."

"Good. I'm glad. And how did they take it?"

Remembering Dad's hesitant silence on the phone when I told him about the nanny position with Lachlan's brother, I slumped a little. "Dad was supportive, but I think a little sad. He's glad I'm here with you, but I think he's worried he's going to lose us both to Scotland, which I told him is ridiculous."

"Don't go making promises, Ree. This place has a way of bewitching you."

"I think we both know you stayed for reasons other than the scenery."

She shrugged, a smug smile prodding her lips, but the amusement fled when she asked, "And how did Mom take it?"

"I don't know yet. She was out. Dad said he'd tell her when she got home."

"Brace yourself."

Yeah, I was pretty sure my mom would be furious. "She's never happy with anything I do."

At my tone, Robyn reached out and squeezed my hand. "Let's make time this weekend. Just you and me. To catch up. To talk about things. Including things you've bottled up that have obviously bothered you for a long time."

"I'm fine," I promised her.

Robyn sighed. "Regan, you can smile and charm everyone

90

into thinking you're the happiest person in the world, but I know better. I know our mom loves us, but I also know she's not perfect. And it's clear you harbor some resentment toward her. So let's talk about it because you're not alone. Wait until I tell you about her and Dad."

Instantly intrigued, I leaned against the doorjamb. "Mac? What about her and Mac?"

Robyn waved me off. "This weekend. When we have time to really talk. Okay?"

"Okay." I nodded. "Will you be all right alone? Where's Lachlan?"

"He's working late tonight. There was a plumbing issue in one of the guest suites at the castle."

"Oh. He plumbs?"

She snorted. "No. He oversees."

"Ah. Yeah, that makes more sense." That afternoon, Lachlan had done as promised and given me a tour of the entire castle and estate. In addition to an impressive suite of reception rooms, the castle held many bedrooms and an entire staff quarters on the other side of the first floor where the kitchens, mews, and security department were located. We then took a golf cart to the separate gym and members' homes dotted around the huge estate. I could tell by the way Lachlan talked about the place that it was his pride and joy and that he had his finger firmly on the pulse of everyday life here.

"I will be fine." She ignored my teasing. "You better go if Thane is expecting you."

<hr/>

THANE

Regan Penhaligon stood in the dusky light of the evening sunset. On his doorstep. With luggage at her side.

Fifteen minutes ago, he'd only just gotten Eilidh and Lewis to sleep, so the sound of his doorbell ringing at nine o'clock did not amuse him. As he tried to work out why she was on his doorstep, he listened for the sounds of waking children.

"Regan?" Thane was pretty sure he was scowling at her.

Her eyebrows shot up, confirming it. "Bad time?"

"Well, nine o'clock at night is generally a bad time to ring anyone's doorbell."

"Oh." She winced. "We're used to fairly long days in the summer in Boston, but nothing like this. I keep forgetting how late it is since it's still daylight out. I mean, it only just gets dark at eleven o'clock. That's wild."

He waited for her to stop rambling and explain her presence.

Regan's smile wobbled at his stony nonresponse, making him feel like an utter arse.

"Sorry." He shrugged apologetically. "What brings you next door?"

Her brows pulled together. "I start tomorrow."

"Yes ..."

"Well ... don't you want me to move into the guest house tonight?"

Now it was Thane's eyebrows that almost hit his hairline. He'd assumed because Regan was living next door that she wouldn't want to move into the annex. "There's really no need."

Disappointment flooded her expression. Another surprise. "Oh."

"You want to live in the annex? While it's fairly comfortable in there, it's not a luxury guest suite with incredible views of the Ardnoch Firth."

"I just thought it would make things easier for the job and ..." She glanced over her shoulder at his brother's home. "I don't want to cramp their style." Regan looked back with a little shrug. "They don't need me sharing their space for six months. They just got engaged. I thought if I lived in the guest house, we'd all have our space."

Her consideration toward Robyn and Lachlan was nice to see. He stepped back to allow her inside. "Come on in, but be quiet. The kids just went down."

She nodded and walked past him, suitcase rolling at her side. Thane reached for it, brushing her hand away from the handle. Regan seemed perturbed by the gesture, but realizing he was taking the luggage from her, she gave him a grateful, dimpled smile.

Thane nodded and followed her as they moved through the house. When they reached the main living area, she waited for him as he pulled open a drawer in the kitchen and grabbed the spare key to the annex with a key and fob to the main house. "Yours," he murmured, presenting it to her. "This way."

He led her down the narrow corridor behind the main staircase, the one that led to a tiny sitting room with an enormous picture window they called "the snug," a downstairs restroom, and the utility room. A side exit door led out from the utility room. Smirking, Thane said quietly, "You'll soon be well acquainted with this room."

Regan threw him a grin as she took in the piles of laundry waiting to be done. "Good thing you pay so well."

Chuckling, Thane opened the side entrance and hauled the suitcase down a paved path toward the annex. He and Fran built the guest suite with her parents in mind. She wanted them to have a separate place they could live when they made the long drive from the Borders to the Highlands to visit. Tragically, Fran's dad, Heath, died of cancer only months after Fran's death, and her mum, Liz, of a heart attack three weeks after her husband passed. Thane knew Liz's heart just couldn't take the stress of losing her husband and only daughter within months of each other.

Thane had talked about redecorating the annex, hoping it would suppress some of those sad memories. But he'd never had time. Not with working from home while also caring for Eilidh and Lewis.

One day he'd returned from dropping the kids at school to find a team of decorators in the guest building. Lachlan had sent them and paid for the whole thing.

Always looking after him.

"I'm kinda excited." Regan pulled him out of his musings. She grinned as she put the key in the door.

He followed her in. "Keypad." He stopped her in her tracks and tapped the small box on the entrance wall. "Code to set the alarm when you leave is 2324."

"2324," she repeated.

"To alarm it on exit, put in the code and then press the A button." He pointed at it and she nodded. "To alarm the annex when you're sleeping, punch in the code and hit the B button."

She frowned. "What if I need to get up to pee?"

His lips twitched. "The night alarm is only triggered by force on the doors and windows. But there's also a smart device in the annex that will do it for you. I'll show you."

"Nice." Regan nodded, wide-eyed. "But can I check out the rest of the place first?"

Laughing softly at her impatient giddiness, he nodded and gestured for her to go ahead. The small hallway/mud-room led into the primary space. There was a farmhouse-style kitchenette along the wall to the right, and next to that a two-seat sofa facing a wall-mounted TV. It was hooked up to a DVD player and to the TV service the main house used.

Beyond that was the king-size bed overlooking sliding glass doors that led out into the yard. She had a partial view of the water at this angle. A dividing wall next to the bed hid a small walk-in and a stylishly refurbished bathroom.

He waited in her tiny sitting room, placing her luggage by the sofa as she wandered through the annex.

"Holy …" He heard her say as she stepped into the bathroom.

When Regan reappeared, she grinned at him. That damn gorgeous smile of hers made it difficult not to smile in return. "You were holding out on me, mister."

Thane raised an eyebrow. "How so?"

"This place"—she gestured—"is amazing."

"You think so? It's half the size of Lachlan's guest room."

"So what?" Her big, shining brown eyes danced around the space. "Look how gorgeous and cozy it is. And that bathroom! I think I might never come out of that walk-in shower."

An image of her naked, water sluicing down her no doubt beautiful body, entered his mind out of nowhere, and he guiltily threw it off. Where the fuck had that come from? He scowled at himself.

"Are you okay?" she asked.

He nodded, unable to meet her eyes. "Fine, fine. Eh … okay … so"—he gestured to the TV—"you've got access to all the channels plus the streaming apps on here. We set up the Wi-Fi. Password is *RescueRiders*. Both *r*'s in capital letters, the rest lowercase. Eilidh chose it."

Regan chuckled. "Maybe you should make your password more difficult."

"So Lachlan doesn't steal it?" he teased.

He saw understanding dawn, and she grinned. "Right."

They didn't have any neighbors around to tap into their broadband services.

"This"—he pointed to a tablet mounted to the wall beside the kitchen—"is the smart home device. You can voice activate it and it'll turn the lights on and off, put the window blinds up and down, even set the alarm. It will switch on the underfloor heating," he continued, pointing at the floors. "It's on a schedule, but you can change the settings on here. Or just voice activate it. If you have any issues, let me know. The voice activation will switch on any technology in the annex."

"Very high tech. I never noticed this in the main house." She studied the tablet curiously.

"It was an experiment in here. I hoped it would convince Fran to put it in the main house, but she thought it would make the kids lazy."

"She was probably right." Regan stole the words from his thoughts.

He cleared his throat. "Anyway, I wasn't expecting you to move in, so nothing is stocked except some basics. I'll leave money for you tomorrow so you can get what you need."

Regan frowned. "You don't need to do that. You're paying me well enough. I can get those things myself."

He nodded. "Speaking of, you need to open a bank account so I can pay you."

"Sure thing."

"Right. Well. That's all I can think of at the moment." Turning on his heel, he strode toward the exit. "The kids are up at seven for school, so I'll need you here around six thirty to make their breakfast. I'll get them up and out of bed before I leave for work."

"I can do that if you need to leave earlier."

"I can manage." He liked to be the one to wake them in the morning. He never wanted six thirty in the evening to be the first time in the day his babies saw their dad.

"Okay. Thanks again."

96

He turned at the door as he opened it. "You're the one helping me out of a jam."

Regan gave him another dimpled smile. "We're helping each other."

"Right, right. The key and fob I gave you will let you into the house via the side entrance. Just swipe the fob over the white box on your right as you enter, and it will deactivate the night alarm."

"Great. Will do."

"Okay. Night, then."

"Night," she called softly as he followed the paving stones back to the house. "See you in the morning."

He lifted an arm in a good-night gesture without looking back, and a strange uneasiness fell over him as he let himself into the main house. Perhaps it was just the action of trusting another human being, one he didn't know all that well, with the care of his children. Letting her into his home. Lachlan had called him as he was driving back from work to tell him Regan had hashed everything out with Robyn, and the sisters were in a good place again. That had made him feel better about offering Regan the job, and Lachlan, who had grown even more mistrustful of people since Lucy's betrayal, seemed to warm to his soon-to-be sister-in-law.

There had also been a hint of envy in Lachlan's voice as he spoke of Robyn's reunion with her sister. Thane knew his brother well. He was thinking of Arran and Brodan. He worried they were losing their younger brothers.

Walking around the house, Thane switched off lights, checked the doors and windows, grabbed a glass of water, and set the night alarm before making his way upstairs.

He quietly peeked into Eilidh's room to find her spread across her bed like a sea star, already deep in dreamland. Love ached fiercely in his chest. She'd been so excited to hear Regan was their new nanny, he'd wondered if she would even fall asleep. But he shouldn't have worried. Eils could fall asleep just about anywhere.

Moving onto Lewis's room down the hall, he found his son curled on his side, his cheek cradled in his hand, and the ache grew stronger. Even Lew seemed content that Regan would look after them. His son, for such a wee boy, didn't welcome new people into his life. And he was strange with those who appeared and disappeared out of it. Thane could only assume it was the effect of losing his mum so young. Something he'd never wanted to have in common with his son.

While Lachlan worried about Brodan and Arran, Thane did, too, but he was also angry with them. He never used to be. He was always the one tempering Lachlan's irritation, reminding him their brothers wanted to find themselves outside the boundaries of the Adair family. Now, not so much.

He had nothing against them going out into the world and living their lives, but where was their love and consideration for family? Their youngest brother, Arran, had been terrible at communicating with them for years. They never knew where he was or what he was up to until he turned up at Christmas or maybe for a month during the summer. He barely knew his niece and nephew.

Brodan, the second-youngest brother, never used to be so bad. When he first moved to LA to work as an actor, he kept in touch every week. He came home whenever he could.

But something had changed over the last year.

Brodan had pushed them all away and was often in the tabloids, earning a reputation as the bad boy of Hollywood. It made no sense. Brodan had never been the wild, partying kind, even at an age when that was expected. He was smarter than all the siblings put together, always had his head stuck in a book, and had openly admitted he didn't understand the fascination with drugs and alcohol.

Thane, like Lachlan, was most definitely concerned about their middle brother. But even through the frustration of his younger brothers making them worry and missing out on his children's lives, Thane had hope that one day, they'd come home.

It was something he and Lachlan spoke of often, but as he walked into the large master suite he'd designed for him and Fran, Thane missed getting into bed beside her warmth and unloading all his worries. Fran was ever practical and sensible and always made him feel better.

Sitting on the bed, he stared at the framed photograph on his bedside table of him and Fran at uni.

They'd been together a year at that point. She sat on his knee in the student union, laughing up into the camera with him as he held her close. For a long time, he couldn't look at pictures of her. Couldn't bear the god-awful black hole of pain that opened inside him.

Time didn't heal all, but it dulled the grief until he could look at photos, could talk to Eilidh and Lewis about how they'd inherited their mother's beautiful dark hair, could fill them in on all the things they'd missed about the mother they never got to know.

To his shame, there were even days he didn't think of his wife. The first time he realized he hadn't thought of her for days, the guilt really fucked with him. For weeks after, he snapped and growled at everyone until Lachlan finally got it out of him what was wrong.

As always, his brother reassured him. Reminded him it had happened when they lost their mum and their dad. That it was normal.

Life moved on.

But then there were days when the grief hit again.

Not like it was in that first year. Everything ached back then. His chest, his gut, even his jaw and gums ached with the tension of his grief.

Now it came back as a deep pang of longing.

Like tonight.

Tonight was the first in a very long time he wished he were rolling into bed beside Fran. The Fran from university. The girl who'd loved him and adored him and never dreamed of being disloyal to him. But that wasn't fair, was it?

Thane laid back on the empty bed, the one he'd replaced when he couldn't get back into the one he'd shared with Fran. He turned to look at the pillows next to his.

In the end, it didn't matter whether she was the Fran from university or the Fran who upended his entire world before she fell pregnant with Eilidh. She was Fran. The mother of his children. And it would have been a beautiful miracle to go to bed at her side that night.

The sudden emptiness was strange.

Almost as if it had come out of the blue.

Or brought on by the redhead living in his annex.

Her smile popped into his mind, and his gut twisted.

Sighing, Thane pushed up off the bed and set about changing into his pjs. No more of this maudlin rubbish. So he was wary of people after Lucy—that was only natural. But Regan was Robyn's sister. And Robyn was one of the most trustworthy people he knew, so he had to trust in Robyn's judgment. There was no need to be uneasy about Regan's presence in their lives.

Eilidh and Lewis were thrilled. Especially Eilidh. She'd fallen in love with the American already.

But Regan was leaving in six months.

Aye, there was the rub.

He'd have to make sure Eilidh and Lewis knew Regan's

stay was temporary. And he'd have to do it in a much better way than how he'd communicated about Lucy's betrayal.

His head nipping with too many concerns, Thane was glad to fall into bed so he could read for a bit. He should be in his office working on the extensive project his firm had just taken on—a commercial revamp of Aberdeen's shopping district—but Thane had already decided not to work himself into an early grave for someone else's company. He'd work the hours he was being paid to work. End of.

Opening the crime thriller he was halfway through, Thane tried to fall back into the story ... but the words weren't penetrating. His gaze drifted to his bedroom window, his thoughts returning to Regan in the annex.

He hoped she remembered how to set the alarm properly. Not that there was a significant chance of anything happening to her on the edge of Caelmore, but Thane was more security conscious after their old family friend and Ardnoch Estate's mechanic, Fergus, and Lucy terrorized Ardnoch.

"She's fine," he muttered to himself, turning back to his book.

Fifteen minutes later, he gave up with a muttered curse under his breath, threw the book on the floor, and switched off the light, hoping sleep would come. It didn't. On nights his brain was overactive, he used to fuck Fran until they were both exhausted. That was early on in their marriage. After Lewis, their sex life changed.

A lot of things changed between them.

8

REGAN

The sound of the lapping sea filtered through my consciousness, waking me before my alarm. As late as night had fallen, day broke early, sunlight filtering through the cracks between the automatic blinds. Blinking against the light, I smiled at the sound of seagulls crying.

I'd left a window open last night because it was a little stuffy in my small apartment, and I decided I'd do it again tonight. The sounds of nature as a wake-up call was pretty fantastic.

"Turn on lights," I said loudly, and all the lights came on in the guest house. I could get used to this. "Turn on coffee."

A whirring sound from my left drew my attention, and I saw the red light blinking on the coffee machine. I grinned. "Oh, yeah, I could *really* get used to this."

Since I was up earlier than I needed to be by half an hour, I dallied while making coffee. I took my phone off charge with the adapter plug from Robyn. "Open blinds," I commanded and then snuggled into the sofa to watch the large blinds on the sliding doors open. From here, I had a partial view of the sea beyond.

Sipping my coffee, I unlocked my phone and checked my emails.

Nothing. Just spam.

Without social media, there was no one to expect emails or texts from. The only meaningful friendships—or friendships I'd thought were meaningful—had been with my high school best friends, Xavier and Riko. Riko had gone on to art school on the West Coast, and we'd lost touch by the end of her freshman year. Xavier had gone to New York to intern with a CFDA designer, and we'd stayed close—until I went backpacking and started keeping secrets from him. I tried to call him when I returned to Boston, but his boyfriend answered and told me "to stop calling, bitch, Xave doesn't want to hear from you."

I cried a lot, but I stopped calling.

And the "friends" I'd made on my backpacking trip weren't people I could count on for any real support.

I literally had no one.

Except Robyn. And my mom and dad.

Deciding quality over quantity was way better, anyway, I pushed away melancholy thoughts, finished my coffee, and got ready for the day.

~

An hour later, coffee consumed, shower experienced in my amazing luxury walk-in (that was just as good as the one in Lachlan's guest suite), hair blown dry, and outfit chosen for my first day on the job, I was ready to go. Deciding comfort was a factor, a shopping spree was in my future to supplement my wardrobe. I wore one of only two pairs of skinny jeans I'd packed, along with a T-shirt tucked in the front but loose at the back, and too-big sneakers I'd borrowed from Robyn.

I let myself into the main house and deactivated the alarm, strolling quietly into the laundry room first where I separated colors from whites. Putting a bunch of colors in first, I finished up in there (for now) and wandered into the kitchen. It was only six o'clock, and no one else seemed to be up yet.

Deciding to get coffee ready for Thane, I fiddled around with his fancy coffee machine until I figured it out. After making myself a cup, I decided no other coffee would ever do again. His was amazing. Then the photos on the wall again caught my attention. After Thane got icy and nonresponsive to my question about his wife, I hadn't wanted to look at the photos too closely in front of him. Alone now, I took my time studying the gallery wall of beautifully framed black-and-white shots.

There were tons of cute photos of the kids and a few of Thane and Fran, some from when they were very young until right up to near her death, I assumed. Again, I wondered how she'd died. Fran was a very pretty brunette, and although I couldn't tell their color from the black-and-white photos, her light eyes were striking against her dark hair.

It was Thane who surprised me, though.

In the photos of him, younger and beardless, he was shockingly hot.

Not that I couldn't already tell he was good-looking. But that massive beard hid a very sexy guy who looked a lot like his brother. Staring hard at him in the pics, I realized Thane's eyes differed from Lachlan's and were his most attractive feature. They were piercing and intense and soulful and ... *hot.*

Disturbed by how sexy my new boss was, I stumbled away from the photos and told myself it was just the photographs. I didn't think that about him in real life. The beard totally wasn't my thing.

At the sound of floorboards creaking above, I set about unloading the dishwasher.

Knowing I'd be too busy later preparing the kids for school, I decided to do their lunches now. I searched the pantry and guessed at what they'd like. Sandwiches made, I then went in search of their lunch boxes. After scouring the kitchen, I finally found cute lunch bags discarded in the mudroom. Eilidh's was pink with a unicorn riding a rainbow and an attached pocket for her juice bottle; Lewis's had *Pac-Man* printed all over his.

I strolled through the hall and stopped at the sight of Thane standing in the kitchen, sipping his coffee. He wore a white shirt and dark gray suit pants, again so incongruous to his unkempt hair and beard. Without turning, his striking eyes slid to the side to look at me over his cup as he drank.

Strange flutters burst to life in my belly.

First-day jitters, I told myself.

"Morning." I pushed through the weirdness and gave him a small smile. "I was just making the kids' lunches." Moving past him, I returned to my spot at the island.

"Good morning. What did you make?" Suddenly I felt the heat of him at my back as he looked over my shoulder.

He smelled good. Not spicy or musky or "cologney." He smelled fresh and citrusy. So he was a body wash over cologne kinda guy, huh?

Regan, stop thinking about how good he smells.

"Uh … peanut butter and jelly sandwiches." I half glanced over my shoulder. "Is that okay?"

"They've never tried them together like that. It's an American thing. So we'll see." He thankfully moved away, but only to open the fridge and return with two different yogurts. I finally looked up at him and found myself caught in those amazing eyes.

Why had I not noticed how truly spectacular those eyes were?

I really wish you'd stop noticing now!

"Strawberry for Eilidh." He handed me a yogurt. "Or raspberry or anything with berry in it. No peach, no banana, no vanilla or chocolate … and nothing with bits in them." His eyes danced with humor. "Eilidh has an issue with food textures."

I grinned, putting the strawberry yogurt in her lunch bag. "Noted."

"Lewis will eat anything, but right now he's on a chocolate pudding kick." Thane gave me the little pudding cup. "If he doesn't stop eating them soon, though, we'll need to force switch him back to a healthier option."

"Okay. I can do that. What else should go in?"

He reached for his coffee, and my gaze followed the movement. His large hands looked strong, his skin naturally olive-toned, long fingers but big knuckles, veins popping across the top. I wondered if his forearms were veined and strong too.

More flutters in my belly. I guiltily looked away.

Stupid, stupid, stupid.

I had a thing about nice hands on a guy. Nice hands turned me on. And Thane's were just about the nicest, most masculine pair of hands I'd come across.

They're just hands.

And he's your boss.

And stop thinking the word hands!

What. The. Actual. Fuck.

"You okay?" Thane asked.

"Huh? Yeah. Of course, why?"

He studied me with narrowed eyes. "Because you didn't respond to my answering your question."

Oh my God.

That's right, Regan, zone out on the first day on the job. "I'm sorry. What was your answer?"

Thane frowned. "You're sure you're okay? Did you sleep well in the annex?"

"Like a dream," I assured him. At his continued frowning, I didn't want him thinking I was a flake, so I blurted out, "I was staring at your hands."

His lips parted in surprise. "What?"

Oh, Jesus. Well, you've said it now! "The reason I didn't hear your answer was that I noticed you have ... hands."

Amusement lit up his blue eyes, and I could tell he was struggling not to laugh. "That's right. I *do* have hands."

Flushing with embarrassment, I rolled my eyes at myself. "Right. You have hands. I meant you have *nice* hands."

"I have nice hands?" he repeated, still scrutinizing me with a sexy smirk on his beard-surrounded lips. I really wanted to take a trimmer to that thing.

Realizing I was staring at his mouth, I flushed harder and looked down at the kids' lunches. With a blasé shrug, I replied, "I notice nice hands on people. Probably comes from my god-awful attempt to draw them for about a year of art class in high school. Hands are hard."

"Hands *are* hard." I didn't have to look at him to know he was laughing at me.

"Anyway, you were saying about the kids' lunches?"

"Well, hang on a minute." He stepped closer and held out his left hand before us, his fingers splayed. "Are they nice enough to do some modeling, do you think?"

I gave him a pretend dark look at his drollness.

His eyes sparkled down at me. "Do you think I should start

wearing gloves? Are my hands a danger to people's libidos? Am I causing unwitting chaos every time I bring these puppies out? I mean, if people start daydreaming about them, like you just did, while they're in a car with me, it could—"

I shoved him playfully. "Shut up!"

Thane gave a bark of attractive laughter, winked, and set his coffee cup down in the sink. "There are snack packs of fruit in the fridge. Grapes for Lewis, raspberries for Eilidh. Stick those in. Fruit juice packs are in the pantry. I'm going up to wake them before I leave."

As he took the stairs two at a time, I tried to ignore the uncontrollable butterflies in my belly.

"Oh, hell," I muttered under my breath, hanging my head in despair.

Ten minutes later, Thane returned downstairs, and I tried to be more professional. "If you let me know what time you get up in the morning, I can make your coffee so it's ready," I said as he filled a to-go cup.

"Thanks, but no need. Just switch the coffee machine on." He disappeared down the hall and returned a minute later in a fitted leather jacket that was just so yum—

Looking away, I focused on cleaning the kitchen. "I had a coffee. Hope that's okay."

"Of course." He approached, forcing me to look at him. I kept my expression blank and didn't stray from his face. Not that it helped with my sudden problem. "Help yourself to whatever you like. And if the kids are not down for breakfast in ten minutes, go get them. Sometimes Eilidh needs help to get ready in the morning too."

"No problem. I'm going to braid her hair today. Maybe a fishtail—or a mermaid tail, as Eils prefers—or I could do a braid crown ..."

He didn't ignore my inane rambling. In fact, he didn't

seem to find it inane. His expression softened. "I don't know what that is, but I'm sure she'll love it."

Oh, boy, the tender look was even worse than the laughter.

"Okay, you better go, right?" *Go, leave, now!*

"Breakfast: cereal. No need to get fancy. I always treat them to a big breakfast at the weekend. Cereal is in the pantry. Lew likes Corn Flakes, no sugar. Eilidh likes Froot Loops."

"Got it." I gestured toward the door. "I have everything handled, I promise."

Thane frowned. "We haven't gone over your domestic duties."

"Do laundry, clean house, cook dinner, right?"

"Right." He eased backward. "But just lightly dust in my office. I want nothing moved."

"You got it."

"And Eilidh likes her bears arranged on her bed and around her tepee exactly so."

My mouth trembled with laughter. "She and I will have a good talk about that."

His eyes widened, as if a thought just occurred to him. "The kids are learning to clean up after themselves, so if their rooms are a bomb scare, no dessert after dinner. That's the rule and they know it."

"Good to know."

"Lachlan should have a car for you in the drive, and Robyn said she'd guide you to the school so you know where you're going."

"Great." I was a little nervous about driving in a foreign country.

"And—"

"Thane," I cut him off. "We'll manage for one day. And then you and I can talk tonight. You're going to be late for work. Don't worry—Eilidh and Lewis are in excellent hands. I promise."

Anxiety flashed in his eyes, but he quickly shrugged it off. "Right. See you tonight."

I waved, ignoring the fact that his adoring, caring dad thing was *extremely* appealing.

When the door closed behind him, I slumped against the counter.

"You can just stop that kind of thinking right now," I muttered, irritated with myself.

~

I'd inhaled a bowl of cereal between getting Eilidh and Lewis ready for school. After a far too lengthy discussion about what I'd put in their packed lunches (and a promise to have a serious conversation about their likes and dislikes when they got home from school), I'd just gotten them into their shoes when the doorbell rang.

It was then I remembered Robyn was guiding us to school. My nerves dissipated at the thought of having my sister near. The familiar and comforting was always nice in an unfamiliar situation.

"You're here!" I threw my arms around her as soon as I opened the door.

My sister seemed a little bemused but hugged me. "You okay?"

I pulled away, nodding, walking back to the mudroom. "Yeah, yeah, yeah, just first-day jitters."

The kids were already making their way down the hall toward the main living room, so I stopped and waited.

Eilidh's pretty face lit up at the sight of Robyn, and she went running to her for a hug.

"Hey, sweetie," Robyn greeted, lowering to her haunches

for the hug. She caressed one of Eilidh's fishtail braids. "Look how gorgeous your hair is."

Her big eyes sparkled. "Ree-Ree did it! They're the best pleats ever. Maisie can't make fun of my hair now."

"Who makes fun of your hair?" I queried before I asked Lewis if he had everything he needed.

He nodded while Robyn reached out to tug on his hand. "Hey, you."

He gave her a small smile.

"Maisie!" Eilidh answered, turning to me. "You have to meet Maisie, Ree-Ree. She's my first best friend. Anna is my second best friend. Well, Maisie *was* my first best friend, but now *you're* my first best friend, Maisie my second, and Anna my third. But we won't tell them that."

Heart melting in my chest, I met Robyn's gaze, and she grinned at me.

"You're my best friend too," I whispered loudly in her ear, "but don't tell Robyn."

"Robyn can hear you." My sister pretended to be affronted, making Eilidh giggle.

"Right, do we have everything?" I asked them again.

They nodded.

"Okay, then." I grabbed the house keys off the kitchen counter and gestured for Robyn to lead the way.

To my shock, she led us to two Range Rovers. Hers, I recognized, a shiny black Evoque. The one behind it was larger—a silver Velar.

"You're kidding, right?" I said as she smirked and handed me a key fob.

I took it, dazed.

"Lachlan's fleet at the estate is all Range Rover," she said, as if that explained everything. "Trust me, you want an SUV that can handle the roads here."

"Is this your car, Ree-Ree?" Eilidh ran up to the silver

vehicle and slapped it.

My eyes bugged out as I turned to Robyn. "I've never even driven on this side of the road, and you want to put me in a $70,000 car for my first try?"

Seeing my genuine anxiety, Robyn grimaced. "I'm sorry. I should have known it would freak you out. I've just accepted that Lachlan is crazy generous. Um ... okay, here's what we'll do: you'll follow me carefully to the school, and then once we've dropped off the kids, I'll take you for a driving lesson."

"I have household duties."

"You'll get them done. If you're going to be driving the kids around, I'm sure Thane would agree it's important that you know what you're doing. Especially on roundabouts."

Trying not to freak out, I nodded. "Okay. Okay. Right, well, we need to get the kids to school."

Once Eilidh and Lewis were happily loaded into the back of the luxury vehicle with its black leather seats and new car smell, I went to get in the passenger side. "Nice start," I muttered to myself, rounding the hood. The next problem occurred, however, when once I'd gotten my seat and mirrors adjusted, I didn't know how to turn it on.

"There's a big button by the wheel." Lewis pointed at it from the back.

Great. A seven-year-old was offering driving instructions.

Finding the engine start button, I pressed it and nothing happened. Except a message binged on the fancy little screen behind the wheel. I needed to put my foot on the brake, it said, before starting the engine.

Sweat gathered beneath my arms and in my palms. Finally, I got the car going and put a thumb out the window to let Robyn know we were ready.

To be fair, the fancy SUV drove like a dream, so quiet, and glided down the narrow country road. While Lewis was silent, Eilidh chattered constantly but thankfully was happy for me to just make agreeable noises now and then as I concentrated on following my sister and sticking to the correct side of the road.

It was so weird!

When we slowed on approach to a roundabout, my pulse leapt. Robyn switched on her right turn signal and I followed suit, and we drove onto the circle the wrong freaking way! Except it was the right freaking way here.

"Oh my goodness," I said under my breath.

"Are you okay?" Lewis asked, interrupting Eilidh's monologue about how her friends were going to react to her hair.

"Fine, fine," I assured him. The kids didn't need to know the person looking after them didn't know how to drive in Scotland.

To my everlasting relief, less than ten minutes later, we arrived at the school. It felt like a year.

Robyn turned into a large parking lot adjacent to the school and by a miracle found us a few spaces.

Sweaty and a little shaky, I got out of the car and unbuckled Eilidh while Lewis got himself out. "Come around my side," I called to him, and he did so. Giving him a tender smile, I turned to Eilidh and lifted her out of the car. She threw her arms around my neck before I could lower her to the ground.

"Can you come to class with me?" She pouted.

I was pretty sure that face got her anything she wanted, but unfortunately, she couldn't have this. "I'm sorry, gorgeous, you know the rules. No parents and no besties older than five allowed."

Her frown was so deep, a person could arrange coins along the ridge in her forehead.

I snuggled her close. "But I'll be here to pick you up from school, and guess what I'm making for dinner tonight?"

Eilidh's eyes lit up. "What?"

"Chicken nugget mash."

Her voice deepened as she pressed her forehead to mine. "Chicken nuuuuuuggets."

As I laughed, the tender pull in my chest was so deep, it hurt.

And I realized something scary.

It was the first day on the job ... and I was already in love with these kids.

~

"This is wrong," I said as Robyn and I got out of our SUVs. We'd parked them on the main square outside the Gloaming after the driving lesson. "I'm supposed to be working."

"And you will work," Robyn promised. "But first, you're having coffee and breakfast with your sister." Suddenly, she frowned as we walked down Castle Street. "Is that ... how can—Dad?" she called out.

Following her gaze, I saw Mac walking down the street toward us. "I thought he was on a trip."

"I thought so too." She picked up the pace and I hurried alongside her.

A woman ahead of us passed Mac with her stroller and glanced over her shoulder at him, obviously checking him out.

I chuckled, and Robyn groaned. "Seriously. It's every-where we go. Women fall all over him."

"You have a hot dad."

"Don't say that." She shoved me playfully. "He's like a stepfather to you. That's like me saying Seth is hot."

"My father is very handsome," I replied defensively.

"Yeah, he is. But there's a difference between noting a father or father figure's handsomeness versus his hotness."

I nodded in agreement. "I won't say Mac is hot again."

"Please don't." Mac drew to a halt before us, having over-heard that last sentence. He gave me a teasing look. "It's weird for me."

Face burning with embarrassment, I shrugged it off. "Hey, it's weird for me too."

"Speaking of weird"—Robyn rescued me by changing the subject—"aren't you supposed to be in California?"

"I got to the airport, and they told me my flight out of London was canceled. Hurricane over the Atlantic. Had to reschedule the meeting for next week."

"Oh. Well, what are you up to right now?"

"I was going to grab coffee and a pastry from the bakery. You ladies?"

"It's Regan's first day as Thane's nanny."

Mac raised an eyebrow as he looked at me with those penetrating hazel eyes. Robyn's eye color was an exact match to her father's, and today the sunlight made his (and Robyn's) a forest green. "You're looking after Eils and Lew?"

"Yeah." I heard the slight note of concern in his voice and assured him, "I'm a good nanny."

"So I've heard," he finally said after a long moment studying me. "Congratulations on the new job."

"Dad, why don't you have breakfast with us?" Robyn asked.

"I really should get back," I argued, guilty about slacking on my first day on the job.

"The housework will still be there when you get back."

"Robbie—"

"Robbie's right." Mac stepped toward us and then gestured across the street to a café. "No harm in having some breakfast first. And you and I haven't had a chance to really talk."

I wasn't sure that was a bad thing. I still didn't know how I felt about Mac, even if he and Robyn were on great terms.

Still, for my sister's sake, I followed them into the café. And Robyn was right. The owner, Flora, an attractive woman around Mac's age, flirted ferociously with him while we ordered. As soon as she left the table, Robyn shook her head at her dad.

He shrugged as if to say "what?"

"She is a married woman," Robyn teased.

Mac grinned a wicked smile I'm sure devastated women of all ages. "There's nothing wrong with a little harmless flirting."

"Just not in front of me again."

Eyes gleaming with amusement, Mac shook his head and turned to me. "So, how are you liking Ardnoch so far?"

We exchanged small talk while we waited for our breakfast to arrive. As soon as I'd put my fork into some scrambled egg, my straightforward sister said, "Let's cut to the chase. Regan is out of the loop on a few things about you and me." She gestured between her and Mac. "And I want it all cleared up."

Mac swallowed a bite of his breakfast roll and nodded in agreement.

They both looked at me. I asked, "You mentioned something about Mom and Mac?"

Robyn exchanged another look with her dad and then exhaled slowly. "Mac wrote to me for years, tons of letters. He sent gifts—not just to me but to you too—and she sent them all back to him without telling me."

I stared at her in disbelief. Since the age of fourteen, my sister believed Mac had completely abandoned her. While she hid her pain from the rest of the world, I was the one whose arms she cried in when his rejection cut her to the

116

soul. And now she was telling me he'd kept in touch, and Mom had hidden it.

"No." I shook my head, sitting back in my chair, the food in front of me at once unappealing.

"I have the letters. The gifts." Robyn gave her father a melancholy smile. "Mac kept them."

Seeing the pain flicker in Mac's eyes, anguish he didn't hide, my heart lurched. "Please tell me this isn't true."

Robyn grimaced. "Mom admitted to it. When I came back to Boston, we talked it all out, and she apologized."

"And you forgave her?" I huffed.

"I'm trying to, yeah." My sister reached for my hand. "I don't want you to hold this against her. She ... Mom is not a bad person. She's just ... she just thought she was protecting me."

"No, she was protecting herself."

"Ree—"

"I can't believe this." I shoved my plate away. "All that time that was lost between you and Mac because she lied."

"You have to remember," Mac spoke now, "I hurt Stacey deeply when we broke up. She didn't want it to end. And when I left for California, she saw it as me abandoning Robyn too. Yes, she made it impossible for me to see my daughter. Yes, she lied and hid my correspondence. But she genuinely believed she was protecting Robyn."

"That's the thing about Mom," I seethed. "She doesn't see the world and the people in it as they really are. She sees them as how she's made up in her mind she wants them to be."

"Don't we all?" Robyn asked softly.

"No. The rest of us judge people based on their actions, not on how we perceive those actions based on our own fucked-up insecurities. Pardon my French."

"This is about more than just Stacey keeping letters," Mac deduced, watching me carefully.

"It is," I agreed. "It's about her projecting this idea of who I am onto me since before I was even allowed to develop into the person I wanted to be. Robyn was the capable, responsible one. I was the silly, frivolous, wild child. And that's not me. And it wasn't Robyn's place to parent me, but Mom put that on her too. It's like she turned me into a problem that didn't even exist but then made sure she had someone else to blame when I messed up. That's wrong."

"You need to talk to your mother," Mac advised sternly. "You can't go around with this resentment hanging over you, Regan."

I knew he was right. The intensity of my reaction to Robyn's revelations about Mac's letters surprised me. "Do I have to right away? It'll ruin my job vacation," I joked.

"Not right away," Robyn answered. "But soon."

"I'll talk to her when I see her again," I decided. "This isn't a discussion you have over the phone." As if on cue, my cell beeped in my purse. "Sorry, let me just check that."

I opened it to discover a text from Thane, and weirdly, it soothed my agitation.

Bringing takeout for dinner. Chinese. Arro is joining us and you're welcome too. Just let me know what you'd like.

I smiled, realizing he was giving me an easy time on my first day by buying takeout. As I texted back that I'd love to join them, along with my selection, I didn't realize I was grinning until I looked up and saw my companions studying me.

My cheeks flushed. "It's just Thane. He's doing takeout for dinner, which means my workload just got easier today." I played off my reaction to his text as happiness about the latter.

But Mac narrowed his eyes ever so slightly, and it was as

if I were caught like a rabbit in headlights. Was that suspicion in his expression?

No way.

I'd just replied to a text. Nothing else. My feelings for Thane were … so what if I … ugh!

I wrenched my gaze from Mac's and listened to Robyn talk about a hike she wanted to take me on when I had a day off.

Seriously.

My sister's dad saw way too much.

9

THANE

"You seem in a better mood."

Thane turned from watching the slowly lowering sunset across the water to meet his brother's gaze. They were sitting on Lachlan's comfortably furnished, raised back deck, beers in hand, enjoying the gorgeous summer evening. A half hour ago, his brother had texted to ask if he fancied a beer out back. He'd just put the kids to bed, and at Eilidh's demand of a bedtime story from Regan, Robyn's sister was still at the house. Thane had tried to tell Eilidh that Regan had to go as it was past her working hours, but Regan shushed him, happy to do as Eilidh asked. She seemed disinclined to return to her annex, and he didn't mind her presence. It was actually nice not being the only adult in the house.

"Go have a beer," she'd said as they descended the staircase. "I can stay here in case the kids wake up."

"You don't need to do that. I'm not paying you to work after hours, Regan."

She'd given him a droll look. "Either I watch a Friday night movie in the guest house, or I watch it here. There's no difference other than you can go have a beer with your brother if I do it here."

Reassured, Thane left her in front of a romantic comedy, curled on his big sectional.

"Regan's lifted the atmosphere in the house," he answered his brother. "She's taken the kids' minds off Lucy. That whole thing was confusing for them. I think *I* made it confusing for them."

"Isn't it confusing for *you*?" Lachlan prodded quietly before taking another sip of beer.

Low-level anger burned in his gut as he looked out at the water. "I wasn't the one she stalked."

"What she did, how she could lie so brilliantly, fucked with my head. If it weren't for Robyn, I'd have become even more of a mistrustful bastard than I already am. As it is, I find it difficult to trust anyone new coming into our lives because of what she did."

Lachlan's confession didn't shock Thane. They were so close in age, they were more like twins. While they rarely discussed their emotions with other men outside of the family, they'd never held back from telling each other what was going on in their heads. Most of the time.

"Regan arriving hasn't been easy," Lachlan continued, and Thane experienced a twinge of something strangely like defensiveness. But before he could voice it, his brother said, "But I trust Robyn, and she trusts her sister. She believes Regan has owned up to her mistakes and that she means well … I'm glad you put some trust in her, for Robyn's sake, but I wouldn't blame you if you were struggling, in general, to trust people."

Thane frowned. "Like I said, Lucy was stalking you, not me."

"There was something between you. She admitted to us she had genuine feelings for you."

That low-level anger flamed brighter. "Is that woman capable of genuine feelings?"

"I don't know. Fuck, I hope so."

"Nothing happened between us," Thane said, turning to Lachlan. He knew his brother suspected he and Lucy had slept together, but it had never gotten that far. "We kissed. Once. After the ceilidh last spring. That was it."

"Did you have feelings for her?"

"Why are you asking this now?"

"Because I don't want you stewing over this shit. I don't want any of us stewing over this shit. The trial looms, and with it a media storm, and all that won't die until the trial is over. I don't want it consuming our lives until then. So, we get the poison she put in us out. Now. Before it goes any deeper."

Marveling at the change that had come over his brother since Robyn's arrival, Thane felt a prick of envy. That was what a good woman's love could do. He knew it firsthand.

He also knew firsthand what her betrayal could do.

"Well … Lucy … did you have feelings for her?"

Thane smirked unhappily. "She was a knockout, charismatic Hollywood star. And I'm a mere mortal. What do you think?" Despite knowing she'd been in his brother's bed, Thane had been extremely attracted to Lucy Wainwright. She was the kind of stunning that was almost untouchable, but she'd seemed so down-to-earth. The type of woman who knew how to make any man comfortable in her presence. Lucy had also always been sweet to his children.

While he'd been on dates since Fran's death and had slept with other women, Lucy was the first woman he'd been more than just physically attracted to. Thankfully, his feelings hadn't developed beyond affection.

The thought of what might have happened had he let her any deeper into his life enraged him.

"She fucked with your head," Lachlan surmised.

"I let her near my kids," Thane hissed. "That's what fucks with my head the most. The time she spent with Eilidh. Filling her mind with who knows what. And then having to explain to them that Lucy won't be around anymore because she tried to hurt their aunt and uncle ... let's just say that was a confusing mess of a conversation for us all. I didn't know what I should tell them and it was ... just ... fuck, it was a mess."

Silence fell between them, and Thane took an agitated pull of his beer.

"Regan's not Lucy," Lachlan suddenly said.

Thane's head whipped toward his brother so fast, a burn of pain flared up the side of his neck. "What?"

He shrugged. "Just saying. In case that's on your mind. She *is* a beautiful redhead."

"Do you think I would have hired Regan to look after my children if that was what was going on in my mind?"

"'Course not. I just meant ... I don't know." Lachlan sighed wearily. "I'm just worried about her. Robyn thinks if we all make Regan feel at home, feel embraced here, she might settle down."

Thane snorted. "She's living in my annex, looking after my kids. How much more do you want me to embrace her?"

His brother burst into laughter. "Fair enough."

Grinning, Thane stared out at the water again. A door closing in the distance sounded, followed by the hum of music. Lachlan glanced over his shoulder, toward the side of the house. When he looked back, he wore a small, almost imperceptible smile. "Robyn's working."

His brother had built a separate building for Robyn's photography business.

"I'm glad you found her," Thane said. And he genuinely was. Lachlan deserved someone special like Robyn.

Lachlan looked somber of a sudden. "I love her so much, I can barely contain it. I don't know how you did it, Thane. How you got up every day and kept going after you lost Fran. I'm humbled by you."

Emotion burned in his throat. Thane reached out and patted Lachlan's shoulder. He didn't know how to tell his brother that in the end, he hadn't had with Fran what Lachlan had with Robyn. There was no point. It didn't change the fact that a woman he loved, the mother of his children, had died abruptly and he'd grieved over her deeply. Still grieved for her.

After a few moments of silence, Thane said, "You're going to let Eilidh be a flower girl, aye? Until Regan showed up, it was all she talked about."

"Of course." Lachlan grinned the smile of a smitten uncle. "We'll make sure she gets the dress she wants … Eils likes Regan, then?"

"Oh, aye." Concern niggled in Thane's gut. "So does Lewis. You know he doesn't take to folks quickly, but I can tell he likes her. I explained to them that it's just temporary, that Regan goes back to the States in six months, but I'm worried about how attached they already are to her, and it's only been two days."

"If Robyn has anything to do with it, her sister will be here longer than six months."

"What do you mean?"

"She thinks this place will be good for Regan."

It would make his life easier if Regan could stick around longer than six months. "At her age? I doubt this place will keep her interested for long. Still, you should see my house. It's gleaming. All the kids' stuff is organized and tidy. I come home to dinner ready. Even my office … she cleans it without messing anything up in there."

Lachlan grinned at him. "Sounds like *you're* enjoying your nanny housekeeper."

Although he knew his brother meant nothing sexual, Thane felt a flush of physical longing.

Just the beer, he told himself, unable to meet his brother's eyes.

"It's nice not living in chaos."

However, when he returned to the house an hour later, he found Regan curled up asleep on his couch. He'd noticed her dress that morning, wondering what happened to her comfortable jeans and T-shirt, which was more appropriate for her daily tasks, but had made no comment since she could wear whatever the fuck she wanted.

But now he was definitely noticing the dress. It had ridden up high so he could see the curve of a very pert ass beneath it. Her gorgeous hair spilled across the sofa cushions.

His gut tightened with need as he took in the sight of the sleeping beauty on his sofa.

She looked sleepy and comfortable …

And sexy as hell.

Reaching for the throw over the back of the couch, he brought it down over her, careful not to touch her.

She was too young for him.

Not to mention his brother's soon-to-be sister-in-law.

And he was her boss.

That she was a beautiful woman must be ignored.

Switching off the TV, he stood back, not making a move to leave, apparently hypnotized by the sight of her lovely face relaxed in sleep.

Earlier, he'd watched her face as she animatedly read a book to Eilidh. She was brilliant at acting it out and doing all the voices, and she'd even made him chuckle.

The image of her laughing face, those dimples deepening in her apple cheeks, made him harder.

"Fuck," he muttered as he quietly stumbled upstairs. "Just a bit drunk," he reassured himself. That was all. He wasn't actually attracted to his twenty-five-year-old nanny.

He was a better man than that.

10

REGAN

S *till getting nasty side-eye from thirsty single moms.*

    I tried not to smirk as I sent off the text to Robyn. A couple seconds later, my cell buzzed in my hand.

Lachlan wondered what I was laughing at so I told him. He thinks it's hilarious. Is prob gonna tell Thane.

Oh, no. He wouldn't. *He better not.*

It was bad enough hiding my ever-increasing crush on the man. He didn't need to know there was a group of single moms at Ardnoch Primary School who clearly had Thane in their sights. Over three weeks ago, at the end of my first complete week working as the nanny, and after these moms had eyeballed me at the school gates every morning and afternoon, two of them made an approach to ask who I was. At first, I thought they were just looking out for Eilidh and Lewis. While the school was big enough to accommodate all the outlying settlements around Ardnoch, it wasn't massive. And I already knew from Robyn that everybody knew each other here. Naive me thought they were being friendly.

"I'm Regan Penhaligon." I'd offered a hand to the attractive older blond who introduced herself as Michelle.

"Any relation to Lachlan Adair's fiancée?" her brunette companion asked.

"Her sister."

"And you're … watching the children for Thane?" the blond queried.

"I'm his new live-in nanny."

Abruptly, the atmosphere turned frosty and their smiles grew tight. They dragged their gazes down my body in that way women did when they wanted you to feel judged.

And there I was thinking how awesome their Scottish accents were and how I liked Michelle's modern take on preppy style.

Then it got worse. "*Just* the nanny?" The brunette arched an eyebrow.

I raised an eyebrow right back at her. "No. I also cook and clean."

Having been taught by the master (Robyn) how to out-stare someone, the brunette lost our match and looked away, her lips pursed.

Michelle gave me another tight smile. "You're awfully young to be a nanny, are you not?"

Damn, she had a cool accent. It was a thicker brogue, a bit like Mac's. Pity her accent was cooler than she was.

"I'm twenty-five."

"Oh, you look younger than that." The brunette's expression was suspicious, as if she didn't believe me. What the hell?

"Aye, we thought you were just out of high school."

Yeah, right. What was going on here?

"We've known Thane a long time," the brunette said haughtily. "We really do miss him at the school gates. Will he not be coming back, then?"

My suspicions built. "Not in the immediate future."

The bell rang, and thankfully the women scampered back

to their companions who leaned in to hear what they'd discovered in their reconnaissance mission. I rolled my eyes and tried to forget them, excited for Eilidh and Lewis to come out of the school.

"Don't worry about them," an English-accented voice said.

I'd glanced to my left to see an attractive guy grinning mischievously at me. He had longish brown hair and dark eyes. "Excuse me?"

He jerked his chin in the direction of Michelle and the three other women. "Thirsty single mothers."

"Excuse me?" I repeated.

"Thane Adair is sexy, wealthy, and a single father. Not just any single father—a widow. Bleeding hearts love that. Plus, he's an Adair. That name has gravitas in these parts."

My suspicions were confirmed. "They all have their sights set on Thane?"

"Yes." The man smirked, his eyes dropping down my body but not in the insulting way Michelle and her friends' gazes had. "They're not happy to hear you're living with him as his nanny."

At my confused expression, he chuckled. "You have looked in a mirror, yes?"

The blood in my cheeks turned hot. As arrogant as it might sound to admit it out loud, I knew I was pretty. I'd never lacked for boyfriends. But I'd never prioritized physical appearance. The guys I'd dated all had one thing in common: charisma. Other than that, they'd been totally different in the looks department. Some typically good-looking like Maddox, and some made attractive by his inner sexiness rather than overt handsomeness.

Anyway, I hadn't expected to find myself back in high school in a small village in the Scottish Highlands, hated on because I was dating the sexiest guy in school. And this time, I wasn't even dating him—I was working for him.

"Jesus," I muttered, throwing them a look. "They think I'm a threat?"

"Aren't you?"

Perhaps it was because I hadn't quite been able to talk myself out of a crush on Thane that I snapped, "Of course not. Thane's a gentleman. He's my boss, that's all."

The guy raised his hands, his gaze flicking to the school doors as the kids flooded out. "Hey, I meant nothing by it. I'm Will, by the way. My fiancé works for Thane's brother at the estate. Jock. He's on the security team."

Jock, as in Sarge? "You're Sarge's fiancé?"

Will chuckled. "He told me you call him that. And yes. That little munchkin running toward me is Adam!" he said, just as a boy who looked like a mini version of Jock jumped into his arms. "How was school?"

"Fine." The boy eyed me shyly. "Glad it's over."

I smiled at him, but I was watching for Eilidh and Lewis.

"Your little one is just coming." Will pointed out Eilidh in the crowd. "She and Adam are in class together, so I'm sure we'll see each other again."

I'd waved goodbye to Will and Adam just as Eilidh ran up and wrapped her arms around my legs. She threw her head back, grinning up at me, and announced, "It's Friday!"

Shaking myself out of the memory of that first full week as Thane's nanny, I shot the four women a look. Even though I knew all their names now, I kept referring to them as the thirsty single moms since Will first called them that. Will, I'd discovered, was an artist, and not only did I fall in love with his paintings, but I was kind of in love with him. We grabbed a quick coffee after school drop-off twice a week when we'd chat about everything and nothing. He'd told me all about Jock getting his ex-girlfriend pregnant and how they'd met when Will moved to Ardnoch to set up his gallery. He didn't go into too much detail, but I could read between the lines that Jock had a tough time accepting he was bisexual. Eventually, though, he came out to his family and moved in with Will.

During all of it, he'd battled for full custody of Adam because of his ex-girlfriend's heroin addiction. There was so much evidence of neglect that he won.

Will was a great buffer between me and the thirsty moms, but he, Jock, and Adam were on vacation in the Caribbean for two weeks, so I was alone at the gates this week.

My sister didn't text back, which meant Lachlan was totally telling Thane about the moms. Not that it mattered. If they were this obvious with me, how obvious were they with Thane?

Another glance over. I caught the brunette's eye—her name was Laura—and smiled.

She frowned like she didn't know what to do with that.

Whatever. Looking down again, I sent Robyn a link to a wedding designer in Edinburgh. While I'd been nannying and housekeeping my ass off this past month, I'd also been helping Robyn plan her wedding. Everything was going smoothly, considering they were getting married at Ardnoch Castle and using the estate's resources for that. But we still had bridal-party wear, décor, music, band, invitations, and all that to sort out. They were having a spring wedding, only seven months away.

Two minutes later, the bell rang and I put my cell away. For once, Lewis reached me first.

"Hey, buddy, good day?"

He shrugged. "It was okay."

I rested a hand on his shoulder, pulling him to my side and inwardly cursing Mrs. Welsh to hell. While Connor's mom filed a complaint and Mrs. Welsh had issued an apology, she was still "impatient and mean." I felt powerless, hating that Lewis disliked school so much because of her. In fifth grade, I had an awful teacher who made me feel stupid all the time, and she'd seriously made me hate school. Until that year, I'd loved school. I didn't want that to happen to Lewis.

"Since it's Friday, I thought we'd grab an ice cream from Morag's. What do you think?"

He gave me a small smile and a nod. As we waited for Eilidh to detach herself from an excited huddle in the middle of the playground, Lewis moved closer into my side.

It was subtle, but it happened.

My hand tightened on his shoulder.

Finally, Eilidh broke away from her friends and skipped to us, her fishtail braids with the pink ribbons tied at the ends flying up around her. "We started a girl band!"

Taking her hand, I chuckled. "Yeah? What are you guys called?"

"Don't know yet. I like the Unicornies, but Maisie likes the Mermaids."

Walking the kids toward the car, I tried hard to keep a straight face. "Well, that's a big decision to make."

"Not really." She shook her head adamantly. "Unicornies are better than the silly mermaids."

"Are you the lead singer?"

Eilidh gave me a look as if to say "well, duh," and this time I couldn't help but laugh. As I opened my eyes, I caught sight of Michelle watching me as she loaded her kids. Deciding not to let the scrutiny bother me, I led my charges to the Range Rover and filled Eilidh in on the ice cream plan.

Just as she did with chicken nuggets, she announced *ice cream* to the world in her monster voice. Even Lewis giggled.

11

REGAN

T he drive to the beach was a mere twenty minutes from the house. It was on the opposite end of the coastal line, so we drove through the village to get to it. I'd been to the beach with Robyn on weekends; as much as I could, I tried to give Thane space with Eilidh and Lewis on my days off. If I wasn't with Robyn (because I was trying to give *her* space with her fiancé), I was hanging out with Arrochar or Eredine or both. We'd taken day trips to Inverness, and they'd gotten me back into hiking by showing me trails through the Cairngorms. Of course, I'd needed to outfit myself with new gear from the outdoor clothing store, and that hadn't been cheap. But it was worth it.

As the weeks flew by, I found myself more and more familiar with the villagers, and between my friendships with Arro, Eredine, and Will, my restored closeness with Robyn, and a job I loved, Ardnoch was starting to feel like home.

The only downside to the whole thing was my feelings for Thane. I couldn't remember the last time I'd crushed this hard on a guy. And never one who was so off-limits. One way I tried to avoid said feelings was to avoid said man, and the best time to do this was on the weekends.

However, it was the middle of October, and the entire country was experiencing this crazy heat wave. Not that anyone other than Scottish people considered temperatures in the low seventies a real heat wave, but the Scots around me marveled at it, determined to take advantage, including Eilidh and Lewis. They'd decided they wanted to spend Saturday, the first official day of their October school vacation, at the beach, but they'd guilted Thane into allowing me to accompany them. I wanted to say no, but when they were looking up at me with those puppy eyes … argh. It was Lewis who did it for me, and I think for Thane too. Over the past six weeks, he'd grown increasingly demonstrative in his affection for me. Last night, when I was cleaning up dinner and preparing to take off to the annex, Lewis suggested I come to the beach with them the next day. And gosh, one look at Thane and I knew neither of us could deny him.

So there I was, playing happy family with Thane Adair.

I just had to pray none of the thirsty moms were at the beach, or this would give them something to chew on.

"I knew it would be busy," Thane muttered under his breath as he parked in the last free space in the lot above the sand dunes. "October break. Everyone and their mother are staying at Gordon's caravan park."

Glancing to my left, I saw the entrance to a trailer park up ahead. "Is that where Robyn stayed for a while?"

"Yeah, in Gordon's private caravan." He glanced over his shoulder at Eilidh and Lewis in the back of the SUV. "You ready?"

Eilidh beamed, her teeth pressed together in a maniacal smile that made me chuckle, while Lewis was already unbuckling his seat belt. They both had their swimwear on under their clothes, but I'd foregone it. I'd worn a summer dress, even though I thought it was breezy. If the kids wanted to go in the water, I'd go in with them, but I was definitely not wearing a bikini in front of Thane.

I hopped out to help Eilidh while Thane grabbed the cooler, blanket, and picnic hamper from the trunk. However, as soon as I opened the passenger door, Eilidh said she wanted to wear her sandals instead of her sneakers. I'd packed them in a bag filled with extras (clothing, shoes, and towels).

"One second," I told her and rounded the SUV.

Food was scattered in the rear of the vehicle. Thane looked up from repacking the hamper. "Bloody lock broke," he grumbled.

"Is the food okay?"

"Some of it's a bit bashed."

"That's fine." I patted his shoulder in assurance and immediately regretted it when I felt his hard muscle. Flushing inward, I rounded his side and bent into the car. "Where's the bag with Eilidh's sandals?"

"I don't—there it is." He pointed to the darkest corner of the deep cargo area.

Unfortunately, we both moved in to get it at the same time and our cheeks slammed together. I felt the surprisingly soft tickle of his beard.

"Sorry!" we both exclaimed and jerked back. In the flailing, Thane's knuckles brushed across my right breast, and I sucked in a sharp breath of awareness.

Our eyes collided, and I swore I saw heat in Thane's before he looked away. His voice sounded a little hoarse as he said, "Let *me* get the sandals."

Body tingling, cheeks burning, I stepped away and tried to look anywhere but at his ass. I succeeded. I failed, however, at keeping myself from ogling the perfect V-shape of his back from his trim waist to his broad shoulders. Over the last six weeks, despite trying to avoid being alone with Thane as much as possible, I'd picked up on his habits. And keeping fit was one of them. He had a small gym off his bedroom that he got up at the crack of dawn to use a few times a week. He said I could use it anytime I wanted. The offer had made me laugh.

"Not a fan of working out?" he'd asked with an amused smile on his beautifully curved mouth.

"I'm more of a yoga, Pilates, hiking kind of girl. MMA training is as close to a workout you'll ever see me do."

But I was more than happy to enjoy the visual fruits of other people's labor at the gym.

"Here." Thane hauled the bulky bag toward the top of the cargo space. "What on earth is in here?"

"Extras," I explained. "Of everything."

At his questioning look, I made a face. "We're on a day trip to the beach with two children under eight. If we get through the day without needing at least three things out of the extras bag, I will be shocked."

He grinned, his eyes crinkling attractively at the corners. "True enough."

I ignored the flutter in my belly and dug through for Eils' sandals. I moved to haul the large bag out of the car.

"I'll get that." Thane reached for it.

Gently swatting his hand away, I walked around him. "You're carrying everything else."

"Dad," Lewis said behind me. "I can help."

"You take the towels, son," Thane said.

Once I'd gotten Eilidh into her sandals, all four of us trundled down the sand dunes onto the fairly busy Ardnoch Beach. Blankets, locals, and tourists dotted the stretch of luxurious golden sand. I didn't blame everyone for descending upon the beach, though I preferred walking it with Robyn when hardly anyone was there.

But today, the cloudless sky had turned the water of the North Sea an almost Mediterranean green-blue. The soft sand was a white-gold up near the sand dunes, only to ombré into a rust orange where the shore continually lapped at it. The beach was secluded into a large cove, curving outward at opposite ends until it disappeared into the jutting green cliffs beyond.

"God, this place is beautiful," I said, even as I shivered from the cool breeze blowing toward us from the sea. I clasped tighter to Eilidh's hand as we slid a little down the dunes. Lewis walked on my right, between me and his dad.

Thane, who seemed as unperturbed as everyone else by the breeze, smiled. A hot pair of Ray-Bans hid his eyes from me. "Is She seducing you, then?"

All I heard was the word *seducing*.

"Huh?"

He chuckled, looking forward. "Scotland. Is She seducing you as She did your sister?"

"I think we both know it wasn't Scotland that did the seducing," I teased.

Laughing, Thane nodded and was about to reply when Eilidh beat him to it. "What does *sepuducing* me?"

Having momentarily forgotten children were *always* listening, I blanched and covered it with a bright smile. "Charmed, honey. It means to charm someone. You know, make them like you."

I was pretty sure Thane shot me a grateful look, but it was difficult to tell behind those sunglasses.

We found a spot a little down the beach, near the dunes, and out of nowhere Thane produced an unfamiliar, multi-colored object and unfolded it. It consisted of four wide strips of stretched canvas with poles slotted in between each so it could fold in different directions. He placed it into the sand like a wall that curved around our towels.

Looking across the beach I realized most people had these or little colorful tents.

"What is that?"

"The windbreak?" He raised an eyebrow. "You don't have these in the US?"

"Nope. We have umbrellas and cabanas to fight off the *sun*. Not the *wind*." I grinned at the thought.

However, when we sat behind it my goose bumps disappeared now that we'd blocked out the breeze. In fact, it was downright toasty under that fall sun.

Windbreaks. They were kind of genius.

I set about slathering Eilidh in sunblock while Thane did the same for Lewis. I tried not to think about the picture we made, all four of us. Like a family.

That way lies danger.

"There's Anna! There's Anna!" Eilidh jumped up and down, the frills of her swim dress bouncing around her waist. Following her gaze, I saw she was right. One of her best friends, a little pixie blond girl, was on the beach with her mom and her big sister Rosie.

"I see Connor as well," Lewis said, craning his neck to look down the beach.

"Don't you want to sit with us for a bit?" Thane asked, sounding a little put out.

Smiling to myself, I took Eilidh's hand. "They can sit with us at lunch, no?"

He reluctantly agreed, and we walked away from our spot, me to deliver Eilidh to Anna, with a promise from Anna's mom to watch her while they played, and Thane to do the same with Connor and his dad.

We met back on our blanket, behind the windbreak and I was suddenly very much aware of being alone with him. "I feel unloved," I joked to break the tension I was sure only I felt.

Thane chuckled. "It's just strange they're both at that age where they want to go off and play with their friends. Not that long ago, they didn't want to leave my side."

"They're still babies," I assured him as I covered up with sunscreen. I'd deliberately chosen a dress with a high back so I wouldn't need anyone to help me out.

What I hadn't been counting on was Thane whipping off his T-shirt.

But why wouldn't he when he looked like that?

The man wasn't muscled to the max like some male model. There was definition, yes, but if I didn't know he worked out, I'd just assume he was naturally built that way. There was nothing overworked about his physique. He was ... too sexy to be my boss.

Damn it.

Not knowing where to look, I turned to stare out at the water as he covered himself with sunblock. Apparently unable to control myself, I glanced at him out of the corner of my eye just as he realized he'd made an error in judgment by whipping off his shirt.

He couldn't cover his back in sunblock without help.

And I was a complete opportunist with no self-preservation whatsoever. "Need a hand?"

Thane made an exasperated sound. "If you don't mind."

My pulse increased as I took the sunblock and walked on my knees until I was behind him.

His broad back stretched before me, smooth, olive skin over healthy muscle. And there was a tattoo on his right shoulder that I'd never seen before—a Celtic knot symbol.

Taking a deep breath that I hoped Thane couldn't hear, I slathered cream on my fingers and then pressed my palms to his strong back. For a moment, I didn't move my hands. I was afraid if I did, I'd *caress* him.

Thane turned his head slightly, as if he sensed something

was wrong. I shook myself out of crazy crush mode and smoothed the lotion into his skin. It was going well until I noted how tense his shoulders were.

"You need a massage," I said, subconsciously kneading my fingers and thumbs into the too-tight muscle.

He grunted. "Fuck, that feels good. Had that knot there forever."

Frowning, I rolled my thumb against the area I thought he meant. "Here?"

The sound of deep pleasure made me smirk, and I continued to knead at it.

"You're good at this," Thane offered after a few seconds, his voice rumbly and hoarse.

I wondered if he sounded like that after sex?

Tingling between my thighs at the very thought, I had to stop from pressing my breasts to his back.

I was losing my goddamn mind. *Control yourself, woman!*

I tried to focus on anything but the low groans falling from his lips. "What does the tattoo mean?"

Thane tensed for a moment and then relaxed into my touch again as he replied, "It's Celtic ... it's the sigil for curse breaking."

Surprised, my hands fell away from his shoulders and he turned, forcing me to move back.

"Not what you expected?" He rubbed a hand through his beard, looking almost boyishly embarrassed.

Not from Thane. Mr. Practical and Sensible. Mac was the one filled with tales of magic and fairies. I shook my head. "What does it mean to you?" After my many talks with Robyn over the past six weeks, she'd confessed much to me about her relationship with Lachlan. One reason he'd held himself back from a genuine relationship with Robyn was that he was convinced the Adair men were cursed to lose the women they loved. He'd been irrationally terrified (not so irrational, I guess, especially considering their circumstances) that Robyn would die if he loved her back. Was Thane referring to the same family curse?

"Has Robyn told you much about our family?"

Wanting to be honest with him, I nodded. "She's entrusted me with some personal things. I know about the Adair curse. Or so-called curse."

"It's something Lachlan came up with. Something that got into his head and almost ruined his chances with Robyn. The stubborn bastard." He said the insult with affection I'd seen openly expressed between the two brothers. They were very close, like me and Robyn. "He thinks it goes way, way back. Our great-great-grandfather lost his wife to influenza six months after they were wed. He married again, but how much he'd loved his first wife and never truly recovered from her death was a tale passed down through the generations. His son lost his wife to childbirth and he never remarried. Then my mother died in childbirth, and our father never got over it. Our aunt Imogen stayed with us, helped raise us, but when she died, I think it finished our father."

"Then Fran died," I whispered, emotion thickening my throat. I still didn't know how she'd passed. Robyn said it was up to Thane to entrust me with that information. That no one was coming out to say if she died of cancer or in a car crash or something that happened every day made me think her death had a darker edge to it.

"Then Fran died," Thane repeated grimly. "Lachlan became convinced we were cursed, but I refused to believe that." I could sense his penetrating stare through his dark sunglasses. "I refuse to be controlled by some greater fate. So I got the tattoo as a reminder not to let myself go down that path." He shrugged and scratched his beard. "Seemed a good idea at the time. Now it just seems ... silly, I suppose."

"No, it doesn't. It's so easy to fall into the trap of

believing you don't have control over your life—if we don't have control, then we don't have to hold ourselves responsible for our failings, or even our successes. Some people use that as an easy way out. Or, like Lachlan, they let fear control their choices. I respect you haven't allowed that to happen."

We shared a long look, the air electric between us. "You haven't either," he murmured. "You took control of your life, yes, when it felt like it was spiraling?"

"Exactly." I hadn't divulged anything to Thane about why I'd taken off on Robyn, and I found myself wanting him to know, to understand. If Robyn didn't think I was a coward, I was sure Thane wouldn't either. And I wanted him to know that I really did understand his tattoo. That I understood him.

And so, somewhat guarded from view thanks to the windbreak, my eyes on Eilidh playing in the distance, I confessed to Thane why I'd left Robyn after she got shot. I didn't go into detail about Austin—that was a conversation I hoped we'd never have to have—but I explained how I'd let my fear keep me away from her.

"I was ashamed of my cowardice," I ended.

Thane leaned into me, his voice gruff. "You are not a coward. You were very young, and you didn't know how to process your emotions. Emotional intelligence takes time. Do you think I was emotionally mature and self-aware at twenty-two, twenty-three?" he said. "You learned faster than many of us do, Regan."

Grateful, I reached out without thinking and placed a hand on his bent knee. "Thank you for saying that."

His large, strong hand covered mine, and goose bumps shot up my arm despite the lack of breeze. I inhaled sharply, and Thane's fingers tightened on mine.

"Thane!" A shrill female voice jolted us out of the

moment, and I glanced up to see Michelle, one of the thirsty moms, stalking toward us.

Sliding away from Thane, my heart raced.

I'd totally forgotten we were sitting in public, touching each other.

"Michelle." Thane looked up at her. "How are you?"

She shook two ice-cream cones at us but put way more jiggle behind it than necessary so that her impressive boobs shook in her cute bikini top.

I hated her.

Side-eyeing Thane, I tried not to glare. I couldn't tell where he was looking, but a possessive growl of jealousy sounded in my head. *He better not be looking at her boobs.*

"The ice-cream van arrived, and the kids wanted some. Connor's dad watched them while I ran off to get them. I saw Lewis. He's getting so big. And handsome. Just like his dad."

Thane cleared his throat. "Aye, well ..." He trailed off uncomfortably, making me laugh.

"It looks like your ice creams are melting there, Michelle," I said.

She wore sunglasses, but I still knew she was glaring at me. "Regan. I didn't see you there."

I guffawed under my breath, but the way Thane turned slightly to look at me, a small smirk on his lips, told me he'd heard me.

At my non-answer, Michelle threw a strained smile at Thane. "I hope to see you at parents' evening. Maybe even before then. We all miss you at the gates."

"That's kind."

When Thane said no more, her smile wavered and she threw us a quick bye before hurrying off with the melting cones.

Silence fell between us for a second.

Then I burst out laughing.

Thane half laughed, half groaned as he leaned back on his hands.

"Could she be any more obvious?" I huffed.

"Every time." He rubbed a hand over his beard. "It's the one thing I don't miss about working from home. Enduring those bloody pickups and drop-offs at the gates with those women."

My jealousy eased. "You're not interested in any of them? They're attractive."

Thane's amusement fled. "No. They're only interested in the Adair name and the money they think comes with it."

Frowning, I shook my head. "I think *you* might have something to do with it too. I'm sure Lachlan's already told you they've been giving me the stink eye for the past six weeks."

His lips twitched. "He mentioned something."

"They think I'm doing more than nannying for you," I blurted.

Despite those damn sunglasses, I could feel him *looking* at me. My body reacted to his unintentional smoldering, and my dress was suddenly too tight across my breasts.

"Ignore them," Thane finally replied. "They like to gossip."

"I do ignore them," I promised. Then, because I was a glutton for punishment, I asked, "So there's no one you're interested in dating?"

For a second I thought I might have crossed the boss/employee boundary, but Thane eventually answered, "I don't date often. I don't want lots of women coming in and out of the kids' lives."

What about sex? He was a virile, hot-as-hell man in his prime.

As if he could read my thoughts, he grinned, and it was too wicked. "There's a difference between 'dating' and *dating*. I 'date' more than I *date*. If you catch my drift."

Oh, yeah, I caught his drift. There was that jealousy rearing its ugly head again. Was he "dating" someone right now? All this time, while I was crushing on him, was he fucking women any chance he got? But when? All he did was be a dad and work. What if it was someone he worked with?

Oh my God, I was driving myself crazy.

Turning to look back at Anna and Eilidh dancing on the beach, I let their cuteness cut through my irrational annoyance.

"What about you? You haven't met anyone special yet?" Thane asked.

Yes! I wanted to shout in his face. *And he's oblivious!* Instead, I shrugged. "Nope. Not yet."

"I find that hard to believe."

The note of admiration in his tone made me turn back to him. I swear to God, I sensed his eyes on my body.

But that couldn't be right. Right? "You do?"

His mouth twisted into a self-deprecating smirk as he looked toward the water. "Aye, surely some young surfer or lead singer of an indie rock band wanted to take you on adventures with him."

Is that what he thought? That I wanted some irresponsible, wild, adventurous, "fun" youth? After what I'd just confessed to him? Irritated, I replied, my voice a little hoarse, "I want a *man*, not a boy."

Now it was Thane's turn to inhale sharply.

"Ree-Ree!" Eilidh came flying at us and threw herself into her dad's arms, despite it being my name she'd called.

Thane caught her and cuddled her close.

Taut with tension, I didn't know whether her interruption relieved me.

"What do you want Regan for, Eilidh-Bug?" her dad asked, smoothing stray curls around her face.

Damn, he was such a hot dad.

And I was such a perv.

Focus, focus, focus. I grinned at Eilidh as she chattered about how Mac said there were mermaids in the water and would I take her down to see them.

"Uncle Mac was talking about the loch at Ardnoch, darling," Thane told her. "This is the firth that leads into the North Sea."

"No mermaids?" she asked, big-eyed.

He shook his head.

"Can we still go in?"

"Regan isn't dressed for the water, but how about I take you in and then when we come back, we'll have lunch?"

Eilidh agreed, and Thane stood and swung her with ease onto his shoulders. Her giggles pealed across the beach, drawing stares.

And some stares remained on the daddy eye candy. Smirking, I reached for the hamper. "Why don't you check on Lewis, see if he wants to go down to the water with you?"

"Will do. Say bye-bye to Regan." Thane waved Eilidh's hands for her, making her giggle harder.

"Bye, Ree-Ree!" she squealed, and I laughed as they wandered down the beach in Lewis's direction. When I reluctantly drew my eyes from them, my gaze landed on Michelle, thirsty mom number one, and I didn't need to see behind her sunglasses to know she was glowering. Her pursed lips gave her away.

Damn these Ardnoch moms and their territorialism.

∼

A little later, after lunch was eaten and food had settled in our guts, when the beach had cleared some and wasn't nearly so busy, the four of us took Lewis's ball down near the shore and played soccer. I hated to say it, because I was all about girl power, but Eilidh and I were useless. She and I spent most of the time giggling hysterically at our terrible skills.

"It's not soccer, Ree-Ree!" Lewis yelled for the hundredth time. He'd taken to calling me his sister's pet name a few weeks ago. "We call it football here!"

"Right, right!" I held up my hands defensively. "I forgot."

"You can't be Scottish if you keep calling it soccer."

The implication being that he wanted me to be Scottish?

Before I could stew over that, Eilidh ran at the ball, grabbed it in her little hands, and threw that thing with impressive might down the beach. "There!" she yelled, like she'd finally accomplished the goal of the game.

Laughing, I took off after the ball. "I'll get it!"

I watched as it bounced down the sand toward a guy running on the beach. He saw it and stopped to retrieve it before it went into the water to be lost for good.

"Thanks!" I called and then slowed as I neared.

I then became extremely aware that he was young, shirtless, and built. And not in the way Thane was naturally built. This guy had a freaking eight-pack.

My inner flirt came out before I could stop it. "Good thing you were Baywatching it down the beach." I took the ball from him. He had the most stunning green eyes I'd ever seen.

He grinned at me. "Aye, good thing. Just visiting?"

"The accent? No." I turned and gestured to where Thane and the kids were waiting. "I live here. I'm a nanny."

The green-eyed hottie nodded and then held out a hand. "Jared. McCulloch."

Having been told the tale of how the Adairs had an antagonistic relationship with Collum McCulloch, the local farmer of Thane's father's generation, I grimaced. Robyn said Collum held a grudge against the Adairs because of land the

Adair ancestors allegedly stole from his family. "No relation to Collum?"

"Granddad, I'm afraid." He squinted past me. "Since that looks like an Adair you're with, I'm guessing you've heard that bloody ridiculous story."

"Yeah, I have. I'm Regan. Robyn Penhaligon's sister. I also heard that your grandfather helped save my sister's life, so I'm thankful to him." It was true. Lucy and Fergus had kidnapped Lachlan and lured Robyn onto McCulloch land. She'd actually thought Collum was behind the attacks on Lachlan, but nope. Collum had helped rescue them that day.

"You would think something like that might mend fences." Jared sighed.

"You would think. I know Robyn would prefer it."

"Aye, my granddad's quite fond of your sister, though the stubborn bugger will never admit it."

That was nice to hear. I smiled. "Maybe things will get better over time." Seeing a trickle of sweat run down his neck, I was aware of his half-dressed body again and stepped to the side. "I'm sorry, I interrupted your jog."

Definite flirtation twinkled in those gorgeous eyes. "I'm quite happy for you to interrupt me anytime."

"Regan!"

Thane's bark startled me, and I turned to see him giving me the universal sign of "hurry the fuck up."

Frowning at his uncharacteristic impatience, I smiled at Jared. "I better go."

"Yeah, I'm going to head back." He jerked a thumb over his shoulder. "I hope I see you around, though."

He was clearly a less complicated option than Thane. But despite his beautiful eyes, nothing seemed to penetrate my almighty crush on my boss.

"Yeah," I replied noncommittally, waved, and hurried back down the beach to the waiting trio.

"Who was that?" Lewis asked, his nose wrinkled.

"Jared McCulloch." I handed over the ball.

"Collum's grandson?" Thane asked.

Finally, I looked at him, still confused why he'd barked at me. "Yeah."

"What did he want?" He sounded sullen and suspicious.

I shrugged. "Nothing. He just saved the ball."

"He didn't need to," Lewis said, sounding as sullen as his father.

Confused by how the jovial atmosphere had turned, I took Eilidh's hand and followed son and father up the beach. Without discussing it with anyone, Thane started packing up our things.

"We're going?" Eilidh's lower lip trembled into a pout. "I don't wanna!"

"Anna has gone home. It's time to go back to the house and get cleaned up for dinner at Uncle Lachlan's," her father said. "Eilidh, don't start." He preempted her tantrum.

"Hey." I swung her into my arms, settling her weight on my hip. "I can do your hair all fancy for dinner tonight."

"Yeah?" Her eyes grew big and excited.

"And I bet your dad will let you wear one of your nice dresses."

Her gaze flew to her father. He gave her a smile and a nod and returned to collecting our gear. Tantrum averted.

Once the kids were settled in the back of the car, I helped Thane load the rear.

Out of nowhere, he said, his voice low, "Jared McCulloch is making a bit of a name for himself around the village."

I pulled back from tucking the cooler into the back of the car and straightened to meet Thane's eyes. He'd taken off his sunglasses, but I still couldn't read his expression. "Name for himself?"

"As a ladies' man. Made his way through the small pool of

single women here and is now working his way through Inverness."

Understanding dawned. "We were only talking."

Thane shrugged, like it didn't matter to him. "I know. I'm just saying." He slammed the hatch down and I flinched from the almost aggressive action. However, he didn't say another word, just rounded the car to the driver's side.

I stared after him.

"Are you getting in or walking?" he called sarcastically back to me.

Without a word, I got into the passenger side and tried to figure out if Thane was jealous or if I was simply projecting how I wanted him to feel.

There was nothing worse than starting the day flustered, and that was exactly what Thane was doing. Eilidh had been sick through the night but was bright and bubbly this morning, confirming his suspicions that she'd eaten too much junk food. He'd finally wrangled the confession out of her that she'd snuck downstairs after he'd gone to bed to eat out of the bags of sweets he'd bought for the kids to take to the Halloween party at school the next night.

Her stomach only held it down for an hour before it wanted back out again.

And Thane was knackered. There was nothing worse than holding your wee girl in your arms while she cried and begged you to make her feel better. Thankfully, after throwing up a few more times, she fell asleep. She woke early and seemed as full of beans as ever.

While her father felt like he'd been dragged through a hedge backward.

The whole thing had thrown him off, and before he knew it, despite Regan being there to take care of everything else, he found himself running out the door, late for work.

After parking his car in the underground garage, Thane dashed into the lift that would take him up to the company's floor. The building was new and modern, and it stood out in the small city center with its black tinted glass.

Pre-twentieth century architecture mostly made up the skyline of Inverness with an eclectic (and unsuccessful) mix of midcentury brutalism. Just a few minutes' walk from the train station, right in the center of town, his architectural firm rented the eighth floor of the new building.

To his growing impatience, the lift stopped at reception to let more people on. One of those was Keelie Tanner. The attractive brunette smiled, her eyes lighting up at the sight of him as she practically pushed two men out of the way so she could stand next to Thane. He tried not to show his amusement.

"Keelie," he greeted her.

"Good to see you. How are you?" She studied him as if he were the most fascinating man on earth.

And Thane wasn't entirely immune to that. What man would be? It was flattering as hell. Keelie worked as a financial advisor on the floor above his. She'd started chatting one day in the elevator and sometimes she'd stop by his car when he was leaving at night to see how his day had gone. Through those small interludes, he'd learned a fair bit about her. She was a single mum after going through a divorce three years ago, and it was nice she understood the trials of single parenthood. And something he hadn't really thought about but seemed to stick in his mind now as he looked at her, Keelie was his age—thirty-seven—though she'd just turned it in June, and his thirty-eighth was in two weeks. Lachlan's birthday was a mere six days before his, so the family had planned a birthday dinner for them both next weekend.

Still, less than a year between him and Keelie.

That was appropriate.

Not that he was thinking of dating Keelie. As nice as she was, and as much as they got along, Thane wasn't in the mood for dating anyone.

"So what do you think?" she queried just as the elevator stopped at his floor.

Thane had no idea what she'd asked. "I'm sorry, Keelie. Eilidh was ill last night. I've barely slept, I'm like a zombie, and I'm running late. I'll catch you later, yeah, and we can talk then." He got out of the lift as Gary from payroll did. Thane hadn't even realized he was on the lift with him.

"How are you?" He gave the payroll admin a polite smile.

"That was brutal," Gary answered in return.

Thane tensed. "Excuse me?"

The young man smirked. "How you blew off the MILF on the lift."

"MILF ..." Thane scowled as he realized who Gary was referring to. "Keelie?"

"Aye, her. I might use that trick to let down a bird in the future."

"Wait, what?" Dread filled Thane's gut.

Gary's eyes widened. "You actually weren't listening to her, were you? Mr. Adair, she asked you out. In front of everybody."

Fuck.

Cursing himself, Thane bristled all the way to his office. He didn't want to date Keelie, but he couldn't believe his woolgathering had mortified her in front of a lift filled with people. He'd have to find her later and apologize.

Something else to look forward to.

Five minutes later, his day grew worse when Thane realized he'd left his portfolio and 3-D model at the house. "No, no, no." He needed the damn thing for an important meeting with their client in forty-five goddamn minutes. He pushed away from his desk and groaned. While he had most of it on his computer, the folio was filled with hand-drawn additions to the digital files, as well as notes and photograph clippings. The visuals helped with the presentation.

"To hell with it." He'd have to reprint the digital drawings and do what he could.

His desk phone rang, the blinking red light telling him it was reception. What now? "Adair," he answered abruptly.

Brian, the company receptionist, answered, "Good morning, Mr. Adair. I have a Regan Penhaligon at reception. Shall I send her along?"

What was Regan doing here? Was Eilidh okay? His heart raced. "Yes, yes." He slammed down the phone and hurried to meet her halfway.

As he spotted Regan rushing down a corridor, checking left and right, searching for his office, his heart slowed at the sight of his portfolio and model in her hands. She'd come all the way to bring them to him?

"Regan?"

Her head turned toward him, and he ignored the way his gut twisted when their eyes met.

Regan heaved a sigh of relief as they drew to a stop before one another. Her light, floral perfume tickled his nose. When she was working, she'd taken to wearing a uniform of jeans and a sweater now that it was chillier outside. Today she wore a long, camel-colored wool coat over her jeans and somehow made it look chic with her Converse. Her hair spilled around her shoulders in perfect, silky red-gold waves. Thane realized over the weeks that she was just one of those women who looked well put together, no matter the occasion.

"Your phone is switched off," she said, her eyes big and round, lashes fanning with the almost accusatory doe look.

"It is?" *Fuck.*

"Yeah. I spotted your model on the dining table about

twenty minutes after you left and tried to call you to come back for it, but I went straight to voice mail."

"Who's watching Eils and Lewis?"

"Robyn. She took them to school. Don't worry, Eilidh is much better and insisted on going because she didn't want to miss the Halloween party tonight."

"You didn't have to come all the way out here," he said, marveling that she'd driven all the way to Inverness. Regan was still wary of the roads here. Though familiar with Ardnoch, she hadn't driven farther afield.

"I thought you had that meeting?"

"I do." Thane took his work from her, their fingers sliding together with the transfer. He placed the model on the floor at his feet. "I'll worry about you driving back now."

Her expression softened. "I'll be fine. I got here, didn't I?" She frowned. "Though I'm pretty sure I'm parked illegally."

Thane grinned. "It's Lachlan's car. He'll get the ticket."

Her laughter filled the space between them, and his gut tightened again.

Bloody hell.

"Adair." A booming voice made him wince seconds before a hand came down hard on his shoulder.

Christ. He knew who it was without looking.

Paul Urquhart: mediocre architect and arsehole extraordinaire.

"Paul." He sent an apologetic look to Regan, and she frowned in confusion.

"And who is this?"

Thane tensed and turned to his colleague. Paul studied Regan with the same heated sneer he'd give a lap dancer. The man was pure sleaze. Thane knew and hated this, but he'd never wanted to punch him as much as he did at that moment. Needing Regan gone from Paul's presence, he opened his mouth to dismiss her. But she spoke first.

She held out a hand. "Regan. Thane's nanny."

Paul couldn't even hide his surprised delight. He shook Regan's hand, enfolding hers in both of his. *"Enchanté*, Regan, nanny of Thane."

Something took over—obliterating his manners—at the sight of Paul touching Regan. Thane grabbed him by the bend of the elbow and yanked him off her.

"Regan, thank you for the portfolio, but we're done here," he clipped out impatiently.

She flinched. "Sure. I'll see you later." She marched away, her coat fluttering behind her. Regret filled him.

Thane squeezed his eyes shut. He had a headache coming on.

"Nanny." Paul's slithering tone prodded his eyes open again. He grinned lasciviously at Thane. "That's your nanny?"

"What of it?"

"Does she live with you?"

"Paul," he warned.

His eyes lit up. "She does!" His gaze shot down the corridor to where Regan had disappeared. "How do you sleep at night knowing prime pussy like that is under your roof? Unless ..." He winked at Thane. "Aye, nobody would blame you if you were paying her a wee bit extra to take care of Daddy. Look at your face." He barked out a repulsive laugh. "Don't feel guilty, Adair. Women are all sluts. You'd just be giving her what she wants."

Later, Thane would blame it on lack of sleep.

Whatever the reason, one minute Paul was on his feet, the next on his knees, clutching his bloodied nose.

~

It had been a horrendous day.

Beyond shattered, Thane walked into the house to find it

quiet. Aromatic spices suggested dinner was ready or almost. Regan, to everyone's surprise, had proven to be a damn decent cook.

However, Thane was used to Eilidh running to greet him, or at least the sounds of his children's voices filling the large house. Instead, he heard music playing low.

Striding into the living area, he found Regan with her back to him at the stove, stirring a pot while another simmered. She'd scraped her hair into a ponytail that brushed between her shoulder blades. As she shifted, the hem of her cropped sweater revealed the smooth, golden skin of her slender back. Thane swallowed hard as he realized how much he was noticing (and enjoying) the way her jeans highlighted her firm, round arse.

Yanking his eyes away, he looked to the living room and saw it was empty. Eilidh and Lewis were nowhere to be seen. The only noise came from the smart speaker that sat at the end of the kitchen counter. A woman's low-toned voice sung out of it about two people finding each other in the stars.

"Where are the kids?"

Regan shot him a quick glance over her shoulder before returning to the pot. "Halloween party tonight, remember? I dropped them off at school twenty minutes ago."

Unease filled him at her emotionless tone. "Did you get them ready okay? No drama?"

"No drama. They looked adorable. Robyn took some great photos."

He could imagine. Eilidh wanted to go as a unicorn, and Regan had sourced a pastel, rainbow-hued dress with a tutu skirt that came with matching unicorn wings and a unicorn headband with a horn. Eilidh loved it so much, he thought she was going to pass out with excitement when she saw it. And Lewis hadn't wanted to dress up, but all his friends were going as Marvel characters and they wanted him to go as

Ant-Man. Again, Regan had sourced the costume for them. Thane felt shit that he'd missed them going to the party, but he'd see them when he picked them up later. "We'll need to add the photos to the wall if they're that good."

"They're that good." There was that emotionless tone again.

Thane dragged a hand down his beard, the long hairs reminding him he needed to trim the damn thing. But that would be after he smoothed things over with Regan.

"I'm sorry I snapped at you." He stepped into the kitchen. "It wasn't you I was angry with. It was Paul. He's a sleazebag, and I didn't want him talking to you."

"Bit of an overreaction, no?" she replied, refusing to look at him.

Irritated that he couldn't see her expression, he sighed. "Will you be an adult and face me when I'm talking to you?"

With angry, jerky movements, he watched Regan turn the stove down and then whip around, her arms crossed over her chest. "I am not one of your children. Do not speak to me like that. Ever."

After the utter swine of a day, Thane did not want to argue with her. "I apologized. The mature thing to do is accept it."

Regan's eyes flashed, but as quickly as her ire appeared, she banked it. Using that annoying monotone again, she replied, "You're right. My apologies. I'll just get out of your hair. Your dinner is ready. You just need to plate it up."

His heart hammered stupidly fast and as she moved to march past him, he reached for her without thinking. Thane wrapped a hand around her elbow, jerking her to a stop. Those gorgeous, warm brown eyes flew to his, and he saw what she was trying to hide.

Hurt.

He'd hurt her feelings.

Thane experienced another sharp pang of regret. "Regan, I'm sorry. I'm being a bastard. It's not an excuse, but I've had a hell of a twenty-four hours. I'm sorry. I didn't mean to take it out on you by being a condescending prick."

To his relief, she relaxed under his hold. Her eyes wandered over his face and sharpened. "What happened?"

"Just a long day." He released her, and her attention dropped to his hand.

"Thane." She reached for him, gently cradling his right hand in hers. His knuckles were swollen. The look she gave him demanded answers as she repeated, "What happened?"

~

"I told you, I'm fine," he said, but secretly he enjoyed Regan fussing over him.

After he'd explained about hitting Paul, miraculously avoiding criminal charges but not avoiding the conversation with his boss about why he'd hit Paul, Regan had pushed him down onto the sofa and told him to wait.

Thankfully for Thane, Allan, his boss, liked him and did not like Paul. Both he and Paul received warnings for their behavior and that if anything like it happened again, they'd both face termination.

Knowing it could have gone so much worse, relief filled Thane.

Regan handed him a beer. "Take with your left hand, please."

He grinned and sipped his beer, feeling better already. "Thanks."

She flicked him a dark look as she sat down close beside him. "Right hand."

Thane's lips trembled from holding back another grin as

he did as she demanded. Out of nowhere, she produced a small bag of frozen peas and crushed them over his knuckles.

"Fuck," he bit out at the shock of the cold.

"We need to get the swelling down." She held it over his hand.

"I can do it," he said, though he wanted her to.

"You can't drink a beer and hold ice over your hand."

"Considering how angry you are, I'm surprised you don't just leave me to it."

She shrugged, relaxing into the sofa. Drawing her knees up, they touched his outer thigh. "I feel bad you had a nightmare day."

"It's better already." He took another swig of beer, watching her over the top of it.

Regan smiled softly, her dimples just teasing an appearance. She was so beautiful, it knocked the wind out of him sometimes.

"I can't believe you punched a guy in the face."

Scowling, Thane looked away. "He deserved it."

"What exactly did he say about me?"

"Nothing worth repeating."

They sat in silence for a moment. "Well ... thank you for defending my honor."

At the teasing note in her voice, Thane replied, "I was defending both of us."

She frowned but as just as quickly, her confusion cleared. Her lips parted on a little "oh." "He insinuated you and I ..."

Thane grunted his yes.

"He's not the first one. Even Lachlan knows there's gossip around the village about us."

Anger and something a lot like guilt had him barking as he slammed his beer down on the nearby coffee table. "Who else is gossiping? I thought it was just those bloody women at the school?"

Regan tutted and moved a little closer, drawing him back against the couch. "No need to get worked up about it. They're just spreading their jealous bile from the school gates to the entire village. Everyone thinks you're sneaking into my annex at night."

The imagery her words conjured caused an instant reaction in his body, and he flew from the sofa before he did something they'd both regret.

"Your hand." Regan jumped from the couch just as he moved to walk away, and they collided.

Thane instinctively reached out to steady her as she dropped the frozen peas to grab onto his arms. They tensed against each other, her body tight to his. He could feel the sharp rise and fall of her breasts, hear her quickened breathing, smell her skin.

"Bloody hell," he muttered hoarsely as their fiery gazes connected.

And there it was, clear as day for him to see in those glittering, chestnut eyes.

Regan wanted him.

For a moment, a lust more powerful than he'd ever experienced clouded his mind. His hands seemed to move down her waist with a mind of their own, tracing the gentle curve of her hips to her tight arse. He gripped her in his hands and pulled her deeper against him, and she gasped at the feel of him hard and throbbing, pushing at her soft belly.

Bending his head toward her, desperate to taste her—finally—Thane was a mere whisper from her mouth when she broke the silence.

"Thane," she moaned his name with so much need, a savage possessiveness flooded him.

"Thane, you in?" Lachlan's voice cut through the house from the front entrance.

It was like being hammered by five thousand bags of frozen peas.

"Fuck," he cursed, unable to believe what he'd just been about to do.

Regan stared up at him in confusion and then something like disappointment.

Oh, hell.

Before he could say another word, she slipped away, hurrying down the corridor behind the stairs, toward the side exit.

Still aroused, Thane scrambled for a large cushion on the sofa, snapped up the bag of peas, and sat down, covering his lap with the former and his knuckles with the latter.

Just in time.

His brother strode into the living room. "Robyn said the kids were at a Halloween party, so I thought I'd stop by, see if you fancied grabbing some food." He frowned, his eyes going to the stove. "Looks like you're already sorted for dinner, though."

"Aye. Regan left it for me. Isn't there a Halloween bash at the estate tonight?"

Lachlan shook his head as he wandered over to the stove. "We agreed to skip it this year after, well, Fergus and Lucy."

Thane understood. One of Lachlan's security guards had been murdered on the estate only a few months ago. The creepy Halloween party they usually put on at the castle would seem in poor taste this year.

"Chicken curry," Lachlan announced, stirring the pot. "Enough for two."

Thane laughed, trying to sound normal. "Grab us both a plate." He held up his bruised knuckles and peas. "Had a bit of an incident."

His brother frowned. "I'll plate up, you explain. Want another beer?"

"Can't. Picking up the kids from the party in a wee while."

"Can't Regan do that?"

Scowling, he snapped, "No, Regan can't do it. She's not my beck-and-call girl."

Raising an eyebrow, Lachlan set out two plates. "I never said she was. You're in a fucking mood."

With a sigh, Thane slumped into the sofa. "It's been a day."

"Tell me."

It took the length of the story about Paul for reality to cool his libido. He did not, however, mention his interlude with Regan. What the hell had he been thinking? He'd almost kissed her. Though burying his arousal in her stomach seemed worse than a kiss, anyway.

"I can't remember the last time you lost the plot like that," Lachlan observed as Thane sat down at the island with him to eat. His brother ate a forkful of chicken curry and rice. "Regan cook this?"

Thane nodded.

"She's not bad at all."

"I know. She's been a godsend."

And I'm the vile bastard who nearly took advantage of her.

"Is that why you cracked Paul in the face? Or is the village gossip getting to you?"

"How bad is the gossip? I wasn't even aware of it until tonight."

Lachlan shrugged. "People daren't say to my face, but you know I have my ways. They're all twittering about you being shacked up here with an attractive younger woman." Seeing Thane's horrified expression, Lachlan frowned. "It's just gossip, and you haven't let the village gossip bother you for years."

"They're nosy, bored, pains in my arse."

"Aye, well. Even so … you haven't been quick with your fists since you were a boy."

It was true. When he was younger, Thane was always in some kind of fight. He was quick to anger whenever someone said shit regarding the people he cared about. A lot of the anger was from loss, but he'd mellowed with age.

"I would have punched that git, Guy, if you'd given me the chance. But you beat me to it." He referred to Arro's ex-boyfriend, Lachlan's former chef at the estate. Lachlan discovered he'd beat up Arrochar and had not only fired him but had taken a nasty swing at him too. Thane found out after the fact, once Lachlan's security escorted Guy out of Ardnoch.

"Still. Sounds like you're protective of Regan."

Concerned Lachlan could tell she'd gotten under his skin, he shrugged. "Don't you want me to be? She's family. I'm just defending her as I would Arro or Robyn."

"It's appreciated." Lachlan gave him a serious nod. "I'm glad it didn't cause too much trouble for you."

Too much trouble?

That was an understatement.

Regan *was* trouble.

But only because he wanted her.

Like really, really was seriously lusting after her.

His nanny.

His brother's soon-to-be sister-in-law.

His employee, thirteen years his junior.

Never again, he vowed.

Thane was not that hotheaded youth anymore. He was a grown man with children and responsibilities and a respectable reputation within their community. He could control his attraction to an inappropriate woman.

Never again.

Thane could only hope Regan understood that. At any rate, he planned to make sure she did.

13

REGAN

I was twenty-five years old.

You would think by now, especially after what I'd been through, that I wouldn't be naive enough to assume that just because a woman got a man's dick hard that it actually meant anything.

And boy, was Thane out to prove it didn't.

My hurt was a deep, hot, wounded ache in my chest that I hadn't expected. I had a crush on the guy, but after his treatment that morning, I worried my response meant it had developed into something more.

When he'd held me in his arms yesterday, I thought I was going to come out of my skin I was so desperate to have his mouth on me, his hands touching every inch of my body. Never had I been that turned on. And I'd read some smokin', spectacular sex scenes in romance novels.

Now, Thane was not only acting like nothing happened, but he was treating me with cold politeness.

The kids weren't up yet. I was in the middle of setting out their breakfast dishes and juice when Thane, dressed in a suit, came hurrying down the stairs. When I offered him coffee, he didn't even look at me and just coolly told me he could get it himself. Then he disappeared upstairs again instead of chatting like he normally would before waking Eilidh and Lewis.

I blinked at the sight of him now.

He'd trimmed his beard. Like, really trimmed it.

And it looked amazing.

Was he trying to kill me?

"Your beard," I said.

His eyes flicked up before moving away as he grabbed his car keys off the hook on the wall near the photo gallery. "Excuse me?"

"You trimmed your beard."

"So I did." He walked out of the kitchen toward the front entrance.

Was that it?

I wasn't even getting a goodbye?

Tears stung my eyes, and I quickly blinked them back as I heard the front door slam shut.

"I hate men," I whispered harshly. Even the best of them couldn't escape the asshole gene when it came to sex and attraction.

~

THANE

He was thirty minutes from Ardnoch before he stopped fighting with himself to turn around and drive back to the house.

Now it was too late. He couldn't be tardy for work after yesterday's debacle with Paul.

Still, his gut churned with that awful feeling he got when he knew he'd done something wrong.

He'd handled Regan badly. There was a difference between reminding her they should act professionally around one another and acting like an insensitive bastard. Leaving without saying goodbye was fucking rude.

"Arsehole," he muttered for the hundredth time as he pulled into the parking lot. How did he apologize now without getting her hopes up?

Would her hopes even be up?

He was assuming Regan gave a shit if he wanted to sleep with her.

"She gives a shit," he said under his breath as he got out of the SUV. If he was being honest, they'd been dancing around their attraction to each other for weeks. That day at the beach, they'd most definitely been flirting, and when he'd seen her flirting with Jared McCulloch, he'd acted like a jealous arsehole then too. Thane thought he was past all the games and possessiveness at his age.

"Thane Adair?" A man stepped from between two vehicles in front of him, drawing him out of his thoughts.

Thane abruptly stopped walking.

Guard up at the suspicious behavior, and with the punch he'd given Paul in mind, Thane glanced around to see if they were alone. They weren't. A few other employees were making their way to the lift. Relaxing slightly, he asked, "Who's asking?"

The man drew nearer. His huge, dark eyes were haunted behind his round spectacles.

But Thane suddenly recognized him. Dread and anger and grief and despair and possessiveness fired within. "What do you want?"

"To talk with you. About Eilidh." He slurred the words.

Rage consumed him, and he took a menacing step toward the man. "You will stay away from my daughter."

Desperation lit up the man's face. "But she isn't yours, is she? She's mine."

A quick look around the lot told him they were alone now. Thane lunged at him, grabbing him by the shirtfront. He cried out, but Thane ignored his pleas, hauling him through a gap between cars to slam him against a concrete pillar. The smell of whisky wafted strongly off the bastard.

"Just because you fucked my wife doesn't mean a goddamn thing. Eilidh is mine!" He was so furious, spittle flew from his mouth as he raged, "I don't know why you crawled out of the woodwork now, but I'm warning you to crawl the fuck back in, or I will ruin your goddamn miserable existence. And you know I can." He pushed him harder into the pillar. "Do you understand me?"

The man nodded as his trembling hand reached to straighten his glasses.

His fear doused some of Thane's rage, and he stumbled away. "Get out of here ... before I do something we both regret."

14

REGAN

"So Arrochar wants to host us all at her place on Saturday, since she's doing the cooking. But I thought you and I could try baking the cake." Robyn folded the clean laundry as she spoke.

I glanced at her and frowned before turning back to my ironing. "I told you, you don't need to help me. This is my job."

"Yeah, but I'm not doing anything right now and these kids have more clothes than a Kardashian."

I shrugged. "Thane likes to make sure they have everything they need."

"I know."

At Robyn's silence, I looked up. She narrowed her eyes, expression ponderous.

"What is it?"

My sister scrutinized me some more. "You sounded a little defensive, that's all. In fact, you've been a little short all morning."

"If you mean about the Adair brothers' birthday plans, then it's because I'm not sure us baking a cake when we have no prior experience beyond the odd tray of brownies is a good idea."

"No, I just mentioned the cake. You've been off all morning."

My pulse raced at Robyn's probing stare. I hemmed and hawed over whether to tell her about Thane. I worried she'd judge me as that impulsive, irresponsible woman who had dated an asshole after running away from another asshole. However, I also needed someone to talk to. Someone I could trust. Someone whose advice meant a lot to me.

"Okay, I'm getting worried." Robyn pushed away from the laundry room counter and stood right in front of the ironing board so I had nowhere to look but into her eyes. They were golden today beneath the room's bright spotlights. "Talk to me."

Sighing, I placed the iron down. "Robyn ... when you started your affair with Lachlan, did you ever think you were doing something wrong? Like he was an inappropriate choice because he was Mac's friend and boss?"

My sister seemed surprised by my question but considered it. "Well, yeah, I think more so on Lachlan's part because I was Mac's daught—oh my God, you have feelings for Thane." She guessed, her eyes big and round and absolutely not revealing whether she was horrified or surprised.

I grimaced. My sister was way too smart for her own good. "If I said I did?"

Robyn blinked like an owl for a few seconds and then exhaled slowly. "Okay ... well ... I'd have to ask what kind of feelings? *Feelings*-feelings or lusty feelings?"

Relieved she wasn't acting creeped out about it, I relaxed. Marginally. "At first I thought it was just a crush. He's sexy and nice and he's got that accent—"

"Oh, I know all about the accent thing, trust me."

I gave a huff of laughter. "Right? And he's adorable with

Eilidh and Lewis. It was the first thing that struck me about him was the way he looked at his children, like they were his universe."

"They are his universe."

"I know. And I thought I just had a typical female reaction to being in proximity to a smokin'-hot single dad. I mean, it's one of my favorite tropes."

Robyn's lips twitched with laughter.

"I was absolutely determined to ignore the lusty feelings he was eliciting in my southern region."

"Thanks for the overshare."

I grinned unashamedly. "You're welcome. As I was saying"—my humor fled as I remembered Thane's coldness toward me that morning—"there have been times these past few months when it seemed like we might be flirting with each other a little … and I even told him about why I left you when you got shot."

My sister raised an eyebrow, obviously surprised I'd divulged that to him.

"And he's entrusted me with some of his history. Things I don't think he discusses with many people. We get along amazingly. It's like we fall naturally into sync, as though we've all been a family forever."

Concern entered Robyn's eyes.

"I know," I hurried to say, "I know, before you say that those are dangerous ideas to have. But I'm finding it harder to ignore how I feel. Until … well, you know how I rushed to his work yesterday to drop off his portfolio?"

She nodded.

"There was this sleazy colleague that Thane wanted me away from as fast as possible, and he was kind of an ass about it. He apologized when he got home and then told me he smacked the guy in the face for making a crude crack about me being the nanny, and, well, he didn't tell me the details but I could guess what was said."

Robyn nodded. "Lachlan told me last night. I was shocked. Thane always comes across as the levelheaded brother, but Lachlan said when they were younger, Thane was kind of a scrapper."

I filed that information away, coveting it, as I did anything about Thane. Seriously, I was borderline obsessed. "I was icing his hand afterward, and we had this moment. There was touching ... of my ass. More like a manly, hot, grabbing of my ass, actually." I shivered remembering it.

"Keep the details to a minimum." Robyn scowled. "You are my baby sister, and I do not want to have to kill Lachlan's brother before our wedding."

I chuckled unhappily. "Well, that was all that happened. He was about to kiss me when your stupid fiancé walked in, and I ran away."

"I will let the stupid comment pass since you're clearly upset."

"I *am* upset. Here I'm thinking, there's no denying Thane is attracted to me, too, because I had evidence of said hard-on digging into my stomach—"

"God save me from baby sisters who have no filter."

"—and being a complete naive fool, barely sleeping because I'm daydreaming that something special might come from this, and all he's thinking is 'How can I make it as clear as possible that I'm repulsed by my reaction to my nanny last night?'"

Robyn frowned, her amusement gone. "What did he do?"

The hurt rose to the fore, and I couldn't meet her eyes. Instead, I smiled breezily. "He was kind of cold to me this morning, no big deal."

"Regan, it's me you're talking to."

I met her loving gaze and instantly dropped my guard. "It

hurt." I shrugged, trying to pull back the ridiculous emotion I experienced over a guy just because he'd acted monosyllabic and short with me. "I'm making a bigger thing out of it than it was."

Robyn leaned on the ironing board and reached for my hand, her expression concerned and tender at the same time. "If there's one thing I know really well, it's Adair men and how they think. One thing I love about Lachlan and Thane is their sense of honor and responsibility. Having a sense of honor is a dying trait, and it's appealing when you find it in someone. But it can also make a person pretty hard on themselves. Lachlan gets tetchy when he thinks he's failed someone or failed himself. And I can see Thane being that guy too."

"What are you saying?"

She squeezed my hand, her sympathy making me uneasy. "I'm saying, how would it look if he seduced his twenty-five-year-old nanny?"

I pulled my hand away. "When you say it like that, you make it sound crude and dirty. It's not."

"No, but that's how some people will see it. And you are his employee, Regan. His much younger employee, and he has two children he needs to protect. Even from village gossip."

My brows pulled together as my agitation built. "It's not wrong if we have feelings for each other."

My sister gave me a pained look. "Sweetie, I think any man would be lucky to have you, and any man who can't see that is a fool … but there's a possibility that all this is for Thane is a physical attraction. Baby girl, you are gorgeous. Could fit right in among all those stunning, famous actors running around the estate kind of gorgeous. He would have to be dead not to see that. And react to it."

The hurt flared again. It had never crossed my mind that all it would be for him was physical attraction.

Why would it be anything else?

He was a professional, intelligent, sexy, wealthy single father.

And I was a flailing college graduate who had abandoned her family because she couldn't face the harsh realities of life.

"No. No." Robyn tugged my chin to bring my eyes to her. "Whatever it is you're thinking right now, get it out of your head."

"I'm a moron," I whispered.

"You're not a moron. Don't say that."

"Should I quit?" The thought of leaving Eilidh and Lewis killed me.

Robyn frowned. "No. They need you, Regan. They ... Eils and Lew are so happy, and I see a difference in Thane too. He's more relaxed, less stressed."

"I have to leave in four months, anyway."

"Actually ... not really. I've been looking into it, and you could apply for a UK ancestry visa. Those allow you to stay for five years, as long as you can prove you have a work placement, which I'm sure Thane would provide."

Surprised, I asked, "What's a UK ancestry visa?"

"It applies to anyone who has a grandparent who was born in the UK. And you do, on Seth's side. While his dad's parents were born in Boston, his mom's parents were born in the UK. In Newcastle, to be exact."

"Is that what you have because of Mac?"

"No. Because my dad was born here, even though I was born in the States, I automatically have dual citizenship. Yours is something you have to apply for."

"I think we need to sit so I can process this."

Two minutes later, I sat on a stool at the island facing my big sister. "I have grandparents living here?"

Robyn winced. "They're both passed now. But that means you have relatives living in the UK, if you ever wanted to look them up."

"Oh. That's cool." I smiled. "So this means I can apply for this visa thingie?"

She nodded, excitement lighting her eyes. "I spoke with Seth, and he gave me his grandparents' information so I could trace them. Mac helped. We found out two weeks ago, and I just … I didn't know how to bring it up because I didn't want to pressure you into staying."

"Dad knows about this? Is he okay with the idea?"

"He's not thrilled, but he sees a massive difference in you. Says you keep in touch more with him now than you did in Boston, and you sound happy. That's all he wants. And he knows how close you and I are. I'd forgotten how much we need each other. Not that I'm pressuring you." She rolled her eyes. "That sounded like pressure."

I was so grateful Robyn wanted me to stay. "It's not. And I would do it in a heartbeat, but … maybe this whole Thane thing is a sign I shouldn't. It's not exactly responsible."

"Please," Robyn huffed, "a person cannot help who they're attracted to."

"I wouldn't call it attraction. It's more like a desperate, savage need to be naked with him and have him do a lot of dirty things to me."

"I have a gun," she reminded me stonily.

I burst out laughing, pulling her in for a hug as she glowered. "I'm sorry, I'm sorry. I'll stop saying stuff like that."

"Please, please do."

Wiping tears of laughter from my eyes, I settled back on my stool and groaned through my amusement as reality returned. "What do I do, Robbie?"

She stared at me, her expression serious. "I don't know what's between you two, but I've never heard you moon over a man like this. Is it ideal? No. But neither were Lachlan and me. Neither are other people," she said a little mysteriously. "And all you can do is sit by and watch them waste something special because they're afraid it's inappropriate." She shrugged, her gaze focusing again. "I don't know. Maybe I'm biased because I'd like you to stay, and because I think Thane is one of the good ones. I just … I don't think you should run this time."

I winced a little at the reminder. "I'm sorry."

"I didn't say it to be harsh. I trust you would never start something with Thane, knowing what this family has been through, if you planned to take off as soon as things got tough."

"Never," I promised. "I would never do that, Robyn. Not to the kids. Not to Thane. Not to you."

"I know." She nodded. "I believe you."

Tears stung my eyes. I hadn't realized how much I needed her to say that.

She squeezed my hand. "I told you I wouldn't hold the last two years against you, and I won't. We'll never move on that way. I am proud of who you've become. I'm proud of how you handle Eilidh and Lewis and the love and friendship and support you give them. I'm proud of how seriously you take your job, and I don't want you thinking that your feelings for Thane diminishes that. We can't help who we want. And who knows how Thane feels about you? What I do know is that if it is just physical on his part, if he is holding back because he thinks it's inappropriate, his mind can't be changed if you leave."

As her words sank in, hope blossomed in my chest. I bit my lip against a giddy smile.

Robyn saw it and shook her head at me. "Jesus, you've got it bad."

"You can't tell Lachlan. Or anyone. This stays between us."

My sister took my words to heart. "I don't like keeping secrets from him, but I don't want him jumping to conclusions about this."

"Thanks. And thank you … for trusting me. For trusting that this isn't just a flavor-of-the-month kind of thing. I am happy here. I do feel things for him that I've never felt before."

"I can tell." She considered this and then said, "Does that mean you'll apply for the visa?"

I laughed at her persistence, overjoyed by it, in fact. "That means I will definitely think about it."

15

REGAN

Arrochar's house was a midcentury bungalow in a well-kept, well-designed residential area a few blocks from Castle Street. The first time she'd brought me to her house for coffee, I was surprised, expecting her to be living it up in a stylish, modern home like Lachlan and Thane.

I knew (didn't everyone?) that the middle sibling, Brodan Adair, was a famous Hollywood actor. Not that I'd say this to Robyn, but I thought he was an even better actor than Lachlan. My soon-to-be brother-in-law was great at the action-hero stuff. He really sold it, and he'd been seriously fun to watch beating up bad guys. Brodan, while he'd started out in similar style movies, had branched into more serious roles. And the man could act. Also, he was probably the most classically handsome of the Adair brothers. Lots of people got Brodan Adair mixed up with the guy who played Captain America.

Between the celebrities in the family, Lachlan's and Thane's large, contemporary homes, and Ardnoch Castle itself, I kind of got wrapped up in the idea of the Adairs as lairds and lady of the manor.

Arro shot that vibe to hell. In a good way. She was a forest engineer and did not rely on her growing inheritance (thanks to Lachlan's successful turnaround of their family estate) or their reputation as pillars of Ardnoch society. Low-key, funny, sharp, and kind, Arro was as down-to-earth as they came.

And she loved her family.

That was evident as I walked into her house holding Lewis's hand while Thane carried Eilidh. The smell of food made my stomach twinge with hunger. A glance in the large dining room revealed a beautifully laid table for the birthday celebrations. We strolled into a living room filled with blue and silver streamers and balloons that made Eilidh antsy with excitement in her father's arms.

Sitting around the living room were Lachlan, Robyn, Mac, and Eredine. We were the last to arrive because two seconds out the door, Eilidh wanted to change her dress. She decided it wasn't her prettiest dress and she should wear her prettiest dress for her daddy since it was his birthday party. There were tears. Unable to resist her adorable reasoning, I'd hurried her into the house so we could put her in her favorite dress.

Which was the unicorn dress I'd bought her for Halloween, minus the wings and headband.

Today wasn't actually either of their birthdays. Lachlan was thirty-nine on Tuesday, and Thane's thirty-eighth was the following Monday.

"Hi, all," Thane greeted everyone. "Eilidh, go say an early happy birthday to Uncle Lachlan." He lowered her to the floor.

Lachlan was sitting in the snuggle armchair with Robyn. It was cozy. Eilidh thought so too. She lunged at them like a bat and landed on her uncle's chest.

"Oh, f—" He cut off the obvious curse word as he caught her, his eyes closed in pain.

"She hit the family jewels, huh?" Robyn teased, her lips twitching with the urge to laugh.

Amusement bubbled inside me as Lachlan's eyes popped open and he glared at his fiancée. All the while he cuddled his niece. "Not funny," he mouthed.

"Uncle Lachlan, I wore my unicorny dress for you," Eilidh announced as she cupped his face in her hands.

His expression softened. "And you look beautiful, angel."

"I thought you wore it for me?" her dad teased as he gestured for Lewis to follow him to the end of the sectional.

"I wore it for you, too, Daddy." Eilidh looked worried he'd think otherwise.

Lewis didn't let go of my hand.

Thane's brow furrowed as he lounged down beside Eredine. "Come sit, buddy."

Instead, Lew looked up at me. I flushed with the awkwardness. While Thane had been in a horrible mood with me all week, he'd been civil in front of the kids. If the kids were there, he at least talked to me. If the kids weren't there, then I got monosyllabic grunts in lieu of conversation.

Lewis … it was like he sensed something was going on, and he'd gotten a little clingy lately.

"Go sit with your dad, honey." I led him toward Thane, but he gripped my hand harder, and I stopped.

"Lewis?" Thane asked.

Everyone grew quiet, making it extra awkward.

"There's no room for Ree-Ree." Lewis glowered at his dad.

"Oh, I'll move up." Eredine smiled sweetly and moved closer to Arro and Mac on the couch.

Avoiding my sister's questioning gaze, I sat, Lewis nestled between me and Thane. Eilidh became aware two of her favorite people were sitting together on the couch and launched herself off Lachlan and at Mac and Arro.

I turned to Eredine. "Hey, I haven't seen you all week. How you doing?"

My friend shrugged. "It's been really quiet at the estate. It usually is this time of year and then it picks up again around Christmas."

That was not really what I asked, but I didn't expect any other answer. While Eredine was sweet, and a fantastic listener, she was guarded and closed off and most definitely difficult to get to know. Outside of the Adairs, she didn't seem to have any real friends here in Scotland. Eredine was a giant mystery. Even more so when I realized why she was so familiar.

When I was around seventeen, eighteen, I followed a lot of social media influencers. One of them was a freestyle dancer who posted videos of her solos and sometimes group dances. They did a lot of pop-up performances in public places. Her online name was Cadenza, and she had around two million followers. One day she just stopped posting, I stopped following, and I never thought much about it again.

However, Eredine Willows was Cadenza's spitting image. I knew it was a coincidence because no one else noted it, and honestly, Eredine was nothing like Cadenza in personality. Cadenza had a cocky confidence that was extremely attractive; Eredine was the opposite. Shy, reserved.

Robyn told me Eredine was always guarded, but the Lucy situation had made her throw up barriers a mile high. I could see that. And I was patient. I was following Robyn's footsteps and not bulldozing my way into her life. For Eredine, we had to be stealthy. Slow and steady would win that race.

We sat around chatting for a while and then seeing the kids were getting antsy, Arro clapped her hands and announced it was time to eat. Everyone offered to help her in the kitchen, but we waved the guys off since it was their birthdays. The women found themselves alone in the kitchen.

I noted the gender division. "Let's not make a habit of this, or they might get ideas."

Robyn snorted. "They know us well enough by now not to make us into the 'little ladies.' Lachlan wouldn't want to, anyway. He likes me—"

"Stop." Arro put a hand up near her face, and Eredine and I laughed at Robyn's stunned look. "He is my brother, and as far as I'm concerned, my brothers are as chaste as monks."

"I wasn't going to say anything dirty." Robyn raised an eyebrow as we followed Arro's lead around the kitchen. "Unlike some people"—she shot me a look—"I am a lady."

I guffawed. "What did I do?"

"You always provide too much information."

"Ooh, about who?" Arro asked. "Do you have your eye on someone?"

I wanted to shoot my sister a killing look, but I knew that would be too obvious. "No. Robyn's talking about past boyfriends."

"Well, good luck here, anyway." Arro made a face. "Living in a small village doesn't exactly make it easy to meet someone. Look at me. Look at Thane."

She didn't say look at Eredine, but I knew we were all thinking it.

"Speaking of my brother," Arro said to me as I followed her into the dining room with the huge bowl of roast potatoes, "is something wrong between you two? I sense a distinct chill."

I shrugged off her comment like it was nonsense, giving her one of my breezy smiles. "Not at all. We're great."

She narrowed her eyes like she didn't quite believe me. "Guess I was wrong, then."

Deciding that a week was enough time for this nonsense between me and Thane to have gone on, I knew I'd have to chat with him and clear the air. To be honest, his behavior had put a damper on my feelings. It was illuminating to see how much of an asshole he could be. I was done trying to be understanding about his position in all this.

Despite Thane's determination to treat me like I didn't exist, dinner was great fun. Food was involved, so it meant Eilidh sat still throughout the whole thing and enjoyed being the center of attention. Lewis insisted on sitting next to me at the table, so I spent a good part of the meal talking with him about the video game he was playing with his friends online during the hours he was allowed. He was irritated because his friends' parents let them play longer than he was permitted, and they kept wanting to play this particular game without him. To distract him from his irritation, I asked him to explain the entire game to me.

He did. In detail. And I loved him so I tried not to die of boredom.

At one point, I glanced up from our discussion to find Thane watching us with a furrow between his brows. He looked away as soon as our eyes met.

After dinner, it was gift-giving time, and I experienced a brief flutter of nervousness in my belly. I'd helped the kids pick out their gift to their dad, but I'd bought Thane something just from me a few weeks ago. When we were still friends. I wasn't sure how I felt about giving it to him now.

Especially in front of everyone.

We settled in the living room, Eilidh tucked on Thane's lap because she was a little sleepy after the food, and Lewis by my side. Lachlan opened his gifts first.

Robyn had given him a photo I'd taken under her direction down on the beach. It was a gorgeous black-and-white headshot of her looking at the water. She'd almost backed out of the gift, thinking it was cheesy and vain, but I'd convinced her to stick with it. Sourcing a frame that matched the interior of his office at work, she added the photo and wrapped it.

I was nervous for her because I could tell by the way she was biting her lip that she still had doubts. When Lachlan opened it, he just stared at it. She shifted uncomfortably in the large armchair beside him.

"It's ... I thought you could put it in your office or some-thing ... but it seems stupid now. I—"

"I love it." He turned to smolder at her, and I felt a mix of happiness and envy. Once again, I couldn't help but think how amazing it would be to have a guy love me like Lachlan loved Robyn. But deep down, I didn't believe that would ever happen. A guy might love me ... but not like that. Robyn was the kind of woman who inspired that kind of love.

"You do?" She still seemed unsure.

"You're beautiful." He stared at the picture. "I love it," he repeated, and then frowned. "But who took it?"

"Regan."

He smiled at me with his eyes. "You captured her perfectly."

I grinned. "I know."

Lachlan laughed softly and then leaned into Robyn to brush a kiss across her mouth. "Later," he murmured, but we all heard him.

"Speaking of ... I have another gift for you, but—" Robyn smirked at me, mischief in her gaze. "I left it in the *bedroom*."

While the adults groaned at the insinuation, I smiled so hard my cheeks hurt. "It doesn't bother me like it bothers you. But I appreciate the effort."

"Damn you." She narrowed her eyes, trying not to laugh.

"I have no idea what's going on." Lachlan turned to Thane for answers.

He shrugged. "Don't look at me."

"Just sister stuff," Robyn assured Lachlan.

"So ... *is* there another present in the bedroom?" He raised his eyebrows in expectation.

"Isn't there every day?"

Lachlan grinned. "Yes. My mistake."

Robyn gave him a sassy nod. "You know it. But yeah, there is actually another present in the bedroom."

"Is it a cuddly toy?" Eilidh asked.

Shooting my sister a look for speaking in innuendo in front of the kids, she blanched and smiled apologetically before turning to Eilidh. "Yeah, sweetie. That's exactly right."

"I want to see!"

"Some other time, Eils." Thane cuddled her close. "It's Uncle Lachlan's present, remember."

"Right, well." Mac stood and handed over a tall, slim gift bag to Lachlan and another to Thane. "What do you get the men who have everything?"

It turned out expensive whisky, which they both were extremely happy about.

More gifts were shared. Lachlan got a tie from me, a sweater from Arro, a kilt pin from Eredine, and new earbuds and an arm strap for his phone from the kids so he could listen to his music while running. It was Lewis's idea, I informed Lachlan, and his nephew couldn't look more pleased by how "chuffed" his uncle was.

Lastly, Thane gave his brother a compass.

"It was Dad's. Do you remember? He said it belonged to our great-great-grandfather. I found it in the attic a few months ago when I was clearing stuff out. A guy in Inverness restored it."

The gift obviously blew Lachlan away, and the brothers did that guy thing where they were all gruff about their emotions and battered each other on the back when they hugged to lessen the sentimentality of it all.

It was kind of adorable.

And then it was Thane's turn. He got a matching kilt pin from Eredine (which I thought was cute), a different sweater from Lachlan's from Arro, a swanky beard grooming kit from Robyn, and a fancy watch from Lachlan.

"For your new start back at work. Turn it over," his brother said.

Thane did so and read, "*Novis Initiis.*"

"New beginnings," Lachlan explained.

As he looked at his brother, Thane's eyes brightened. Something only they seemed to understand passed between them. "It's great. Thank you."

Now my gift seemed weird in comparison. Instead of handing over the entire gift bag, I delved into it and took out the present from the kids. I gave it to Lewis to give to Thane.

"Happy Birthday, Dad." Lewis hopped off the couch to lean into his dad's legs. "It was my idea."

"Mine too!" Eilidh frowned deeper than any human had ever frowned before. She turned to her father with that ferocious scowl. "Mine too, Daddy."

Thane kissed her forehead. "I know, Eilidh-Bug. Now let's have a look and see what it is."

"It's LEGO," Eilidh announced, squirming excitedly, and we all couldn't help but chuckle. "Can I play with it too?"

Desperately trying not to laugh, Thane nodded as he ripped open the wrapping. "Of course." He studied it, his eyebrows lifting. "It might be a wee bit difficult." He looked at Lewis. "I didn't even know LEGO did this stuff."

It was adult LEGO. A complicated set with plans for a contemporary, all-white architect's studio. "I thought it would look great in your office once it's built. And it's supposed to be a stress reliever."

Thane flicked me a look. "Right."

"Ree-Ree might have helped with the idea too," Lewis admitted.

Their dad gave me a vague look of thanks.

I tucked his gift from me behind my legs.

~

Thane and Lachlan swapped stories about their misdemeanors as teenagers; Lewis and Eilidh were in Arrochar's TV room watching a movie because they'd gotten bored with the adults. Mac helped Arro clean up the kitchen. Even Eredine joined the warm conversation between my sister and the brothers.

I wasn't really in the mood. Abandoning my spot on the sofa, I thought I'd go check on the kids and passed through the hallway to do it. A glance in the kitchen, however, stopped me in my tracks. Arro and Mac were standing near the sink, side by side, but they were pressed together, heads turned to each other, murmuring in conversation. Mac stared down at Arro with such tenderness, I felt like I was intruding upon something.

Their body language was *not* the body language of two *friends*.

Oh my God.

How the hell had I missed that?

Probably because you're obsessed with your asshole boss.

Hurrying away before they caught me watching them, I tucked this revelation away and considered asking Robyn about it later. Or maybe I shouldn't. Maybe no one else knew. Maybe I was making something out of nothing.

Peeking into the den, I found Lewis sitting cross-legged in front of the TV, engrossed in a Marvel movie while Eilidh slept on the sofa. Not wanting to disturb them, I closed the door softly and pondered my next move. I couldn't go into the kitchen to help Arro and Mac because it definitely seemed like I'd be interrupting. And I didn't want to return to the sitting room because Thane's insistence on making me feel like I didn't exist was …

Well, it was horrible.

Looking down the hallway, I noted the side entrance that probably led to the backyard. It was cold out, but it was dry.

And I could do with some fresh air.

~

THANE

Regan disappeared fifteen minutes ago and hadn't come back. At first, he'd thought she'd gone to the kitchen to help Mac and Arro, but they'd returned with drinks for everyone and she wasn't with them.

He noted Robyn frowning at her empty spot on the couch, more specifically at the floor. Thane peered around Mac's legs and noted the gift bag.

When he looked up, Robyn stared intensely at him.

He squirmed with guilt.

"Where's Regan?" Eredine asked, cutting through Lachlan and Mac's conversation about security plans for the Hogmanay ceilidh at Ardnoch Castle.

"I don't know." Robyn moved to push up off the large armchair she shared with Lachlan. "I'd better check."

"Let me." Thane stood. "I need to look in on the kids, anyway."

Regan was probably with them.

A muscle ticked in Robyn's jaw, but she nodded and lowered beside Lachlan.

Robyn's strange intensity worried him. Had Regan told her sister about ... the incident? Damn it. It was nothing. Something that shouldn't have happened.

Or maybe she's just picking up on the fact that you're being an absolute bastard to her sister.

Guilt rode Thane's every step. Once he'd put up his guard with Regan, he hadn't known how to stop for fear he might cross the line with her again. And it was more than that. That man's appearance last week had put Thane in the foulest of moods. Had he taken it out on Regan?

Remorse sharpened in his chest.

He'd been so lost in his concerns about that man and Eilidh that he hadn't been paying attention to what he was doing to Regan.

Forced to socialize with her now, it was glaringly obvious that beyond the teasing between her and her sister, Regan had lost her sparkle. She didn't want to sit around and laugh with them, and that was out of character. Regan was an optimistic, happy person who lit up any room she was in.

Had he dimmed her light with his behavior?

He'd acted like a typical fuck boy, flirting with her for weeks, touching her ... and then icing her out. He hadn't been a dick like that to women even in the arrogance of youth. It was appalling he'd do it now.

Was that why Lewis had clung to Regan so much this past week? He sensed Regan's unhappiness?

Was his boy worried she didn't want to be with them anymore?

What if she doesn't?

Who would want to stick around for a boss who treated her like a mere servant?

If any other man did that to a woman he cared about, he'd have more than a few strong words for him.

The idea of Regan returning to the States made his pulse race with panic. Eilidh and Lewis needed her. Their lives were running so much smoother with her here, and she made them happy. Robyn had mentioned something about an ancestry visa a few weeks back, and it had given him hope perhaps Regan might stay on as their nanny for longer than six months. They were already in month three of her stay, almost halfway through.

A quick look in the TV room told him Regan wasn't in there with the kids. The downstairs bathroom door was open, and she wasn't in there either. As he stepped into the kitchen, he bumped into Robyn.

She held up the gift bag that had been lying on the floor.

Bemused, Thane took it and looked inside to see a book-shaped gift inside.

Robyn gave him that stony stare of hers. "Regan's gift to you."

He frowned. Why hadn't she given it to him during the present opening?

"She's sitting out in the backyard in the cold because she'd rather do that than sit in a room with you," Robyn said bluntly. "Fix that, please."

It was a command.

Ashamed of his behavior, he nodded like a scolded schoolboy and made his way to the French doors that led out into the back garden.

And there she was.

Her red hair gleamed gold in the autumn sunlight as she sat on one of Arrochar's garden chairs, staring out into the woodland behind his sister's house. Thane noted the protective way Regan sat with her knees drawn to her chest.

Sensing movement behind her, she glanced over her shoulder and tensed.

Only weeks ago she would have turned and given him her glamorous smile and those appealing dimples.

"Fuck," he muttered under his breath and walked around her to sit down on her chair's twin. "Hi."

Regan drew her knees in even tighter. "Hey." Her eyes dropped to the bag in his hand, and she stiffened.

"Robyn said this is from you to me."

She tucked her hair behind her ear. "It's just silly …"

Wanting to put her out of her obvious misery, and also intrigued by what the gift could be, Thane took the object out of the bag. It was thick and soft. Unwrapping it revealed a dark leather journal with an inscription on it. *"Loyal Au Mort."*

"I … um … I noticed you have all these loose papers and sticky notes lying around the office, and a lot of them seem to be your thoughts on the same project." She gestured to the journal as he opened the soft leather binding to reveal the lined paper inside. "It might better for you to put all your ideas in one place so you don't lose them."

It was incredibly considerate, and he felt even more of a shit than before.

"Lachlan told me this is the Adair Clan motto."

"Loyal Au Mort." He traced the words embossed on the front. "Faithful unto Death."

"I like it. It speaks to who you guys are. But … I don't know." She shifted uncomfortably again. "It seems stupid now."

Because she saw him differently now?

Why did that prick his pride more than he liked?

"It's not stupid," he replied gruffly, his pulse thundering in his ears. "It's perfect. Thank you."

When she wouldn't meet his gaze, he knew he had to do

major damage control, or he was going to mess up things between them for good.

"I'm sorry I've been such a bastard to you. You don't deserve that."

Regan shrugged and gave him a wide smile that didn't reach her eyes. "It's fine."

She was lying.

Hiding how he'd hurt her.

Not wanting to be vulnerable with him.

And who could bloody blame her?

"Last week, the man my wife cheated on me with suddenly approached me at work," he shocked himself by blurting out.

Regan's reaction was physical. Her knees fell away from her chest as if her strings had been cut. "What?"

"No one knows. About any of it. Not even Lachlan."

Eyes wide, she shook her head. "Thane, I won't tell anyone."

He sat back in the chair, the cold air nipping at his cheeks. And it all just spilled out, like he couldn't contain it any longer. "It was before Eilidh was born. I didn't suspect a thing. Nothing had changed between us. Not our family dynamic, not our relationship. There had been a rough patch before it. Fran seemed discontent and I couldn't work out why. But soon enough, I thought something had clicked into place for her because she seemed happier than ever. I just assumed she was finally growing into family life," he grunted, remembering the brutal wound of discovering the truth. "I wanted to surprise her at work for Valentine's Day. She had been working late a lot at school, and I thought she deserved a wee break. So I packed a hamper with nibbles and champagne to take to her. Arro was babysitting Lewis.

"The school was near empty when I got there. Her door

was open. No one was in the classroom. But I could hear muffled noises coming from within her supply cupboard."

"Oh, Thane." Regan dropped her head in sympathy.

He gave her an unhappy smirk. "Opened the door and found her colleague Sean McClintock fucking her up against the shelves."

Regan squeezed her eyes closed as if she felt his pain. "I'm so sorry."

"We had the prick and his wife over for goddamn dinner. He'd held my son in his arms. And it turned out for six months, they'd been cheating on us."

Regan shook her head. "But you forgave her?"

Remembering the months of emotional wreckage Fran had wrought, Thane confessed quietly, "It wasn't that easy. McClintock took off. Didn't want to lose his wife, so he left for a school in Moray. I was still trying to figure out what I wanted, and Fran was desperately trying to convince me she loved me."

"Then why cheat on you?"

"She said it wasn't about not loving me. It was the thrill. After we had Lewis, she'd felt old. Said she was worried she'd missed out since she'd only ever been with me."

"What the hell?"

"I know." Fran's confession had hurt like hell. True, she was a virgin when they met, and he had been with other girls before her, but few. And never had he thought he'd missed out by settling down with Fran. "But she said the idea of losing me woke her up. That she wanted only me. I was still deciding whether to give her another chance when she told me she was pregnant with Eilidh."

"Thane?" Regan sat forward on the chair, reaching to grip his wrist as realization dawned on her. "No. I ... see you in Eilidh. No way. She's yours."

193

"I know she's mine." His heart banged in his chest at the very idea of someone trying to take her from him.

Regan relaxed. "You did a test?"

"No." He yanked his arm out from under hers. "I don't need a bloody test. No test needs to tell me what I already know in my gut. Eilidh is *my* daughter."

She seemed to process that, and whatever conclusion she drew made her expression soften to pure tenderness. The tightness in his chest eased, and he had the seductive thought that it might be fantastic to pull her into his arms and bury all his worries and frustration in her.

But he couldn't.

Not this woman.

"I'm telling you this because McClintock approached, like I said. He was drunk, and Eilidh was the reason he'd come to me. I quickly shut him down, but it put me in a bear of a mood. I'm sorry. You don't deserve to take the brunt of it."

Concerned, she sat forward, her elbows to knees. "Did he threaten to take action about this?"

"I've worried all week that's where the conversation was heading, but I think I scared the shit out of him. Haven't heard from him since."

"Why now?"

"I don't know. I don't care. It's not happening."

At his dark tone, Regan gave him a grim nod. "Agreed. I'm glad you scared him off."

Seeing her reaction, her genuine fondness for his family, made him feel even worse about his treatment of her. "Do you accept my apology, then?"

She cocked her head and her hair spilled down her shoulders, the copper glinting brilliantly in the low afternoon sun. In the shadows, her eyes often looked dark brown, but today their color was a warm, glossy chestnut with red and gold tones to match her hair.

They'd been dull only a short time ago. The light was back.

Thank God.

"I won't put up with it again. I'm nobody's punching bag, Thane."

He winced slightly. "I know that. It won't happen again. I'm ashamed it even did."

Her expression softened and then turned quizzical. "Does that mean you weren't treating me like that because of … the hands on my ass thing?"

Flushing, Thane rubbed the back of his neck. How did he explain this tactfully without hurting her feelings even further? Deciding she deserved his honesty instead of his avoidance, he leaned toward her. "That can't happen between us, Regan. Ever."

Her brow puckered. "You're attracted to me too. I felt it. In more ways than one."

At her mischievous comment, he threw her a quelling look.

She grinned wickedly and goddamn it, all his blood rushed south.

"Regan," he warned. "I'm serious. There's no point in denying that I think you're beautiful. I'd have to be half dead not to react to you pressed up against me." He quickly threw the memory out. "But I'm your boss, and you're too young for me. It could never be anything but sex between us, and that's not happening."

Thane waited impatiently for her reaction. She studied him for what seemed like a very long time, and he worried about her being out in this bloody cold garden with no coat. Finally, she threw a glance over her shoulder at the house, then turned to lean into him. Her voice low, husky, heat in those gorgeous eyes, she asked, "Who said it had to be anything serious? We want each other, and we're both adults.

Why can't we just satisfy those urges without making a big deal out of it?"

The blood was definitely rushing out of his brain because there was a part of him that wanted to give in, to say screw it, and crawl into her bed that night to bury his loneliness inside her.

Shaking his head at the selfish thought, Thane stood, putting distance between them. He clutched the journal in his hand and gestured with it. "Thank you again for the thoughtful gift, Regan. But I'm going to say this one more time: it can't happen between us. Now either we agree to put it behind us, or we'll need to reassess your position as the children's nanny."

"Thane." She stood with a huff of anger and tried to reach for him. He pulled away from her and ignored her hurt expression. "I don't get how you can be so great one minute and then so cold the next."

"Probably because every time I'm myself with you, you cross the line," he snapped. She was pushing him to lose control. He wanted to, and he hated himself for it. "I'm trying to be a good man. A good father. I don't need to make village gossip the truth and turn this into something sordid. For the last time, I'm asking you to act professionally toward me from now on, to treat me as you treated the other fathers who employed you, unless, of course, you get off on harassing older, unavailable men."

He regretted it as soon as the words left his mouth.

Regan jerked back as if he'd physically hit her, and he clenched the hand not holding her gift to stop himself from reaching for her.

"Message received loud and clear. I'm sorry if my behavior came across as harassment. It won't happen again." She strode away from him, her spine stiff, and disappeared inside.

Feeling a burn in his chest, Thane turned his back to the house to gather himself. Trying to be a good man, he'd said. To everyone but her, it would seem.

"Thane!"

Taking a deep breath, he turned to the house to see Mac standing at the French doors. "Regan isn't feeling well, and Eilidh's still asleep in the den, so I offered to take Regan home. Just wanted to say bye before I left."

Thane tried not to react to the news that he'd chased her out of Arro's house. "Right. Okay, then. Thanks, Mac. And thanks again for the whisky."

"No problem. Hopefully see you before your birthday, but if I don't, have a good one."

"Thanks." He waved his friend off and braced himself for returning indoors.

He couldn't look at Robyn, but he could sense her watching him. Judging him, probably. Pondering the many ways she could unman him with her martial arts skills.

And he'd deserve it.

Lewis grew stonily quiet at the news Regan had gone home without them. Eilidh woke up as he put her into the back of the car, and the first person she asked for was Ree-Ree. She cried, reminding him how little she was, when he didn't produce her nanny (and to be frank, her best friend) immediately.

His daughter thankfully fell back asleep as they made the short drive back to Caelmore. Lewis gave him one-word answers to his questions, so he stopped asking.

The silence gave his thoughts time to wander.

And it suddenly occurred to him he'd confessed Fran's betrayal to Regan. She was the only person he'd trusted with it. Why? And then why insult her afterward?

He sighed heavily. He was a mess.

Maybe he wasn't protecting himself from Regan by pushing her away. Maybe he was protecting her.

Sounds like a shitty excuse, a voice that sounded an awful lot like Regan's said in his head.

As he pulled up to the house, an overwhelming sense of remorse and melancholy filled him at the sight of the lights on in her annex. Thane decided the fact that the woman had him so tied in knots was a sign that he *should* keep his distance.

Lewis got out of the car before Thane had even taken off his seat belt, and he watched his son stare toward the annex as he walked to their front door. Thane saw to Eilidh, lifting her from her seat. Her little arms circled his neck, and she pressed her cheek to his.

His chest expanded with emotion. "Come on, little love," he whispered. "Time for bed."

"Will Ree-Ree be there too?" she whispered sleepily.

He winced. "Regan's already asleep, Eilidh-Bug. But I've got you."

She snuggled deeper into him, apparently too tired to argue. Thank God.

Flicking one last look in the annex's direction, Thane decided he'd have to fix things *again* with Regan. He could be civil and kind and friendly toward her without giving her hope of more.

And there was one surefire way to get the message across without treating her so undeservedly.

"**Y**ou did what?" Robyn demanded as I tried to get out of her choke hold.

Slapping her arm to let me go, I gasped with relief as she abruptly released. My decision to take her up on an MMA session because my Wednesday morning was suddenly free didn't seem like such a good idea. I growled in irritation. "You are impossibly strong!"

"You okay?" *Now* she was concerned.

"Fine." I waved her off before falling backward onto the mat. Splayed like a sea star, I stared up at the private gym's ceiling.

Robyn stood over me, her hands on her slender hips, one eyebrow raised. "Repeat what you just told me."

So I did, which was pretty much the entire conversation with Thane in Arro's backyard the previous weekend, minus what he'd confided about Fran's affair. That shocking revelation was going to take longer to process. It also made me empathetic toward Thane when all I wanted to do was hate him after what he'd said to me. I didn't want to judge a dead woman ... but how the hell could she cheat on Thane Adair? Was she nuts?

You hate him, remember!

Yes, I hated him. And hurt for him in equal measure. Ugh, it was so complicated.

But Robyn knew none of that, and she wouldn't ever find out from me. What I'd told her was my suggestion to Thane that we have no-strings-attached sex.

"Are you crazy?"

I had a feeling it was a rhetorical question.

"It just slipped out!"

"That's like having sex with someone and saying we didn't mean it, it just slipped in."

"Ew, Robbie!" I laughed. "It's not at all the same thing."

Robyn huffed and kneeled beside me to pull me to sitting. Her brow knit together. "Seriously. Why would you suggest that to Thane?"

"Why not?" I deflected. "You and Lachlan started off with a sex-but-zero-commitment affair."

"Yeah, but we didn't even like each other, let alone have *feelings* for each other."

"Not true. I know you can't just have sex with some random."

My sister considered this and amended. "There were things I liked about him, but there were more things I didn't like about Lachlan. But I couldn't deny that I had never wanted to have sex with a guy more in my life. Would I have fallen into bed with him if I had emotional feelings for him, knowing he only wanted sex? No. That's asking for trouble. As it was, it was horrible thinking I'd fallen in love with him and he didn't feel the same way. You suggested having sex and zero commitment with a man you actually care about. Why?"

I winced, dreading the truth, so I posed it as a question.

"Because I thought that if we got close enough, he might develop feelings for me?"

She gave me her best "big sister is disappointed in you" look.

Ouch.

"You're setting yourself up to get hurt. And you're being dishonest. With yourself and with Thane. That's not fair to either of you."

Shamed, I looked away. "It just came out ... without me thinking it through. It's a moot point, anyway. I kind of actually detest his guts right now." Sort of. Like seventy/thirty in the hate/sympathy ratio.

Robyn grimaced. "That's not good. What happened?"

I told her what he'd said to me at Arro's.

A dark cloud fell over my sister's face. "Shit. It looks like I'm going to be a parent sooner than I'd thought."

Confused, I blinked rapidly. "Uh, what?"

"Well, someone is going to have to adopt Eilidh and Lewis after I kill their father."

Even though I knew she was joking, there was a serious, hard glint in her eyes. "Robyn, it's fine. I'm fine." I beamed at her. "You know me. Water off a duck's back."

"Why do you do that? Why do you lie to me?"

I flinched. "I'm not ..." Shaking my head, I shrugged. "Because if I told the truth half the time, I'd cry. People don't want to know if you're sad or hurt or angry or depressed, Robbie. Not even so-called friends. They just want you to say that you're fine so they don't have to expend emotional energy on you."

Hurt flickered across her face. "And you think that's how I am?"

"No." I hurried to assure her, realizing belatedly how it had come out. "No. I meant I picked up on that a long time ago with other people, sometimes even with Mom, and I've just gotten into the habit of being happy-go-lucky no matter how I'm really feeling because I know most people don't want to hear the truth."

"You don't have to do that with me."

I stared at my sister, blinking back tears. "I know that. I do."

"So hit me with the truth."

I sucked in a breath and shakily exhaled it. "He hurt me. He made me feel ... like I had imagined it. He used the word *harass*. I spent the night crying in my bed like a sixteen-year-old because I was so scared I was doing to him what Austin did to me."

"That is completely different." I could hear the sharp edge of genuine anger in Robyn's voice.

"I know that now. I've had four days of giving the bastard the cold shoulder to come to that conclusion myself. He said what he said so he didn't have to deal with me anymore, and he didn't care if he hurt me to do it."

"I doubt he didn't care," Robyn said, surprising me.

"Really?"

"I'm angry at him for speaking that way to you, but I can't imagine he's happy with himself about it."

"Where's his apology, then? He's not giving me the silent treatment anymore, but he didn't apologize for what he said." I shook my head, looking toward the water beyond the cliff. "I should quit, but every time I think about it, I cannot imagine leaving Eilidh and Lewis."

"Or Thane."

"No, he can go fuck himself, preferably with a glove made of splinters."

Robyn threw her head back in laughter, and I couldn't help but laugh too. Then she reached for my hand, squeezing it. "Do you know how brave you are?"

Instantly, my smile fell and I tried to pull away. She wouldn't let me. "Don't."

"No, I will." Robyn leaned toward me. "Do you think for one second that I would have told Lachlan I wanted him if he hadn't made the first move?"

"Of course, you would. You're the most courageous person I've ever known."

She looked modestly uncomfortable with the praise and shrugged. "Maybe I'm okay with situations like kidnappings and break-ins and shootouts ... but when it comes to my heart? Regan, it took me ten years to get up the courage to find Mac. And I never told a guy I loved them after Josh Horner broke my heart. I didn't even try to let a guy in until Lachlan. And he wasn't very nice to me at first, so I would most definitely have *not* made myself vulnerable to him. If he hadn't mauled me"— she raised her eyebrow with a smirk—"in Gordon's trailer that first time, and then again in his office and again—"

"Got it. Lachlan is a horndog. Moving on."

She grinned cheekily. "My point is, he made the first move. But you ... you put yourself out there with Thane, even after he'd treated you not very nicely and with full knowledge and awareness that the idea of you two together is a little controversial. You still did it. You still followed your feelings—"

"And my libido."

"My little sister doesn't have a libido, and putting yourself out there with him is really brave. I'm proud of you."

Her words were like water on a thirsty seedling. "Thank you."

"Now that we've established you're brave ... my sister is nobody's punching bag—"

"I said those same words to him!" I exclaimed.

"Good. Now live by them. If you're mad at him, be mad

and stay mad at him until he mans up and apologizes for being a dick. But once he apologizes, you move on. Thane goes back to just being your boss, and you take care of those kids. Don't let him put you off the ancestry visa."

"I told you I'm thinking about it, and I won't let him put me off. That's not a decision I'm going to make based on a guy."

"No. Just make it based on your sister who wants you here to help plan her wedding and see her get married and be there the day she finds out she's pregnant and the day you become an aunt and—"

"I get it." My eyes filled with a different emotion. "I don't want to miss those things either. I'm just … what kind of life could I have here? It's not the remoteness that bothers me, or the small town. It's just … I still want to meet someone, eventually. Someone who wants me in return." I looked down at my sneakers. "If he's out there."

"He's out there, Regan. You just need to stop renting space in your head to Thane Adair. You'll see things clearer once you do, and I promise, I was kidding before. No more pressure from me. Stay or don't stay, I just want you to be happy."

～

With my sister's advice fresh in my mind, I braced myself for Thane's return from work that night. Determined not to stop with my icy response to him until he apologized, I kind of got myself worked up about it. Even more so when I picked up the kids from school. As I started the engine, Lewis announced, "Eilidh and I know what we want to do for Dad's birthday."

"Oh, yeah?" I asked, staring at them in the rearview mirror. "What's that?"

"Dad talks to us about the bird show at the castle that looks like something out of Disney. Dad said he would take us next summer, but we thought we could go at the weekend."

Castle like something out of Disney? I didn't know what castle he was talking about. "I'll mention it to your dad."

"You have to come!" Eilidh said, kicking her legs with the words.

Inwardly, I grimaced. There was no way in hell I was spending a day out with Thane. Trying not to wince at the lie, I replied, "I can't, honey. I have plans this weekend."

"What plans?" She crossed her arms over her chest and jutted her chin sternly at me.

"Noneuhyurbusiness plans," I singsonged.

She giggled but a quick glance at Lewis revealed he wasn't laughing. He stared out the passenger window, his brow furrowed in thought.

He was quiet for the rest of the drive and while I settled them at the dining table with their homework and a snack. After I started dinner, I sat down with them to see if they needed help with anything. Not that they ever needed much help. Thane's children were smart as whips and quick too.

While the Scottish system had adopted a play-based strategy for primary one and two classes, Eilidh still got some reading, spelling, and math work sent home a couple times a week. Not a lot. We usually blew through it in twenty minutes. Lewis, now out of the play-based learning years, had transitioned with no issues. As Eilidh kept herself busy drawing on a tablet, I watched over Lewis as he did his multiplication homework.

"Very good," I murmured as I watched him do it with ease. He seemed to whiz through his math work while he took a little more time over spelling and language questions. To be fair, spelling and language posed a slight learning curve for me, too, considering the differences between British and American English.

"What are you doing this weekend?" Lewis surprised me by asking.

He looked up from his booklet to stare at me like a little interrogator.

I swallowed hard, not wanting to lie to his face. "The truth is, I'm not going to crash your weekend with your dad. This weekend is all about his upcoming birthday and spending time with the two people he loves most. It's not fair to your dad to keep involving me in family days."

Lewis frowned. "But ... don't you like Dad?"

Shocked by the question, I nodded. "Of course, I like your dad. That's why I'm not crashing his birthday plans with you two. Now finish up. I'm going to check on dinner." I left the table before he could ask more questions I didn't know how to answer.

At around six o'clock, just as I was setting the table for dinner, Thane returned home. Over the past few months, I'd taken to eating with the family. We'd all fallen naturally into the habit. With Robyn's words in mind, however, I left my plate aside for now. If Thane apologized, I'd put my plate out and eat with them. But if he didn't, then maybe it was time to draw some lines in the sand. The kids would find it weird at first, but they'd get used to my not being there.

As always, Eilidh ran to greet Thane at the front door, and I tried not to let his tender hello to his daughter melt my resolve. He wandered into the living area with her in his arms as usual and smiled over at Lewis first. "Hey, buddy. How was school?"

"Fine." Lewis shrugged and turned back to the television.

Thane frowned and then looked at me in question. I shrugged.

"Eilidh, go sit with your brother for a minute." Thane lowered her to the floor, and she skipped across the room to throw herself on the couch at Lewis.

"Eils!" Lewis giggled, pushing her off, and I relaxed at the sound.

"Can I have a word?"

I glanced over at Thane. "Now?"

He gestured down the hall. "Now."

"Dinner's ready."

"I'll be quick."

Pulse picking up at his request, I followed him down the hall and into his office. When he closed the door behind him, I got worried. "Is everything okay?"

"Yes and no." Thane stared directly into my eyes. "I owe you an apology for the way I spoke to you at the weekend. I took too long to say sorry, and I'm sorry for that too."

Relief flooded me, but I nodded in agreement.

He nodded back, his expression stern. "It was unbearably rude of me, and it won't happen again."

"Apology accepted."

Thane exhaled slowly, relieved. "Good. The second thing is, I wondered if I could pay you overtime to watch Eilidh and Lewis this Friday night?"

I answered without thinking. "Of course." Then I thought of that McClintock guy who had approached him about Eilidh. "Is something wrong, something going on?"

"No, no." Thane dropped his gaze as he rubbed his hand over the back of his neck. "I ... I have a date."

Honestly, I didn't think I could have flinched harder if a cannon had exploded behind me.

He wanted me to work overtime so he could go on a date?

And I'd agreed.

I was so infuriated and hurt and disappointed, I couldn't even look at him or speak. Instead, I walked out of his office and back into the kitchen. Attempting not to tremble with rage as I plated up the homemade macaroni, I also pretended I couldn't sense Thane watching me.

"Dinner is ready, kids," I announced as I walked into the kitchen to get my purse and car keys.

"Where's your plate?" Lewis asked.

I grabbed my stuff and looked over at the three of them as they settled at the table. "I have plans tonight." Forcing myself to enter Thane's space, I walked past him to kiss Lewis and Eilidh on the head. "Enjoy dinner, cuties. I'll see you in the morning."

I didn't acknowledge their father and walked out the front door, not knowing where to go. I could drive to Eredine's and confess it all to her. Or Arro and not confess anything. Or I could do what I really wanted and just be with Robyn.

Decision made, I strolled next door and hoped Lachlan wouldn't mind me crashing their evening. It turned out Lachlan wasn't home from the estate yet.

Perfect.

Over a glass of wine and a salad I wished was my home-made macaroni, I told my sister about the apology followed by the date bomb.

She gaped at me for a second and then shook her head in despair. "These Adair men … emotionally constipated, I tell you."

"So what are we? The laxative?"

Robyn gave a bark of laughter, and I grinned despite my inner turmoil.

"I don't want to be anyone's laxative, Robbie. It's not cute."

My sister laughed so hard, she snorted.

When she finally calmed, wiping tears from her eyes, she said, "I've missed you."

I smiled tenderly at her. "I've missed you too."

Reaching over to squeeze my hand, she asked, "So, what are you going to do?"

"What would you do?"

"Well …" Her amusement faded. "Before we knew it was Lucy behind Lachlan's stalker, we thought the stalker put her in the commercial fridge."

"I remember." Jesus, what a psychopath. Robyn would never use that word, but I was all too happy to. The bitch tried to kill my sister.

"Lachlan started spending all his time with her, and I was hurt and jealous, even though I tried to tell myself they were just friends. But knowing they had history … well, to me it looked like he had realized how he really felt about her."

"That must have sucked."

"No, what sucked was walking into his bedroom to find Lucy in silk lingerie lying on his bed while the two of them watched movies, like that was perfectly acceptable." I could hear the residual anger in my sister's voice, and I didn't blame her.

My jaw dropped. "What?"

"I told you, emotionally constipated. I left, he followed me, and we got into it. Turns out he"—she flicked me an unreadable look—"thought it was me who'd been taken, that it was me he'd find in the fridge. When it wasn't, when it was Lucy, he felt—"

"Relieved," I guessed. I saw the way the guy looked at my sister. She was his world. He must have been terrified that night.

"Yeah." Robyn raised her eyebrows. "Yeah, he was relieved. And he felt—"

"Guilty," I guessed again.

She quelled a grin for a mock stern look. "Am I telling the story, or are you?"

Chuckling, I waved her on. "Continue."

"Anyway, my point is, he hurt me by choosing her when I needed him, and even though he did it out of guilt, *I* didn't know that. And I didn't cover up my feelings to spare his or hers or anyone's during a difficult time. I just let it all hang out. I told you I never would have made the first move with Lachlan, and that was the truth. But once I was in it with him, I couldn't lie about how I felt. And I believe it was my honest reactions throughout our whole affair that allowed things to progress naturally and for Lachlan to slowly but eventually work out his own feelings about me."

"So you're saying I should react honestly?"

"Yes."

"What if my honest reaction is to be so mad, I can't even look at or talk to him?"

"Then do it."

"It's not very mature."

"Neither is punching someone, but I was this close"—she squeezed her forefinger and thumb together—"to punching Lachlan in the junk that night."

I chuckled. "I don't blame you." I wanted to say it was also a big red flag about Lucy. Hanging out on Lachlan's bed in her lingerie when she knew Robyn was sleeping with him? Yeah, no true friend did that to another friend. I, of course, didn't say that to my sister because that would be incredibly insensitive considering how badly she'd been blindsided by Lucy.

We sat in silence for a moment, eating dinner, sipping wine, and then I said softly, "This date with whoever this woman is … You can't say now he isn't deliberately trying to hurt me, Robbie. Maybe it's time to walk away. I don't want to work for someone I don't like."

"Is that honestly what you want to do?"

Despite my sympathy for what he'd been through, at the moment, dislike for Thane clouded everything. "Maybe. It's like what you said about how you felt about Lachlan at first. Just because you were physically attracted to him didn't mean you liked him."

"You used to like Thane. More than, I think."

Hurt was an angry burn in my chest. "That's when I used to think he was one of the good ones."

Robyn sighed. "Is he going about everything the wrong way? Absolutely. But I don't think he's deliberately trying to hurt you. He *is* one of the good ones."

I scowled at her.

She gave me a sympathetic look, and I knew I was about to get a brutal dish of honesty from her. "I don't think he has a spiteful bone in him. He probably just thinks this is the best way to move forward. I mean, was he a dick about the date? Not really. Did he apologize for last weekend? Yes. Maybe this is just his way of clarifying that he wants you both to move forward in a professional capacity and that nothing romantic is going to happen between you. If he's in denial about that, there's not a lot you can do. I told you to act naturally. And do that. Who knows how things will turn out? So consider where Thane really might be coming from on this before you decide how you're feeling."

I slumped, knowing I needed to listen to her.

Needed to move on.

But I didn't care if Thane's behavior seemed rational to everyone else. I'd considered it. I got it. But I also knew what was between us. He knew! And I was hurt. And mad as hell.

"You're right." I nodded. "And I promise once I have a handle on them, I won't hide my emotions."

17

THANE

Dimming the headlights before he swung into the driveway, Thane took a sobering breath. He parked and switched off the engine but made no move to get out.

If he'd thought Regan was giving him the cold shoulder before he announced he was going on a date, he'd been wrong. Her attitude had been downright temperate compared to the subzero chill directed at him these past two days.

She hadn't eaten with them last night again, and it visibly upset Eilidh and Lewis. He could tell Regan felt awful but that she also needed to create boundaries, and he understood that too. Thane didn't like it, but he got it.

However, the children were noticing the way she ignored him or clipped her answers anytime she couldn't ignore him, and it was bugging the shit out of him.

When he'd departed for his date with Keelie tonight, he'd left the three of them watching a movie. The kids just thought he was spending time with Mac. Thane never told them when he dated. There had never been anyone he was serious enough about to justify bringing them into his children's lives.

Eilidh and Lewis had said goodbye, and Regan didn't even look at him. He'd stared at her for a second, the muscle in his jaw ticking with irritation at her petulant behavior. Obviously not wanting to create even worse friction in front of the children, he'd left her to it.

And then endured a terrible date.

Thane was distracted. Regan's attitude was maddening, and he couldn't stop stewing over it. He barely listened to a word Keelie said over dinner, but thankfully, the woman was so self-involved, she didn't even notice he'd barely spoken. In fact, when he walked her to her car, she said almost dreamily, "Wow, you're such a good listener, Thane. I hope we do this again."

He'd given her a polite smile and a nod, opened her car door for her, and watched to make sure she was safely on her way home before he walked to his car. And he had the entire drive from Inverness to mull over the situation. So the date hadn't gone well. It had still served its purpose.

But now he dreaded going into the house to relieve Regan of babysitting duties. He dreaded her coldness.

He missed her smile.

Squeezing his eyes closed, Thane pinched the bridge of his nose, rid himself of feelings he couldn't afford to feel, and shoved out of the car. Inside the house, he found the entire space dimly illuminated by the kitchen under-cabinet lighting. It was past midnight, so Eils and Lewis would be abed.

The TV was a murmur in the large room, flickering light over Regan. She was asleep on the sectional with a throw over her. Thane approached quietly, his hands in his pockets. It didn't seem that long ago he'd found her like this on his couch when she'd just arrived in Scotland.

But it had been weeks.

Weeks for her to crawl under his skin.

He'd give anything for the freedom to reach out and stroke her cheek, brush his thumb over that lush lower lip of hers.

A hot, dark need built within him.

And then, as if she sensed him watching her, Regan stirred, and he retreated.

She blinked rapidly until those beautiful brown eyes focused on him. The adorable sleepiness iced over and regret replaced his desire.

"Oh, you're back." She sat up, pushing the throw off to stretch.

His gaze dropped to her breasts as her top tightened over them, and he glanced away. "Yeah. Eils and Lew okay?"

"Fine. Asleep. Night." She stood and brushed past him without another word.

Irritated, Thane turned to watch as she grabbed her keys and phone off the kitchen counter and disappeared down the corridor toward the side exit.

That was it?

Fuck that.

Thane hurried to catch up with her. "Wait," he whispered loudly, just as she was about to disappear out the door.

Regan halted but didn't look back at him. "What?"

His hands clenched and unclenched at his sides. Still speaking low so he didn't wake the children, he bit out, "Is this how it's going to be from now on?"

Finally, she looked at him. "What do you mean?"

"This"—he gestured between them—"our friendship. It's just over, then?"

She raised an annoyingly perfect eyebrow and gave him an even more irritating, pitying smile. "I'm just following orders, boss. You asked me to treat you how I treat the other fathers I've worked for. And despite your insinuation that

I'm an immoral tramp who tries to fuck unavailable older men—"

He flinched.

"I have always been professional. And this"—she gestured between them—"is how I treated the other fathers I worked for. Believe it or not, a couple of *them* tried to fuck *me*, and I politely declined before politely handing in my resignation."

His anger toward himself shifted to the bastards who'd done that to her.

"So, you're not the first dad to grab my ass and get a hard-on over me."

Her words whipped him like a lash, eliciting many emotions, and none of them good.

She gave him a bitter smirk. "You're just the first I was attracted to because I thought you were one of the good ones. My mistake to confuse a good father with a good guy. So you can stop worrying if I'm going to 'harass' you again. I'm over it."

Fury building, Thane drew in a breath. Still, his words came out in a rasp, "You said you accepted my apology."

"I did, didn't I?" She considered this and then her eyes narrowed. "How was your date?"

At her pointed question, he huffed. "You're jealous I went on a date with Keelie?"

Regan gave him a big smile that didn't reach her eyes. "Why would I be jealous? I feel sorry for her. You used her to drive a point home to me, didn't you? You hurt me, and you maybe even hurt her without caring beyond the fact that it made your point. So as far as I'm concerned, that canceled out your last apology."

"Regan ..." He didn't know what to say. She was right. And this was a mess. "Maybe ... maybe it's best I look for another nanny."

She flinched like he'd hit her, and he almost reached for her.

"You'd take Eilidh and Lewis away from me?"

Something twisted in his gut. "Regan."

"Right." She exhaled shakily. "Right. Yeah, you should do what is right for you guys. I'll, um ..." He saw her lower lip tremble, and she couldn't meet his gaze. "I'd appreciate it if you'd give me plenty of notice, though." Then she hurried out the door before he could answer.

"Fuck." He marched to the exit but all he saw was the annex door closing behind her.

Shutting the side entrance, he turned the lock and leaned his forehead against the cool wood. She tried to hide he'd made her cry.

He kept hurting her, and he didn't know how to stop. Other than to find a new nanny.

It would devastate Eilidh and Lewis.

"Fuck, fuck, fuck." He hit the door but not as hard or as loud as he wanted to.

Robyn wouldn't thank him for it either. Consequently, neither would Lachlan.

And Thane would no longer have the mornings to look forward to. When he'd wake up, knowing she was downstairs in his kitchen, putting the coffee on for him.

Her smile a better start to the day than anything else could ever be.

"Thane, you're fucked, man," he whispered to himself as he finally headed to bed.

~

REGAN

I laid in bed the next morning, trying not to think about the fact that Thane had most likely already posted an ad for a new nanny housekeeper. I'd failed. Again.

I'd spent all night thinking about things, and my conclusion: I was mad at my boss for not wanting to be in a romantic relationship with me.

When I said it to myself like that, I sounded like a crazy person.

I was mad at my boss for not returning my feelings.

Yup. Wasn't sounding any saner.

I was going to have to swallow my pride, wasn't I?

The alarm clock read six in the morning. Thane and the kids slept in a little later on Saturdays. But I needed to talk to him. I needed to fix things before it was too late. Because if I applied for the ancestry visa—and I had been leaning more and more toward doing so—I'd need a job. And this was a great job when I wasn't acting like a wounded ex-girlfriend.

Ugh. I threw off my bedcovers, mortified by my behavior. Had Thane given me mixed signals? Yes, he had. Had he said some extremely not-nice things to me? Yes. And had he hurt me? Also yes. But were we in a relationship when he did all those things? Had he made me any promises?

No!

No, he had not.

And I think that was what Robyn had been trying to remind me without wounding my feelings.

Shit.

When was I going to grow up?

"Now." I stood, nervous but determined. "You start now."

Hurrying into a pair of jeans and a tee, I quickly brushed my teeth and scraped my hair back into a ponytail. I wore no makeup but who cared? I was no longer trying to make Thane see me as desirable.

Letting myself into the house, I switched on the coffee

machine out of habit and then quietly made my way upstairs. The butterflies in my belly raged to life as I stopped outside Thane's bedroom. Of course, I'd been in his room to clean, and the master suite had the best views in the house. To my surprise, it was a very masculine space, making me wonder if he'd changed the décor after Fran died.

I had noted the picture of them on his nightstand. Something that humbled me now that I knew about her betrayal.

The reminder that he'd confessed something so personal to only me (not even to his siblings!) confused me again. Why would he confide in me if I weren't more than the nanny?

Down that road, danger lies.

Drawing in my breath, I knocked on his bedroom door. "Thane," I said as loudly as I dared.

I heard movement almost right away and then the door swung open and there he was, sleep rumpled in his pajamas. He stared warily at me. "Regan?"

"Downstairs." I nodded toward the stairwell. "Please."

He nodded and followed me downstairs.

Once in the kitchen, I settled on the opposite side of the island from him to give us space.

"What is it?" he asked, his brow furrowed, his beautiful eyes filled with concern. "Has something happened?"

"No. I just … I'm sorry for how early it is, but I couldn't sleep and I just …" I took a breath to control my nerves. "I wanted to apologize for my behavior." My cheeks burned with embarrassment and shame. "I haven't been acting like myself, and I've treated you unfairly."

Thane frowned. "You're not at fault here, Regan. I sent out the wrong signals. I'm sorry."

Ignoring the sting of his rejection, I shook my head. "No. I should have gotten over it when you asked me to, and I just kept dragging it out. You're a grown man, and you can date whoever the hell you like and … I don't want to lose this job."

I tried to smile through my fears, tried to do the easy-breezy Regan thing, but tears brightened my eyes as I thought about Eilidh and Lewis. "I adore those kids." I gestured upstairs, my tears spilling over to my everlasting mortification. "This is a great job, and I love being near my sister and—"

"Hey, hey, hey." Thane interrupted me softly, holding his hands up and taking a step toward me. Then he stopped himself, looking a little helpless. "Please don't cry. We'll figure this out, okay? You can keep the job. We'll figure it out. I don't want to lose you either. It would devastate the kids."

I swiped at my cheeks, irritated by my emotional display. "I'm sorry. I didn't mean to cry. I'm not a crier or someone who uses tears to get their own way. That's not—"

"Regan."

At his authoritative tone, I stopped talking.

He pressed his lips together in a kind smile. "Maybe, from now on, we just go forward assuming the other only has the best of intentions. How does that sound?"

Relaxing somewhat, I nodded. "That sounds good."

"Good. So are we starting over, then?"

"I'd like that very much."

Thane released a heavy sigh of relief and grinned. He was so sexy I could cry again. I stubbornly ignored the butterflies in my belly.

"Good. That's great. So ... will you join us at Dunrobin Castle today?"

Stunned, I didn't know what to say. When he suggested starting over, I thought we'd set boundaries, not return to how we were before the hands-on-ass drama. Dunrobin Castle was the one Lewis had mentioned earlier in the week. It was in a place called Golspie, on the North Coast, about thirty minutes north of Ardnoch. The kids had never been to it before despite its proximity.

"I don't want to intrude."

"Well, the kids have been pestering me all week to invite you. I didn't because of how things were between us, but not because I didn't want you there. Eilidh and Lewis enjoy having you around, and I just want my children happy."

Why, oh why did he have to be such a wonderful dad?

"But no pressure." He hurried to say. "If you need boundaries, we can do that."

And let him think I was so crazy about him, I couldn't be around him?

I still had some pride, for God's sake.

"No, it's fine." I shrugged, like it was no big deal. "I'll come hang out with you guys."

Regan Penhaligon, you are such a masochist.

18

REGAN

I'd returned to the annex to shower and dress. When I went back into the main house, I found Thane in the best mood he'd been in since McClintock had approached him. I assumed the man hadn't been in touch again, but I made a note to find a private moment to ask. Other than a quick double glance at my legs when I walked in (I was wearing one of my preppy short dresses with thick tights, a pair of cute ankle boots, and an emerald-green, double-breasted pea coat I'd purchased online with my nice new salary), he'd treated me with nothing but friendly civility.

Eilidh and Lewis were happy I was joining them on their day out, but as always it took us twice as long to get them ready as we figured. By the time we climbed into Thane's SUV, it was already midmorning.

"What's so special about this castle?" I asked as we drove through the village. "It can't be as spectacular as Ardnoch." Not that I'd spent as much time there as I would've liked.

Thane smirked. "Ardnoch will always be special. Even if it was drafty and miserable to live in when we were children."

Surprised, I said, "It was?"

221

"Oh, aye. It was nothing like how you see it now. Lachlan invested a lot into the castle and estate to make it the grand, luxurious building it's become. But when we were children, it was baltic—freezing," he clarified. "Some fireplaces were unusable because nests and other critters blocked the chimneys. We'd congregate around the one in the reception area with blankets and books and games." He grinned like the memories weren't so bad. "We were what you call land rich but cash poor."

"I can't even imagine that."

"Lachlan knew changes had to be made after our father died. Dad had raised us to be very aware of our responsibilities as Adairs. We were custodians of a rich history. And Lachlan felt that responsibility deeply, but he knew if he didn't do something, we'd lose everything. We owned land all over the Highlands and even in the Lowlands, some of it particularly lucrative because of its resources. Lachlan sold it all, divided the earnings between us, and then he invested his Hollywood earnings into the estate. Created the club. A percentage of its earnings goes toward the rest of our inheritance."

Impressed by my sister's fiancé, I said, "He's very savvy. I mean, the club's reputation precedes itself."

Thane grinned. "My brother is a born showman. And the club is just one big show."

"So if Ardnoch is better than Dunrobin, why are we going?" Lewis asked.

Thane glanced at him over his shoulder before returning his eyes to the road. "In just a few minutes, you'll see why."

Intrigued, we waited, and then as we turned a bend on the coastal road that followed the cliff's edge, Thane pointed out the window. "There, do you see it? Eilidh-Bug, do you see it?"

I sucked in a breath. In the distance, stretching up above

the trees, perched near the cliff's edge, was a castle straight out of a storybook. It was white with conical spires.

"Oh, Daddy!" Eilidh gasped as she caught sight of it.

I turned to look at her in the back seat, grinning at how big her eyes had gotten. "Isn't it beautiful?"

She nodded, amazed. "It's the *Beauty and the Beast* castle!"

"I've seen it before," Lewis piped up. "We've driven this way before, Dad."

"We have. But Eilidh was too young then to notice it. Do you like it, Eils?" her dad asked.

"Yes!" She gave me an excited "well duh" look that made me giggle.

I sat back in my seat and shot Thane a grin. "She likes it."

His pleased smile made my heart flip in my chest.

"It's the seat of the earls and dukes of Sutherland," Thane told us. "And the Adairs have some family connections to them."

I raised an eyebrow. "Seriously? Are you guys aristocracy?"

"Not quite. We're what you would call landed gentry. That means—"

"I know what it means."

He raised an eyebrow.

I shrugged and admitted unashamedly, "I read a lot of historical romance."

Thane shot me a quick look, saw I was serious, and then grinned that stupidly sexy smile of his. "Okay, then."

"So not aristocracy, but you have links to them?" I prodded. I found this fascinating. British royalty and aristocracy were like something out of a fairy tale.

"Yes. We have an ancestor who married the younger brother of the Duke of Sutherland."

"Are we there yet, Daddy?" Eilidh asked impatiently.

"Nearly, sweetheart. Nearly."

As Thane turned off the road, the castle appeared before us, imposing and beautiful. There were cars parked on the wide drive before it. Upon closer inspection, I saw the castle wasn't white but more of a sandstone. Still, it was freaking beautiful. "It's amazing," I whispered.

"It's inspired by a French chateau," Thane said, "which is why, Eilidh, you think it looks like something out of *Beauty and the Beast*. The castle gardens were inspired by the gardens at the Palace of Versailles. It was a fort back in the day, but in the Victorian era, the earl hired the famous architect Sir Charles Barry." He looked at me. "He designed and rebuilt the Houses of Parliament after they caught fire."

I raised an eyebrow. "Impressive." I could see why Thane, the architect, loved this place so much.

"Very. He turned Dunrobin into what it is now, and he also designed the gardens."

"Ree-Ree …" Eilidh got our attention with her worried tone. She stared at us from the back seat with that deep frown furrowing her brow.

"What is it, sweetie?"

"I'm not dressed right!"

Confused, I studied her for a second in her adorable red winter coat and matching hat. Underneath she wore a navy dress and navy ankle boots. The kid couldn't be any cuter. "You look beautiful."

"But I'm not dressed like a princess." Her eyes flew toward the castle. "I should have put on my unicorny dress."

Thane and I looked at each other, both of us clearly trying not to laugh at how cute she was. Then suddenly I realized how close our faces were. As if Thane realized it, too, a strange, hot tension sparked between us, and we jerked back in our seats.

"You're perfect, sweetie," I said, scrambling to unbuckle

my belt and get away from my boss. "Come on, I'll help you out."

Once Thane had paid for our entrance, we walked into the castle, Thane's hand on Lewis's shoulder as he talked to him about the castle's history. Despite his age, Lewis hung on to his father's every word. Eilidh, while old enough to appreciate the castle's beauty, just as Thane knew she would, was too young to take much of anything else in.

So while her dad lingered with her brother over every little thing in the rooms that were open to the public, I took photos of everyone with my camera phone and only stopped Eilidh at the parts I thought she'd like. Like the room with the old-fashioned ceremonial clothing. She seemed right at home in the opulent drawing room and wanted to touch anything shiny. Thankfully, Eils, despite her big personality, listened when she was told not to do something.

Okay, so she listened after the third time I told her with a sharpened tone not to touch. And that was only after she shot me a dark look that made me want to laugh. But I didn't. Because if she knew how funny I found her antics, she'd never again see me as an authority figure.

We were standing in the fanciest dining room I'd ever seen, and it was like I'd stepped into one of the period dramas I loved so much. A hot breath suddenly whispered across my ear, and a rumbly, masculine voice said quietly, "I'll take Eils if you want to have a proper look around now."

Goose bumps prickled my neck, and I couldn't look at Thane as I nodded. "Sure, that would be great."

"I can take you around," Lewis offered.

"Sounds good."

"Come on, Eilidh-Bug." Thane grasped her hand. "Do you like the castle?"

"Can we live here?" I heard her ask as I followed Lewis out of the room.

For the next half hour, Lewis led me back into rooms I'd hurried through with Eilidh, and I discovered not only had he been listening to his dad but he had retained nearly everything Thane had told him. Smart as a whip.

Once we were done, we headed downstairs and found Thane waiting with Eilidh. "Did you enjoy it?" He grinned down at me.

Squeezing Lewis into my side, I replied, "With the best guide in the world showing me around? Of course."

Lewis blushed a little but grinned when his dad smiled proudly at him. "Right. Time to see the gardens. The falconry display is on in twenty minutes."

"What's fall-rony?" Eilidh asked as we wandered the grounds.

While Thane tried to explain to his five-year-old daughter about the ancient art of using birds of prey to hunt, I peered over the edge of the top tier of the back of the grounds, amazed. Thane had not been kidding. The castle was perched above the lower gardens with many steps down to get to them. Despite being tiny in comparison, the landscape had the same beautiful order and formal grandeur of Versailles. Beyond that was the sea, gleaming like a tranquil mirror.

Though it was a cold November day, only a very slight sea breeze blew past, the sun cutting through the iciness to create perfect, crisp salty air. My favorite kind of day. Thane lost Eilidh's interest five minutes into the garden walk, and she took off with Lewis to run around instead. I captured photos of them with my phone, and Thane approached me while I snapped a picture of them staring up at a fountain. They did so in the same manner, and with their dark curls, there was no mistaking they were siblings. Thane leaned into me to see the picture, and I caught a whiff of his fresh, citrusy scent.

"Can you send that to me?" he asked.

"Sure." I met his gaze, swallowing hard at his nearness. "I'll send them all to you."

Our eyes held for a moment too long.

"Ree-Ree!" Eilidh shouted, breaking the tension.

Ignoring the butterflies in my belly and the worries in the back of my mind, I hurried to Eilidh just in time to talk her out of climbing into the fountain.

By the time we arrived for the falconry display, Eilidh was mulish, bored, and hungry. She was done with the fairy-tale castle. "Just a while longer," I assured her, lifting her into my arms.

It was clear Thane really wanted to see the falcons, so I handled her while he and Lewis moved closer in the small crowd that had gathered around the falconer and his Peregrine.

"I don't like the bird." Eilidh held on tight to me.

"It won't hurt you, sweetie," I promised but took a few steps back. "Better?"

"No, I'm hungry," she growled in her monster voice. Not so cute when she was on the verge of a tantrum.

"Eilidh, we won't be long."

"I want to go now!" Her voice got louder, her scowl deeper.

I gave her a stern look as she tried to slide out of my arms. "Eilidh Adair, today is your dad's day. This is for his birthday. And your dad doesn't ask a lot from you, so you're going to behave and let him enjoy his day."

She pouted, her eyes brightening with tears, but to my relief, she clamped her lips closed and snuggled her head against my chest.

"Good girl," I whispered, turning to look toward the show.

Instead, I caught Thane staring at me. His eyes smiled and he mouthed, "Thank you."

I smiled back, wishing my heart didn't race at a mere tender look from him.

Thankfully, he turned back to the display. It was pretty awesome, but Eilidh was getting heavier and more restless in my arms by the second. I was grateful when it ended.

"That was really cool, Dad," Lewis said as they followed us up toward the castle.

"Glad you enjoyed it ... do you fancy stopping in at the tearoom for something to eat?"

"YES!" Eilidh yelled.

I winced. "Eilidh, my ears."

"Sorry!" she said, not sorry, and then slipped out of my arms like an eel before I could stop her. She made to rush precariously down the stairs to be with her father, and my heart leapt into my throat. Thane, however, quickly dove forward and grabbed her up into his arms. Happy to be there, as well as delighted food was on the agenda, she let him carry her with no complaints up the steps.

A little out of breath when I reached the top, I bugged my eyes out at Lewis who grinned at me. "I think I need to start running with my sister."

"Nah, you're just old," he teased.

I guffawed, horrified, and glowered at Thane as he laughed. "If I'm old, what are you? Ancient?"

That just made him laugh harder.

Sexy bastard.

Trying to get Eilidh to sit down in the tearoom was a nightmare. There was a glass cabinet filled with cake, and she just wanted to stare at it. Not that I didn't understand the fascination. Eventually, after promising she'd get a piece of whatever cake she liked, we got her to sit down at a small table. And by small, I mean, my knees kept knocking against Thane's.

The proximity was driving me nuts.

I tried to ignore it as we sat and talked with the kids about the castle and then about school. While the rest of us were eating scones with our tea, Eilidh had, of course, decided on a piece of messy chocolate cake. "You'll spoil your lunch." I tried to tell her.

"It's Daddy's birthday. There should be cake," she argued.

"Fine, then you can share a piece with your dad."

Thane's lips had twitched at having been given no choice in the matter, but we both knew Eilidh would be sick if she ate the entire thing. As it was, she got most of it on her face. Trying to avoid cake crumbling onto her new red coat, I pulled baby wipes from my purse and swiped at her face as she continued talking about the argument she'd had with a boy in her class over how Marvel films weren't for girls.

"But I said, I watch all the Malver films with Lewis—"

"Turn your face to me, sweetie," I murmured, tilting her cheek.

She did as I asked but kept talking. "—and how can it not be for girls when there's one with a girl called Captain Malver!"

"It's true," Lewis agreed, for once engaged in one of Eilidh's many retellings of her school-day "discussions."

As I got the last of the chocolate off her face and tenderly brushed a stray curl behind her tiny ear, I felt heat on my cheek. Glancing at Thane, I found him watching me with an intensity that made my breath catch.

"Ree-Ree, I need a wee-wee!" Eilidh announced loudly, breaking our staring match.

Thane pressed his lips together to stop his laughter at the answering titters around the tearoom, but his gorgeous eyes glittered with amusement.

Lewis giggled around a bite of scone, and I cut Eilidh a half-amused, half-stern look.

She grinned with her teeth comically pressed together.

"Eilidh Adair, we do not call it wee-wee, especially since it rhymes with my name."

"But that's why I *should* call it wee-wee."

I narrowed my eyes, and she mirrored my expression. This kid! "If you need to use the restroom, what do you say?"

She opened her mouth, and I just knew she was going to repeat the Ree-Ree/wee-wee thing.

"Not that," I cut her off and heard her father choke on his amusement. Shooting him a quelling look only made his shoulders shake harder.

Eilidh sighed like a world-weary eighty-year-old. "Fine. Ree-Ree, I need to use the restroom even though I don't need to rest, I need to wee-wee."

Thane coughed into his fist to cover up his laughter.

I couldn't look at him. "Okay." I stood, dropping my napkin on the table. "You're too smart for your own good, kid."

"I know." She hopped up from the table and took my hand.

"We call it a restroom because it's a polite word for it," I told her as we made our way through the tearoom, following the sign for the ladies' toilet off the entrance.

"But I like the word *wee-wee*."

"You do now. However, believe me, when you're my age, calling it that is not cute."

She continued to argue about this the entire time we were in the bathroom. I waited outside her stall door, interrupting her thoughts on how funny the word *wee-wee* was to ask how she was doing. She'd answer and then continue her monologue. If I never heard the word *wee-wee* again, I wouldn't be sorry.

Though she *was* hilarious.

"Do you think Daddy will have ate the rest of my cake?" Eils asked, her brow furrowed as we washed our hands and stepped out of the restroom.

"Eaten, sweetie," I corrected. I was so busy looking down at her, I missed the person crossing our path and collided with him. My head flew up as the hand not holding Eilidh's hit a hard chest. "Oh my God, I'm so sorry."

Green eyes stared into mine, and familiarity hit me. "Regan, right?"

"Jared, hey." I stepped back a little, tightening my grip on Eilidh's hand.

Noting her, the yummy young farmer looked down and asked, "And who's this?"

Turning uncharacteristically shy, Eilidh pressed into my side and buried her face in my coat. Huh. "Uh … this is Eilidh. Eilidh, this is Jared, Farmer McCulloch's grandson."

She nodded and lowered her eyes to the floor.

Surprised, I looked up at Jared.

He just grinned. "Shy one?"

Not usually. "Uh … what are you doing here?"

"Oh, just dropping off some produce for the kitchens. You showing the kids the castle?"

"Yeah. And having cake." I ruffled Eilidh's hair lightly. She still didn't look up.

Jared searched my face for a second. "I was hoping we'd bump into each other again."

I smiled noncommittally.

"I have to get back. I have other deliveries to make, but … can I have your number?"

Oh my God. I had not been expecting that. No messing around with him, huh?

Uh …

He gave me a sexy half smile. "I just want to take you out for a drink. No pressure."

I thought of Thane waiting for me back in the tearoom.

About the tension still crackling between us.

Or was it all in my head? Thane had made it clear where we stood.

But once he apologizes, you move on. Thane goes back to just being your boss, and you take care of those kids. I remembered my sister's advice.

Move on.

Right.

"Sure." I grinned, nodding, even though my stomach was in knots.

Jared pulled out his cell, and I rattled off my number. He tucked the phone back into his work pants, stared at me like he had a lot more than a friendly drink in mind, and backed away. "I'll call you."

"Great." I gave him a little wave and then led a strangely quiet Eilidh back to the tearoom.

"All good?" Thane grinned at us, and I felt a stupid prickle of guilt.

"Yeah."

"Ready to go, then?" He stood. "I've already paid."

I frowned. "I was going to pay for your birthday."

He gave me a look as if to say "nonsense."

Letting it go, we gathered our things and walked back to the car. I should have known by how quiet Eilidh was that she was stewing over something. But I was so distracted by what had just happened, I wasn't paying enough attention. It wasn't until we were all in the car and Thane was about to turn on the engine that Eilidh asked loudly and somewhat sullenly, "Why is that pretty man going to call you, Ree-Ree?"

I squeezed my eyes closed for a second as silence descended over the car.

Ignoring Thane's stare, I looked over my shoulder at Eilidh, who looked confused and upset. She clearly didn't understand what had passed between me and Jared, but she knew she didn't like it. Shit.

"What's Eils talking about?" Thane asked quietly.

I flicked him a look. "We bumped into Jared McCulloch in the hall. I gave him my number." I met Eilidh's gaze. "It's what friends do, sweetie. We exchanged numbers so we can hang out."

"Like you and me hang out?"

"Sure!" I knew my voice was too high with my lie.

She frowned. "But … I'm still your *best* friend. He can't be your best friend."

For some stupid reason, tears pricked my eyes. "My bestest buds in the entire world—you and Lewis. Promise. No one is replacing your spot as my besties."

Eilidh side-eyed her brother. "I'm your *bestest* best friend. Lew is your best friend." She looked back at me now that she'd asserted herself at the top of my priority list. "Daddy is your other best friend. So that man can only be a *friend* friend. Okay?"

Lewis scowled ferociously out the window.

Oh, boy.

I really shouldn't let Eilidh think she had authority over my friendships, but that knot in my stomach tightened at her mention of Thane. The children were starting to see us as a unit. And if the last few minutes were anything to go by, they were territorial about that unit.

Which meant they were too young to understand the imaginary lines drawn in the sand between "nanny" and "family." It didn't help if the two adults kept blurring those lines.

I shouldn't have come today.

That is it, I decided as Thane started the car. *No more*

spending weekend day trips with them. It wasn't fair to the children in the end.

Eilidh had a short attention span and started talking about how hungry she was again. Considering it was past lunchtime and they'd only had a scone and cake, Thane promised we'd stop in at Morag's to see if she had any sandwiches left.

Morag, the bubbly, pink-haired owner, was delighted to see the Adair kids. She brought them behind her chilled counter to help her make their sandwiches. Thane and I stood in a weirdly tense silence, watching.

Then I asked just loud enough for him to hear me, "Have you heard any more from that McClintock guy?"

"No," Thane replied just as quietly. "I think my message got through."

Yeah, I wouldn't want to mess with Thane Adair while he was in scary, protective Dad mode. "Good."

A few seconds passed. "Jared McCulloch. Really?"

At his sneering tone, I stiffened. "What does that mean?"

"It means"—he turned to me, his eyes glinting with hard irritation—"I already warned you he's slept with every woman from here to Inverness."

"I'm not looking for marriage, Thane. I just gave the guy my number."

A growling sound rumbled from the back of his throat. "You're better than that."

My spine straightened. "Better than what?"

"Casual sex with a most likely disease-ridden farmer."

I gaped at him. He sounded like a pretentious, elitist prick. "You don't think he's good enough?"

"No, he's not," he hissed, leaning too close. "And not because he's a farmer but because he's a silly wee fuck boy." His eyes darkened to smoke. "Definitely not the *man* you said you wanted."

Was he jealous?

After the angst we'd just been through and promised to get over, *he* was dragging us back into it. Robyn was right. I so wanted to junk-punch him. Shaking my head in disbelief, I walked away before I said something I'd regret. "I'll wait in the car."

~

THANE

Watching Eilidh fall asleep in her bed, Thane stood and finally allowed himself to think about what the hell he was doing. As he walked quietly from her room toward Lewis's, he berated himself for how the afternoon had turned out.

After his discussion with Regan this morning, *he* was the one who had thrown out the mixed signals again. But every time he thought he had a handle on his attraction, some little thing pushed him over the edge. The way she was with Eilidh and Lewis, always taking care of them, consciously and subconsciously, proving they were constantly on her mind.

What father wouldn't appreciate that in a woman?

Her thoughtfulness at the falconry display, realizing he was looking forward to sharing that with Lewis. And teaching Eilidh to be considerate, teaching her that some things would not be about her so that she realized as she got older, if she loved her family, she'd be content with putting them first when needed.

And Regan's sense of humor and how Eilidh had only gotten wittier since Regan had come along. Learning from her in ways Thane didn't mind at all.

The way Lewis was opening up from that serious, shy boy

he'd been before her arrival. How much happier he seemed.

Then there were the things he noticed as a man.

The way he and Regan looked at each other and seemed to know exactly what the other was thinking.

The way her body was aware of him, how her back slightly arched whenever he got too close, causing her breasts to push up, her arse to push out. She didn't even realize she was doing it, the movement was so subtle. But Thane was aware. Aware of the way her eyes dropped to his mouth as often as his lowered to hers.

He wanted her.

Even knowing how wrong it was, how complicated, how it would be construed by everyone else as something sordid and indecent, Thane wanted Regan Penhaligon, and he didn't know how to make it stop without pushing her out of their lives completely.

And he'd been seething with jealousy ever since Eilidh let it out of the bag that Regan had given her number to Jared McCulloch.

Peeking into Lewis's room, he was surprised to see his son's light out. Lew was asleep. Usually, he waited for Thane to come and say good night.

That meant returning downstairs already.

To where Regan had insisted on cleaning up the kitchen after a night of showing him and the kids how to make homemade pizza to end their day of "celebrations." It was so good, and the kids loved it so much, Thane was considering getting an outside pizza oven.

Of course, it would have been an even better night if Regan wasn't so pissed off she couldn't even talk to him. He knew Lewis had noticed because he'd grown quieter as the night wore on.

Damn it.

Reaching in to close his son's door, Lewis's voice stopped

him.

"Dad."

"Hey, bud, thought you were sleeping." He crept into the room.

In the light spill from the hallway, Thane watched his son turn to look at him—and he was glowering.

Uh-oh.

"What is it, Lew?"

"Ree-Ree seems mad at you."

Thane tensed. "We're fine, buddy."

"You were mad at her, and now she's mad at you."

Christ, his seven-year-old was too perceptive. "No, we're good, Lew."

His son glared harder. "She's going to go away. And it's your fault." His voice broke as he buried his head in his pillow.

Oh, fucking hell. Rounding the bed, Thane sat down and placed a hand on Lewis's shoulder. His son pushed his face deeper into the pillow.

"Lew, Regan and I are friends. She's not going away. Not just yet. But you know, wee man, that she's your nanny. She's not part of the family," he reminded him gently, even as each word caused an ache in his chest. "You have to be prepared for that."

Lewis took a shuddering breath and turned to look at him. Thane's heart broke at the sadness in his son's eyes. "Why do people always have to leave?"

No, Thane was wrong. Now his heart fucking broke. He'd never wanted his children to have the childhood he had. To lose their mother.

Determined that when Fran died, he wouldn't crumble like his own father had, he'd poured every ounce of his soul into fatherhood. Thane had thought he was doing not too bad a job, but the ordeal with Lucy, perhaps his handling of it, seemed to remind Lewis of loss. Not for him—Lew had never really taken to Lucy (Thane should have seen that as a warning sign)—but for his wee sister who'd thought the actress hung the moon and the sun. Thane was only grateful that his daughter was resilient and had been quick to transfer her affection to Regan.

"I don't want you to think that," Thane whispered, lying down beside Lewis to tuck him into his arms. He burrowed into his dad, and Thane held him tighter. "Not everyone leaves, Lew. I'm not going anywhere. Neither is Uncle Lachlan or Aunt Arrochar, or Aunt Robyn and Uncle Mac." He didn't mention Brodan or Arran. They'd grown too unpredictable for him to make any promises on their behalf. The reminder agitated him.

"What about Ree-Ree? She's Aunt Robyn's sister. Why can't she stay?"

Thane exhaled slowly, feeling the loss of her already. "Because she's young, Lew. She's got her whole life ahead of her. She needs to go off and experience the world a bit before she settles down. Not to mention, her parents live in America. Her life is back there."

And there it was.

The truth.

No matter her attraction to him, Thane knew that no twenty-five-year-old would want to settle down in a remote Scottish village with a man thirteen years her senior and play mum to his two children. Christ, Fran hadn't wanted it, and she'd *chosen* it.

"I want her to stay," Lewis whispered sadly.

"I know, buddy. But try not to think about her leaving. It's not for a while yet. And she's here now. Just enjoy having her with us for now, okay?"

Lewis nodded, but Thane knew he didn't understand. How could he? All he knew was that a woman he cared about because she so obviously cared about him was temporary. And that made little sense to a boy who was raised on the belief that his mother loved him and hadn't wanted to leave him and if it had been up to her, she never would have.

Knowing his son was going to take Regan's leaving as proof she didn't love him, Thane squeezed his eyes closed, tightened his hold on Lewis, and stayed with him until he fell asleep.

However, the longer he lay there, the more he stewed. Lewis wouldn't have fallen asleep with tears in his eyes if Regan had treated Thane with civility and professionalism tonight. Yes, he'd been a prick at Morag's, and he'd admit it, but she couldn't act like that around the kids. They were too perceptive, and she should know that by now.

Unfortunately for her, when he came downstairs, she was still there.

Heat licked through him at the sight of her in her prim little dress with its not-so-prim fucking hemline. As she bent over to load the last of the dishes into the dishwasher, he caught a flash of her arse. Sadly, the thick tights she wore covered it.

She stood and shut the washer, not looking at him as she wiped down the sink. "I had a hard time getting the flour out of the couch. I don't know how it got over there. But I got it. I cleaned everything up." Regan threw down a dish towel and grabbed her purse off the stool at the island. "I'll see you Monday." Finally, she looked at him as he refused to move from her path.

Her eyes widened at whatever she read in his expression. "Are the kids okay? You were up there awhile."

Seething, he licked his lips and took his time so he didn't lash out at her. "You cannot give me the cold shoulder in front of the children."

Regan narrowed her pretty eyes. "I didn't."

239

"You did. Lewis picked up on it."

Guilt flickered across her features. "Is he okay?"

"No." Thane took a step toward her and another as she retreated. "He's worried about you leaving."

"I'm not going anywhere."

"Yet. He needs to be prepared that you'll eventually leave. But until then," he said, bowing his head toward her as the island forced her to stop, "I expect a civil tongue." His gaze dipped to her mouth, and his hands clenched at his sides. "In a civil mouth … from now on. At least in front of them."

She jutted her chin stubbornly. "Does that mean you're going to stop acting like a crazy person?"

"Excuse me?" he bit out.

"You … did we or did we not have a discussion this morning that cleared the air, only for you to act like a jealous ass over Jared McCulloch?"

"Just like you were jealous over the idea of me sleeping with Keelie."

She grimaced. "And round we go again. Just admit that Keelie was a ploy. You were never going to sleep with her. You're too much of a gentleman."

The damn woman had a way of pushing him to the boiling point with very little effort. And for some reason, it pricked his damn male pride that Regan saw him as some buttoned-up, controlled, gentlemanly figure. If only she knew.

He leaned into her, their mouths almost touching, and she inhaled sharply. "How do you know I didn't sleep with her? A man has needs."

Hurt flickered in her eyes, but she buried it beneath fire. That he could deal with. She pushed against his chest to move him, but he pressed deeper into her personal space.

"Did you sleep with her?" she demanded.

"No," he immediately admitted.

Satisfaction lit her expression, and then something more dangerous. "No, because sleeping with any woman would just be an attempt to screw away your problem."

"And what problem is that?" he asked gruffly, heat pooling in his groin.

"That you can't stop thinking about me," Regan whispered, lowering her hand from his chest but only so she could move her body into his. He swallowed hard at the feel of her soft curves. Her breathing hitched. "We can go around and around in circles for days, weeks … but it won't chase this away, Thane. You want me. It isn't convenient. It's complicated … but it's unavoidable."

"You're my children's twenty-five-year-old nanny," he argued, even though the fight had left him.

"You keep saying that like I'm eighteen." She reached up to cup his cheek, her fingernails scraping along his beard. "I'm not a child, Thane. I'm a woman. For Christ's sake, there's ten years between Robyn and Lachlan, and no one bats an eyelash."

"It's different. She's older," he said, even as his head bent toward hers. "This is madness."

"Then let's just be mad," she whispered back before pulling his head that last inch down to her mouth.

She kissed him like he was water and she had been thirsty for weeks. Ravenous, deep, wild kisses that ignited his blood. Her hands were just as hungry, searching beneath his sweater. His stomach contracted as her cool fingers caressed his bare skin, and he groaned, losing all control.

He took over the kiss as he wrapped a hand tight around her nape and devoured her, while his other slid down her slender back and under her dress to cup her tight arse. He kissed her harder, reveling in the way she took as good as he gave, her thumbs rubbing his nipples.

Pleasure pain radiated from where his dick strained

against his jeans zipper. Irritated by the tights in his way, he pushed down into them so he could cup one of her supple, round cheeks in his hand. He bent his knees ever so slightly as he pulled her into his erection, wanting inside her so badly he was about to come like a callow youth.

"Fuck." He broke the kiss and released her.

Her hands were still under his top as she stared up at him, flushed, aroused. Confused.

Her fingers moved over his chest and just that simple touch sent a lightning bolt through his groin.

Thane squeezed his eyes closed as he reluctantly reached under his sweater to remove her hands.

"Thane?" Regan whispered.

He wanted to hear her scream his name as she came, not whisper it in confusion and worry.

She was right. They could go around and around, denying what they wanted and having multiple jealous fights over the course of the next few months. Or ... he could have of her what he could before she left him.

His eyes flew open, anticipation thrumming through his blood as he made up his mind.

Regan stared unblinkingly at him, waiting for his next move.

"Just sex," he said gruffly. "No promises, and no one can know."

Surprise slackened her features. She hesitated so long, he could barely hear anything over the blood rushing in his ears. Then to his relief, Regan nodded slowly. "Okay."

Satisfaction slammed through him, and it took every ounce of willpower within him to not pick her up and throw her down on his sofa to have his way with her. Instead, he thought of her misconceptions about him as a gentleman. Best to disprove her of that now. "Go wait for me in the annex," he demanded. Her eyes widened slightly. "Clothes off. Keep your underwear on because I want to take it off. And lights on so I can see you. When I get there, I expect you on the bed with your legs spread."

Her chest heaved with surprise; her nostrils flared with arousal.

He leaned down to brush his mouth over hers. "I need to make sure the house is secure." His hand slipped under her dress, and he touched the damp heat between her legs, making her bow into him with a moan. He licked at her lips, and she tried to chase him with her mouth, but he retreated, taunting her. Then he rubbed her through her tights and underwear, and she gasped. "Don't touch yourself until I get there. Your orgasms are mine now."

Before he lost his mind and just took her against the island, he strode quietly upstairs to check on the kids once more.

Doubts niggled at the back of his mind.

What people would think if they knew the gossip was now reality …

How they desperately needed to keep this from the kids …

What a selfish bastard he was letting his desire dictate his actions.

But Thane ignored the doubts … especially the one that whispered how, if it was just about physical attraction, he'd never jeopardize his reputation, his honor. If it was just about screwing some hot young thing, he could do that anytime.

It was about her.

Regan.

About burying everything inside her and watching her shatter around him with the immensity of it.

And doing it for as long as he had her.

No matter what it cost.

19

REGAN

I laid there, panting, so excited I trembled with it. The ache between my legs was hot and almost painful. Months of longing had culminated to this point, and all I could think about was having Thane inside me.

I was almost mad with the need of him.

His orders had been a shock, but to my surprise, one my body reacted to. My instinct was to buck against a man's command, and if it had been anyone but Thane, I would have. But as it turned out, *his* bossiness made me exceptionally hot.

Lying in my underwear, I felt a little shy, a little weird at first, but as soon as Thane stepped into the annex, everything disappeared but my need for him. He was right. This thing between us was almost a madness.

Nostrils flaring as his eyes devoured me on my bed, Thane walked toward me slowly, his arousal obvious through the pajama bottoms he'd changed into.

"Look at you," he said gruffly, running a hand down his beard. His expression was a little dazed, as if he wasn't sure I was real.

"I want to look at you," I replied softly.

In answer, Thane tugged off his T-shirt and dropped it on the floor by the bed. Then his bottoms followed, and I sucked in a breath. I'd forgotten how much I liked his body. All that natural power, not overly muscled, but strong and so goddamn masculine my body reacted everywhere. His fiery gaze, the way his features had hardened with lust, made me tingle hotly between my legs. My breasts were heavy, my nipples tight.

Jutting proudly between his muscled thighs was an impressive, pulsing erection.

All for me.

Thane produced a condom as if out of nowhere, opened it with his teeth, and rolled it on. But I'd barely had time to ogle him when he crawled over me, bracing himself above me in the bed, falling between my already open thighs.

He stared into my eyes, studying me intently, and I marveled at how weird this didn't feel. Shouldn't it feel weird, lying in my lingerie beneath my naked boss?

The first time with someone new was always strange. Vulnerable was probably a better word. I'd felt vulnerable, except for my drunken one-night stand with Austin, which I barely remembered. This ... this with Thane, though, I'd remember forever. I wasn't vulnerable at all. I was relieved. That I'd found him.

This beautiful, kind, funny, sexy, sometimes irritating, emotionally suppressed Scotsman whose love for his children only made me adore him more.

I loved him, I admitted to myself as he stroked my cheek with his thumb.

And if all he wanted from me was this, then I'd take it. I'd take these memories we were about to make, and they'd just have to last me a lifetime.

Emotion choked me, and I could feel the tickle of

oncoming tears, so I reached up and kissed him hard before I fell apart in his arms. Thane groaned and pressed me back down onto the mattress to take control of the kiss, and I happily allowed it. I loved the taste of him on my tongue, loved the way his beard was soft, not scratchy, and the feel on my skin was sexual and arousing. I hoped I'd get to feel it between my thighs.

As if Thane heard the thought, his lips broke away from my mouth to kiss a path down my body. When he reached the rise of my breasts and discovered I'd put on a bra that clipped open in the front, he looked up at me with amusement glittering in those beautiful, desire-filled eyes.

I bit my lip to stop a stupid, goofy grin, and suddenly Thane was over me again, crushing my mouth beneath his as he stole hungry, deep kisses. I was a little dizzy and breathless as he released my mouth to return to my bra. He removed it with quick efficiency, and I pulled the straps down my arms. The inexpensive but sexy, lacy number flew across the room. Then his hot mouth covered my right nipple and he sucked.

My back bowed as I cried out at the sharp pleasure that echoed between my thighs. Lost in his loving, I could only writhe beneath him as he moved between each breast, sucking, laving, until I was swollen and aching. And then his lips followed that invisible path down my stomach, while his big hands stayed at my breasts, caressing and squeezing until I thought I'd go mad with the need to release.

Finally, Thane reached the apex of my thighs, and his hands left my breasts, but only to push my legs open wider. He looked up at me, his features taut with hunger. And as he stared into my eyes, his thumbs met in the middle over the lace of my underwear. I gasped as he pressed down.

My hips arched off the bed into his touch, but he only rubbed his thumbs over me once more before he stopped. I lifted my head to complain, but the feral look on Thane's face as he gazed up my body halted me. No man had ever looked at me like that. Like he'd lose his mind if he didn't have me. I experienced a squeeze deep in my lower belly, and my stomach shook with it.

Thane's eyes dropped, catching the movement. Something snapped inside him. His fingers brushed my lower belly, curling into my underwear. He wrenched them down my legs, and I whimpered with excitement.

I heard Thane's grunt of satisfaction seconds before the tickle of his beard on my inner thighs and the touch of his tongue at my apex.

Need slammed through me, and my hips pushed into his mouth. Thane gripped them, pressing them back to the mattress and then he devastated me in the best way possible.

Oh my God, so this is what it feels like—I arched into him—*when a man knows what he's doing.*

He studied my body, my reactions, and just when I was about to reach blinding satisfaction, he'd pull back a little, torturing me. "Thane," I pleaded, reaching for him. My fingers slid through his thick hair and tightened. Thane grunted at the slight pull, and then his tongue returned. I shuddered, but it still wasn't enough. Again, the damn mind reader sensed it, and two thick fingers pushed gently into me.

That was it.

It was all I needed.

I cried out his name as I came, wonder flooding through me as the powerful release swept over my body.

Shaking my head on the pillow, I couldn't believe it.

"Never," I whispered, touching a hand to my forehead. "Never, ever," had it been so good.

Suddenly I felt the heat of Thane's body, the hair on his legs tickling mine, his stomach brushing across my belly as he moved upward. His harsh need made the pulsing inside me quicken again as he wrapped his hands around my wrists to pin my arms above my head. When I tried to move them, I couldn't. He held me captive.

I gasped, my breasts tightening, tension coiling deep in my belly. I hadn't expected to enjoy the sensation of being held down.

But with Thane ... everything was different.

His lips brushed mine, softly, sweetly, surprising me considering how hungry he seemed, and then he was there, throbbing hot between my thighs. Leaning all of his weight on my wrists to hold me down, he pushed into me.

I gasped his name in pleasured pain at the burn of him stretching me.

Our eyes held, my breath scattered as he moved inside me, the feel of him so perfect it electrified my lower spine.

And he began to thrust.

Hard.

His expression turned even darker with want and after only a few drives inside me, he released his hold on my wrists, slipped out, and got on his knees. Thane reached for the back of my thighs, gripping them in his hold so my hips and ass came up off the bed.

And then he powered into me.

My hoarse shout echoed around the annex, and Thane grunted in satisfaction as he fucked me.

There was no other word for it.

And it was glorious.

I didn't know what to do with my hands. I wanted to touch him but I couldn't reach. I couldn't do anything. He was so strong, so determined, so ... primal.

Watching him, watching him watch me as he drove into me, was the sexiest thing I'd ever seen in my life. I gripped the sheets as he pounded into me, hitting this place inside no man had. And in that moment, I was nothing but hot skin and sex. I wasn't cognizant of anything but the intensity of his body inside mine and the coiling bliss building within.

I exploded.

After years of reading romance novels, I finally understood what that meant.

"Thane!" I cried, shuddering and shaking against his thrusts. The sensation was so sexy, so raw, I never wanted it to end. It was like it *would* never end.

"Regan, fuck!" Thane growled, and I watched him bare his teeth like an animal as his hips stilled against mine. He throbbed in me, bowing into the release in hard, jerking shudders.

As if he couldn't hold himself up any longer, Thane rested his cheek on my stomach and tried to catch his breath.

He still pulsed inside me.

Possessiveness and satisfaction mingled as I stroked his back, his skin damp from our exertions.

I wanted to tell him it was the best sex I'd ever had, but even that didn't sound perfect enough for what I'd just experienced.

After a while, he pressed a sweet kiss near my belly button. Thane lifted onto his hands to look down at me. His face was relaxed, sated, but I could see his busy brain working behind those soulful eyes. Before I could say a word, he kissed me. Not a chaste, sweet thank-you, but a deep, possessive kiss that promised we weren't done.

However, apparently we were. Thane retreated to watch my face as he eased out of me, something masculine and smug in his expression as I moaned.

He got out of the bed and stood in the bright lights of the room. As he strode unashamed of his nakedness to the bathroom, most likely to deal with the condom, I squirmed on the sheets, wanting him back inside me.

Jesus, I was addicted.

When he came back out, his attention returned to me. His eyes flickered over my body, and his jaw clenched.

He wanted me again too.

Thane walked around the bed and said, his voice gruff, "I have to get back to the kids."

God, of course. I touched my forehead, feeling stupid and irresponsible for forgetting Eilidh and Lewis. My desire for him made me a selfish, sex-mad woman.

I sat up as he dressed, pulling the sheet over me, that vulnerability I hadn't felt the entire time now sliding over my skin.

Was that it? Had Thane scratched his itch and now we were done?

My only answer was a non-answer. He bent over me, kissed me softly, almost chastely, then kissed the tip of my nose before hurrying away.

"Lights off," he commanded, and the annex turned dark seconds before he slipped back out into the night.

That was it?

Stupid tears pricked my eyes as I pulled my knees to my chest. I ached between my legs from where he'd been moments ago.

For me, it had been earth-shattering. Enlightening. A stupendous awakening.

Sex had been good for me before, but I hadn't known it could be like what I'd read about.

Mind-blowing.

But maybe it hadn't been for Thane. Maybe what he had in the past with Fran, a woman he'd *loved*, meant what he'd just had with me was the equivalent of a jerk in the shower.

I winced at the thought and shook my head. No, I was being silly.

Yet I despised Thane's ability to make me doubt myself, to

feel insecure. I'd never really overanalyzed if a guy I was with had enjoyed sex. The mere act of them coming suggested they had. But it wasn't just about Thane enjoying sex with me.

I wanted him to have experienced what I just experienced.

Something beyond an orgasm.

Love. The word whispered in my mind, and I swiped angrily at a tear. Determined not to let his abrupt departure twist up my head beyond anything but the need to return to his children, I pushed out of bed and found my way to the shower in the dark.

20

THANE

H is skin heating as his thoughts turned to last night,
Thane reached out and twisted the knob on the
shower to cold. "Fuck," he grunted as ice-cold water cascaded
over him. But he needed it. He groaned as the image of
Regan sprawled before him, taking him, her face flushed
with pleasure, refused to leave his mind. Thane leaned his
forehead against the cool tiles. He attempted to get a hold of
himself.

He had sex with his nanny last night.

With his twenty-five-year-old nanny.

With his twenty-five-year-old, soon-to-be sister-in-law
of his brother.

"And you knew that and did it anyway," Thane murmured
as he got out of the shower to dry off. And if he was being
honest with himself, he had every intention of doing it again
and again and again until she left or grew bored with him.
That didn't really say much for his self-respect, but as long as
he got to make love to Regan Penhaligon again, his self-
respect could go fuck itself.

Thane moved into the bedroom to dress. It was early. The

kids wouldn't be up for a few more hours as he let them sleep in on Sundays. The weekends were when Regan most often went next door to see Robyn or spent time with Eredine and Arro. Sometimes even with Will, Jock's fiancé. All this he knew, because whether she realized it, Thane listened to every word that came out of her mouth.

And he didn't want her to spend this Sunday with someone else. He wanted her in his house, even if he had to pretend like all she was to him was the kids' beloved nanny.

Aye, he remembered the night before and grew heavy with need all over again. If it wasn't so contaminated by his doubts and guilt, last night with Regan would have been one of the best goddamn nights of his life. He'd come so hard he thought his heart was going to explode.

As soon as the thought crossed his mind, his attention caught on the photo of him and Fran on his nightstand. A different guilt knotted his gut. He'd loved Fran. Adored her. Thought there was nobody like her … until she cheated on him. The sex had been great too. No complaints there.

Yet never, not even with the woman he'd forgiven and promised to spend the rest of his life with, had he ever experienced such an animalistic, desperate need to be inside someone as he had last night with Regan. Everything went out of his mind. Everything but her body, her reactions, the way she felt coming around him.

He stared at Fran smiling back, and his gut tightened even harder. "It's just sex," he promised her, as she had once promised him. "Doesn't mean anything."

Thane tensed as he remembered the sound of Fran's dry laughter. *Liar*, he swore he heard his dead wife purr in his ear.

REGAN

It was a beautiful day. Much too beautiful for November. Unseasonably warm. Eils and Lew loved it, tearing across the sand, chasing each other on Ardnoch Beach. We had the whole place to ourselves.

"Slow down!" I shouted, hurrying to catch up with them. They'd gotten fast. I couldn't seem to get within closing distance of them, the wet sand resistant to my attempts. Realizing they were growing farther away, panic set in. "Eilidh, Lewis, come back!"

"Daddy!" Eilidh screamed joyfully, and I followed her gaze to see Thane standing waist deep in the sea, beckoning her.

It was too deep.

"Thane!" I tried to catch up, to warn him. Why couldn't he see it was too deep?

"Eilidh!" Lewis shouted now as his sister rushed into the water.

Then Thane was there, lifting her up into his arms, and catching Lewis in his other. Relief flooded me. The waves crashed gently against his waist, but he didn't move, a powerful, solid, stalwart protector.

I loved him. I loved them all. So much.

Smiling as they waved, I continued to attempt to reach them, but they never seemed to grow any closer. "Come to me!" I yelled through frustrated tears.

A powerful arm banded around my waist, pulling me into a hard body. Austin's fake smile filled my view, and I struggled against his hold. "What are you doing here? Let go!"

"Shh," he hushed, hauling me into his arms and pressing my cheek to his chest. "It's okay, Regan, I've got you. This is where you belong. They're not for you. But I want you. I'll always want you."

I tried to yank out of his hold, but he kissed me and I couldn't pull away, couldn't breathe.

He let me go to say my name, over and over.

Then he kissed me again. Gentler this time.

His beard tickled.

Beard?

I felt another tickle on my cheek, and when he released me, it was Thane. Not Austin. I sagged with relief and then sighed into his kiss.

"Regan, wake up," *he murmured against my mouth.*

The tickling sensation grew more insistent.

"Regan, wake up, *mo leannan*."

There was a tickle across my lips again and then the shivery brush of Thane's mouth against mine. My eyes flew open, and I stared sleepily into his gorgeous blue-gray eyes.

"Finally, she wakes," he murmured.

He kissed me, this time parting my lips to touch his tongue to mine. Reality intruded, and I realized he'd woken me up and was kissing me before I'd brushed my teeth. Breaking the kiss, I covered his mouth with my hand as a barrier between us.

Scowling up at him, I grumbled, "I have morning breath."

"I could give a fuck." I think he said against my hand. He rolled his eyes as it came out garbled, curled my hand into his fist, and bent down to cover my mouth again.

I tried to resist, but it was futile. Moaning into the taste of him, coffee and toothpaste, I slid my hand up his back, pulling him down onto me as I opened my thighs to him.

"I didn't come in for that," he huffed as he broke the kiss, thrusting against me, his words incongruous to his actions. Desire darkened his expression, and he shook his head with a dry smirk. "I only meant to bring you coffee."

I turned my head on the pillow and saw the steaming mug on my small nightstand. "How thoughtful."

He braced his hands on either side of my head and then reached with one to brush my hair off my face. Last night it had taken me awhile to fall asleep, I was so filled with doubt and insecurities. However, as he looked down at me with tenderness, knowing the first thing he'd thought to do this morning was bring me coffee, check on me, I melted beneath his touch.

"I have to get back in case Eils and Lew wake up," he said, regret in his eyes.

"Well, thank you for the coffee," I whispered, unable to speak any louder. Knowing if one of us didn't break the intense staring match, he might end up naked on top of me again, I pushed myself to sitting, and Thane leaned back from his seat on my bed to give me space.

Not a lot. As I reached for my coffee and sipped, his hand came to rest possessively on my thigh. My nightdress had risen indecently high, but considering what we'd done last night, it didn't matter. Thane's fingers stroked toward the crease in my leg, and I sucked in a breath.

His eyes heated.

"I thought you needed to get back to the kids?"

"I do." Thane reached out and took my cup, grinning at my nonplussed expression as he placed it back on the nightstand.

"Hey, I wanted—oh!" I reached out instinctively to grab his shoulder as he suddenly slipped beneath my underwear to press his thumb over me.

Then he was kissing me. Rough and hungry as he played me. Fingers, thumb, circling, pushing, he gave me the dirtiest, wettest kiss of my life. My fingernails dug into his wide shoulders as I arched into him, panting against his kiss as the tension inside built, and built, and built—

I exploded, and he captured the sound of my cries in his mouth, his groan a delicious rumble down my throat as I throbbed around him.

Finally, he released me to pepper kisses along my cheek

and down my neck as he removed his hand from between my thighs. I clung to him, trying to catch my breath. "What was that?" I panted.

"That was my version of 'good morning,' *mo leannan*."

My eyes flew open. Was that an endearment? "What does *ma le-ow-nin* mean?"

He grinned at my attempts to pronounce it and kissed my nose. "I need to get back." He avoided answering me.

"Wait." I grabbed his arm to stop him. Sliding a hand along his jeans-covered thigh, I grinned. "What about you?"

He covered my hand as I reached for the good stuff and squeezed his eyes closed as he gently removed it. "We can't. Don't have time." That stormy gaze met mine. "Later. Tonight."

Anticipation thrilled in my belly. Last night wasn't just a one-off for him, then. "Absolutely." I edged closer to cup his cheek, to draw him back to my mouth. My kiss was gentle, tender, not meant to incite anything more when I knew he had to leave. It was a thank-you. "Last night was the best it's ever been for me," I confessed against his mouth.

His grip on my hip tightened, and he seemed to swallow hard before replying gruffly, "Good." He pressed a quick, hard kiss to my lips and shot off the bed, marching across the annex in the space of a second.

I blinked rapidly, feeling like I'd just been punched in the gut.

Good?

Good?

That was his reply.

Also known as, "I'm pleased for you, but it wasn't the best I've ever had."

Hurt was a burn in my chest as I drew my knees up.

"Why don't you come over today?" I was aware of him stopping at the door, staring back at me, but I couldn't quite look at him. "We're just having a lazy Sunday, but I know Eils and Lew would love for you to hang out with us again."

I had no plans.

I could absolutely hang out with them.

Speaking to his shoulder, I gave him a tight-lipped smile. "I have plans."

"Oh?"

Ignoring his question, I reached for the coffee as I stood. "Thanks for the coffee." I saluted it in his direction and rounded the bed to disappear into the bathroom, where I was pretty sure I was going to cry in the shower like a big baby.

Out of sight, I dumped the mug on the sink, not really seeing anything, only hearing his "good" in my head over and over as I brushed my teeth.

Not long later, as I reached to pull the hem of my nightdress up, I was halted by the brawny arm that encircled my waist. I squeaked in surprise as Thane pulled me back against his hard, now-familiar chest. His lips brushed my ear, and he said in that deep, delicious voice, "Best sex of my life."

I stiffened.

And then turned my head to meet his eyes.

There was something guarded in his.

"You don't need to say that." I shrugged, feeling horribly vulnerable.

"I'll never lie to you," he promised, his hold on me tightening. "Best fucking sex of my entire life. By a long shot."

And just like that, I melted.

His expression hardened, though. "But we agree it's just sex. You'll get in the shower, get dressed, and abandon your nonexistent plans to come spend the day with us. We'll go on as before, friendly in front of the kids, so Lewis knows everything's okay, but nothing more. And then at night"—he hardened against my behind—"I'll sneak in here so we can have more of the best sex of our lives ... and that's it. Agreed?"

I refused to acknowledge the chill in my heart. Instead, I concentrated on the one thing I had from him that no other woman had apparently had, not even his late wife.

I turned in his arms, his arousal brushing across my ass as I did. "What time is it?"

Thane frowned. "Nine o'clock."

Good. I unbuckled his belt. "The kids won't be up for another hour at least."

He sucked in a breath. "Regan ..."

But his willpower was already out the window as I released him from his jeans and underwear and lowered to my knees. He cursed under his breath, his eyes blazing, chest heaving as his hands clasped my head. I hadn't even touched him yet.

Thane's long groan, the way his stomach rippled when I touched him, was the most empowering feeling in the goddamn world. At that moment, I was absolutely everything to him, and just as I'd decided last night, I was going to take (or give, as it so happened) all I could while it lasted. No matter what happened between us, I'd always have this of him. The best sex of his life.

It wasn't everything, but it was something.

The computer screen before him was a blur of lines, his mind somewhere far beyond. With Regan. He could still smell her perfume, feel the slide of her silken hair across his skin, feel the tight, hot sheath of her. His want for her was driving him to distraction. While he was a man, and there was a part of him that got off on sneaking into the annex each night to be with her, Thane couldn't rid the dread that had settled over him since they'd agreed on their sex-with-no-strings arrangement.

In fact, the dread had only worsened since that first night. The only reprieve he had from it was when he was inside Regan. Nothing else penetrated his thoughts but the over-whelming need that consumed him in those moments.

"Thane!"

Jarred from his now daily daydreams about his kids' nanny, Thane turned from his computer screen to see Keelie standing in the doorway, frowning at him.

"Sorry for shouting, but I said your name a few times and you didn't respond."

Fuck.

This was getting out of hand.

"Sorry about that." Then it occurred to him Keelie was in his office. On their floor. "What brings you down here?"

She closed his door and walked over to his desk.

Thane felt awkward. When he hadn't called Keelie back, he'd presumed she'd understand what that meant. That was how the dating game worked. Unless she was here about something else.

Keelie perched on his desk and gave him a somewhat self-deprecating shrug. "My friends told me I should leave it alone, but I like to know for certain where things are at. I can't play the usual bullshit dating games. I'm not very good at understanding the rules."

Oh, boy.

"I thought we had a really nice time at dinner, but … you haven't called. So … I just thought I'd check if maybe I was supposed to ask you out next? And if so, would you like to go on a second date with me?"

Thane admired her courage and straightforwardness. To be fair, her self-involved nattering on their first date could have just been nerves. And in another life, maybe he would have gone on a second date with her. But she deserved honesty. "I had a nice time, Keelie, but I think we're better off as friends."

Disappointment darkened her eyes, but she smiled through it. He felt like shit. "Oh. Of course." She pushed off his desk, smoothing her skirt. "Well, I appreciate you being up-front."

"I'm … sorry." Thane winced as she winced. An apology was the wrong move. It was pitying. Fuck. "I mean—"

"It's fine." She backed up toward the door. "I need to … I need to get back to work."

Keelie fled his office as if the hounds of mortification were nipping at her heels.

Thane buried his head in his hands and muttered a string of curse words. Regan was right. He'd used Keelie and hurt her. What an arsehole.

The rest of the day passed painfully slowly. Now he was distracted by his own bad choices. Even Regan noted at dinner he seemed troubled. He waved off her concerns as he pondered what the hell he was doing with his life. With Regan. The chances he was taking with his family with this affair. But when she gave him a sultry look before she left the house for her annex, his addiction to her took over.

And when he let himself into the annex that night to find Regan lying naked on the bed, waiting for him, everything else ceased to exist.

Regan Penhaligon had seduced him past the point of no return.

22

REGAN

Except for Thane's birthday that following Tuesday, our affair fell into a strict routine. That doesn't sound like it could be hot, but it was *so* freaking hot, he'd become my obsession.

We went about our lives as we had before, except friendlier and nicer to each other than we had been the past few weeks. This seemed to appease Lewis, and he stopped being so watchful of us all the time.

But at night, when the children were asleep and secure in the house, Thane slipped into my annex for an hour. Sometimes he made love to me like he actually loved me. Those were the dangerous nights. Strangely, for the sake of my heart, I preferred the nights he was bossy, when he moved me about the bed the way he wanted and fucked me until I saw stars. On my knees, riding him, on his knees, on our sides, upside down, twisted like a pretzel, hands tied together above my head. The man knew how to screw every which way. I'd never have guessed he was so wild. It was the best surprise.

And all I kept thinking was what a moron Fran had been. How the hell could she cheat on Thane Adair?

The only exception to our routine was the morning of his birthday. I'd snuck upstairs with breakfast before he could wake. But he didn't want the scrambled eggs on toast I'd brought him. He wanted me. It was the first time we'd had sex in the house, and having to stay super quiet was strangely erotic for us both.

Afterward, Thane looked guilty as hell, and I knew he worried about Eilidh and Lewis discovering our secret. He was cooler toward me because of it, and once more my feelings were wounded. I ignored the somewhat *used* sensation crawling across my shoulders as I vowed not to enter his bedroom without invitation again.

I was his dirty little secret.

It never seemed like that when we were together, but sometimes, like when I was standing at the school gates, I felt it. The thirsty moms didn't pay me attention anymore. They'd long moved on. But I still remembered their gossip. I knew what they'd think of me.

I could tell myself I was a grown woman who could do whatever the hell she wanted with whomever she wanted, but it was hard to remember that on days like this morning. For a moment, I'd totally forgotten where we were. The kids were sitting at the kitchen table eating breakfast, and Thane was behind the island, his ass facing into the kitchen. As I passed him to put my mug in the sink, I'd reached out without thinking and caressed said ass. It wasn't until he turned sharply to glare at me I even realized what I'd done.

I flicked a guilty look at the kids, relieved they weren't even paying attention, but Thane glowered at me like I'd just murdered the family pet.

Dirty. Little. Secret.

Whatever he saw flash across my expression softened his

264

with confusion. Heart pounding, I skirted around him, keeping my distance. "I'm just going to put a load of laundry on before the littles get ready."

I had been in there only a few seconds when I felt him.

Glancing over my shoulder, our eyes locked as Thane leaned against the doorjamb. He looked down the hall before turning and whispering quietly, "I'm sorry. I just …"

"No, I'm sorry. I wasn't thinking."

"I get it." He crossed the room to still my hands as I sorted the laundry. "I have moments where I'm itching to touch you … but we can't. Yeah?"

Dirty. Little. Secret.

I blinked hard out of the memory, glaring at the school as I waited to collect Eilidh and Lewis. Will was a few yards away, talking animatedly with another parent, so I didn't have him to distract me from my dark thoughts.

Two weeks.

It had only been two weeks since Thane and I started our affair.

And I was wondering how long I could hack the emotional roller coaster I was on.

Jared called last week to ask me out, and I made up some excuse about how I wasn't looking to date while I was in Scotland. He didn't seem to care. I mean, it took him long enough to call. Instead, he told me to call him if I changed my mind.

Robyn … my sister knew something was up. She kept asking if I was okay and giving me these long, searching looks. Usually, I would just tell her about Thane. But I'd promised him I wouldn't tell anyone, and I didn't want to break my promise, even though I'd kill for my sister's sensible and loving advice.

Rather, I had to rely on what I thought she might tell me.

And she'd tell me that if the affair only made me feel good

when we were having sex, if it made me feel horrible about myself when we weren't having sex, then I needed to end it. I needed to be honest with Thane that I was not cut out for zero commitment. Not with him. I thought I could. I thought something was better than nothing.

It had taken less than fourteen days to realize how naive I'd been.

Loving the man who only wanted to screw you … it was like taking five knives in the chest every day.

I had to end it.

The thought made me want to scream in rebellion, but for the sake of my sanity, I knew I had to end it.

The bell rang, snapping me back to the moment.

Focus. When Eilidh and Lewis were around, I didn't have time to worry about the state of my relationship with Thane. I thanked God every day for them—the best little distractions a girl could hope for. If I was obsessed with their father, I was a goner for them. But that was the kind of love a girl could live with.

Grinning at the sight of Eilidh hurrying down the front steps into the yard, my eyes wandered past her to find Lewis. So focused on finding her brother in the crowds, I didn't notice the man approach.

By the time I did, it was too late.

As my attention returned to Eilidh, she'd just stepped through the gates when the stranger swung her into his arms, making her shriek.

What the hell?!

"Hey!" I yelled, panicked, launching myself toward them.

The man's eyes flew to me, wild and mad behind his round glasses as Eilidh beat his head and screamed, but I swore adrenaline made me fly into super speed. I shrieked at him to let her go, and he backhanded me so hard, I stumbled onto my ass.

266

"Oi, you!" I heard Will shout, and I scrambled to my feet, ignoring the throbbing in my cheek. Will grabbed at the man's hair, distracting him enough so I could tug Eilidh by the waist out of his arms. He slammed an elbow into Will's nose just as I got Eilidh free, and he lunged at her again. I pushed her away in instinct and put myself between them, trying to focus beyond the discombobulation of a complete stranger attempting to steal my child in front of hundreds of witnesses.

"Back off!" I yelled, shoving him away.

He grabbed my arm, trying to twist it, but Robyn's lessons kicked in. I slammed the base of my palm in an upward strike into his nose. I wasn't strong enough to break it, but it stunned him long enough to loosen his hold. Spinning toward Eilidh, now in Lewis's protective little arms, I found my shoulder jolted back in a painful jarring yank.

"Give her to me!" he roared like an animal as he clawed at my throat from behind. The smell of whisky was overwhelming. "Give me my daughter!"

McClintock?

Oh my God.

Throwing my entire weight behind it, I sank my elbow into his face and stumbled toward the kids as he grunted and released me. I was aware of bodies rushing at us, at him. We were being protected by the other parents, so I pulled Eilidh and Lewis into my belly, covering them as much as I could with my body. Like a cocoon. A fist slammed into my temple, momentarily dazing me as I heard McClintock scream Eilidh's name again.

Eilidh and Lewis sobbed as they burrowed into me, as my back and head were punched and kicked as he tried to beat his way around me to get her. I ignored the pain, refusing to budge. The cacophony of those around us blurred into white noise.

And then the hitting stopped as abruptly as it had started.

"Regan, you're okay." Michelle bent her face into mine.

I glanced up and behind her, shocked to see McClintock flat on the ground, held down by Will and all the thirsty moms.

Kids were crying around us, scared out of their minds.

"Eilidh. Lewis." I dropped to my knees as they threw their arms around me. My face and body throbbed with pain, but it didn't matter. They were safe. Relief and adrenaline made me tremble as much as they did. I tried not to cry with rage that McClintock had scared the hell out of them.

"The police are on their way." Michelle rubbed my shoulder soothingly. "Do you know who he is?"

"Eilidh!" McClintock wailed, glaring at us from the ground where Will and the ladies had him pinned. "My daughter!" He sounded like a wounded animal.

I blanched, feeling everyone stare at us as I lied, "No, I don't know who he is."

~

THANE

It took everything within him not to drive like a maniac all the way from Inverness to Caelmore. Killing himself to get home to the children and Regan wouldn't do anyone any good. But the adrenaline coursing through him made it very hard to control his foot on the accelerator.

The only thing that reassured him was that Lachlan and Robyn were with them.

Sean McClintock had tried to kidnap Eilidh at the school gates.

Lachlan had called him. His brother had rushed to the school when Jock informed him via Will that McClintock was being held in a citizen's arrest while they waited for the police. His brother was there to see the bastard arrested, but Thane was waiting for contact from the police. He would see the piece of shit put away for this.

According to Lachlan, if it hadn't been for Regan's quick actions and help from the other parents, Sean might have gotten away with Eilidh. The very thought sent a cold shudder down his spine. Thane didn't know the details yet. He did know he owed Regan more than he could ever pay back.

He skidded to a stop outside his house, his thoughts solely focused on its occupants. Bursting through the door, Thane rushed into the main living space, dizzy with relief as his children jumped from the couch beside Regan and Robyn and rushed him.

He dropped to his knees, taking in every inch of them before they slammed into him. Physically, they were fine, but as they clung to Thane, they cried, the sound unbearable. Tears filled his eyes as he pulled them tighter to him, vowing he would never again take for granted the singular feeling of his children embracing him. Thane pressed quick, desperate kisses to their heads as his tears threatened to fall.

A hand on his shoulder brought his head up, and he looked into Lachlan's concerned face. "They'll be all right. They've just had a fright," his brother assured him.

Eilidh and Lewis pulled away from his embrace, Lew wiping at his cheeks while Eilidh's face turned purple with anger through her tears. "That bad man hit Ree-Ree, Daddy!"

Thane's heart leapt into his throat. "What?" He stood, glancing from Lachlan's stormy expression to across the room where Robyn had her arm around Regan on the sofa.

She had an elbow to her knee and a bag of frozen peas pressed to her eye.

"Regan." He moved toward her, and the children ran across the room before he could get to her. Eilidh scampered onto the couch to press against her while Lewis took the seat next to his sister, his serious focus on Regan.

Thane approached, aware of Robyn at her other side, but unable to take his eyes off Regan. She watched him warily and lifted her head from the frozen peas. Her right cheekbone was swollen. It would bruise.

Renewed rage flooded him. They'd all just returned from the minor injuries unit in nearby Golspie, but Thane had assumed it was routine after something like this to have everyone checked over. Lachlan hadn't mentioned that McClintock had attacked Regan.

The reminder that Thane couldn't sweep her into his arms and bury his face in her throat so he could feel and hear her pulse rushing, alive and healthy, was a gut punch. Instead, all he could do was lower to his haunches before her and place a comforting hand on her knee.

"Are you all right?"

She gave him a wry smile. "Eilidh is all right, so I'm all right."

At the disagreeable sound Robyn made in the back of her throat, and the way her eyes blazed, he could see she didn't think so. He turned back to Regan as she shot her sister a quelling look, and he noted the bruise at her temple.

"What the—" He cut off his curse just in time as he stretched to push her hair back. Barely able to hear over the blood rushing in his ears, he demanded, "What exactly happened?"

Regan brushed his hand away and gestured subtly with her head toward the children. Her eyes said "later."

"Ree-Ree's going to be okay, right, Daddy?" Eilidh stared up at him soulfully. Lewis wore the same expression.

"I'm fine." She turned, switching the frozen peas to her other hand so she could pull the children into a one-armed hug. They both tried to plaster themselves to her side, and his gut tightened at how shaken up they all were.

He stood abruptly, leashed fury burning his nerve endings.

McClintock was going to fucking die for this.

"Robyn, why don't you call out for some food?" Lachlan was suddenly at his side, his hand on his brother's shoulder. "I'm going to take Thane outside for a minute."

"I'm not leaving them," Thane growled.

"You need a minute. And I need to fill you in on what happened."

He looked down at his family. Regan lifted her chin, her expression sympathetic. "Go. We'll be okay for another few minutes."

"I've got them," Robyn assured him.

As he reluctantly followed Lachlan out onto the deck, he snapped, "This better be quick."

His brother didn't answer him. He led Thane down the deck and across the yard into his garden.

"Lachlan, where are we going?"

He glanced over his shoulder at Thane, his expression as cloudy as Thane's. "Trust me."

Despite the impatient fury boiling inside him, he followed Lachlan into his house and upstairs to the home gym that made Thane's look pathetic in comparison. Lachlan led him over to the corner—to the boxing bag.

"Robyn's." Lachlan tapped it. "I put it in here for her. It's where she leaves everything that frustrates her. It got used a lot in the first few days of Regan's arrival. And it'll be the first place she comes tonight." His eyes darkened. "One parent,

271

Michelle Kingsley, told us McClintock grabbed Eilidh at the gate, but Regan rushed him. He backhanded her, and that's what drew Will's attention. He moved in to help, and Regan got Eilidh free from McClintock. Will got hit and McClintock went for Eilidh again. Regan hit *him*, dazing him long enough to get her arms around Eils and Lew, protecting them with her body. That's when the other parents descended on him, but the bastard got a few more kicks and punches in to Regan's head and back before they subdued him."

The imagery his brother created made Thane sick with fury; at the same time, his chest ached with gratitude.

"There was no way he would have gotten Eils," Lachlan assured him, his eyes bright with pride. "Regan would have died before letting that happen."

Thane found it hard to swallow, his throat so thick with emotion.

"I misjudged her," Lachlan admitted softly. "I wanted to believe in her for Robyn's sake, but there was always a part of me waiting for her to show us who she really was."

He thought of Regan using her body as a shield to protect his children and felt like his heart might explode. "This is who she really is," he replied hoarsely.

His brother nodded. "The question is why she needed to protect Eilidh. Who is McClintock, Thane?"

"The man Fran had an affair with," he bit out, knowing the truth was unleashed now, no matter what.

Lachlan looked away for a second, the muscle in his jaw ticking. "She cheated on you?"

"Aye. He was a colleague at her school. I caught them a few months before we found out Fran was pregnant with Eilidh. It had been going on for months."

"And you forgave her? Why didn't you tell me?"

Hearing the disbelief in his brother's voice, Thane bristled. "She was my wife and my son's mother. I had to try. Especially when she told me she was pregnant again. And I didn't want you to treat her differently. The only person who knows is Regan."

Lachlan's eyes widened slightly at that detail, but then something else seemed to occur to him. He exhaled slowly. "Is Eilidh McClintock's?"

"No," Thane growled.

"You did a paternity test?"

"No. I don't need to." Thane took a menacing step toward his brother. "She's *my* daughter."

"And if she's not?" Lachlan pushed.

"Lachlan, brother, unless you want my fist in your face rather than that punching bag, don't say another word."

Realizing Thane couldn't even entertain the thought of another man being Eilidh's birth father, Lachlan let it drop. He pushed the boxing bag toward him. "Let it go here. You can't go back into the house the way you are now. You're seething. And the kids need you calm."

Taking Lachlan's advice, Thane shrugged out of his jacket, whipped off his jumper and the shirt beneath it, and brought his fists up to his face. Instead of the boxing bag, he saw McClintock. He saw McClintock terrifying his children. Punching Regan. Regan shielding them while she took blows to her head and back. His rage flooded out of him, and he roared as he threw a punch powered by its intensity.

By the time the worst of it drained out of him, sweat soaked his hair and skin.

Head bowed, hands on his hips, Thane whispered, trying to choke back the tears, shaking with the force of it. "What if she isn't mine?"

Arms came around him, and he found himself pulled into his big brother's embrace. "We'll deal with it … and you won't lose her. We're not losing her. I won't let that happen.

Whatever it takes, Thane, I mean it. Whatever favors I need to owe, whatever palms need greased, laws fucking broken—I will do it. Nobody is taking our wee girl from you."

Thane tightened his hold, needing to believe more than he ever had that Lachlan Adair could do anything he set his mind to.

23

REGAN

"Freaking wonderful," I muttered as I looked into the mirror above my bathroom sink. The kids had been reluctant to let me out of their sight, but as we'd sat on the couch waiting for Thane and Lachlan to finish whatever they were doing, I'd felt cramps in my lower stomach.

With everything that had been going on, I'd lost track of the time, but sitting there, I realized what date it was.

Excusing myself to the annex bathroom where I kept my toiletries and stuff, I discovered my suspicions correct.

My period had arrived.

Perfect.

Nothing like holding a frozen bag of peas to your face and a heating pad to your belly as a visual representation of how shitty your day was going.

Walking back into the main house just as Thane and Lachlan did, Thane ran his eyes down my body and back up again, a deep scowl scoring his brows. "Where were you?"

"I needed something," I said vaguely, not wanting to announce to the room about my period. Then noting both he and Lachlan had changed shirts and Thane's hair was wet, I frowned, "Where were *you*?"

His attention moved to where Eilidh and Lewis were curled on the couch, watching a movie with Robyn. When he turned to me, he looked so shattered, I wished I could embrace him. "Expelling some of my anger."

Fuck it.

I walked over and put my arms around him, pressing my cheek to his chest, and not giving one shit what his brother or my sister thought. To my relief, Thane closed his arms around me.

Tight.

He took a shuddering breath. "Thank you," he whispered. "What you did today … I can't ever repay you for that."

Lifting my head, my heart in my throat and most likely in my eyes, too, I whispered back, "You never have to thank me for that."

Thane's gaze dropped to my mouth, and for the first time since the attack, I couldn't feel the throbbing in my cheek. All I could feel was the promise of his lips on mine.

The doorbell rang, breaking the moment. We both blinked rapidly, guilt flooding me as I remembered where we were. Pushing away from each other, I caught Lachlan's eyes over Thane's shoulder and experienced more than a twinge of concern at the suspicion in his expression.

Before anyone could answer the door, it burst open and Arro's voice carried toward us. "We brought food! Where are my babies?"

"Aunt Arro!" Eilidh and Lewis clambered off the sofa and dashed across the room to meet their aunt as she strode into the room with Mac at her back. She beamed and dropped to her knees to pull them in for a hug, but as soon as they couldn't see her, her expression filled with anguish. She looked up at Thane as she hugged them, and her brother approached to squeeze her shoulder in reassurance.

"Food," Mac said, his own countenance grim as he placed bags of takeout on the island. To my shock, my belly rumbled. I didn't think I'd be able to eat so soon after what happened. Mac's eyes caught mine and zeroed in on my cheek. "You all right?" He came to me, and before I could answer, he pulled me into his powerful, comforting embrace.

And that was how we got through the next few hours.

The family closed ranks.

They distracted the kids, making them laugh when I didn't think they could laugh so soon after, and they fed us. I was more grateful for them than I could say, especially when two police officers knocked on the door around an hour after their arrival.

To my gratitude, Thane wanted me with him in his office to speak with them. Lachlan was present too.

"We're sorry to interrupt your evening after a day like today, Mr. Adair," the constable who'd introduced herself as PC Diana Kerr said. "We just wanted to update you on the situation with Mr. Sean McClintock, the man who attempted to kidnap your daughter this afternoon."

Thane nodded impatiently.

The male officer, PC Brian Shanks, had been staring at Lachlan in awe the whole time. Now that I knew him, and because people in Ardnoch were so used to him, I forgot Lachlan was famous. The officer finally dragged his attention away from Lachlan at the silence and found his colleague subtly glaring at him. The officer whipped his head to us, his expression a little sheepish. "Uh … do you know Mr. McClintock?"

I wanted to reach for Thane's hand. Instead I placed it more subtly on his back to remind him I was there for him.

He was tense and hot beneath my touch, but he also leaned into it.

"He was a colleague of my late wife's."

The officers nodded and PC Kerr said, "Did you know that Mr. McClintock's wife and daughter were killed two months ago in a car crash? Mr. McClintock, it seems, was driving the vehicle in question and survived, while his wife and child did not."

Oh my God. I shared a disbelieving look with Lachlan, and he scrubbed a hand down his face, visibly distraught.

Thane bowed his head and exhaled a curse before replying gruffly, "No, no, I didn't know."

That was why he'd shown up at Thane's work too.

"Mr. McClintock is being detained while the charges are brought against him for attempted kidnapping."

"What if I don't want to press charges?" Thane shocked me by asking.

PC Kerr gave him a compassionate but tight smile. "I'm afraid we have enough evidence from witnesses, Mr. Adair, to proceed with charges regardless. If you have concerns, you're free to contact the procurator fiscal as the case goes forward."

Thane nodded. "Okay. Thank you, Officers."

At the door, PC Shanks gave Lachlan a somewhat embarrassed look. "I hope you don't mind me saying, considering the circumstances, but I'm a big fan of your films."

Lachlan gave him a tight-lipped smile. "That's very kind, thank you."

"I'm sorry for your troubles today." The officer gave us a sympathetic nod and followed his colleague out to the patrol car.

"I swear, if he asked you for a selfie, I was going to hit him," Thane growled, his frustration palpable. And we both knew it wasn't about the starstruck police officer.

I turned to Lachlan. "Can you give us a minute?"

Lachlan studied us, then gave me an abrupt nod before he left us alone.

I took hold of a somewhat dazed Thane's hand and led him back into his office, closing the door to give us privacy.

"Fuck." He shrugged in disbelief.

I pulled him into my arms like I'd wanted to all night, pressing kisses to his cheeks, across his bearded jawline, my fingers digging into his shoulders. "It's okay," I murmured over and over as his arms banded around me.

He buried his face in my throat with a groan and breathed me in. I sighed at the touch of his lips near my pulse.

We stood like that for a while.

Holding on to each other.

Finally, Thane exhaled a heavy sigh and straightened. Studying my face with those beautiful, soulful eyes, he brushed my hair gently from my cheeks, his thumb tracing the outer edges of where Sean had hit me. When our eyes met, he looked at me with such tenderness, my lips parted in surprise.

Could he ... did he feel—

A knock on the office door jolted us apart seconds before Arro stuck her head in. "Food is getting cold and the kids are asking for you."

Thane nodded, not meeting his sister's gaze as he pulled the door open. "Right, coming."

She watched him march away and then turned to me with a frown. "You okay?"

I nodded because there was nothing else to do.

"You need more ice on that cheek." Arro grabbed my hand to lead me back into the kitchen where she proceeded to mother hen me almost as much as Robyn did.

I didn't mind. Not in the least.

And I thanked God for all of them as we congregated on the huge sectional after dinner, a movie playing for Eilidh and Lewis while the adults talked about anything but what had happened.

~

Everyone left before nine o'clock so we could put Eils and Lew to bed. Robyn and Lachlan were the last to go, and my sister was so reluctant to leave me, Lachlan had to manhandle her out of the house.

The only reason she allowed him to was because of Thane.

"I don't want you sleeping in that annex alone tonight. You'll stay with us," Robyn had commanded.

"She's staying here," Thane replied. "In the guest room. I think the kids will appreciate her being close tonight."

Robyn couldn't argue with that. She kissed my good cheek, hugged me tight while I ignored the new aches in my upper back and right side, and took Lachlan's hand as he led her out.

Once everyone had gone, Thane and I ushered the children upstairs to bed, but Eilidh and Lewis grew subdued again. We took turns tucking them in—me with Eilidh first while Thane was with Lewis, and then we swapped.

"And you'll be just down the hall?" Lewis asked for the second time as I got up to leave.

Bending over, I kissed his forehead and promised him once more I would be.

Meeting Thane outside their rooms, he shook his head and whispered wearily, "I just lied to my children."

"They asked who he was?" I guessed, wondering when one or both of them would. To be honest, I thought they'd shown immense restraint to not ask again sooner. They'd asked at the school, but I'd avoided answering in all the chaos.

Thane nodded grimly. "I told them he was just a man who had lost his family and was in pain. That the pain made him confused about who Eilidh was." He looked away.

I cupped his cheek, bringing his focus back to me. "They don't need to know anything else."

"What if they do?"

Knowing what he alluded to, I shook my head. "We'll cross that bridge *if* we get to it." I pressed onto tiptoes to kiss him lightly and murmured that I needed to retrieve some things from the annex. Five minutes later, I crept upstairs with a small bag of necessities to find him waiting for me.

"I'm going to turn on the alarm." He brushed his fingers along my stomach as he passed me to go downstairs. I'd never been more grateful for the security system. As it was, I hated I couldn't sleep in Thane's arms tonight. I didn't want to be alone.

But that wasn't reality, so I entered the guest room at the end of the hall, the easiest room in the house to clean since all it needed was dusting and vacuuming. After brushing my teeth, I changed into my nightie. I was about to turn the bedcovers back when I heard behind me.

"What are you doing?"

The gruff whisper spun me about. Thane scowled at me from the doorway.

"Going to bed," I whispered.

The man actually rolled his eyes. "Don't be daft." He crossed the room and took my hand in his, leading me out.

"What are you doing?"

He didn't answer. He just dragged me into his room and closed the door. Technically, that *was* his answer.

"What about the kids?"

Thane removed his borrowed shirt. "I'll wake you before they wake up." I opened my mouth to argue as he unzipped his suit pants and he cut me off. "Regan, I need you with me tonight. Please, don't argue."

"I have my period," I told him regretfully.

Thane scowled over his shoulder as he pulled the duvet back on the bed. "It's not about sex. I just need you close."

And like that, I melted into a metaphorical pile of goo. He needed me. Hiding my giddy grin, I got into his bed and almost sighed with relief at how comfortable his mattress was.

"I'll be back in a second," he murmured before disappearing into his bathroom.

Despite the utter shittiness of the day, snuggling up against Thane's pillow, inhaling his scent from the sheets, was a fantasy come to life. I was in his bed. Invited.

And then my eyes hit the photo of him and his wife on the nightstand.

Every day I passed the photos on his gallery wall downstairs. They didn't bother me. They were of Thane's entire family. And I couldn't erase his past with Francine without erasing Eilidh and Lewis, and the very thought made me breathless. Besides, even though I had issues with his dead wife cheating on him, I wouldn't want to erase her. Not just for the kids but for her. Eilidh and Lewis were hers. She lived on in them. And they needed to be surrounded by her memory. I wouldn't want to take that from her or them ever.

But the photo on his nightstand was different. It wasn't about Eilidh and Lewis. That was for him.

Even after her betrayal, he obviously adored her. So much so, all these years later, she still slept beside him at night.

Jealousy was an ugly, ugly emotion. Even uglier when you were jealous of a dead woman.

Ashamed, I turned around, tucking my good cheek under my hand and closing my eyes against the reminder that, despite Thane's need for me tonight, he would never love me like that.

A tear escaped beneath my closed eyes before I could stop it.

"Hey, hey." Suddenly the mattress depressed, and I opened my eyes to see the blurry vision of Thane getting into bed with me. "I'm here." He pulled me into his hard, warm body, kissing my tears. "It's over."

Realizing he thought I was crying about today was a relief. So I cried harder, clinging to him, hating the voice in my head that urged me in a nasty voice to enjoy his attention while I could.

"You're killing me," he groaned, pressing a kiss to my head. "I should have been there."

More shame flooded me and I shook my head, swiping at the tears. "No, no, don't do that to yourself. I'm fine, I'm fine. It's just been a long day. And I get emotional when I have my period."

His thumb pressed gently under my chin, forcing me to tilt my head to look at him. "By all accounts, you were bloody magnificent today ... and I'm so grateful for that, *mo leannan*. But you should never have been in that position. Even not knowing about Sean's loss, I should have known by his behavior that day in the car park to be on alert. Even the slightest hint of danger to Eilidh or Lewis ... I should have been more cautious."

"How?" I argued.

"I don't know. Asked one of Lachlan's security to shadow you while I investigated Sean myself. Instead of burying my fucking head in the sand and hoping it would just go away."

Even as I pressed kisses to his chest to soothe him, something niggled at the back of my mind, pushing forward, making my heart beat fast.

Feeling me tense, Thane asked, "*Mo leannan?*"

"I have to tell you something." I pushed into a sitting position, forcing myself to meet his gaze.

He frowned warily. "Okay?"

Taking a shuddering breath, I hated I had to explain to Thane what an impulsive moron I'd been, but he was right. Burying my head in the sand, hoping Austin would go away, was selfish and irresponsible. There had been nothing in months, and Robyn said Autry was monitoring him periodically ... but he ... Thane should know about his existence. Just in case.

In hushed words so I wouldn't wake Eilidh and Lewis, I told him about the backpacking trip, the group of friends, the impulsive one-night stand, and the harassment that followed.

One time, maybe four or five weeks into the job as Thane's nanny, he'd asked me why he never saw me on my phone, on social media. "I thought your generation couldn't exist without it?" he'd teased. I'd given him a vague bullshit answer. Now I told him the truth.

"I had to delete all of my socials. My email. Block my number. When I was living in California, I was like a ghost." I smirked unhappily. "But I don't miss talking to people who don't really care about me. Or checking my follows or likes. And not just because it keeps him out of my life, but because ... I don't need the validation like I did when I was younger." *I have everything I need when I'm with you.*

Thane studied me, his eyes bright with concern as I went on to tell him about dating Maddox the asshole, and Austin's return and his creepy, stealthy stalking at the coffeehouse.

"But since I've been here, nothing. Robyn knows, and her

cop friend is keeping tabs on him." I reached for his hand, squeezing, hoping he'd forgive me. "I didn't say anything because of everything that happened with Lucy and Lachlan. It isn't on the same level, and so I thought it was stupid to worry you. But I see it was selfish to keep it from you. You need to know about these things for the children's sake. I'm sorry."

He shook his head, and I sighed with relief as he pulled me into his arms. "It's fine, it's okay. At least you didn't keep it to yourself—you told Robyn. That's good, Regan. I'm glad. I'm just sorry you had to go through that."

"You're not mad at me?"

Thane made a hoarse sound that was half amusement, half pain. "You protected my daughter like she was your own today, *mo leannan*. You could steal off into the night with all my money and I couldn't be angry with you."

God, I loved him so much. He had such a big heart. Caressing his chest where said heart beat a little fast within, I asked, for perhaps the hundredth time, "What does *ma le-ow-nin* mean?"

He was quiet for a moment as he stroked my upper arm with his fingertips. "Does the meaning matter?"

His question stopped me in my mental tracks.

When he used the endearment I was pretty sure was Gaelic, his voice grew softer, his tone tender.

I smiled at the realization. "No." I snuggled deeper into him. "It doesn't matter."

THANE

Two hours later, Thane woke up from a light sleep for the fourth time. His heart raced too hard. Regan had rolled out of his arms in her sleep and sprawled on her back, her chest rising and falling gently. Even so, he couldn't hold back the urge to press his fingers lightly to the pulse at her throat.

Relieved to feel the steady, gentle throb, he slipped out of bed while she slept and checked on Lewis. His boy was asleep, his soft snores music to Thane's ears. Then he checked on Eilidh. Usually she sprawled much like Regan was right now in his bed. But tonight, as if her subconscious still had her gripped in today's terror, his little Eilidh-Bug was curled into a protective ball.

Throat thick with too many emotions to name, Thane sat down on the bed and sang softly in her ear. When she was a baby, it was the only thing that would make her sleep. After a while, her little body relaxed and she rolled onto her side, her tiny fingers touching his knee.

He covered her hand and brought it to his lips, pressing a kiss to the back of it.

Fear unlike anything he'd experienced overwhelmed him.

What if she wasn't his?

She's mine, he raged inwardly. No piece of paper could tell him differently. Blood or no, Eilidh Francine Adair was his daughter, and he'd fight to the death for her if it came to it.

A creak near the door drew his head up. Regan stood in the dim light. "Is she okay?" He barely heard her question, it was so quietly asked.

Kissing Eilidh's hand one last time, he laid it gently down on the bed near her chubby little cheek and stood slowly so as not to wake her.

He pulled her door until it was almost shut and then slid a hand around Regan's waist. As he led her quietly back to bed, he ignored the feeling of rightness that settled over him.

She wasn't his wife or Eilidh and Lewis's stepmum.

She wasn't permanent, he reminded himself.

And so before he let her drift back to sleep, he rolled her onto her back and kissed her until they were both breathless.

Another memory to keep him warm when she was gone.

24

REGAN

Thane didn't want me to return to the annex. To appease his worries, I moved some of my things into the guest suite. This also reassured Robyn, but I was concerned how it looked to Eilidh and Lewis. They loved the idea of me being so close, but with Thane still keeping his distance whenever we weren't alone, I wasn't sure if I should dig myself any deeper into the children's lives.

Who was I kidding?

I was as deep as you got without actually being married to their dad.

The mere thought made my pulse flutter, so I threw it out of my head immediately.

I focused on the historical romance on my e-reader. For the past week, I'd gone to bed in the guest room, only for Thane to sneak in when he was sure the kids were asleep. I'd still had my period, so we did nothing but cuddle, and when I woke in the morning, he was always gone. While I waited for him every night, I read.

Whenever I was having a strenuous day or week (or month!), I liked to reread my favorite books. There was something comforting not only about a happy ending but also in going through the emotional angst of a couple's roller-coaster relationship, enjoying their pain and passion, because you already knew how it ended. Romance novels were my version of comfort food, except better because they had hot, fantastical sex.

Well, what I thought was fantastical until Thane came along. I smiled smugly. As I got to a sexy scene in the novel, hot tingles awakened between my legs.

"What are you reading?"

"Oh!" I startled.

Thane stood over the bed, his arms crossed, grinning at me. I hadn't even heard him come in. "Whatever it is, you're engrossed."

I grinned back, happy to see his smile. He'd laughed with the children throughout the week so things would be normal for them, but he'd been gloomy with worry when we were alone.

"A book." I turned back the duvet on the other side of the bed and patted the mattress.

Removing his T-shirt, Thane rounded the bed, never taking his eyes off mine. Despite the approach of December and this month's bitter introduction to a Highland winter, Thane's home always sat at a comfortable temperature. And he always ran a little hot.

In more ways than one.

I missed him.

And my period was over.

But I wasn't sure anything physical was on the table for us while I was under his roof.

"Is it a historical romance?" He slid into bed beside me and wrapped an arm around my shoulder to draw me to his side. All the while he peered curiously down at my e-reader.

I grinned at him. "You remembered I like those."

He nodded, his eyes smiling into mine. "Let's have a look, then."

Feeling mischievous about what he was about to read, I bit my lip and held the e-reader up to him. The tingles between my legs grew insistent as I watched his eyebrows raise as he read. Thane's hand slid from my upper arm to around my waist, and as his eyes moved over the screen, said hand pressed into my stomach.

Heat licked down my inner thighs, and I swallowed hard, my mouth suddenly dry. "What do you think?"

Thane spoke while he still read, his voice gruff. "It's ... fuck ... it's ..."

"Arousing?" I supplied.

He looked at me, his lips quirking. "Very. Is this how you get your kicks?"

I narrowed my eyes at his teasing. "They're not just about sex."

"Oh, really?"

"No." I gestured with the e-reader. "They're funny and romantic and the heroines are relatable and sometimes they even make me feel like I'm not alone. Romance novels can be witty and emotional and make me cry but in this great, cathartic kind of way."

He studied me intensely, his gaze probing, sharpening at my words.

Realizing I was veering the conversation away from where I wanted it, I grinned. "And the sex ... People call it smut or mommy porn, but there are different kinds of romance. That stuff is great, but I like the ones where the romance, the connection between the couple, is what makes the sex so hot. And it's sex through a woman's eyes. It's the kind of sex we fantasize about."

At that, Thane's brow furrowed and he looked back at the e-reader screen. Even through his beard, I could see a muscle tick in his jaw. I smoothed a hand over his face, guessing where his thoughts were. Leaning up, I pressed my breasts against him and whispered near his ear, "You make my sexual fantasies come true."

He twisted to look into my eyes; his darkened with desire.

I smiled and gestured with the e-reader. "This is just the appetizer these days while I wait for you to come to me."

"Do you read these every night before I come to you?"

"Not always, but often, yeah."

His gaze dropped to my mouth and then to my chest. He inhaled sharply at the sight of my nipples hard against the silk, his hand on my stomach clenching the fabric and unintentionally drawing it tighter. "When you say appetizer ... do you mean these books make you wet?"

My breathing quickened in time at his bluntness. "Sometimes."

"Are you wet right now?" His other hand dipped beneath the duvet, and I shivered at the touch of his fingers sliding up my thigh. When he reached my center, pushing past my underwear, his features hardened with want. "That would be a yes, then."

I arched into him. The e-reader fell from my hand as he played me with precision.

He knew my body as well as he knew his own.

"*Mo leannan*," Thane groaned as he kissed me. He rolled into me and I could feel him throbbing with need.

"What about the littles?" I panted as his lips scattered kisses down my throat and he pulled my nightdress straps down my arms to get at my breasts.

Thane looked up at me, his breath on my hard nipple making me thrust against his fingers. "I need to fuck you, or I'm going to lose my mind. We'll just have to be quiet."

"I'm on the pill," I blurted out. "And I ... I had a health

check a while back. After Maddox ... there wasn't anyone after him, until you."

Thane's eyes flashed, clearly happy with the idea of no barriers. "I'm clean. There's been no one but you for longer than I care to say. So I guess we're both going to have to try *very* hard to be quiet."

I tried. As he kissed and made love to every inch of me, I panted behind my hand and swallowed the cries that wanted to escape. Even with his head between my thighs, his tongue licking and sucking me to orgasm, I clamped a hand over my mouth and muffled my release. Even at the feel of him, heavy and powerful above me, gliding inside, perfect and thick and exactly what I needed, I bit back my gasps.

But when he suddenly pulled out to flip me roughly on my hands and knees, take hold of my nape to whisper in my ear how hard I made him, how he couldn't get enough of me, using dirty, sexual words he'd never used before, I lost my mind. As wild and playful as Thane was in bed, he wasn't a talker.

He was acting out the scene from my romance novel.

Love and passion exploded within me, and I had to bury my face in the mattress, my fingers clawing at the sheets because my scream of release was unstoppable.

"F-f-fuck," Thane stammered as I came in forceful throbs around him. His grip on my hips turned bruising as he climaxed with a hoarse yell, juddering against my ass even as he collapsed over me. "What the fuck, what the fuck," he murmured breathlessly against my shoulder.

Blood pounded in my ears as I came down from the release, and I mewled as Thane pulled out. I turned and opened my mouth to speak, but he braced over me and pressed a finger to my lips, his wide eyes on the bedroom door.

My heart stopped as I realized Thane had been loud in climax.

We waited, our ears pricked, trying to hear over our racing pulses.

Finally, his gaze came to mine. "I think we're fine," he whispered.

"You were loud," I admonished, grinning smugly.

Thane grinned back. "Couldn't be helped. I've never felt anything like it when you came." He fell down beside me on the bed, looking a little dazed as he cuddled me into him.

"*I've* never felt anything like it." I caressed his damp skin and the happy trail that followed a path to one of my favorite physical attributes of his.

Thane's hand moved under my arm to cup my breast. "I think you took everything I had."

I chuckled, settling my chin on his chest. We smiled at each other, giddy with endorphins. "I should clean up," I whispered.

"And I think I need to tell every man I know to get his partner hooked on romance novels."

I pushed up and straddled him on my way to crawl across the bed to the bathroom. I paused and leaned down to brush my lips over his. "Most of them would just take advantage of the fact that their partner was turned on ... they wouldn't go out of their way to recreate the fantasy. It was so hot, I'm never, ever going to forget it."

Something flashed in his eyes, something grim, something I didn't like, but he hid it as he pulled me deeper into the kiss. At the sudden urge to tell him I loved him, I kissed him harder, drowning the words.

Thane groaned and rolled me onto my back, and we had to be quiet all over again.

25

REGAN

The next morning I woke up and Thane was gone, like always.

And like always, I hated it.

Ignoring the now-constant ache in my heart that was only ever lightened when we were together-together, I got ready for the day as usual. Despite news that Sean McClintock had voluntarily checked himself into rehab, Lachlan had two of his security guys shadowing me and the kids wherever we went. Any gossip that might have arisen from Sean yelling about Eilidh being his daughter was cut off when word got out he was an old acquaintance and a grieving father who'd focused on Eilidh because she was close to his daughter's age.

As for the thirsty moms (who I now felt guilty about calling thirsty moms), we'd come to an understanding. I think I'd gone up in their estimations, and they'd certainly gone up in mine when they'd rushed to my defense. They were now just Michelle, Ava, Laura, and Heather. We'd never be close, but we exchanged hellos and friendly smiles at the gates now. Will joked it was a Christmas miracle.

Robyn's twenty-ninth birthday on the upcoming eighth gave us another excuse to have everyone over for dinner without alerting the children to the fact that we were still closing ranks. But I knew Arro and Mac were as worried as we all were and wanted to stay close. Much like Lachlan and Thane, Robyn wasn't really the birthday-celebration type, so we planned to have the family (plus Eredine, who counted as family) over at ours a week from Wednesday.

That night we'd put the kids to bed, and I was snuggled on the couch, pen and notebook in hand, figuring out what of Robyn's favorite dishes I wanted to cook next week and thus what ingredients I'd need. Thane was a little farther away on the couch than I'd like, but we'd come to a silent agreement not to get too cozy, even when Eilidh and Lewis were abed, in case one of them woke up and came downstairs.

Tapping my pen in thought, I looked up to find him watching me instead of the TV. I couldn't quite read his expression, but I liked his eyes on me. "Hey," I said softly with a smile.

His countenance turned from thoughtful to tender. "Hi."

I wanted to crawl across the couch into his lap, and Thane must've been able to read the desire because he murmured a regretful, "I know."

Then tell everyone, I wanted to say. *Screw them. We're not doing anything wrong. We're grown adults. Shit happens. Feelings happen.*

It seemed so obvious.

That it wasn't obvious to Thane was a reminder that whatever I was to him, I wasn't forever. I knew I was more than just sex to him. There was no doubt in my mind, especially after the past week. But it wasn't love. Clearly.

Which was devastating, considering I knew with

certainty that I would never love anyone the way I loved Thane Adair.

"What is it?" Thane asked, frowning.

Realizing my expression might give me away, I shrugged and smiled breezily. "Nothing. I was just wondering if you have a middle name. I noticed on Lewis's report card that his is Stuart. After your dad, right?"

"Aye. All the living Adair men have Stuart as a middle name." He gestured to himself. "Thane Tavin Stuart Adair."

I smiled genuinely this time because it suited him to a tee to have two middle names. "Very distinguished."

He gave me a mock reproving look. "Lachlan is Lachlan Lennox Stuart Adair. Brodan Bryce Stuart Adair. Arran Alexander Stuart Adair. And Arrochar is Arrochar Vivien Adair after our mother. She was the only one to escape the dreaded double name."

"So that's why Lewis and Eilidh only have one middle name?" I had noted that Eilidh's middle name was Francine, after her mother.

He nodded. "Do you have a middle name?"

I grinned. "I do. And it's not an easy one to guess."

"What is it?"

"I'm named after my great-grandmother. As you know, we Penhaligons are of Cornish stock, and I have a very Cornish middle name." I actually liked it. "It's Demelza. Regan Demelza Penhaligon."

Thane considered me for a moment. "It's beautiful. And it suits you well."

It seemed like such a random, silly conversation about middle names, but on the back of the feelings I'd been having before it, I was suddenly claustrophobic. Trapped by a future Thane had already determined we would not have together.

I would never stand at an altar and say, "I, Regan Demelza

Penhaligon, take thee, Thane Tavin Stuart Adair, to be my lawfully wedded husband."

And it hurt like a motherfucker.

Like the angel I was beginning to think she was, Arrochar again demonstrated her perfect timing. Her ring tone on Thane's phone cut through the air. I'd been seconds away from letting my feelings burst forth before she saved me.

Thane frowned at whatever Arro said down the line. "I don't think that's a good idea ..." he sighed. "I know they do it every year, but I don't want them out of my sight."

"What is it?" I asked.

"Arro, wait a second." Thane heaved another sigh as he muted his cell. "Help me find a diplomatic way to tell my sister no."

I frowned. "To what?"

"Every year, Eilidh and Lewis spend the first weekend in December at Arro's. They help her put up the Christmas decorations and watch Christmas movies. They love it because she decorates early. Not as early as Robyn, mind you." He gently judged.

"Hey, we're sacrificing Thanksgiving by living here, buddy, and that's when we traditionally put up the tree. It's just weird to you strange Highlanders. To Americans, it's perfectly reasonable."

Thane's lips twitched with amusement at my defense of my sister, who had decorated their house last weekend. "Fine. But I still don't want the kids spending a night away from me."

Honestly, I didn't either. "Just tell her no."

"I'm not being unreasonable?"

"Maybe. But you're their dad. You're allowed to be."

He gave me his "I want to kiss you" look, and I had to bite my lip against a pleased smile. Unmuting the phone, he put it to his ear. "I'm sorry, Arro. I'm just not comfortable with it this year ... Uh-uh ... Mac? ... Well, would he be there all night?" He muted the phone again. "She said she can convince Mac to sleep on the couch."

I nodded, remembering what I thought I might have witnessed the birthday weekend at her house a few weeks ago, wondering if he'd really be sleeping on the couch. Either way, he'd be there, and the rest was none of my business. But it would be really naughty of the Adair siblings if they were simultaneously screwing around with someone complicated and out of their age bracket. Come to think of it, there was the same number of years between Arro and Mac as between me and Thane. Huh. Okay.

Jesus, Mac had Robyn so young.

"Regan?"

"Hmm?" I blinked out of my wayward thoughts.

"What do you think? About Mac?"

"Uh. Yeah, I think that works."

"You sure?"

"Yeah."

Thane considered it a moment and then put the phone back to his ear. "All right, then." He scowled, and I heard her voice rise a little on the other end of the line. "I'm not being sexist ... no, it's not that ... If you'd said Robyn was staying with you, I would have agreed to it then too. It's not about being a man, Arro."

"It's about being a badass," I murmured. Because let's face it, my sister was a *badass*.

"Exactly," Thane agreed with me. "No, I was talking to Regan ... Yes, she agrees ... Arro, I love you, but I'm tired and I don't want to argue over semantics. Eilidh and Lewis can stay with you if Mac is there, and I don't care if that makes me an arsehole. All I care about is feeling comfortable with the idea of my children staying somewhere not under my roof. Mac's presence makes me comfortable." His expression softened. "Thank you ... yeah ... I'll drop them off ... or you can pick them up ... Yeah, that's fine ... Good ... okay ... yeah... love you too." He hung up and gave me a look. "Sisters."

I grinned. "You wouldn't change her for the world."

Thane grunted, but I knew I was right.

~

THANE

Lowering down to his haunches, Thane pulled Eilidh into his arms and brushed wisps of hair back from her face. "You excited to stay with Aunt Arrochar?"

He just wanted to be certain, now that it was happening, that his children really were fine with being out from under his roof for the first time since McClintock's attack.

Resilient as ever, Eilidh beamed. "We're going to put the tree up and bake cookies and watch Santy Claus movies andandand and Aunt Arro says we might watch *Nightmare of Christmas* this year!"

Understanding she meant *The Nightmare Before Christmas*, Thane looked up at his sister who was joking around with Lewis. He glanced at Mac who watched him in his usual intense way. Mac Galbraith saw everything. Mac shook his head as if to say, "I won't let them watch it," but Thane wanted it clear to Arro.

"Arro," he said, drawing her attention, "they're not watching that movie."

His sister practically pouted. "But it's my favorite, and surely they're old enough now. Lachlan let me watch it when I was Eilidh's age."

"And then had to let you sleep in his bed that night because you had nightmares."

She frowned. "I don't remember that."

"Well, I do. Another five years."

"Five years." She shot Mac a look and whatever she saw in his face, she sighed and turned to Thane. "Five years," she promised in disappointment.

"But I want to watch it, Daddy." Eilidh frowned and then gave him the monster voice. "*Now.*"

"No," he growled back and then pretended to bite her face and neck and tickled her with his beard and kisses until her peals of giggles rang through the house. Best sound in the goddamn world.

Movie forgotten, Thane hugged Lewis and kissed him on the head. "Be good." Not that his son was anything but. Lew was his wee serious angel and Eilidh his charming wee devil.

"They'll be fine," Arro assured him as Mac took the kids into the kitchen to get started on the baking.

"It's good of Mac to do this. I'll thank him later."

"It's not a hardship for him," Arro said defensively.

Thane nodded. "I know. He loves the kids."

She smirked. "Right."

"Eh?"

"Nothing." She pulled him into her arms and gave him a squeeze. "Go. Enjoy your free night. Have a whisky with Lachlan or something."

As Thane got into his car a few seconds later and drove back toward Caelmore, he was agitated but knew leaving the children with Arro was the right thing for them. They had to keep acting normal, or they would think there was still something to be worried about.

A distraction, he mused. He needed a distraction.

And he knew exactly what kind of distraction that was.

For the first time since their affair started, Thane and

Regan had the house to themselves. They could be loud. And he planned on giving Regan many, many reasons to be very loud indeed.

Letting his mind wander to the woman in his life, to the frustrations of having to curb his instinct to reach for her throughout the day, to the worries that they had less than two months left before her visa was up, Thane became focused on one thing: making tonight a night she'd never forget.

An almost savage possessiveness gripped him.

"Hey." Regan turned to him from the dining table when he strode into the house. "I'm just setting the table—" Her next words were swallowed in his kiss.

She tasted of chocolate. Sometimes he saw her sneak a piece before dinner but never in front of Eilidh and Lewis. She wanted to be a good example. Always thinking about them, loving them, protecting them. Him too. And in less than eight weeks, she'd be gone. And he would feel her loss more deeply than he could admit to himself most days.

Throwing the painful inevitability of the future out of his mind, Thane kissed her harder and Regan whimpered, her tongue stroking his in return.

And Thane was lost.

His kiss turned hungry as desperation came over him, and he pressed his body down the length of hers. He gripped her ass, urging her closer, his arousal straining against her belly. His hand slid down the back of her thigh, and he hiked up one leg against his hip so he could be where he needed to be, snugly between her legs.

Fuck, he loved her little dresses, but he hated the goddamn tights she wore with them.

"Thane," she panted, breaking the kiss. Her head fell back and her eyes fluttered with the sensation of him thrusting against her. Her cheeks were flushed as she moaned and dug her hands into his shoulders. She flexed her hips against his, and his nerve endings caught fire.

He needed inside her. Now.

Knowing how wildly she responded to him when he was rough, Thane stepped back but only to spin her around and bend her over his kitchen table. Lust was a haze across his mind as she cried out. He gripped her nape and pressed her down into the table while his other hand pushed up her dress and ripped at her tights.

She pushed against him as if to get up.

"Stay down," he panted as he unzipped himself.

Regan trembled beneath him, whimpering. She pushed up again, and he assumed she was arching into him, ready to take him.

Remembering how hotly she reacted to him holding her wrists down in bed, he pressed her back down and shoved his way between her legs.

"No!" she suddenly cried out, pushing forcefully against him. "No!" This time the word broke on a sob.

Her panic was the equivalent of ten buckets of ice over his head and body. Thane released but gently reached for her, her sobs scoring through him. He felt like he had razor blades in his throat as he choked out an anxious, *"Mo leannan."*

But Regan shoved at his hands, crying, her face red and streaked with tears.

Thane retreated completely. Regan pushed off the table and ran past him upstairs.

Chest heaving as he attempted to catch his breath, pulse racing, Thane tried to figure out what the hell had gone wrong so quickly. He'd been rough with her before—she'd told him she loved it when he lost control. He'd taken her on her hands and knees many times ... he'd even held her down.

Thane looked at the table.

Always in bed.

They'd never had sex anywhere but in bed.

Fear churned in his gut.

He'd triggered her.

And someone was going to fucking die if it was for the reason he feared it might be.

~

REGAN

Panic clawed at my throat, and I couldn't catch my breath. The memory had hit like a lightning bolt as soon as Thane pushed me onto the table and told me to stay down. Then the terror was all I felt. It didn't matter that it was Thane and that I loved him and knew he'd never hurt me. All I could remember was that night in Ho Chi Minh City a year ago. A night I'd buried so deep inside, I'd forgotten about it.

Sobbing in the guest-room bathroom, I couldn't get a handle on the violent heaving of my chest, and while no more tears fell, I couldn't catch my breath. The more I panicked about it, the worse it got. Oh my God, I was going to die.

I'm going to die, I'm going to die, I'm going to die. Tears blurred my vision.

"Regan, breathe." Suddenly Thane was on his knees before me. "You're hyperventilating, *mo leannan*. Cup your hands."

I heaved for breath, staring at him, unfocused, confused.

He cupped his hands around his mouth. "Like this. Try to concentrate on breathing slowly into your hands. Look at me."

Hands shaking, I watched him as he took slow breaths in and out. A calm filtered through the chaos in my head, and I mimicked him. Eventually my breathing calmed, and the terror dissipated.

But the reality remained.

All that I'd buried, deep, deep within … it wasn't buried anymore. And there was no escaping it because I could tell looking into Thane's sad, worried eyes that he knew. Exhausted, I crawled toward him and rested my head on his chest.

His arms came around me as he sighed with relief.

He then lifted me off the bathroom floor. Looping my arms around his neck, I let him carry me into the bedroom.

"Okay?" he asked before settling us on it.

Tormented that he felt he had to ask, I sucked back more tears and nodded.

He laid back against the pillows and pulled me into his arms, and I snuggled into his chest. "I'm sorry." His words were rough with emotion. "I didn't mean to frighten you."

I shook my head as I met his eyes. "Don't. You did nothing differently from what we've done before."

Thane's eyes narrowed. "It was the table, wasn't it?"

I flinched as an image hit, my face pressed to the sideboard in that hotel room in Vietnam. Focusing on Thane's eyes, I admitted, "Yes."

Distress ravaged his features and he choked out, "Did someone rape you, Regan?"

A tear slipped down my cheek as I curled a fist into his shirt. "Almost."

Thane's eyes brightened with sadness, but rage too. "Was it him?"

I nodded, and every time I blinked, another tear fell.

26

REGAN

H*o Chi Minh City*
Last New Year's Eve

District 3 was loud with music, voices, laughter, screams, and drunken revelry. We were delighted when we discovered the Vietnamese celebrated the Gregorian New Year. None of us wanted to miss it. Now I wished more than ever I'd gone back home to Boston to celebrate with Robyn and Mom and Dad. Instead, I'd stayed and made a mess of everything.

Western New Year was over, but with Lunar New Year upcoming on February 1, the city was still bright with color and celebration. I stared forlornly down at the streets filled with people and lights and lanterns. Vietnam knew how to celebrate in style. I'd never seen anything like it. The lights that hung from the buildings and lampposts and wound around the trees were on par with the most impressive Christmas displays. The lights on the street below looked like bright pink flowers and golden birds, while streams of fairy lights sparkled between them. It was truly something.

And yet, here I was, alone in my crappy hotel room because I'd stupidly slept with Austin Vale on New Year's Eve.

Our friends had gone to a party tonight. I'd tagged along, thinking surely Austin had gotten my not-so-subtle hints that our drunken night together was a mistake. What had been annoyingly clingy behavior since had degenerated into obsessive. I finally blew up at him tonight when he got in my face for flirting with another tourist. I hated that he pushed me, and I was mean to him. Or that Desi's boyfriend, Liam, had to tell Austin to back off and then walk me back to the hotel because my night was ruined. At least Austin knew the score now. I just hoped he'd give me a wide berth or I might have to ditch my backpacking companions.

They were a fun group, but I realized I wouldn't really miss any of them if I left.

Maybe that was a sign I should leave.

That I should finally pull my shit together and face my big sister.

She hates you.

Tears burned my eyes. "I'd hate me too," I muttered.

Robyn would never have needed a guy to walk her back to her hotel room. She'd never sit on a strange, crappy bed that thousands of other people had slept on, wallowing in self-pity.

"You're sad without me."

The familiar voice made me jump. My heart thumped in my throat as I launched up off the bed, spinning to face Austin. He closed the hotel room door behind him and turned the lock.

"How did you get in here?"

"You taught me how to pick a lock, remember?" He grinned, waving a couple of bobby pins.

Damn it. So I had. A few months ago, in Spain, Austin and

I had worked together at this bar in Málaga. The boss was a creepy British guy, a total asshole. He kept a locked room on the premises, and it became a running joke among a few of us. We'd hazard guesses about what he kept in there, the guesses growing scarier as the weeks went on.

On our last night on the job, Austin and I had a couple of shots for kicks and I told him I could pick locks. I'd read about it as a teen and then practiced until I'd perfected it. I'd taught Robyn how to do it too. That night, I showed Austin, and we broke into the room to find it filled with stock we'd never seen. Expensive cases of whisky and gin, boxes of cigarettes, and cash. Lots of cash. Realizing there was probably something criminal going on, we got the hell out of there and hoped the boss didn't have a security camera in the room.

The next day we were on a bus to Italy, anyway.

And Austin had learned a new skill.

Well done, Regan.

"I want you to leave." My voice shook.

"Not until you tell me you feel the same way. Because I know you do." There was a light in his eyes I'd never seen before. Utter faith. Utter belief.

In us.

Oh my God. He was delusional.

"Austin, we're just friends. Sleeping together was a mistake. I don't want to be in a relationship with you. I'm sorry if that hurts your feelings, but that's just the way it is. Now please leave, or I'm going to call the police."

"Good. Call them. Because if you don't try to love me back, I'm going to kill myself."

Aghast, I stared at him like I'd never seen him before. I felt like I hadn't. We'd been in each other's company for months, and I'd always thought he was just a good guy. Laid-back, great sense of humor, kind of a cute nerd. We had zero chemistry, so I'd only ever seen him as a friend, which was why I was so angry at myself for sleeping with him while drunk. I never would've imagined this would happen after sleeping with him, though. Never.

"You're obviously drunk, right? 'Cause you're talking crazy."

"Don't call me crazy." He gave me a dark look. "It's politically incorrect and incredibly insensitive."

I narrowed my eyes. "So if I'm insensitive ... what do you call a person who tries to emotionally manipulate someone into being in a relationship with them?"

"I'm not trying to manipulate you. I'm telling you how I'll feel, knowing you're denying the truth between us. I don't know what you're running from, Regan, but you don't have to run from me." He crossed the room, and I backed up, my hands raised defensively.

"Don't touch me." I warned. He kept coming. "Austin, don't touch me!" But he reached for me, so I planted my hands on his chest and shoved. "Get away from me!"

"Why are you fighting this?" he asked calmly as we grappled.

Fear and panic set in. I tried to get away from him, but he gripped my wrists tightly in his fists. I kicked at him; he cursed and jerked out of the way, my foot just missing a direct hit to his balls, but he never once let go. He was freakishly strong.

"Let go of me!" I shrieked.

"Not until you come to your senses."

He was so calm. So collected. Even as I struggled in his arms like a wild animal.

I couldn't get past the self-flagellating thoughts that I should have listened to Robyn when she told me to take self-defense classes. *Why didn't I listen to you, Robbie?*

Tears escaped before I could stop them, and Austin tsked, pulling me into his body. "Shh, don't cry. I know it's hard to make yourself vulnerable, but you can be vulnerable with me. I love you so much."

Rage flooded me, and I brought my knee up hard into his gut. His grip on me loosened as he grunted in pain, and I shoved him off, pushing past him, lunging toward the door.

A strong arm banded around my waist a mere second later. "No!" I shouted as I was hauled back against him. He was too strong. How was he so strong? "Stop it!"

"You stop it," he hissed angrily in my ear as he struggled to hold on to me. "I tried to be nice. But it's time to teach you who is in charge here, Regan." Then he swiped a hand across the top of the sideboard where my roommate and I kept our stuff. My perfume bottle smashed on the wooden floor, the smell at once cloying.

"No!" I pushed against the arm that was crushing me, kicking out with one leg, and suddenly feeling nothing but air beneath me seconds before I found myself bent over the sideboard. The breath was knocked out of me as it slammed into my gut. As I struggled to draw breath, I was vaguely aware of the throbbing in my cheek where my face had smacked off the top of it.

I tasted blood.

"You're going to remember what it's like between us, Regan." I heard Austin say over the buzzing in my ears.

Air tickled my backside, and I realized my dress had been shoved up to my waist.

A sense of unreality descended over me as I felt my underwear tear.

No.

This wasn't happening to me.

This happened to other people.

It couldn't be happening to me.

I heard his zipper.

No!

309

I tried to push up off the sideboard, but he had my arms splayed over my head, my wrists crossed, holding me down with one hand, while he used his other—

"No," I whispered hoarsely, pushing against his hold. He had me pinned with the weight of his entire body. *No.*

"Stay down," he demanded.

"No." My voice got louder as I tried to dislodge him with my hips.

"Stay down!"

And then I felt him, ready, pushing between my legs.

Nausea rose up from my gut.

And rage.

I lifted my head and chest just enough, and I screamed as loud as I could. "HELP!"

"Shut up!"

"HELP ME!"

"Regan?!" a girl shouted from the hallway.

Desi.

"DESI, HEL—"

A large, sweaty hand covered my mouth, cutting me off. "Shut up, or I'll kill—what the fuck!"

A loud banging drew my terrified gaze to the door. It shook against the jamb. Another pound and it broke away, splintering off the door frame, flying open into the room.

A frantic Liam and Desi appeared, and I sobbed in relief against Austin's hand.

"You motherfucker!" Liam lunged at Austin and then his weight was off me.

I was aware of Desi's gentle hands on me, of her smoothing my dress down to cover me, her embrace as she held me while Liam threw Austin out of the room. Their words of concern, their questions, became like gnats in my ear, buzzing around.

I was already somewhere else in my mind, planning my escape from Vietnam, from what had just happened.

Nothing happened, I whispered.

Nothing had happened.

You're okay.

Nothing happened here.

27
REGAN

P*resent day*

"Liam and Desi wanted to get the police ... and I should have." I couldn't meet Thane's eyes. "I should have been brave and stayed and pressed charges, but all I could think about was running. Getting as far away from Austin as possible. If I could get away, then it never happened. So that's what I did."

Thane's silence made my heart throb with renewed fear.

Now he knew.

I was a coward.

Finally, I looked up into his eyes. He was furious.

My stomach dropped. "I'm sorry," I whispered.

"You," he bit out hoarsely, "have nothing to be sorry for. I just ... I wish you'd told me. Then what happened downstairs ..."

"No." I reached for his face, scrambling into his lap to straddle him. "No, Thane, no. What we have," I whispered against his mouth, fresh tears falling, "it's the most beautiful thing I've ever had in my life. I don't want this to taint it."

He gripped my hips, squeezing. "Why didn't you tell me, then? Why did you lie to me and Robyn about what happened in that hotel room?"

Shame was this sickening ball in my gut. "Because ... I'm not strong like you. Or Robbie. I'm not brave. And I thought if I just pretended it didn't happen, then he wouldn't have any power over me. I guess I got so good at pretending ... that I really buried it. I buried it like it was just a nightmare. Until now. It flooded up and out of that deep, dark pit I'd put it in."

"*Mo leannan.*" Thane cupped my face in his hands. "Our brains are strange and complicated. But when we bury things that shouldn't be buried, our subconscious always pushes it back into the daylight. And now that it is"—his expression was tender but wary—"you can't pretend anymore. We have to deal with it. And you must tell Robyn. You have to press charges."

I tried to pull away, but he slid his hand around my nape to gently but firmly stop me.

"Please, *mo leannan*. Or I'm going to kill the motherfucker."

It wasn't a threat said in an angry but teasing manner.

He sounded extremely serious.

"You're going to fly to the US to kill him?" I tried to ease the tension between us.

Thane didn't think any of it was funny. "He tried to rape you. He stalked you. And he made you feel like a coward, which you're not."

I looked away.

He took hold of my chin to turn me back to him. "You are strong. You are brave. And I won't let him make you feel like his victim." He nodded. "Yes?"

Considering this, considering the rage I felt in that room, and then how I'd buried what he'd done so deeply that I'd served coffee to that piece of shit for weeks after, something hard and determined slid through me. "You're right."

Pressing a sweet, grateful kiss to his mouth, I sighed into him. "Thank you."

"I did nothing," he said gruffly.

"You did. You were you." I kissed him a little deeper, and his hands flexed on my hips.

"We shouldn't. You should rest."

"I don't want to rest." I kissed his cheek through his beard, peppering soft kisses down his strong throat. "I want to make love to you. All you have to do is sit there and take it."

Searching my gaze for truth, Thane hesitated.

He didn't trust me. Didn't trust me with my own emotions.

How could I blame him?

My inner question made me freeze over him.

Just because I'd buried a trauma didn't mean I didn't know myself.

I *knew* myself.

I glared at him. "Don't patronize me."

"I didn't." He frowned. "I didn't say a word."

"You don't trust me."

"It's not that. I just think it's too soon right now."

"For who?" I slipped off him and slid from the bed. "Me? Or you?"

"Regan." I heard him scramble to get off the bed, but I was already out of the room.

Just as we were about to pass his room, he caught up and pulled me to a stop. "Regan, don't take this out on me. Please."

I glowered at him. "You know what you don't do when the woman you're sleeping with tells you she was almost raped? You don't sexually reject her afterward. It tends to make her feel like used goods."

Thane jerked like I'd punched him. "I never meant it like that."

Remorse flooded me. "I know. I'm just ..."

"I know." He hauled me into his arms, hugging me tight. "Let's take a breath. We'll go downstairs and have some dinner. Yeah?"

I nodded, though I still felt a little rejected.

Rational or not.

Thane took my hand and led me downstairs.

We avoided the kitchen table and ate dinner in front of the TV for once.

The atmosphere was strange between us. Thane kept us physically connected, snuggling with me on the sofa, kissing my head now and then, caressing my arm. And that night when we went to bed, he took me to his.

My heart was in my throat as he switched off the lights and hauled me back against him. I waited.

"Good night."

I couldn't say good night.

I was choking back tears.

Either he didn't want me anymore or he didn't trust me to know what I wanted.

Neither felt wonderful.

Wanting nothing more than to cry myself to sleep, I felt suffocated by his arms because his presence meant I had to hold it in, and now that I wasn't holding anything in, I never wanted to bury my feelings like that again. It was too painful once they exploded. The awful panic attack in the bathroom was proof of that.

Pressing my lips together to stifle the sobs, the tears rolled down my cheeks, hidden in the dark.

So busy concentrating on not making a sound, I didn't

feel Thane tense against me. Seconds later, however, I heard him whisper hoarsely in my ear, "You kill me, *mo leannan*."

And then I was turned as if weightless and hauled over Thane's body as he fell onto his back. My palms landed on his chest and I straddled him in the dark. As my vision adjusted to the shadows, I made him out through the moon-light peeking in around the window blinds.

"Take whatever you need."

Relief flooded me as he grew hard beneath me. An answering throb pulsed between my legs, and I reached for the hem of my nightdress, pulling it off, followed by my underwear.

Thane reached for my bare hips, his long, strong fingers caressing and squeezing as he undulated gently under me. I lifted off him but only to yank down his pajama bottoms and underwear just far enough to free him.

Then I pushed down onto him, and our gasps filled the room as his thickness filled me.

"So good," I panted, leaning over to brace my hands on his shoulders.

"Take it," he grunted, gripping my hips harder now. "Take everything you need."

Wanting his hands everywhere at once, I opted for moving them from my hips to my breasts. Thane groaned and massaged them, his thumbs plucking at my nipples.

"Yes, yes," I gasped, riding him slow but deep. When I twisted my hips at a certain angle, he hit me exactly where I needed him. My hands curled into his shoulders for better purchase as I grew more desperate for the exquisite tension building inside me.

"Fuck." Thane squeezed my breasts harder as his hips flexed under me, his movements constrained by his pajamas and boxers.

It made me hotter. Knowing I could do whatever I wanted to him.

Bending to his powerful chest, I licked at his nipples and then sucked before I bit him gently.

His hips bucked under me and then he sat up, changing the angle of my drives, roughly pulling my hair back so he could clamp his mouth over my breast. The relief of him playing with me as he always had excited me more than anything. We hadn't changed.

He wouldn't let us change.

My fingers scraped through his hair as his mouth tormented me, and my hips picked up pace. Thane released me to lift his head to mine, and we stared into each other's eyes as I rode him. We held gazes, his hot and desire filled, tender, and mine the mirror image.

My fingernails bit into his back as I increased my pace, the pleasure building higher, higher, our breaths mingling as we panted against each other's mouths.

And then that tightening coil inside me snapped, and I arched my neck, crying out my release, Thane's lips pressing against my throat seconds before he groaned in climax.

I shook, trembling as the orgasm melted through my limbs. As I throbbed around Thane's pulses, he kissed me. Deep, possessive, wet kisses that fired my blood.

"Again," I said against his mouth.

He grinned. "I'm not twenty anymore, *mo leannan*. You'll need to give me ten minutes."

I shoved him none too gently back on the bed and slipped off with a little gasp that made him grunt. Then I shifted down his body, pulling his pajamas and boxers all the way off. And I kissed my way back up.

Thane laughed softly in the dark. But his amusement died when my kisses reached his inner thigh. I teased and tormented him until he was begging for my mouth where he wanted it most. And before I gave it to him, I smirked. "That was less than ten minutes."

He gave a bark of laughter that cut off with an abrupt "Jesus!" as I took him deep into my mouth.

We made love until light streamed into the room through the blinds and then finally, exhausted, we collapsed in each other's arms. As sleep drifted over me, I smiled, our shouts of pleasure still ringing in my ears. It was like I'd marked him tonight. Made him mine in a way he could never be anyone else's.

While he had given me exactly what I needed—the reminder that what Austin did to me and what I'd unintentionally done to myself could never taint the connection I had with Thane Adair.

And just maybe ... maybe we wouldn't turn out to be temporary after all.

The next morning when I woke up, the first face I saw wasn't Thane's; he was behind me, cuddling me in his sleep. No, the first face I saw was Francine Adair's, grinning from Thane's lap in the photo on his nightstand.

Just like that, the hopes I'd gone to sleep with—while early-morning dusk and the musky scent of sex-exhausted bodies clouded my reality—deflated.

28

THANE

He couldn't remember the last time he'd slept in this late, but he wouldn't chastise himself for it. And last night had been bloody worth it. Just when he thought sex with Regan couldn't get any better, she'd devoured him, barely letting him up for air.

He grinned, feeling their workout in his muscles as he stretched. Regan had slipped from the bed to use the bathroom a few minutes ago, and he anticipated her return with hot blood in his veins.

Unbelievably, he wanted her again.

Rolling onto his elbow as she emerged from the bathroom in her nightdress, he let his eyes roam over her, his chest swelling with emotion. She was so beautiful, inside and out. Stronger than she gave herself credit for. After she'd revealed her attack, he never imagined they'd spend the night the way they had. But she clearly refused to let that son of a bitch screw with her head any more than he already had, and Thane knew he had to follow her lead on this. He was proud of her.

He opened his mouth to tell her so, but as she neared the

bed, he noted her eyes weren't on him. They were on his nightstand.

Thane looked over to see what had her attention and then froze.

A quick glance back at Regan confirmed his fears.

She was staring morosely at the photo of Fran and him.

It had always been there. Thane had never had reason or want to move it.

But guilt suddenly gnawed at him as Regan dropped her gaze.

"I'm going to put the coffee on." She didn't look at him. Just threw a small smile in his general direction before leaving the room.

It wasn't the first time he'd caught Regan looking at the picture. It was, however, the first time he felt like he'd done something wrong by leaving it there.

Sitting up, Thane scrubbed a hand over his face as he contemplated the situation.

If it were the other way around and he'd spent all night in Regan's bed only to wake up to the photo of another man on her nightstand—his gut clenched at the thought.

Looking back at the picture, he exhaled slowly.

~

REGAN

The photo of Fran was gone.

When Thane didn't come downstairs for his coffee, I sucked it up, deciding I was being a jealous, selfish moron. Last night he'd taken a night that could have gone down as one of the worst of my life and turned into one of the best.

With mugs in hand, I ventured upstairs, determined to shove my confused thoughts about Fran to the back of my head.

When I returned to the bedroom, Thane was dressed in his pjs and sitting on the end of the bed with his head in his hands.

And the photo on his nightstand was gone.

Contrition filled me. I placed the coffee on the now-empty spot and sat down beside him. "You moved the photo."

Thane lifted his head and nodded. "It was time."

"I didn't mean to be obvious about it ... or make you feel bad."

"The photos bother you." He sighed.

"Not all of them. Fran is Eilidh and Lewis's mom. Your first love. She should be here in the house with them, with you. I ... the one on the nightstand is ... it's different from the ones downstairs. Those are about you all as a family. That one is about you and her. I ... I'm not going to lie and say it doesn't make me jealous." I couldn't meet his eyes. "But it also makes me hurt for you. Fran was obviously the love of your life, and you clearly can't move on from her, and I don't want that for you. I don't want you to not be able to love again."

"You got all that from a picture on a nightstand?" His question was defensive, harsh, and it drew my gaze. He glared at me, and I glowered back.

"Not just that. You never talk about how she died. Ever. Why is it such a big secret?"

Thane shook his head, confused. "It's not a big secret. I assumed you knew. That one of the family told you or that Robyn told you as soon as you got here."

Now I was confused. "You haven't been keeping it from me?"

"Why would I?" He turned to me. "I don't talk about it

because it was the worst thing I've ever experienced ... but that's different from keeping it from you."

Fear coiled in my gut. *God, Thane, what happened?* I wanted to ask, but not after what he'd just said. I didn't want to torment him because I was screwed up over loving a man who didn't want to love me back.

Thane sat up straight and stared around the room. Finally, he said, "Everything is different in here. The rest of the house is decorated pretty much as Fran and I decorated it together. But this room ... I had to change it. Paint, floors, blinds, furniture ..." He glanced over his shoulder, a haunted look on his face. "New bed, new mattress ... She died in our bed," he announced abruptly, and I sucked in a harsh breath.

At the awful look in his eyes, my tears spilled over.

"One morning the alarm went off as it always did, and I woke up. I thought Fran was still asleep ... but as I started to wake up properly, I realized there was an unnatural stillness about her.

"She was just ... gone." I saw his disbelief. "And I was in a nightmare. How do you go to sleep with your wife breathing beside you ... and wake up and her body is there, but she's not in it anymore?"

The pain I felt for him burst out in a sob before I could stop it, and he reached for me, catching my tears on his thumbs.

"It was a brain aneurysm," he whispered. "Died in her sleep. Peaceful, they told me. A peaceful way to go. For her. And for that, I will forever be grateful."

"But it was horrific for you." I didn't need to guess. If one day I woke up to find Thane no longer breathing beside me, I'd lose my goddamn mind. "You're so strong." I reached for him, peppering tear-soaked kisses over his face.

He returned those kisses with deeper, more intentional ones.

"Thane"—I tried to move away from him—"maybe we shouldn't." Not after what he'd just told me.

"Francine is not a ghost in this bed." He lifted me under my arms and threw me gently on it. I gasped as he came down over me, his features harsh with need. "And I won't let her become that for you."

~

THANE

Making love to Regan wasn't just about distracting him from memories he'd rather not linger on or making sure she didn't let the truth of Fran's death mess with her head regarding what was between them in this bed.

It was Regan's tears. Her visceral, unconstrained reaction to his pain.

That she might care enough about him to want to stay. And maybe she did. Maybe now, at this moment, she did.

But Thane couldn't trust her mind wouldn't change in a few months or a year or even a few years' time. If he let himself believe in what sparked between them, she'd eventually destroy him.

So he needed to lose himself in her body, in the distraction of their passion.

And mostly, he needed to let go of the self-reproach that plagued him. Remorse for Fran. For her memory. Because as much as he'd never forget what it was like to love her or grieve her … Thane had moved on.

He'd moved on in a way that shook him to his core.

29

REGAN

"**L** ew, remember your homework," I said as he and Eilidh made their way toward the front door.

"Got it," he mumbled.

"Then what's that on the dining table?" I rounded the island and hurried to pick up his math booklet.

I was just tucking it into his backpack as he waited patiently and Eilidh not so patiently announced she wanted to be at school already because "they were writing letters to Santy Claus today" when the doorbell rang seconds before it opened.

Lachlan stepped into the house.

"Uncle Lach-Lach!" Eilidh lunged at him, and he swung her up into his arms. She wrapped her little arms and mitten-covered hands around his neck. "What are you doing here?"

"Princess Eilidh, I am taking you and your brother to school this morning."

He was? "You are?"

Lachlan's azure gaze turned to me. He seemed to study

me as he nodded. "Robyn needs a word. I thought I could take the kids before I head to the castle."

My stomach flipped. I knew what that word was most likely about. Yesterday, I'd asked to speak with her alone, and I'd taken her for a walk on the beach to tell her about Austin's attack in Vietnam. I tried my best to explain that I wasn't intentionally keeping it from her, like I'd explained to Thane. I think she understood. Plus, I told her what triggered it, which meant I revealed my affair with Thane, and my sister was not in the least surprised. She said she already suspected, and Lachlan had made a few comments to her that he suspected the same thing. Panicked about him finding out without Thane's say-so, I made her promise not to confirm it. She was so dazed and angry about Austin, I didn't even know if she remembered agreeing to it.

I knew she was furious at Austin, but I was also afraid she was hiding how mad she was at *me*. She said his attack completely changed the profile she had on him. It took his threat level up a couple hundred notches.

Pulse racing, I stared back at Lachlan. "Oh. Okay."

He nodded and looked at Lewis as he held out his car keys. "Lew, you want to open the Rover and get your sister buckled in?"

Lewis took the keys from his uncle and asked with a weary sigh, "When will she be old enough to buckle herself in?"

Eilidh wriggled out of Lachlan's hold, her expression mulish. "I'll buckle myself in now!"

Her brother hurried after her out the door. "You can't, Eilidh. You won't do it right!"

"I will too!"

"Will not!"

Their voices grew distant as they ran down onto the drive

where I knew Lachlan's security guys were already waiting to escort the kids to school.

All the while, Lachlan stared at me. I squirmed, knowing by the hard but tender glint in his eyes, much like his brother's, that Robyn had talked to him. "She told you."

He gave me a grim nod.

I shrugged, feeling vulnerable. "I'm fine. He didn't rape me. Other people have had it way worse. Look at Robbie. She's been shot three times, attacked, and almost murdered by a psycho."

Lachlan didn't smile at my nervous facetiousness. Instead, he took a step toward me, his voice low as he replied, "And yet, she handled all that like a pro but cried herself to sleep in my arms last night."

Emotion choked me, tears flooding my eyes at the thought of my sister's heart breaking over me. And suddenly, I knew why.

Yesterday, she wasn't angry with me. She was angry with herself.

Damn it, Robyn!

It was not her job to protect me all the time. I shook my head. "She takes on too much."

"It's who she is. It's why we love her. But—and I know I probably don't need to ask this—I want you to do your best to convince her she didn't fail you. Because right now, she's next door kicking her own arse, and nothing I say seems to penetrate."

Seeing his concern and frustration for her, I swiftly crossed the room and hugged him.

Lachlan seemed surprised at first, hesitant, and then he wrapped his arms around me and gave me a sweet kiss upon the head.

I smiled and whispered, "Thank you for loving her the way she deserves to be loved."

His arms tightened just a fraction, and when I pulled away, I saw emotion brighten his eyes.

God, what a gift to be loved by an Adair man. They could be infuriating sometimes, but Lachlan with Robyn and Thane with Francine were proof that when they loved you, they loved you with everything they were.

I'd never been such a confusing mix of gloriously happy for my sister and so envious at the same time.

"I'll talk to her," I promised.

"Good." He brushed my cheek affectionately, like a big brother might, and I decided it was really nice. "I better get the kids to school. You okay?"

I nodded. "I'm going to be fine. I promise."

That promise didn't seem to alleviate his concern, but he had to leave and I had to go see my sister.

I didn't bother knocking. I strode into the house, calling Robyn's name, and when she came hurrying downstairs, I didn't let her speak. I rushed her, throwing my arms around her. "Robyn Penhaligon, what happened to me was not your fault. You didn't fail me, and I won't ever think that. Ever."

"I know that," she murmured, not letting me go.

We swayed a little in each other's arms at the bottom of the stairs. "Then why did Lachlan tell me you cried last night?"

She stiffened and then sighed into me. "He is such a meddler."

Grinning, I shook my head. "Well?"

Retreating, Robyn brushed my hair behind my ear. Turmoil roiled in her eyes, turning them a smoky gray. "I was so mad at you," she whispered, remorse etched into every feature. "That entire time I was angry at you and judging you and feeling like I didn't know you anymore ... and all the time you needed me. You *really* needed me. And I should have tried harder to track you down. I should have known something wasn't right."

"No." I grabbed her hands, squeezing them, my words fierce. "We will not do this. We will not go around and around about the past two years. We both did the best we could at that time. If we feel now like we can do better going forward, great. But we can't go back, and I won't let us self-flagellate over the mistakes. Not when we're here, right here together, closer than ever, despite it all. It's pointless, Robbie. It's not worth it."

She swiped at a wayward tear, shaking her head, something like awe in her eyes. "When did my little sister get so wise?"

"I learned from my big sister."

"No, you're outwisdoming your big sister right now."

"Outwisdoming?" I teased, pulling her into the kitchen. "Come on, we need coffee."

"I'll make it. You sit." Her tone turned serious again. "I have something I need to tell you."

My stomach flipped again as I settled on a stool at the island. "Yeah, Lachlan said. Is it about Austin?"

Robyn glanced over as she switched on the coffee machine. "It is."

"Is it bad?"

"Please don't be angry with me."

I tensed. "Okay …"

"I told Seth."

"Dad?" Horror flooded me. "Why would you tell Dad?"

"Because …" Robyn squeezed her eyes closed. "The day after McClintock attempted to kidnap Eilidh, Seth tried to call you and couldn't get you because of everything going on. So he called me instead. And he mentioned that a man named Austin Vale came to the house looking for you. Said he was a friend you went backpacking with, and he'd just gotten back to Boston and was looking you up."

Nausea roiled in my gut.

Robyn's eyes changed color, golden now with anger. "The fucker lied. Getting antsy waiting for you to come back to Boston. Thankfully, Seth is a paranoid cop and didn't tell him where you were. But I had to explain to him who Austin is. He and Mom need to know that Austin is a danger to you. Seth said he's going to look into the guy's finances to make sure he isn't in the position to come chasing you across the Atlantic."

"Dad never mentioned it." I'd spoken to him several times in the past few weeks. He and Mom were coming to Scotland for the Christmas holidays, courtesy of Lachlan. Dad was having trouble accepting that kind of generosity, but I told him it would be good for them to see how happy Robyn was here.

And our relationship with Mom wasn't the best. We both still had unresolved issues there. I didn't want that. I wanted us to move past them. Now all my worries about seeing Mom at Christmas paled compared to the news that Austin hadn't let go of his obsession.

"His attack on you changes everything. I had to tell Seth, and he's going to call you today. Be prepared because he's going to ask you to press formal charges."

I shook my head, anger and frustration bubbling inside me now. Thane had asked me to do the same thing, and I'd avoided responding. "You of all people know how hard it is to get those charges to stick under normal circumstances. Accusing him of attempted rape in a foreign country a year ago?" I glowered at her. "They'll laugh at me."

"No one is going to laugh at you. But Seth is right ... if Austin hasn't let his obsession with you go, then we need this on record. The charges will more than likely be dismissed before it even gets to court due to lack of evidence, but if we can track down Liam and Desi as witnesses, we might have a shot. And even if we can't and the charges are dismissed, it will be on his record."

"So that if anything else happens ..." I trailed off, shuddering at the thought of anything else happening.

"Nothing is going to. He can't get to you here. I need you to be brave one more time, Regan, and do this, not for me or your dad, but for yourself."

Even though the thought made me want to puke, I knew I couldn't run from it anymore. "Okay."

Satisfied, Robyn gave me a nod and a look that said she was proud of me, and I had to admit, it felt great to make her proud.

After she made the coffee and slipped onto a stool next to me, she said, "I need you to do one more thing for me."

"And that would be?"

"I need you to consider talking to someone. Professionally."

Stiffening at a comment that seemed to come out of left field, I bristled. "You think I need to see a therapist?"

"Don't say it like that." She glared. "I went to therapy for months after I got shot."

"I didn't know that."

"Well, I did. I couldn't cope with it all on my own. I had nightmares about killing Eddie Johnstone."

Eddie Johnstone was the drug dealer who'd shot my sister. She'd fired back in self-defense and killed him.

"It all kind of snowballed. The shooting, my unhappiness with my job, why I became a cop, Mac's abandonment. Therapy was the reason I came to see my dad in the first place. I realized that I'd never have any sense of closure until I knew why he'd left me. Unfortunately," she said, heaving a sigh, "that opened up a whole new can of worms with Mom, but she and I are getting there. At least, we were getting there until I realized how much she'd screwed with *your* head over the years."

"It's just mom-and-daughter stuff," I assured her. "At least she loves us. Other people have it way worse in the parent department."

"True." Robyn nudged me with her shoulder. "My point is, therapy helped."

"And you think I need therapy?" The thought scared me.

As always, my sister read me like a book. "It's not a shameful thing to need, Regan. And you have a terrible habit of either physically or mentally running away from your emotions. You ran away from me because you couldn't deal with how frightened you were at the thought of losing me, and you ran away from your own memories of that night in Vietnam because you couldn't deal with the trauma. And I'm so afraid that you'll repeat it. Anytime life gets really hard or really sad, you'll push everyone away and lock your shit down so tight that one day, it will all explode out of you, and the results could be devastating."

I breathed a little harder because I knew she might be right, though at the same time certain she was wrong. "I won't run. I didn't run when McClintock tried to kidnap Eilidh. I'm not running now, even knowing Austin hasn't backed off like I'd hoped. I'm in love with a man who sees me as something temporary, and it hurts like hell, but I'm not running away."

Robyn's expression filled with sympathy as she squeezed my hand. "That's good. That's great. I'm proud of you, and I hope that doesn't come across as condescending."

"It doesn't."

"I still would like you to see someone. I won't pressure you. You have to make that decision on your own."

Covering her hand with mine, I nodded. "Then I promise I'll think about it."

We fell into silence and sipped our coffees while I pondered the huge conversations that had taken place between us in less than twenty-four hours.

Robyn looked at me. "You're in love with Thane?"

I grimaced. "I tried not to be."

She huffed, "Oh, sweetheart, I've been there. Those damn Adairs."

I snorted. "I know, right?"

We shared a commiserating look.

30

REGAN

To distract us, Robyn joined me while I went Christmas decoration shopping. I'd discovered Thane put up a real tree every year, and it was a tradition for them all to go pick one. However, I'd also learned that he only had one box of ornaments and another with some knickknacks. It seemed Fran hadn't been Christmas crazy like I am. But a large house like Thane's should be covered in festive cheer, so I bought more decorations.

By the time I hauled it all into the house, I was a little worried Thane might be irritated with me for taking it upon myself to buy holiday décor. However, when Thane stormed into the house five minutes after I'd hauled in all my purchases and half an hour before I needed to pick up the kids, it wasn't me he was angry at.

"What are you doing home early?" I tripped over a bag of tree baubles as I hurried out of the sitting room to meet him in the kitchen.

His scowl was as deep as a scowl could be, and it reminded me so much of Eilidh, I wondered how anyone could think he wasn't her dad. And then, like he'd plucked the thought from my mind, Thane barked, "Sean has demanded a DNA test."

Anxiety gripped me. "What?"

Thane waved a piece of paper at me. "From his lawyer. They're taking me to court to acquire a court-ordered paternity test to determine if Eilidh is his daughter."

"What?" I yelled now. "After what he did? Are they crazy?"

Thane threw the letter at the island and it fluttered onto the floor. I picked it up, smoothing it out to read the words written by McClintock's lawyer.

"I spoke with my lawyer on the drive home." Thane exhaled slowly, his hands to his hips, agitation vibrating from him. "She said that due to Sean's erratic behavior, it is unlikely Eilidh would ever be taken from my custody in the immediate future."

"Immediate future?"

That muscle ticked in his jaw as he tried to control his building fury. "Never mind the unbearable fucking idea of losing her later on down the line ... what do I tell her now, Regan? She's five years old—how do I explain this to her? Even if Sean doesn't get custody, what happens if legally she's not mine?"

His chest was heaving, and I could see he was panicking.

Our roles had flipped. Over the weekend, he'd calmed me down. Now it was my turn to be cool and collected and support him.

"Hey, hey, hey." I gripped his arms, forcing him to focus on me. "This will take weeks or even months to get to court, okay, so let's beat the bastards to it."

Thane stilled in my hold. "What do you mean?"

"We'll do it now. Under the radar. We'll take hair from Eilidh's hair brush, and we'll run our own DNA test. The results don't take long, and finally you'll know one way or the other and your lawyer will help you with a plan. Grief does not give him the right to come into your lives and hurt this family."

"No, but being her birth father does."

"Does it?" I snapped angrily. "Because where was he before this? I am truly devastated for the man that he lost his wife and child. It's horrifying ... but Eilidh isn't anybody's replacement. If he wanted her, then he should have tried to claim her long before this. She's claimed now. She's a goddamn Adair, and she isn't going anywhere."

Thane suddenly broke his hold, but only to haul me against him so he could crush my mouth beneath his in a devastating, hungry kiss. I was breathless when he finally released me. Thane pressed his forehead to mine and said, his voice thick with emotion, "Thank you, *mo leannan*."

His kiss, his words of gratitude, made me feel a thousand feet tall.

~

All I could think about over the next week was that damn DNA test. Thane had ordered the test online. It arrived the next day, and we'd surreptitiously collected the sample from Eilidh's hair brush and sent it off, along with Thane's. My worries about Austin were shoved to the back of my mind, and my plans to tell Thane pushed aside too. He already had too much on his plate. I didn't want to bother him with this.

We had lots to distract us. Well, at least, lots to *try* to distract us. Thane was bemused by my Christmas décor shopping spree, but when I dressed the house (leaving the tree for the children to decorate), he was more than happy with the results—especially with how excited and content it made Eilidh and Lewis.

"It's so beautiful!" Eilidh kept shouting as she wandered from room to room.

"I need to pay you back for all this. It must have cost a fortune," Thane had said, grinning as Eilidh tried to make Lewis as delighted over every little ornament as she was.

"It's my Christmas present to you all." I shrugged, staring around at my handiwork.

"You should do it professionally. Lachlan's decorator at Ardnoch couldn't have done a better job."

I smiled at the compliment, and even more so when he broke his own rule and pulled me into his side to kiss my temple in thanks.

That Wednesday was Robyn's birthday, and we had everyone over for dinner, which the kids always loved. Eilidh adored making people laugh, and she did it without even trying, so nights like that pushed the memory of Sean's attack further and further away. Robyn, much like her fiancé, was not a birthday kind of gal, so she confided she was glad Ardnoch's annual Christmas ceilidh fell on the weekend of her birthday week, foiling anyone's plans to do anything more than a dinner.

The ceilidh was at the Gloaming that Saturday night. Robyn had insisted I needed to experience it. As worried as Thane was about the results of the paternity test, I knew he wasn't in the mood for celebrating, so I told him to stay home with the children. However, he wanted to escort me to my first ceilidh and Eredine volunteered to babysit, along with two of Lachlan's security guys. They sat outside in their car so as not to freak out the kids.

Thane didn't want to drop security now that Sean had made his intentions clear. Lachlan, enraged as I'd ever seen when Thane told him about the paternity test, had kept security on the children. He'd also vowed to "crush any fucker who tries to mess with this family." Not gonna lie, it was *hot*. A completely inappropriate thought considering the subject matter, and that he's my sister's fiancé and my lover's brother, but I couldn't deny it.

As for the Christmas ceilidh, I didn't know how to feel about it. Robyn had waxed lyrical about her first one (I later found out that was where she and Lachlan had sex, so no wonder she had fond memories). I think if I'd been drunker and knew the dance steps, I might have enjoyed it more. The beginning was enjoyable when everyone was sober and willing to teach me the folk dances. But the drunker everyone got, the wilder it got, and the more of a crush it became. It was sweaty and crowded; the accordion started to grate on my nerves after a while, and I took an elbow to the temple about five times.

On the plus side, Thane was in a kilt. As were Lachlan and Mac and all the men. But only Thane made my belly flip at the sight of him in his traditional clothing.

I decided after seeing all the village men in kilts that a kilt was like a suit. Some guys wore it, and other guys were worn *by* it. And Thane could wear a kilt.

All three of the men wore a matching kilts of dark green plaid with red, black, and white accents that Thane explained was the Sutherland tartan. While Clan Adair was actually from the Lowlands of Scotland, their particular offshoot of the Adairs had migrated to the north and broken away from the clan. They became more involved in the politics of Clan Sutherland, and their ancestors had opted to adopt the Sutherland tartan in lieu of the tartan worn by Clan Adair. Which was Maxwell tartan. Confusingly.

Thane tried to explain about the clans and allies and dependents but I lost track.

His long story shortened was that his family wore Sutherland tartan in their traditional attire. And while Mac wore a black suit jacket, matching waistcoat, and white shirt, Thane and Lachlan's kilt jackets and waistcoats were a dark gray.

They wore matching sporrans over their kilts, long knee socks that shouldn't have been hot but really showed off Thane's muscled calves, and dress shoes with laces that wrapped around said calves.

So Thane was sexy as hell and definitely fun to look at, especially when he took off the jacket later on.

Also, he got to hold me in public for the dances. He made me laugh, and I made him laugh as I cursed the Gloaming's owner who clapped in my face and shouted the steps like a drill sergeant.

We'd commandeered a round table at the back of the large hall. Mac, Arro, Lachlan, Robyn, Thane, and me. And when I wasn't being hauled around the dance floor, I sat at a table laughing and joking with Robyn's other family, feeling like maybe—just maybe—they were my family too.

Later when we got home, Thane insisted that Eredine sleep in the annex rather than drive all the way back to her cabin, but she refused. I worried about her. Robyn did too. She said that since Lucy, Eredine seemed like she was slipping further away. I'd been so consumed with my own mess, with Thane's, with my feelings for him, that I hadn't given her enough of my time. I vowed when things calmed down a bit to do that, to make an effort, to bulldoze where Robyn refused to bulldoze because it wasn't in her nature to push people. Other than me.

It was definitely in my nature. And sometimes, people needed it.

Lachlan's security guys promised to escort Eredine home, and with the kids asleep long ago, Thane dragged me into his room. He shoved me toward the bed. A little rough, a lot exciting. "I've wanted to kiss and lick and suck every inch of you from the moment you walked downstairs in this bloody dress," he growled.

To be fair, I had bought it to drive him crazy.

It was a departure from my usual preppy style. I'd chosen a calf-length, silk jersey blood-red dress that had a demure neckline but sculpted (like, painted on!) to my body. It left very little to the imagination, despite very little skin showing. However, it was probably one reason I didn't enjoy the ceilidh dancing so much because I couldn't stretch my damn legs in it.

"And I've wanted to put my hand up your kilt since I came downstairs."

Thane grinned wolfishly as he coasted his hands over my ass. "Nothing stopping you now."

Remembering he'd had more to drink than me, I glanced back at his closed door. "You need to remember to be quiet."

"I'm not the one who's going to need to be."

I understood that comment seconds later when he pushed me down on the bed, shoved my skirt up to my waist, ripped off my underwear, and settled his mouth between my thighs to satisfy his hunger.

~

Three days later, I was loading the laundry at around ten in the morning when I heard the doorbell. I hurried to answer it, greeted by our local postal worker, Pauline. She had a few parcels in hand.

"More Christmas presents?" Pauline smiled as I signed for them.

Probably. I thanked goodness our mail always arrived when the kids were at school or I'd never be able to hide their gifts.

"Some mail too." She handed over the envelopes as I struggled to hold on to all the boxes.

"Thanks so much," I said, trying not to drop the parcels.

As I was closing the door with my foot, I looked down at the top envelope, and my heart stopped.

Oh my God, it was here!

Hurrying into the kitchen, I dumped the packages onto the counter and rushed for my cell on the dining table. Hands shaking, I dialed Thane and hoped he wasn't in a meeting, that he'd pick up.

He did on the third ring. "Regan, are you okay?"

Hearing his concern, because I never called him at work —he was always the one ringing me on his lunch break—I blurted out, "It's here. The results just arrived."

Thane hesitated a moment. "Give me a second." I heard some muffled talking on the other end, and I slumped into a dining chair, clutching the envelope. My knee bounced with nerves.

"Right, I'm back," Thane said a little breathlessly. "What does it say?"

Surprised, I replied, "You want me to open it?"

"I can't wait the hour it will take me to get back home. So yes, open it."

Shocked and humbled that he trusted me with this, I switched my cell to speaker, took a breath, and ripped into it. I almost dropped the damn letter I was trembling so hard.

And there it was.

Tears flooded my eyes and I sobbed, "She's yours! She's yours, baby, she's yours!"

I heard the choked noise he made down the line, the sounds of him trying to catch his breath, and I suspected my big, brave Scotsman was crying.

Aching to be with him, I let him take his time to process.

Finally, in his voice gruff, he said, "Thank fuck, *mo leannan*. Thank all the fucks in the world for that."

I gave a bark of laughter through my tears. "We knew it. We knew it in our guts."

"Aye, but now I have a piece of paper I can give to my lawyer so she can tell Sean McClintock he can go rot."

"Yes, you do." Relief melted through me. Now Thane could just enjoy Christmas with Eilidh and Lewis without this cloud hanging over his head.

"I need to phone my lawyer. Can you send me a photo of the results?"

"Of course."

"Then I need to let Lachlan know."

"Good. Yeah, he'll be so relieved."

"And then I'm coming home for lunch so I can celebrate with you. In my bed."

Shaking my head, I rolled my eyes but grinned. "It seems to be your favorite form of celebration these days."

"Oh, it absolutely is. And be prepared. Good news makes me energetic."

"Is that a promise?"

"You fucking know it, *mo leannan*."

And three hours later, I discovered that wasn't a false promise.

341

31

REGAN

The Tuesday before Christmas, I got my first taste of
what living in Ardnoch would be like during the
summer. While I'd caught only a few glimpses of famous
actors in the village over the past few months (and it was
never not weird!), Robyn had warned me that summer and
Christmastime were when the paparazzi arrived because that
was when a lot of members descended upon the club.

And the paps were particularly interested in one of Hollywood's current golden boys, Brodan Adair. That he was
spotted at Inverness Airport had signaled he was returning
home, and the vultures chased after him.

Brodan and Lachlan had to set up security at the bottom
of the country lane into our homes to deter the paparazzi
from coming near the houses. They camped outside the
castle to catch glimpses of celebrities coming and going. Very
few guests ventured into the village, however, when the paps
swarmed.

It was crazy, though. I didn't like it at all. The village took
on a tense vibe. Everyone was in guarded, protective mode,
and I wished the assholes would just leave. Thankfully,

school finished up the day after Brodan arrived, so we only had one morning where the paparazzi surrounded the SUV and had to be pushed back by the security team.

Still, the flash of camera lights into the car was blinding, and I told Eilidh and Lewis to cover their eyes. The kids handled it better than I did, having grown up with this and understanding (Lewis more so than Eilidh) that their uncles were famous. They were too young to see any of their movies, though, so I think it was still an abstract idea for them.

That Wednesday night, the whole crew congregated at Thane's for dinner—Thane, the kids, Robyn, Lachlan, Arro, Mac, Eredine, and Brodan. I noted throughout dinner that Eredine was even more monosyllabic than usual, and Thane's younger brother's gaze was drawn to her more than a few times as he answered questions about his latest movie.

I studied them, but Eredine never once looked over at him.

When she insisted on leaving right after dinner, claiming a headache, Lachlan shot his brother a frustrated look before seeing her to the door. Now I was intrigued. While Ery was reserved, she still liked to be around us and usually left when everyone else did. What about Brodan discomfited her so much?

"So ... you're the nanny."

I turned from my spot in the kitchen where I'd been making hot cocoa for Eilidh and Lewis (a task that multiplied when all the adults decided they wanted their own, with a dash of whisky), to find Brodan sauntering toward me.

A quick glance across the large room told me everyone was on the sectional with the children, laughing and chatting. Thane's attention, however, was on us in the kitchen.

Looking at Brodan, I quirked an eyebrow. "I am indeed. And you're the wayward brother."

It was his turn to raise an eyebrow. "I am? I thought that was Arran."

"I think it's both of you now."

He frowned and lowered his gaze toward the mugs. "Can I help?"

"You can grab the whipped cream out of the fridge."

Those pale-blue eyes of his, the same shade as Arro's, rose to meet mine. His lips twitched, reminding me of Thane. "If I had a penny for every time a woman has said that to me."

I tried not to smile, but he made it difficult. It was already proven that I was not immune to a charming Scotsman. "Just get the cream."

"At your service," he teased as he went to do so.

I looked over my shoulder as he moved across the room to the refrigerator, and I couldn't help but *notice* him. Brodan was as tall as Lachlan but even broader in the shoulders, his biceps sculpted and movie-star impressive beneath his form-fitting cashmere sweater. His waist tapered dramatically in a perfect Captain America V, and I couldn't look too long at his ass because it made me guilty for appreciating it. You could crack a rock, never mind an egg, on that thing.

Like all the brothers, Brodan had sandy-blond hair and, like Lachlan, he sported designer stubble.

Focusing on the hot cocoa, I was a little startled to feel the heat of him at my back as I worked.

"Whipped cream, my lady," Brodan overpronounced the words, making them sound dirty as he placed the can down in front of me. His body brushed my back with the movement.

I stiffened. "Thanks." I tried to move away, but there was little space. He had me sandwiched between him and the counter. If Thane was still watching us, this did not look good.

"Do I make you nervous?" Brodan asked softly.

I turned my head to meet his gaze. "No, but you are in my personal space."

He smirked. "Your personal space smells very nice."

This close to him, I saw something in his eyes that I recognized. Something weary and a little desperate, pushed back under charm and cheekiness. It was like looking in a freaking mirror.

What had happened to him?

At whatever he saw on my face, his expression fell. Wariness settled over him, and he eased back. "So, you're really the nanny?" he asked, and I wondered if it was to distract me from what I'd just seen.

"I think we've established I am in fact the nanny."

Brodan grinned, and it was so much like his brothers', I couldn't help it; fondness crept over me despite him trying to flirt. "You're just wandering around my big brother's house? Day in and day out."

I narrowed my eyes at the insinuation in his voice. "Meaning?"

"You're very beautiful."

"I'm also good at my job." I grabbed the whipped cream, expertly swirled it over the top of two mugs, and then sprinkled them both with chocolate curls. Shoving the cocoas at Brodan, I said through clenched teeth, "Why don't you take these to the niece and nephew you never see? They could do with your attention more than I could."

A flash of anger made his eyes seem bluer, but he took the mugs, gave me an abrupt nod, and marched out of the kitchen.

"Hey, kids! Look what Uncle Bro made you!"

I grimaced and caught Thane's gaze across the room. His expression was unreadable, but when I rolled my eyes at Brodan's audacity, Thane smiled and got up from the couch.

"Need help?" he asked as he strolled into the kitchen.

"Yes, please." I pushed mugs toward him.

Then he touched on my lower back and I looked at him in surprise before glancing over at our guests. No one was looking.

"You okay?" he asked.

"Oh, yeah. Your brother is harmless."

The muscle in his jaw ticked, but he just nodded and took the mugs I'd passed him and carried them over to Robyn and Lachlan. I hoped Thane wasn't jealous of that brief moment in the kitchen. His brother probably flirted with everything in a skirt. And while I could notice how good-looking he was and what an amazing body he had, he didn't inspire a visceral reaction in me. Sometimes I got turned on just from Thane's smile. He did it for me in a way no man ever had. And I wished I could tell him without scaring him off.

~

THANE

Brodan's arrival home for the Christmas holidays filled Thane with a strange mix of relief and agitation. His visits were becoming few and far between, and he didn't know his niece and nephew very well anymore.

Watching him with them made Thane long for the days when they were all together. Natural-born flirts, Brodan and Eilidh gravitated toward one another, and Thane witnessed something wash away from his brother as Eilidh bewitched him. Listening to Brodan's loud, deep laughter at Eilidh's too-quick quips and adorable mischievousness, Thane rubbed his chest where he felt a slight ache.

He missed Brodan. He missed Arran. Arran, who'd called

Brodan to let him know he couldn't make it back for Christmas but to send along his best wishes. His fucking best wishes.

Thane watched as Regan and Robyn returned from the kitchen with more cocoa, the last for Eilidh and Lewis, before they went to bed, and his eyes narrowed as Brodan looked up to watch Regan. His brother's gaze moved down her body, and Thane curled his hands into fists, resisting the urge to bark at him to take his bloody eyes off her.

The jealousy that surged in him when he saw Brodan press Regan into the counter was unbearable. He'd wanted to punch his brother. He hadn't felt that urge since they were kids and Brodan crashed a football into the 3-D model of Edinburgh Castle Thane had spent months building out of Popsicle sticks.

He'd also noticed Regan checking out his brother.

And he hadn't liked it.

He didn't like it one bit.

That was how easy it would be, he'd thought to himself, for her head to be turned once she grew bored playing house with him.

Quietly stewing over the jealousy he hated she inspired, Thane was quiet as his siblings told Robyn, Regan, and the children funny stories from their childhood.

"Uh, how about the time you and Arran crashed my first date?" Arrochar glowered at Brodan.

"They did not?" Regan gaped at her in horror.

"Oh, aye, they did. Blake Burnside asked me out in third year. I was so happy because all my other friends had already been on dates, and I worried no one fancied me. His mum drove us to the cinema in Inverness and was going to pick us up after. And we're sitting in the cinema and Blake had just got up the nerve to take my hand when there's all this scuffling around us. I look to the empty seat next to Blake, and it's not empty anymore. Brodan's in it. And suddenly Arran is in the seat next to me. They mortified me!"

"Where were *you*?" Robyn tried not to laugh as she addressed her fiancé.

Lachlan grinned. "On a movie set somewhere."

"And you?" Regan asked Thane.

Thane found himself smiling, despite his unhappy thoughts. "At uni."

"At uni?" Brodan scoffed. "It was his bloody plan! We were just his foot soldiers!"

Thane cut his brother an annoyed look as Arrochar turned on him. "You did not!"

Rubbing his neck sheepishly, he shrugged. "I couldn't be there to make sure you were all right. And anyway"—he shot Lachlan a warning look—"*I* was only following orders."

"No!" Arro turned on Lachlan, making them all laugh.

Lachlan grinned unrepentantly. "You were fourteen. If boys were going to date you, they needed to know what they'd be facing if they hurt you."

She shook her head. "I didn't get asked out again for two years!"

"Well, that was just an accidental bonus."

Robyn shoved Lachlan playfully on Arro's behalf, and he roared with laughter, setting them all off. Thane caught Brodan watching Regan again as she fell against Arro giggling, her dimples so damn appealing. Any amusement Thane felt died at the definite interest in Brodan's eyes.

Not long later, when Regan announced it was bedtime for Eilidh and Lewis, Thane took them up and settled them in as he always did. Eilidh was more hyper than she'd ever been, and he regretted allowing her that final hot cocoa.

"I don't wanna sleep, Daddy," she growled at him in the monster voice.

"You have to, Eilidh-Bug. It's past your bedtime."

"But I wanna be downstairs!"

"Come on." He lifted her into bed, pulled up the covers, and settled down beside her in one swift move. "I'll read *The Night Before Christmas* to you."

She harrumphed like an eighty-year-old but couldn't resist snuggling into him as he slowly made his way through the Christmas book. Thankfully, despite her excitement, she was also an energetic five-year-old who needed her sleep. Her eyes closed, lashes thick and casting shadows across her chubby cheeks. Thane squeezed her closer, just watching her for a bit, preferring to feel the utter relief of knowing no one could ever take his daughter from him rather than dwell on the panic that one day soon, another female who had become precious to him would slip through his fingers like sand.

A while later, Thane came downstairs to find the adults—except for Arro, who was driving Mac home—had moved on to a glass of whisky. Brodan had somehow insinuated himself into a seat next to Regan. He had his arm stretched along the back of the couch behind her. Thane tried not to let it bother him, considering Regan was engaged in conversation with Robyn, but as he sat down at the end of the sectional, he couldn't stop his eyes from moving to them.

Brodan was chatting with Lachlan but Thane's eagle eyes caught his subtle movement. His brother started drawing circles on Regan's shoulder.

His gut tightened with anger, and he was about to snap at Brodan when Regan suddenly launched herself off the sofa. "Sorry, have an itch behind my shoulder blades. Robbie, can you get it?" She crouched, and while her sister frowned at Regan's randomness, she reached up to scratch her back.

"Got it?" Robyn asked.

"Yeah, thanks. I hate those awkward itches." Regan grinned breezily but Thane recognized it for what it was—a fake smile. When she returned to the couch, she sat down next to him instead.

His gut unknotted.

He wanted to lay his hand on her thigh in an obnoxious, claiming gesture.

Not long later, Brodan's cell rang.

"Damn." He looked at the caller ID. "I need to take this."

"At this hour?" Lachlan scowled.

"It's my agent. He's on LA time. I'll just be a second." Brodan got up and strode toward the bifolds that led outside. "Hey, what's happening?" he asked as he opened the door.

Ice-cold air immediately encased them, and they all shivered. The door closed behind Brodan and the air warmed again.

Five minutes later, when he still hadn't come back, Thane's annoyance grew. It wasn't just about his flirting with Regan; it was the fact that he hadn't seen his family in half a year, and he couldn't go one night without shoptalk? Aggravated, Thane got up and strode toward the bifolds.

"Thane," Lachlan called in warning.

Thane waved him off and slipped outside onto the deck.

His breath puffed in the air as soon as he shut the doors behind him. It was fucking baltic. Shivering, he turned to find Brodan sitting on the stairs at the bottom of the deck. No phone in hand. Just staring out at the blackness beyond. While he could smell the sea and hear it lapping at the rocks below, he couldn't see a damn thing, which was why the kids were never allowed out here in the pitch-black.

"What are you doing?" Thane sat down beside his brother, the icy wood seeping into the arse of his trousers. "It's bloody freezing."

Brodan shrugged. "I like it. I've been filming in a desert for months. This is refreshing. It's home."

The sound of longing in his voice made Thane frown. "Then why are you never here?"

"Because I have a life, a career."

Thane made a huffing sound but didn't reply.

"Anyway, you're all doing well without me. I've never seen Lachlan so happy."

"Aye, Robyn is good for him."

"She's pretty great." He flicked Thane a smirk. "Her sister is tasty. Can't imagine it's a hardship having her around."

That jealousy and anger flared inside him again. "You'll stay away from Regan."

Brodan snorted. "It's just harmless flirting."

"It'll stop. You're making her uncomfortable."

"I'm making her uncomfortable, brother, or I'm making *you* uncomfortable?" All amusement fled Brodan's expression as he stared into Thane's eyes. "I'm not an idiot. Our family might not have noticed, but I certainly have. You watch her like a hawk. And she watches you back. A man doesn't look at his brother like he wants to rip off his head for staring at a woman, unless he himself is fucking said woman."

"Brodan," he warned.

His brother held up a hand to cut him off. "I won't tell anyone." He stood and stared down at Thane. "But have you really thought this through, Thane? She's a lot younger than you, she's gorgeous, and she's barely experienced life. I just …" he sighed heavily. "I don't want you to get hurt. Watch yourself there." He patted Thane's shoulder and strode back up onto the deck to disappear inside.

Thane bowed his head, fighting a million emotions, few of them pretty. Finally, knowing they'd all wonder where he was, he took a deep, calming breath before he forced himself to return inside.

While our mom expected way too much from Robyn in all things, she expected very little from me. I didn't know what was worse—the pressure, or the lack of faith?

What had started out as a joyous reunion at Inverness Airport, a giddy drive to Ardnoch, and a lovely dinner with our mom and dad had changed somewhat the next day. It was Christmas Eve, and while Mac would attend Christmas dinner with us, he'd decided to not be there on the evening of the twenty-fourth. He'd offered to *not* attend Christmas Day, too, because he didn't want to make Mom and Dad feel weird, but Robyn put her foot down. It was her first Christmas with her father in years, and she wasn't missing out.

Ery and Arrochar had also forgone Christmas Eve dinner with us.

Mom and Dad were, like almost everyone on the planet, charmed by Eilidh's effervescent personality and Lewis's reserved adorableness. At the dinner table, I sat next to Dad. I hadn't realized how much I'd missed his big, solid presence in my life. You only had to take one look at us to know where I got most of my genes. Dad was a good man. His work got to him more than I liked, but that was because he was honorable, and unfortunately, sometimes the justice system wasn't. I know he often felt helpless, but he made up for it by being the best goddamn detective he could be.

I was proud of him.

Dad squeezed me into his side, telling me he missed me too. "You seem happy." He grinned with those dimples he'd bestowed upon me.

"I am."

"Good." He kissed my temple and returned to his plate.

I knew that my being happy in Scotland must've been a scary prospect for Dad, but I believed he wanted the best for me, even if that meant there was an ocean between us.

"You'll come stay the night with us at Robyn's," Mom said as we discussed plans for the next day, "after Santa's arrival."

Eilidh's ears pricked up and she looked at me, her eyes big.

"I'm staying here," I replied for more than just my mom's benefit.

Mom frowned as she swallowed a bite of the steak pie we'd bought from the village butcher. "But it's Christmas Eve. You should be with your family. We've come all this way, Regan. Don't be inconsiderate."

My spine snapped at her tone.

"Stace," Dad warned quietly.

"I'm not being inconsiderate," I replied calmly. "I promised Eilidh and Lewis I'd be here to open presents with them first thing in the morning, and that's where I'll be."

"And what about us?"

I could feel Eilidh watching.

"Mom, the kids will be up super early. You won't even be awake. I'll come over after to open presents with you then."

"You're going away?" Eilidh frowned. "You can't go away on Christmas Day! You have to come to Mummy's with us, Ree-Ree."

My plan had been to visit with my family at Robyn and Lachlan's while Thane took the children to the cemetery to visit Fran's grave. They put flowers on her grave once a month, a trip they always took on the weekend and one I'd never taken with them out of respect. They also visited every Christmas, New Year's Day, and on her birthday.

"Mommy's?" Mom frowned, having been told that Thane was a widower.

I shook my head at her to be quiet and turned to Eilidh. "Sweetie, that's family time."

"But you're family!"

"Eilidh, don't shout at Regan," Thane admonished. "Tomorrow Regan will spend part of the morning with her family while we visit Mum. We'll see her in the afternoon. End of discussion."

He'd used the tone the kids never argued with, but Eilidh pouted dramatically and shot me an unforgiving look.

Shit.

Brodan thankfully engaged Mom, asking her in that flirty voice how it was possible a woman as attractive and as young as she could have two grown daughters. Mom, as much as she loved Dad, was not averse to a handsome Hollywood actor fawning over her. Despite Eilidh's upset, I relaxed as the heat of Mom's disapproval cooled under Brodan's attention.

"They're attached to you," Dad muttered beside me, clearly referring to the kids.

"Yeah, we've grown close."

"So what time can we expect you tomorrow?" Mom suddenly pushed.

"Mom," Robyn huffed, "it's Christmas. No schedules or routines. Let's just enjoy it."

"I would if both my daughters were bothering to show up."

"For Christ's sake, Stacey." Dad glowered at her. "Not here."

I glanced down the table at Robyn, and we exchanged a knowing look. Mom wasn't pissed about me not staying the night with them; she was pissed I was here in the first place. She was pissed I didn't check in with her as much as I checked in with Dad.

And she was pissed about the last ten years of my life in which I'd seemed to do nothing but disappoint her.

I hated it, because I'd missed my parents, but I was relieved when they left a few hours later so we could put the kids to bed.

Lewis was a great sleeper and he drifted off, no problem at all, even though I could tell he was excited about Santa.

Eilidh was ... well ...

"But I want to see Santy Claus!" she cried as Thane and I tried to settle her in.

"You need to sleep, Eilidh-Bug. Santa only leaves presents for good children who go to sleep when they're supposed to."

She considered this, pouted, and crossed her arms over her chest. "Not my fault if I can't sleep."

"But you can try," Thane insisted. "And when you wake up in the morning, your stocking will magically be filled with presents and lying at the foot of your bed. And there will be more presents under the tree."

Her eyes widened and she sprang at Thane, clasping his bearded face in her hands. "Daddy, I can't wait! And I don't wanna Santy not to leave me pressies 'cause I'm too excited!"

While I covered my mouth to muffle my amusement, Thane struggled not to laugh as he hugged her to him. "It's okay, Santa will come, but you need to calm down, my darling."

"I'm trying," she whined.

In the end, I used a trick Robyn used to use on me. I picked Eilidh's least favorite book and I read it to her in a soft, soothing monotone. She complained at first, but eventually her eyes drifted closed as she rested against her dad's chest.

"She's asleep," Thane murmured eventually.

With a sigh of relief, he carefully maneuvered her onto her pillow and we slipped out of the room. Downstairs, as I drank most of the glass of milk the kids had left out for Santa, Thane sidled into me at the island. "So … your mother is a bit of a pain in the arse," he opined bluntly.

Keeping my voice low, I shrugged. "I'm used to it."

"You shouldn't have to be."

"She's not awful," I whispered back defensively. "We had a lot of good times with Mom growing up. She's just … mistrustful. She always expects too much from Robyn and never—"

"Expects enough from you," he answered grimly.

My pulse raced at his perceptiveness. "It is what it is."

Thane leaned into me. "If she can't see how bloody wonderful you are, she's a fool."

My stomach flip-flopped at his words, and I leaned in to kiss him. I meant it to be just a peck, but Thane grabbed hold of my waist and pulled me in for a deeper kiss. He groaned, trailing kisses down my throat. "Damn your period."

I grinned, pushing him away playfully. "Just be glad it's here."

We'd been having so much sex, it was a wonder the odds hadn't stacked against us regarding pregnancy, despite using contraception.

Thane chuckled under his breath, even though he wore

the look of a frustrated man. He helped me eat the cookies the kids had left out and then we put the carrots they'd set out for the reindeer back in the refrigerator but left the plate.

The spirit of Christmas filled us as we tiptoed in and out of the house in our coats and boots, hauling in the gifts I'd wrapped and hidden in the annex. All the family had dropped off the kids' presents, too, and I arranged them prettily around the tree. Thane's tradition was to tell the children that their big present was from Santa and the rest were from him and their loved ones.

I placed my presents for them next to Thane's and put Thane's in the pile from his family. He'd disappeared as I perfected the arrangement and snapped a photograph to send to Robyn. The presents overflowed past the tree, and the bike Lewis had asked for was propped against the wall with a big red and green bow on it.

Eilidh's big present from Santa was the Arendelle Castle from Disney's *Frozen*, along with dolls to go with it. She was going to adore it.

Excited about seeing the kids' reactions in the morning, it took me a minute to realize Thane was watching me.

"What is it?" I whispered.

He shook his head, approaching the tree with a Christmas gift bag in his hand. "You just ... you're really into this."

"Christmas is all about kids. The first year I realized Santa wasn't real, the magic went away. But ... this is the first time I've felt it since I was a child. I'm excited they're excited."

Thane stared at me, his expression unreadable.

"What is it?" I repeated.

He shook his head and placed the gift bag down near the presents. I could see a couple of wrapped parcels inside.

"Where did that come from?"

Thane turned and winked at me. "Santa."

"Are those for me?"

He grinned. "I couldn't not buy you a Christmas present or two."

Staring at them greedily, I whispered, "What are they?"

His soft laughter filled my ears as he wrapped his arms around my waist, drawing me back against his chest. "You'll have to wait until the morning to find out like all the other good girls and boys."

Desire flashed through me, sudden and intense, and I blamed my damn hormones and the utter irony of how turned on I got when I couldn't do anything about it.

Well ... I could do *something* about it.

Turning around his arms, I looped mine around his neck. "We're done here. Time for bed."

"Already?" He frowned. "You don't want to sit for a bit?"

"I'm tired," I lied.

His disappointment was adorable and made me feel all warm and fuzzy. I loved he wanted alone time with me, even when it wasn't about sex. The stubborn man definitely cared about me. I just had to get him to admit it. But not during Christmas. The holiday was all about Eilidh and Lewis.

Taking the kids' filled stockings upstairs, we crept into their rooms to drape them over the end of the beds as was tradition among the Adairs. I held my breath the entire time, afraid I'd wake them.

When we were done, Eilidh and Lewis none the wiser, we stopped outside Thane's bedroom door, and he sighed before whispering, "I guess this is good night, then."

Smirking, I pushed him through his bedroom door. "Not quite."

Thane's eyes lit up as he stumbled backward into the room. "I thought you couldn't."

I closed the door behind us and lowered myself to my knees in front of him. "I can't ... but that doesn't mean I can't give you an early Christmas present."

"Fuck," he muttered, his expression darkening with need as I unzipped him. "What did I do to deserve this?"

I couldn't answer. I was too busy making his Christmas Eve extremely memorable.

Afterward, as Thane tried to catch his breath, exerted not just by my generous mouth but by the effort of being quiet, he pulled me to my feet and pushed me toward the bed. "You're sleeping with me tonight."

Shocked, I gaped at him. Since I'd moved into the house, Thane had always visited my bed at night and left after we made love. We'd not spent the night sleeping in each other's arms since the morning after we'd made love all night. And even then, we'd only fallen asleep together out of pure exhaustion.

I suspected I knew why Thane never stayed the night with me, even though my insecurities wanted me to think he was using me. However, I didn't believe that.

Not now.

Now that I knew how Fran died.

I suspected Thane was afraid to go to sleep with me in the bed with him because of how he'd found Fran. And that broke my freaking heart.

"Are you sure?" I tried to keep his hands at bay as he attempted to undress me, wanting to make certain he wasn't pushing himself beyond the boundaries he'd needed for so long.

Emotion roiled in his gaze alongside a fierceness. "Yes."

"The kids will wake up first, though."

"They won't. They've never woken up before seven on Christmas Day. You know they're good sleepers. And I'll wake you up early so you can slip out."

"Thane—"

He kissed me, cutting me off, then murmured against my lips, "I just want to hold you."

When he undressed me down to my underwear, no bra, I quirked an eyebrow, my heart pounding in my chest. "Really?"

Thane gave me that boyishly wicked smile as he pushed me onto the bed. "If I can't be inside you, I can at least feel you naked against me."

I huffed, but I really didn't care. I wanted to fall asleep in his arms more than anything. "Will you set the alarm?"

"I will," he promised.

By the time he got undressed, set the alarm, and climbed into bed beside me, I was giddy with anticipation. This, to me, was just as great as sex. His muscular arm pulled me back into his chest, and I hit his steely warmth. The hair on his legs tickled mine, and I curled my foot around his calf, entangling us. He buried his face in my neck, cupped my breast possessively, and relaxed completely into me.

Certain that he was okay about this, I relaxed too.

Pure contentment lulled me into a deep, deep sleep.

~

"Ree-Ree."

I moaned as a familiar voice cut into my dreaming.

"Daddy?"

An arm laid heavily over my waist. I felt the tickle of Thane's beard on my shoulder and the throb of his morning erection against my ass. I pushed into it with a moan.

"Ree-Ree, Daddy, wake up!"

I tensed and the arm around me tightened too.

No.

No, no, no.

"Santy's been! Wake up!"

A tug at the duvet had my eyes flying open and my hand

reached out to grab hold of it to keep it covering me and Thane.

Eilidh stood at my side of the bed, staring at me with those big, curious blue eyes. They danced with her inquisitive impatience. "Why are you in Daddy's bed?"

"Fuck," Thane muttered into my skin.

Think fast, think fast, think fast.

"Uh, well, I must have fallen asleep here waiting for Santa."

Her eyes widened. "Did you miss him? 'Cause he's been! He filled my stocking and there are lots of nice things in there I want to show you!"

I winced at her loudness but covered it with a smile. "Why don't you go back into your room to wait for me and your dad? We'll be right in."

"But—"

"Eilidh-Bug …" Thane lifted his head from my shoulder. "Do as Regan says. Wait for us in your room, sweetheart."

"Okay!" She began backing away. "But hurry, Daddy!"

Once the door slammed shut behind her, both of us jumped out of bed.

"Oh my god, oh my god, oh my god." I frantically pulled on my clothes.

"It's fine," Thane said, though his expression belied his calm. "She doesn't understand what she saw, and she's too excited to care or remember."

"Are you sure?" I trembled as I pulled on my sweater.

"Positive." He strode around the bed and put his hands on my shoulders. "Just act normal and she'll forget about it."

I nodded, but as I followed Thane out of the room, I feared I wouldn't be able to pretend. It wasn't just that I worried about Eilidh being confused by finding me in bed with her dad. I was angry and depressed that after everything

SAMANTHA YOUNG

that had passed between me and Thane, we were still
sneaking around like we were doing something wrong.

What we had felt more right than anything ever in my
life.

Why couldn't he see that too?

33

REGAN

Thane was right.

Eilidh didn't even mention finding me in her father's bed. She was too busy showing us everything in her stocking (which, of course, we'd already seen because we put it there) while we oohed and aahed.

"Can we wake Lewis now?" she begged in a shout loud enough to wake the dead after Thane said we couldn't open the presents downstairs until her brother was awake.

Her dad and I exchanged a look before Thane went off to check if her shouting had woken Lewis. A couple minutes later, Thane returned with a sleepy Lewis in his arms. Lew held his stocking.

"Merry Christmas, sweetie." I leaned up to kiss him on the cheek.

To my delight, he reached for me. "Merry Christmas, Ree-Ree." Thane handed him over and even though he weighed a ton, I held on tight and gave him a big cuddle before lowering him to the floor.

My heart was full.

And it just kept filling, swelling with the sweet tightness

of too much emotion as the day stretched on. Eilidh and Lewis were beyond delighted with their gifts from Santa and their presents from their dad, me, and the rest of the family. Thane said he loved the photograph Robyn had taken of Eilidh and Lewis on the beach. She'd taken it a few months ago when she, I, and the kids had gone for a walk during their October vacation. It had been a moody day, but the sunbeams had spilled through a break in the clouds, creating this amazing light across the sand dunes. There was water in little pools along the shore, and Eilidh and Lewis had taken great pleasure in making footprints in the wet sand.

They had rushed ahead of us and Robyn had captured a beautiful shot of Lewis turning to reach for Eilidh's hand to help her across a wider pool of water.

As soon as I saw it, I knew I needed to frame it and give it to Thane for Christmas. When I'd seen Lachlan's reaction to the photo of Robyn, it solidified my decision. Under their gruffness, the Adair men were sentimental softies.

Thane's eyes brightened as he caressed the glass protecting the photo. "It's beautiful."

"I thought you could put it in your office, maybe?"

He nodded, looking at me with such tenderness, I cursed the fact that I couldn't just reach out and kiss him. I cursed it even more when I opened his gift to me. He said it was from him and the kids. They'd given me a gift set of my favorite nail polish, a cashmere scarf in an emerald green that looked great with my hair color … and a gift shaped like a book.

"No way." I gaped as I unwrapped it, almost afraid to touch it. "This isn't what I think it is?"

"Lachlan told me about your reaction when you saw it in the library at Ardnoch. The books in there belong to our family. Arro removed all of her favorites years ago. We don't believe in books filling shelves just to gather dust. They should be treasured and loved. I wanted you to have it."

Tears burned the back of my eyes as I stroked the cover of the first edition of *Gulliver's Travels* that I'd admired all those months ago. "I can't believe you would trust this to me."

"I trust my most treasured possessions to you, Regan. Why would I not entrust a book to you?"

I grinned because when he put it like that, I seemed silly. The tears caught in the corner of my eyes, and Thane noted them, his expression so loving, my frustration curled in my fingers and toes. I shoved it down and hugged the first edition to my chest. "I have no words for how much I love this. Thank you."

The kids broke our intense staring match as they asked questions about the book, and I promised to read them a chapter from *Gulliver's Travels* every night. It delighted me they were interested in it.

From there, Thane prepared us a full Scottish breakfast. I looked forward to making Robyn squeamish with a very detailed account of how much I enjoyed my haggis and black pudding (blood sausage). While I'd pretty much eat anything, Robyn couldn't get her head around what the latter two were made of. Considering the scary things she'd faced in life without batting an eye, it was fun teasing her about her weak stomach.

By the time we got Eilidh and Lewis showered, dressed, and ready to leave for the cemetery, I only had a small amount of time to get ready. Delaying going over to see Mom and Dad any longer would only irritate Mom.

When I eventually arrived next door, Brodan's charming anecdotes about Hollywood actors he'd worked with and famous people he'd met had Mom in a good mood, so she didn't notice how late in the day it was. Lachlan was a fortress when it came to Hollywood gossip. It was his business to keep his members' lives private, so he never spoke about the people he'd worked with.

Brodan had no such qualms. We spent the afternoon laughing at his hilarious and often outrageous stories, waiting for everyone to arrive for Christmas dinner.

To my relief, when Mac arrived, Mom was on her best behavior. Dad and Mac exchanged one of those awkward half man-hug things, reminding me they'd been good friends back in the day. Mom and Mac just shared a nod of hello and exchanged overly polite pleasantries.

It was good. Better than anyone could have hoped for, and Robyn was in a wonderful mood.

In fact, it was such a magical day, the best Christmas I could remember in a long time, that I never suspected it could go so horribly wrong.

The first not-so-pleasant moment was just before dinner was served. Everyone congregated in Lachlan's sitting area, but I'd gotten up to retrieve juice for Eilidh and Lewis. Dad followed me into the kitchen.

"Now isn't the perfect time, but I don't know when will be. Can we talk a minute before everyone sits down to dinner?" He nodded toward the front entrance.

My pulse increased a little, wondering what he needed to talk about in private, but I nodded and followed him out.

The door off Lachlan's entrance led to a small room where he kept memorabilia from his work as an actor. Awards, props, that sort of thing, all encased in glass and well looked after. However, it was so typical of my sister's fiancé to keep it hidden away in a room no one ever went into.

Dad stared around for a moment, drinking everything in. Spotting the long broadsword encased in glass by itself, Dad approached it. "Jesus, it's his sword from *The Last King*." He turned to give me a small, awed smile. "I still can't get my head around the fact your sister is marrying a guy whose movies I actually like to watch."

I grinned in understanding. Dad wasn't really a movie

guy. But he liked good action movies, and while Lachlan hadn't branched out into the "serious" movies Brodan had, he had made great action flicks.

"Yeah, it's weird. I still do a double take when I see a movie star in the village. It's like we're living in this weird bubble."

Dad's amusement suddenly died, and he turned to me. "You happy here?"

My stomach fluttered with uneasiness. "Like I said yesterday, I am very happy here, Dad."

"I see a change in you. You seem ... more comfortable in your skin."

That was a good way to describe it. "I feel that way."

Striding to me, he clutched my hands in his and squeezed, pain flashing across his features. "Robyn told me about that piece of shit Austin."

Heart in my throat, I whispered, "Dad, not here."

"I know." He hauled me into a hug. "But I just wanted you to know how sorry I am that you didn't think you could come to me."

Tightening my arms around him, I shook my head against his chest. "Dad, no, please don't think that. I didn't tell anyone. It's hard to explain ... but I buried it. Okay? It was like my *mind* didn't even want to know about it."

"He came to the house again."

I jerked out of his arms. "He what?"

Dad's face was a mask of fury. "I got out my badge and escorted him to his car with a warning to stop harassing you. It took a lot not to fuck him up. And I didn't tell him I knew about Vietnam because I don't want to tip him off before you give a statement. And you *are* giving a statement."

"Dad, you and I both know that statement won't hold up in court."

"I'm hunting down the witnesses. Desiree Jones and Liam

Smith. With names like Smith and Jones, it hasn't been easy. But we've got a few leads. Once we find them, we can get their statement to corroborate yours. But you need to make yours first."

Sick at the thought but even more sick Austin had harassed my parents, I nodded. "Okay. After Christmas."

Relief flooded Dad's features. "Austin shows up at my house again, I'm arresting him."

"What?"

We both turned to find Thane standing in the doorway, his angry gaze on me.

"Austin is back?"

Shit.

In all the chaos of the last few weeks, I'd forgotten to tell Thane about Austin's renewed interest in me.

"Yes. I'm sorry I didn't tell you. I was going to."

"What has he been doing?" Thane stepped into the room, looking between me and Dad.

"Showing up at the house, asking for Regan."

"And you didn't tell me?" He glowered accusingly.

"Is there a reason you need to know about the private business of your employee?" Dad asked, slowly and suspiciously.

Thane took a visible breath, and I could see his mind working behind his eyes, figuring out how to cover his furious reaction to the news. "Because I should know if the woman looking after my children is a safety risk to them."

Wow. Ouch. Even knowing he was just using that as an excuse hurt.

Dad grunted. "I would have thought it would matter because she's your brother's soon-to-be sister-in-law."

"That too."

"Yeah, right." Dad cut me a look that told me he hadn't

bought a word of it. "I hope you two know what you're doing." He walked out of the room before I could reply.

Great. My dad also suspected there was more between Thane and me than we were letting on.

Were we really that bad at hiding it?

"You and I will talk later when the children are in bed." Thane's tone reminded me of the one he used with Eilidh and Lewis when he was displeased.

I opened my mouth to retort, but he was already marching away.

Wonderful.

Merry Christmas!

Attempting to shake off my concerns about Austin's behavior, Dad's suspicions, and Thane's displeasure, I returned to the room and threw myself into helping Arro prepare dinner.

Everything kind of settled again as we sat around the large table, eating and talking while the Adairs got to know my parents. Thane sat between Eilidh and Lewis, and I was directly opposite, sitting beside Mom and Dad. Arro was beside Eilidh, and I was only semi-aware of their conversation about a sleepover for all of Eilidh's dolls at her Aunt Arrochar's when I heard Thane say determinedly, "Eilidh, no."

His tone brought my head up as it cut through the conversations at the table.

Eilidh scowled at her father. "But I wanna!"

"Not tonight."

"What's not tonight?" I butted in.

Thane barely even spared me a glance, but Eilidh shouted across the table, "I wanna sleep over at Aunt Arro's tonight with all my dollies!"

Her loudness killed all conversation.

"Not tonight, sweetie," I replied. "It's Christmas. You spend Christmas with your dad and brother."

"Exactly. You're in your own bed tonight," Thane said, his tone brokering no argument.

"Why can't I sleep where I wanna? Ree-Ree got to sleep in your bed for Santy coming!"

Oh, fuck a fucking duck.

Everything stopped. Cutlery, breathing, my heart. There was an awful silence around the table, and I couldn't look at anyone but Thane, whose expression mirrored my mortification.

"What does that mean?" Mom broke the silence. "What does Eilidh mean?"

"Ree-Ree was in bed with Daddy this morning," Eilidh whispered it now, sensing the bad energy in the room and clearly not understanding it.

I looked down the table to Robyn and saw nothing but concern in her eyes.

"Does she mean what I think she means?" Mom hissed.

"Mom, not here." I turned to her, pleading.

But fury and disappointment filled her expression. "In front of his children?"

Her words made me feel dirty and small. "It wasn't like that!"

"How could you?" Mom pushed her chair back from the table to stand, and I followed suit. "Here's your father giving me bull about how you've changed while you've been here, and we should let you just get on with things, that you're a grown woman! Ha! You're just as spoiled and selfish and irresponsible as ever, and you are coming back to Boston with us."

"Mom, let's go next door to talk about this."

"We're talking about it now!"

"Not in front of the kids."

"Oh, that's rich," she guffawed.

The blood rushed in my ears, my cheeks hot with her recrimination. Looking over at Eilidh and Lewis, seeing their confusion and upset, I said to Arro, "Take the kids next door."

Arro hurried to do so, and Mac strode from his side of the table to help, hauling Eilidh into his arms. Eilidh burst into tears, burying her face in his neck, and my heart plummeted. Mac shot my mom a ferocious glower as he marched away with my girl, soothing her in the way I or her father should be but couldn't because we had to deal with my inconsiderate mother.

Eredine hurried to follow Arro, Mac, and the kids out of the house.

"You're ruining Christmas for the children! You couldn't just leave it alone until dinner was over?" I yelled.

"Are you sleeping with this man?" She pointed at Thane, who stood now, bristling with silent fury.

I couldn't lie. I wouldn't. "Yes."

My mom scoffed. "Then I haven't ruined anything. *You* ruined it for them. You ruined it by doing whatever the hell you felt like doing, never mind that there are children to think about. Always spreading your legs for the first inappropriate man you can find!"

"Stacey!" Dad snapped from his seat beside her.

Her words were like a slap. I flinched and gritted my teeth. "Don't you talk about Eilidh and Lewis. You know nothing about them or my feelings for them!"

"And don't"—Thane's voice was a quiet boom around the room—"you dare talk to Regan like that again."

"Stacey." Dad moved around me to Mom's side. "Calm down. Okay? They're both adults and you're saying things to our daughter you're going to regret. How you're feeling is not about this, and you know it."

"Of course it is. Regan has proven once again she is not an adult. But you"—she turned on Thane as he rounded the table—"how could you do this? Take advantage of my daughter? A grown man, a father!"

"She's twenty-five." Robyn joined the argument. "Seth is right—they are both adults. You're acting like she's sixteen and underage. This is none of our business, and frankly, you're blowing it completely out of proportion. But what's new, Mom?"

"You knew!" Mom accused. "You knew and you let this go on? You allowed this to happen to your sister?"

"Oh, for fuck's sake, don't start that rubbish under my roof," Lachlan warned her. "It is not Robyn's responsibility to police Regan's behavior. Regan is a grown woman whether you want to accept that." He turned to Thane. "But you ... what the hell were you thinking?"

Thane narrowed his eyes, his hands curling into fists at his sides. "Just what Robyn said—that I'm a grown man, and she's a grown woman, and it's nobody's business but ours."

"I'm not talking about that." Lachlan shoved away from the table, his brow furrowed with concern. "I'm talking about the secrecy. The sneaking around. Why not be up-front about it? Did you think we would judge you?"

Mom huffed at my back, and it took everything within me not to pour the nearby jug of ice water over her head just to cool off her psychotic ass.

"No." Thane gave a sharp swipe of his head. "But what was the point? Eilidh finding us was a mistake. It's not permanent between us. Regan will be leaving in six weeks."

I physically stumbled away from his words. He had his back to me, facing Lachlan, so he didn't see my reaction. But my dad put his hand on my shoulder, and he gave me a comforting squeeze. Devastation crashed over me.

I was always just temporary to him.

He would never change his mind.

"Exactly!" Mom pushed past us, and Thane turned to her, scowling like she was a bug he wanted to squash. "She's just drifting from one place to the next, not caring whose heart she breaks, and those kids' hearts are clearly going to be broken." She looked at me. "You've *insinuated* yourself into their lives far beyond that of a nanny, and it is wrong, Regan. It might be the worst thing you've ever done, young lady."

Ignoring her hurtful words, I moved toward Thane. "You don't believe that."

His gaze roiled with a million emotions, but he didn't respond.

"You know I'm not going anywhere. I don't want to be anywhere else." I exhaled a shaky breath, desperation taking control. "I don't want anyone else but you."

Thane's lips parted as his eyes searched mine.

"And I'm sure you believe that, but he shouldn't," Mom interrupted. "Your word is not reliable. Just ask Robyn."

My temper snapped. Whirling on my mother, I shrieked, "For Christ's sake, for once in your life, just shut the fuck up!"

She blanched in shock.

"Amen to that," Brodan muttered under his breath from his spot at the table.

"I can't believe you spoke to me like that," Mom whispered, tears in her eyes.

"As opposed to the way you speak to her?" Thane sneered.

"All right, everyone just calm down," Dad said, pulling Mom into his side and rubbing her shoulder. "We're all hyped up and saying shit we don't mean."

Mom pulled from his hold and came to me, clutching my hands. "Sweetheart, I'm sorry for the way I said it, but we both know there's truth in what I said. You'll fill this poor man's head with ideas and then grow bored and move on."

She squeezed me closer. "You're so young emotionally, and that's okay. That's who you are. You just … you just need to come home and grow up a little."

I yanked my hands out of her grip. For the first time in my life, my mom's behavior truly disgusted me. "You don't know me. You have never known me. You project *your* idea of who I am onto me just as you projected your idea of Robbie onto her. All you care about is not being left behind, and you manipulate things to keep me where you want me— by your side. Well, I'm not who you say I am, and I never have been."

"Regan—"

I pushed past her and grabbed a hold of Thane's arms. He was stiff and unyielding beneath my touch, but I held on. "Please don't listen to her. *You* know me. And if I thought for one second, you could love me back the way I love you … I would never leave you."

It was not how I wanted to confess my feelings to him. But my drama-queen mother had forced us into this situation. And I needed to know I wouldn't lose Thane because of it.

However, as he continued to stare blankly at me, I realized it was too late.

Releasing my grip, I whispered, "You don't believe me."

Something snapped in Thane's expression, and he took a firm hold of my wrist and led me to Lachlan's memorabilia room. When he closed us inside, I opened my mouth to apologize about my mom, but Thane's pitying look stopped me.

My stomach flipped unpleasantly. I already knew what was coming, and it felt like my chest was about to cave in.

"You're only twenty-five, Regan. Why the hell would you want to settle down in a wee place like this with a man whose adventure days involve taking his kids to a local safari every summer? You might think you want this now because the sex is good, but you'd wake up in a year or two years' time and realize what a giant mistake it was. You'll feel stuck. You might even stay for the kids and grow to resent me for it. I won't do that to you. I won't do that to me."

"That's not true."

"No? Well, if that doesn't happen, there's the fact that when I'm sixty, you'll still only be forty-seven, and I might not look so good to you then."

Anger boiled in my blood. "That's not how love works, Thane. You'll always be handsome to me, even when I'm eighty and you're ninety-three, you'll be the most handsome man I've ever seen because it's you, and I don't just see the Adair good looks when I look at you. I see *you*."

He scowled at me in silence.

My heart broke. "You don't trust me to know my own feelings?"

"I've been there before. My experience means I see things you can't."

"Been there before?" I shook my head, not understanding—

And then it hit me.

Fran.

Cheating.

"I'm not her." I glared at him, outraged by the suggestion. "I wouldn't need to get my kicks somewhere else because of something as pathetic as FOMO." I didn't care if I was disparaging Eilidh and Lewis's mom. She'd betrayed Thane because of her fear of missing out, and that he would compare me to her made me lose my mind. "You're *it* for me. You are what thrills me. You excite me in a way no man ever has."

"Because we've been sneaking around like a couple of teenagers. We knew we were doing something we shouldn't, and we were getting off on it."

"Was that all it was to you?" *Please say no, God, please say no or I might crack in two.*

Thane glowered fiercely. "It was that for us both. You're just confused."

As a horrible despair fell over me, my rage so consuming, I couldn't even yell anymore. I could barely get the words out as I sneered, "You condescending bastard."

Ignoring his flinch, I shoved him aside and marched out. I felt brittle. Like I might shatter at the slightest touch. Mom made to move to me, to talk to me, and I put a hand up between us. "Get that woman away from me, or so help me God."

She sobbed like she was the victim, but I couldn't acknowledge her. I only had eyes for my sister, who took one look at me and her face hardened with anger.

"I need to get out of here," I whispered hoarsely. "Before I lose it in front of everyone."

My sister didn't say a word. She exchanged a look with Lachlan, put her arm around me, and hurried us to the laundry room where we put on our coats and boots. The next thing I knew, we were in her SUV. As soon as it drove away from the house, I burst into sobs so hard, they wracked my whole body.

Not long later, Robyn pulled off to the side of the road and reached for me. She cradled my head on her lap like she used to when we were little and stroked my hair as I cried through the pain of my heart crumbling into pieces.

I didn't know how much time passed before the passenger door to the car opened.

"Baby girl." I heard my dad's gruff voice.

Blinking through my tears, I saw Dad sliding into the passenger seat with me. I had to move my legs to let him in.

"Come here, dahlin'."

I pulled out of Robyn's hold and found myself enveloped

in my dad's embrace. In that moment, I didn't feel like the grown-up woman I'd argued I was. But I didn't care. My dad was the safest place in the world right then. And Robbie who tenderly stroked my back. Two of my favorite people in the world were with me, and there was comfort in that.

I realized then that I wasn't only crying because Thane didn't love me; I was crying because of that awful scene my mom had thought was okay to cause. The hurtful words she'd said. The way she always tried to make me feel small.

As if reading my mind, Dad spoke. "Your mom doesn't mean a word she says. It comes from one place: fear. She thinks she's going to lose both her daughters to Scotland, and she'll say and do anything to stop it."

"So she doesn't care if she hurts me?" I whispered.

"Of course, she does. She just ... everything always comes out backward with Stacey. No one will kick her ass more than her in the morning. You know your mom just speaks before she thinks."

"Well ... she's getting her way. I'm not staying." I cried again at the thought of the days, weeks, months, and goddamn devastating years ahead of me without Thane, Eilidh, and Lewis.

I'd been living in a dreamworld for the past few months.

Playing house.

Playing stepmom more than nanny, and we all knew it.

And Thane ... was he really just getting off on fucking around with me, or was he just scared because of Fran?

Either way, I was a fool.

Just like Mom thought I was.

"You really love him, don't you? Him and the kids."

My only answer was to cry harder. I didn't know how to stop. I was frustrated with my reaction, that I couldn't be stronger like Robyn, but I couldn't make the tears stop. Or the pain in my chest or the knot in my gut that tightened so hard, it ached.

Dad kissed my head. "Then don't give up, baby girl. As much as I will miss the hell out of you, it is my job to make sure you're happy. And until tonight, I have never seen you as happy as you have been these past few months."

"He doesn't feel that way about me." Did he?

"Or he's just afraid to take the risk."

I lifted my head, wondering what Dad could mean considering he didn't know about Fran.

At my questioning look, Dad sighed. "You're only halfway to thirty, but that man is closer to forty. His children are his life, and he's settled down in a way he's never *un*settling. He knows he doesn't have time to go gallivanting around the world with you or take you to nightclubs or fancy restaurants every weekend. That's not his life."

Indignation stiffened my spine. "When have I ever said I wanted that? I don't want that! It's empty. And the so-called friends from that life? Where are they, Dad? I don't have any. Other than you and Mom—when she's not being a selfish psycho—I had nothing real in Boston. I have Robyn here. And him … I … nothing is more real than him and Eilidh and Lewis. From almost the beginning, we clicked into place, like we'd been a family forever."

Robyn's hand pressed deeper into my back at my confession.

"Then stay," Dad said, even though I knew it cost him. "Stay and fight for them."

Worry niggled me. "I don't want to harass him."

"You don't need to. You just need to show him you're not going anywhere."

34

REGAN

The longing to wallow was real.

Yet I wanted to prove, not just to everyone else but
to myself, that I could handle fear and grief without running
away like I had in the past. I knew Robyn wanted me to talk
to a professional about why I always ran, and maybe I would
in the future, but for now, I wanted to try on my own. It
wasn't easy. I fought the urge to pack my bags and run
almost every hour of the day. Alone in one of Lachlan and
Robyn's guest rooms, I'd bury my face in a pillow and cry all
the tears I couldn't cry throughout the day.

In the harsh cast of daylight, I held it together as best I
could. My sister's house had probably never been cleaner. I
knew she worried I was bottling shit up, but really, I was just
protecting myself from falling apart in front of my mother.

There was no way to salvage Christmas dinner. I felt
awful ruining it for Eilidh and Lewis. Robyn assured me it
was all right, that Arrochar would make it up for them the
next day. In the UK, they celebrated Boxing Day the day after
Christmas, and it involved another big family meal. They
hosted it at Thane's, and for Eilidh and Lewis, I insisted

Robyn and Lachlan be there. Brodan was leaving the day after, and I wanted him to have uninterrupted time with his family too.

Mom, Dad, and I stayed put.

And I hid in my room.

Robyn said they'd tell Eils and Lew that I was sick and they'd see me later. I'd hoped that was true, that I could convince Thane to let me continue as their nanny.

However, when I texted him to meet me the day after Boxing Day at the annex, I was floored by his coldness. As soon as he walked into the small apartment, memories rushed over me of the past few months. Of our passionate nights here. Of the dreams I'd spun in my head of making a life with him.

My heart throbbed so hard in my chest, I was nauseated.

And he stood about three feet away, his arms crossed over his chest, staring at me like I was a stranger.

Before I could speak, he announced, "I need to make this quick because we're seeing Brodan off at the airport ... I'm letting you go, Regan. I'll pay you for January for the inconvenience of an abrupt termination, but I think this is for the best. You're leaving soon, anyway, and your presence in Eilidh's and Lewis's lives has become confusing for them."

Thane sounded so emotionless. Like it meant nothing to him to cut me out.

Was my dad wrong? Would I be humiliating myself if I stuck around to prove something to this man?

Suddenly angry at him, I stared incredulously. "What have I done to deserve you treating me with such contempt?"

His stoic expression faltered, and his tone softened a little. "It's not contempt. You have done nothing. I'm just doing what's best for my kids."

"By taking me away from them?"

Indignation flashed in his eyes. "You'll be gone, eventually. The longer we let this go on between us, the worse it will get."

"I'm going to be in their lives. My sister is marrying your brother," I reminded him.

"They'll see you once or twice a year when you visit. By then, they'll have—" He cut off abruptly.

Fighting back tears, I couldn't look at him. "Forgotten me."

"Regan ..." he sighed heavily, and I felt like an inconvenient child he was forced to deal with. "I am sorry it turned out this way."

Tightness crawled across my chest, like a stone creature sat atop it. The thought of not seeing him, not touching him, never being in his arms again was unbearable. And the thought of not being there for Eilidh and Lewis as they grew up killed me. I wanted to witness them become the amazing adults I knew they'd be. To send them off to high school, watch them go on their first dates, cry my heart out after dropping them off at college, and spend every Christmas I had left on this planet with them because they were my family.

And it was like a death. The destruction of that dream felt like someone I loved had died.

I guessed I hadn't realized until that moment just how much I'd been hoping our affair would turn into something more, something permanent.

All the while Thane stared at me, veering between dispassionate and pitying.

I didn't know if it was an act to protect himself.

I didn't know what was real anymore.

"I'll give you time to say goodbye to them. Just let me know when you want to do that."

Never.

I never wanted to say goodbye.

Not to them.

Thane was a different story. I wanted to fight for him, but he didn't believe in me. As much as I wanted to ignore that, I'd come too far. How would I ever continue to believe in myself if I continued to love someone who didn't believe in me? Where would my pride and self-respect be then?

Devastated, I couldn't say another word.

Thane took hold of my arm as I strode past him, halting me. Staring at the floor, I resisted the urge to melt into his touch. Almost as if he'd read my mind, he said hoarsely, "You are a very special woman, *mo leannan*. Never forget it."

Then why don't you want me?

I met his gaze. I'd finally asked Arrochar what *mo leannan* meant. And I wasn't his darling, his love, or his sweetheart. I was nothing to him. "Don't call me that." I wrenched my arm out of his grip and marched out of the annex before I burst into tears.

Robyn and Lachlan moved my stuff into their place.

A few days before New Year's Eve, Mom and Dad returned to Boston. They were supposed to stay and attend Hogmanay—the Scottish term for New Year's celebrations—at Ardnoch Castle. It was a big deal that they were invited since only the Adair family could attend outside of the club members. But between Robyn and me giving her the cold shoulder, Mom wasn't exactly feeling welcome, and Dad decided they should go home early. That broke my heart, too, but I didn't know how to fix it. I partially blamed her for losing Thane, and that resentment wasn't going away anytime soon.

I was in my room, reading, preparing to go downstairs and say goodbye to my parents when a knock sounded at the door. "Come in," I called, thinking it was Robbie or Dad since they were the only two who had ventured in to see me over the past few days.

The door opened, and I looked up from my spot on the chaise by the window to find my mom gazing forlornly at me. She was dressed in loungewear, something she only dared wear when she was flying. Otherwise, I got my love of pretty dresses from her, as well as my love of reading. An overwhelming sadness settled over me.

I hated that I resented her.

Without asking, Mom crossed the room and sat down on the end of the chaise. I swung my legs off and sat up, shutting down my e-reader. We sat in silence for a moment, me staring at the floor, she at me.

"I always seem to be apologizing to my kids lately." She heaved a weary sigh.

Maybe don't do shit you need to apologize for.

Mom continued, "I don't know why I do the things I do. Your father likes to psychoanalyze me. Should have been a psychologist, not a detective."

One goes hand in hand with the other.

Mom huffed. "Are you ever going to speak to me again?"

I looked at her. "Are you going to apologize for real?"

Recognizing her expression, the one that said she wanted to reprimand me, I smirked. Mom was so hardheaded, it would be funny if it wasn't so self-destructive.

"I'm sorry," she said, surprising me.

That ache in my chest grew. "Really?"

"Yes. I'm sorry if I've ever made you feel like a failure. I didn't mean to do that. Now, I won't say that I agree with what you've done here. I just won't. But I will say that I have to remember it isn't my place to judge those decisions. You're a grown-up now, and I have to respect that."

"That's your apology?"

"Yes." Mom reached for my hand. "Regan, I blew it out of proportion, and I messed up. I ruined dinner for everyone, and I'm mortified. Your dad is right. That fight was about more than your affair with Thane. It was about losing you to this place." She squeezed my hand. "Robbie was always so independent, from the moment she could walk. And she was …" Sadness saturated Mom's features. "She was Mac's little clone. Adored him. When he was around, I couldn't get a look in. So I knew"—she gave me a wobbly smile—"I knew from when she was a little girl that she'd never be *my* little girl. She'd go off and do her own thing, and I would see her when I saw her. I tried to push her on you too much, hoping your bond would keep her close to us all."

"Mom." I tightened my grip on her hand, not realizing that had been her perspective on Robyn. "Robbie loves you."

"Yeah, I know. But I thought with you, you were all ours. Mine and your dad's. And I was determined you would be ours forever. That you wouldn't be like Robbie and disappear on us." She laughed bitterly. "I guess I pushed you away, anyway, trying to keep you too close. Trying to coddle you, make you think you needed me."

Her sudden self-awareness shocked me.

Or maybe Dad's psychoanalyzing had finally sunk in.

"Now I've lost you to this place too. Or have I?"

"Mom … things between us can't just magically be okay. You hurt me. And you … your actions led to the end of a relationship that meant a great deal to me, whether you agree with it or not. But with time …" I shrugged sadly. "I love you, Mom. That's never going to go away."

"But you are?" she pushed.

I swallowed the hard tears in my throat as I choked out, "It's not going to happen with Thane."

"Oh?"

"But I'm not leaving. Robyn is here, and I don't want to leave her."

Tears brightened Mom's eyes, but she nodded. "You do seem better here. Safer. Your father told me about this Austin person. You know ... I am here if you ever need to talk about that."

I flinched and lowered my eyes. "It's just like how I told it. Nothing more to say." At my mother's hurt silence, I sighed. Now was not the time for her to be my confidante. "I'm sorry."

"Don't be." She patted my hand and stood. "Robbie told us about the ancestry visa you're applying for."

Wait, what? I hadn't applied for it yet.

"Seth was thinking of looking up that side of his family, maybe visiting them when we come back over for Robbie's wedding."

I nodded, dazed, my mind wandering.

"Can I get a hug goodbye?"

I hugged my mom. Still angry at her, still confused, still resentful, but ... she was my mom. And I loved her. "Not goodbye," I promised. "Just 'see you soon.'"

Me crying as they loaded Lachlan's SUV to leave seemed to soothe something in both my parents. I didn't want them to think I didn't miss them when we weren't together. Mom and I definitely needed a breather from one another, but Dad was the calm in the storm. And I'd miss him like crazy.

"We'll see you soon." Dad kissed my forehead. "We'll be back for the wedding."

After they left, I sat in that big house by myself. Brodan was also gone, and Lachlan and Robyn had driven our parents to the airport. I stared numbly at the television until the front door opened a few hours later. As soon as Robyn strolled into the room, I asked her about the visa.

She gave me an appeasing grin. "I might have ... begun the process for you."

Gaping at her, I didn't know how to respond. It was so unlike her to meddle like this.

"What was the harm? And you were wasting time taking

forever to decide." She crossed the large room to the side table near the stairs and opened a drawer. When she returned to me, Robyn clutched an envelope. She handed it over, and I saw it was a letter providing me with an appointment in Inverness next week to have my biometrics taken. "I started the process over four months ago. This letter arrived just before Christmas."

"Four months ago?"

Robyn sighed. "It's not a straightforward process. As it was, we're having to use a connection of Lachlan's to push it through before your visitor visa is up. I had to apply for copies of birth certificates for Seth's maternal grandparents, his parents, his, as well as marriage certificates, and those took a few months to arrive. I also had to collate your income for the past six months, along with your personal information. It's all done. All you have to do is go to this appointment, and we'll have everything we need. Then Lachlan's friend is going to push it through as quickly as possible." She smirked at her fiancé. "Sometimes it pays to be an Adair."

He smirked back and strolled toward the kitchen. "Coffee anyone?"

I stared at the letter. "Don't I need an income for this to even matter? I don't know if you noticed, but Thane kind of fired me."

Robyn's expression softened with sympathy, but before she could speak, Lachlan said, "And I just kind of hired you."

Spinning toward him, I raised an eyebrow. "How so?"

"You want to stay, don't you?"

"Yes. But not for your brother," I clarified, not caring how bitter I sounded. "I'm staying for me. And for Robyn."

My sister sidled up to me and put her arm around my shoulders. "You don't know how happy I am that you're staying."

"I mean it," I promised. I was determined I could live here, despite Thane. "I'm settled here. Even without ..."

"Then it's decided." Lachlan strode across the room and handed each of us a coffee. "Until you can find something more permanent, I have a server position open at the castle. You can start whenever you want."

"Really? You trust me to work there?"

My soon-to-be brother-in-law smiled. "I trusted you with my niece and nephew, so I certainly trust you to work at the club."

It was so similar to what Thane had said only days before that I had to lower my eyes to cover the flinch of pain. Yet if I was staying in Ardnoch, I had to get used to it. I was going to see Thane, Eilidh, and Lewis more than Thane realized at this point.

"Speaking of." Robyn squeezed my shoulder. "The kids are asking for you. There's only so long we can tell them you're sick."

Sipping my coffee, I moved out of my sister's embrace and slumped down on the sectional. "Thane expects me to say goodbye to them. And I don't want to. So ... I'm putting it off."

"My brother doesn't know you're staying?"

I shook my head. "He thinks I'm leaving soon, I guess."

"Then don't say goodbye." Lachlan stared at me with a gleam in his eyes. "It'll only confuse them when you never leave."

"I'll need to talk with them soon, though, about not being their nanny anymore. The very thought nauseates me."

Robyn and Lachlan exchanged a look, and my sister turned to me. "I've got an idea ... why don't you get all dolled up for the Hogmanay party at Ardnoch. It'll be an excellent distraction."

The thought of pasting a smile on and socializing with

movie stars wasn't as appealing as it might have been six months ago. Plus, Thane would be there.

"Thane's not coming," Robyn assured me, as if she'd read my mind. "He's staying home with the kids."

"I don't know." I still didn't think I had the energy to be the bright, bubbly, breezy version of myself. However, I also didn't want to be alone in the house with the objects of my affection a mere stone's throw away.

Something occurred to me. Directing my question at Lachlan, I asked, "I don't suppose you need extra servers for this party, do you?"

35

REGAN

Lachlan wasted no time putting me on his payroll. With employment came the offer to stay in one of the cabins Lachlan rented to seasonal employees just there for the summer. I knew right away he'd discounted my rent and was affronted I was being coddled again until Regan assured me it was just Lachlan's way. He was extremely generous with his family, and he'd be offended if I refused the discount.

Every day on the estate, being away from Caelmore, away from Eilidh and Lewis, my uneasiness grew. It wasn't fair for me to just disappear out of their lives. While I didn't know what I'd say to them, I finally texted Thane the morning of New Year's Eve to arrange a time for me to see them. We decided on the third day of the new year at the play park near the school. I didn't want it to be public, but Thane, for whatever reason, thought it was best. His texts were clipped and no-nonsense. I didn't recognize him in them. In fact, I hadn't recognized the Thane I knew and loved since Christmas Day.

Maybe that would make it easier for me to get over him.

Eventually.

~

"Are you sure you want to do this?" Robyn asked me for the sixteenth time.

I stared at her, looking more glamorous than I'd ever seen her, in a long-sleeved, formfitting, sheer black dress that came to just above her knees. It was saved from being utterly scandalous by the stunning beadwork. The sequined embroidery created an explosion of golds, silvers, blues, and pinks that looked like fireworks. A perfect New Year's Eve dress, an incredible work of art that had been a gift from Lachlan. Robyn wore her hair slicked back in a high ponytail that elongated her eyes, making them particularly sultry. Dark gold strappy heels that made her amazing legs look even more spectacular completed the ensemble.

She was a bona fide hottie.

"I'm sure," I promised, answering her question. "Have I mentioned you look incredible?"

Robyn gave me a sad smile. "You have. And you look super cute in that uniform, but I will ask you again, and it will be the last time: Are you sure you want to work at this party rather than be a guest at it? Because frankly, it's weird that my baby sister is serving people rather than standing at my side, showing all those Hollywood types what genuine beauty looks like."

Tears brightened my eyes. "Have I also mentioned how you're the best friend anyone could ever ask for?"

She smiled and came toward me, her arms outstretched, but I waved her off.

"No, I don't want to rumple you or get my uniform caught on a sequin." I was dressed in the server's uniform. All the waitstaff wore the same traditional getup—white cravat, black waistcoat, coattails, flat-black dress shoes, and white gloves. Only Mr. Ramsay, the maître d'hôtel and my supervisor, and the butler, Wakefield, wore a dark green waistcoat to differentiate them from the rest of the staff. I thought girls in coattails were adorable and applauded Lachlan's decision to be gender neutral rather than make the girls wear uncomfortable skirts and heels. The only thing that was a pain was the cravat. But I'd get used to it.

Robyn halted, her arms flopping to her sides. "Well, if I can't convince you otherwise, I better let you get to work. I'll see you at the party. No gawking at the famous people."

I made a face. "I've seen plenty of famous faces the past forty-eight hours and have been totally cool, thank you very much."

"But this is your first time serving them up close. Don't be dazzled."

"Believe me, Robbie," I said, giving her a melancholy smile, "nothing can dazzle me right now."

At the way her face fell, I hurried to say, "Except you in that dress."

My sister didn't buy my teasing. So I kissed her on the cheek before she could say anything else and hurried out of their private suite.

I couldn't imagine the castle like Thane had once described it—cold and dreary—as I moved through the traditionally decorated hallways that were now warm and inviting. On the staircase, I approached the British actor Angeline Potter and some guy I didn't recognize climbing the stairs hand in hand. They weren't dressed yet for the party, though Angeline's hair and makeup were certainly made up for it, so I assumed they'd be arriving "fashionably late."

"Oi, you, come here," she called as I descended toward them.

"Yes?" I asked as I slowed.

She narrowed her eyes at me as I stopped on the wide staircase beside them. "You're new. I'd remember that face."

"First night."

"How nice for you. Could you be a dear and let Wakefield know I want a bottle of champagne sent to my suite?"

"Sure thing." I moved to walk by her.

"Sure thing?" she called snottily at my back.

I glanced over my shoulder. "Pardon?"

"Darling, you're new, so I'll let it slide just this once. When you're speaking to me, I expect you to be well-mannered. You don't answer 'sure thing.' You reply, 'Right away, Ms. Potter.' Understood?"

Call it the rough week I'd just had or maybe fatigue of being condescended to, but I responded with, "I treat people how they treat me. If you'd like my attention in the future, instead of hailing me like a dog, you might try, 'Excuse me, miss, can you help me, please?'"

Angeline gaped like a gulping fish while her companion covered a smirk with his hand.

"I'll let Wakefield know you want that bottle sent up." I hurried downstairs, my pulse racing a little.

Probably not the best start.

~

"We're going to get this unpleasantness out of the way immediately." Mr. Ramsay cornered me as I placed champagne flutes onto sterling silver serving trays.

At his agitated tone, I turned to him. "Is everything okay?"

"Mr. Wakefield has just informed me that our esteemed guest Ms. Angeline Potter has filed a complaint against you for your rudeness to her this evening." His expression couldn't be any more disapproving. "Now, I understand this is an unusual situation, as we've never had an extended member of the Adair family on staff before. However, I do not care if you are the Queen of Sheba, Ms. Penhaligon. You will not be rude to my guests because you think you can get away with it."

Indignation fired through me, and I sought to stay calm. "I wasn't rude because I think I'm immune to disciplinary action. I responded in kind to Ms. Potter."

Some of Mr. Ramsay's ire seemed to deflate. "It is your first night, Regan, and you are jumping into the deep end. There are more members here tonight than any night of the year. No one does Hogmanay like the Scots, and our members clamber to attend."

I bit back a pithy reply about how only Scottish people technically did Hogmanay.

"During your time here, you will discover some members are more difficult to deal with than others. While no one gets away with outright disrespecting the staff, we cannot stop members from being generally ill-mannered or difficult to please. You must react in those situations with utmost professionalism. I suggest counting to ten in your head before responding."

"Is that what you do?" I asked somewhat cheekily, grinning at him.

A gleam of amusement flickered in his eyes, and I knew he wasn't immune to a little charm. "Back to work, Ms. Penhaligon. Best behavior, please."

"Yes, Mr. Ramsay."

Still, when he walked away, I huffed under my breath. I couldn't believe the snot tattled on me.

An hour later, the dining room and humongous reception hall, transformed for the party, were filled with members. The band was set up on the staircase landing in front of the stained glass window. When I first glimpsed Ashton Solomon, lead singer of the famous indie-rock band High Voltage, I thought I was seeing things. Then I spotted the rest of the band.

Lachlan had hired one of the most sought-after bands in the world to play his Hogmanay party.

Shit, I didn't even want to know what that cost him.

Before the band started, the guests were asked to come outside. As I watched everyone file toward the large main entrance in their coats, a warm hand clasped my elbow and I turned to find Robyn.

"Come on, you don't want to miss this."

"But I'm working," I protested.

"Lachlan said everyone."

"Why? What's going on?" I asked loudly to be heard over the guests.

"Fire is a big part of Hogmanay celebrations. Every year, Lachlan hires fire dancers to put on a kickoff show on the driveway."

Eyebrows raised, I let my sister drag me outside. Lachlan gestured her over to him, and I followed willingly until I realized he wasn't alone.

Arro and Mac looked especially glamorous, Mac like Lachlan in his kilt, and Arro in a green gown that showed off a figure so elegant, she could be an advertisement for diamonds.

They weren't the problem.

It was the other Scot in his kilt.

Thane.

"I thought he wasn't coming," I hissed in Robyn's ear as she forced me along with her.

"Eredine hates Hogmanay, so she offered to babysit. Lachlan made him come."

Wonderful.

As if he sensed my eyes on him, Thane turned from talking with Mac and looked directly at us. He stiffened as his gaze drifted down my body, taking in my staff uniform. I winced as he shot an accusatory look at his brother.

Obviously, Lachlan had failed to tell him I now worked at Ardnoch.

The flicker of orange light caught my attention just as gasps of delight filled the night air. Robyn's hand closed around mine, refusing to let go, as we turned to watch the spectacle of the elegant fire dancers.

"Just ignore him and enjoy this."

Thankfully, the procession of dancers down the long drive was hypnotizing as flames lit up the surrounding darkness. I made sounds of delight and amazement along with everyone else as fire-breathers shot massive fireballs into the air and fire dancers spun by them in aerial cartwheels while they twirled fans of fire in their hands.

Not long before it ended, one of my new colleagues, Andrew, approached to tell me Mr. Ramsay wanted all the staff back inside for serving food. That morning I'd rehearsed with the rest of the waitstaff because we wouldn't enter the party with the trays of food and drink until the castle piper piped in a ceremonial haggis. The members wouldn't be eating that haggis. They'd be eating fancy canapés with haggis wrapped in phyllo pastry drizzled in a whisky cream sauce.

While I envied them the food and drink and cheer, I was gladder than ever that I was working now that Thane was here. The guests would keep me busy, distracting me from looking for him every second.

I had to admit, as the bagpiper led the procession of the haggis, I got goose bumps. The pipes' mournful rendition of "Auld Lang Syne" filled every inch of the reception hall. The servers holding the champagne moved through the crowd quietly. I was one of those servers, and having spotted the Adairs on the far side of the room near the entrance, I stuck to the opposite side. Once all my glasses were taken, I returned to an archway near the back of the hall.

When the piper finished, Lachlan strode up the main staircase and stopped on a step just below the band on the landing. The murmurs settled, and he gestured with his glass. "Thank you, honored guests," his voice boomed around the room, his accent sounding more pronounced tonight, "for being here to celebrate Hogmanay at Ardnoch."

A few cheers came from the members, and he grinned, waving his hand to settle them. A solemnity replaced his smile. "Not for many years has Ardnoch looked forward to a new beginning as it does tonight. The hardships of this year cannot be denied, and we'll never forget them or my friend Greg McHugh."

Greg, I knew, was the security guard killed by Fergus when Lucy was terrorizing Lachlan and Ardnoch.

At the emotion in Lachlan's voice, tears stung my eyes.

"I cannot bring back Greg for his family, but I can thank him for protecting mine. It is a debt I can never repay ..." He took a deep breath and continued, "Despite the loss and trauma of this year, as I stand here, I am nothing but grateful for my many blessings. To be surrounded by you all, friends who have shown me and Ardnoch such support." His gaze drifted to Robyn. "To have Robyn by my side and her promise to stay at my side forever."

Whistles rent the air, making him grin ruefully.

"To have my family here, safe and well," he continued, "it's all any of us can ask. And I wish nothing but the same for you, my friends. Tonight, we let go of yesterday and embrace new beginnings." He raised his glass, and the guests followed suit. "May ye for'er be happy an' yer enemies know it! *Slàinte Mhath!*" He pronounced the Scottish Gaelic for "cheers" as *slanj-a-va*.

"Slàinte Mhath!" the guests roared, and the band broke into the beginning chords of their biggest hit to date.

I watched Lachlan stop to shake hands with guests. All

the while, his eyes were on Robyn. Just a few weeks ago, I'd imagined spending New Year's Eve with Thane. Maybe sneaking away from everyone else to kiss at midnight. As I followed my new colleagues to collect fresh trays of drinks, I scoffed at the very idea. Perhaps in five years' time, I'd be less bitter and at a Hogmanay much like this, I'd be able to clink my glass against his and wish him well.

I winced.

I *did* wish him well.

I would never wish Thane anything else.

But I wasn't quite ready to wish it to his face.

36
THANE

"**B**rother, a word." Thane didn't care if he was being rude as he took Lachlan's elbow and forcefully removed him from his conversation with the famous director, Merriam Burbanks.

"Excuse me," Lachlan said before he was hauled away. "You can let go of me now."

Thane released him, knowing his big brother would follow, as they moved swiftly through the crowd, their expressions warding off anyone who might approach to engage them in conversation. Thane searched through the famous faces to find Regan. She was in profile, flashing her pretty dimples at Roman fucking Bright, of all people. Even in the ridiculous livery Lachlan made his staff wear, she was appealing. And Bright seemed to think so as he stopped her from drifting away with her tray of champagne flutes. His lips were quirked in flirtation. The bastard was married, but Thane knew via Lachlan that the son of Hollywood legend Garret Bright was a well-known womanizer.

His gut twisted as he wrenched his gaze away, stormed from the party, and turned down the castle corridor toward

Lachlan's stage office. Once inside, he waited until his brother shut the door behind him.

"You said she wouldn't be here."

"I said she wouldn't be a *guest* here." Lachlan shrugged.

"You bastard. I can't believe you hired her."

Lachlan stared calmly at him. "Robyn is as good as my wife. Regan is her sister."

"So you hired her? For how long? Until her visa expires?"

"No."

Thane's stomach dropped. "No?"

"She's applying for her ancestry visa. I have a friend at the Home Office who's going to push it through so she doesn't have to return to the States to wait for it. I offered her a position and a cabin here on the estate for however long she needs it."

"With no thought to me or the kids?" Thane seethed.

Lachlan quirked an eyebrow. "I'm sure the kids will be pleased Regan can still be in their lives. Frankly, your attitude to this point has suggested *you* don't give a fuck about her. I didn't think you'd care. But Robyn does. Robyn wants her here, so I'm making that happen."

"Don't give a fuck? Didn't think I'd care?" he whispered harshly, feeling the unfamiliar urge to punch his brother.

He received a hard warning look. "I'm not the one you're angry with."

"Oh?"

"You're angry with yourself, you hardheaded prick." Lachlan cut him a dark look. "A decade of happiness is better than a lifetime of emptiness."

Thane tensed, remembering those words.

"That's what you said to me," Lachlan pushed. "Not even eight months ago. When I came to you about Robyn, you advised me to face my fears and just be with her. Not very good at following your own advice, are you?"

"You love Robyn."

"And by that, I suppose you mean you don't love Regan?"

Sweat dampened Thane's palms and suddenly his bow tie was too tight. "We don't make sense."

"That's a lie and you know it. I have never seen you happier than I have these past few months. I suspected something was between you but couldn't be sure. What I did know was whether you had given in to your attraction to Regan, you were more content with her in your life than you have ever been. *Ever*, Thane."

The truth in his words was soul-destroying. "I have to protect Eilidh and Lewis. If Regan was older, ready to settle down, then it would be a different story. It would be a calculated risk that anyone takes when they're in love. But Regan's too young. Right now, it's just asking for Eilidh and Lewis to be hurt."

"And asking for you to be hurt, am I right?" Lachlan glared at him. "Or I'm wrong. Because you can't love her if you don't trust her. And you obviously don't trust Regan and her feelings for you." His brother shook his head in disappointment and strode away.

As he opened the door to leave, he glanced back at Thane and said grimly, "One day you're going to realize how in love she was with you, that you betrayed her with your mistrust and destroyed the best thing that ever happened to you since the kids came along. And I will be there for you on that day because you're going to need me. But Christ, Thane, you could save yourself a world of misery by just pulling your head out of your arse before it's too late."

Thane flinched, not at the slam of the door as his brother departed in frustration, but at Lachlan's words.

They held an air of prophecy that filled him with dread.

Tonight should have been a good night. The beginning of a new year, as Lachlan had said, after a horrifying one. A night to move on. His children were safe in their beds at home, Sean McClintock was out of their lives for good as per the correspondence Thane had received from the arsehole's lawyer, the pall of Eilidh's paternity no longer hung over him, and a fresh start beckoned.

Except he was still fucking miserable.

"Now what could you possibly have going on in your life to make you brood so?"

Thane looked up from his glass of whisky at the husky, upper-crust voice. Angeline Potter, current young darling of the British film industry, leaned against the castle library door with a champagne flute in her hand.

He hadn't ever conversed with her, only knew her from her films and the odd sighting here and there at the estate and in the village. "Nothing," he replied, in no mood for pleasantries. "Just wanted to be alone."

Not taking the hint, she sashayed into the room, swinging her slender hips. "I know the feeling. That's why I found my way here. It's my favorite room at Ardnoch." She settled into the armchair opposite him and crossed one leg over the other so the slit in her blue dress revealed her pale, lovely leg from stiletto-encased toe to upper thigh. Angeline gave him a sultry but hard look. "My partner disappeared with Lizette Mayfield ten minutes ago. One guess what they're getting up to."

At her bitter tone, Thane murmured, "I would think Angeline Potter wouldn't have to put up with a cheating boyfriend."

"Oh, we're just casual. We're working on a film trilogy together, and the director asked that we pretend to be more serious than we are, you know, for publicity. But you'd think"—she pouted—"that the arsehole could get through one evening without fucking someone else. As if he'd ever be allowed to step onto this estate if it weren't for my membership. And he goes and fucks Lizette Mayfield of all people." She lowered her voice. "I will never understand how she was granted membership."

Thane raised an eyebrow.

"Oh. I don't mean to disparage your brother. I just think he's too kind sometimes." She leaned forward, eyeing him in a way that couldn't be misinterpreted. "I haven't seen the youngest brother, but it seems the handsome gene runs strong in the Adair men. I met Brodan in Cannes once. He's a rather delicious specimen, isn't he? I like my men broody, though." She grinned flirtatiously. "That American of Lachlan's is certainly a lucky woman. Are you married?"

"No." The word was like ash on his tongue. Not in the mood to be Angeline Potter's distraction for the evening, he stood abruptly. "If you'll excuse me, it will be midnight soon."

She gaped at him, as if shocked he was giving up the chance to be with her in private. As he marched away, he heard the rustle of her dress and the click-clack of her heels as she called, "Wait for me. I don't want to miss the fireworks."

Wanting to run from her was completely incongruous to the way Thane's father had raised him, so though he didn't slow down, he didn't run off either. Back in the reception hall, they found many of the guests had donned coats and jackets and were making their way outside again, this time for the fireworks display. It *was* almost midnight.

"There you are!" Lachlan called to him from the main door. He gestured for Thane to hurry.

"I don't have a coat," Angeline whined, reminding him she was at his side. "But I don't want to miss the display."

The gentleman in him shrugged out of his kilt jacket, despite how irritating he found her. He placed it around her shoulders, and she clutched it, staring up at him with wonder in her big Bambi eyes.

"Thank you," she whispered, apparently amazed. Then she grinned and looped her arm through his to snuggle into his side.

Oh, wonderful.

Lachlan glowered at him as they approached, and Thane threw his brother an exasperated "I don't know how this happened" look.

Outside, he couldn't shake her, and as they wandered along with the guests to find a spot to stand on the driveway, he saw Robyn with his sister and Mac. She turned and caught sight of him. Her lips stretched into a smile that faltered when she saw who was on Thane's arm. Her features hardened, and she glared at him as fiercely as his brother just had.

Fantastic.

Sighing, he looked down at Angeline, who now rested her head on his shoulder. How *had* this happened? "Don't you want to find your ... friend ... before the clock strikes midnight?"

"I'm very happy where I am." She lifted her head and squeezed his biceps. "You feel like a man. He feels like a boy. I like the difference."

Her words struck so close to something Regan had said to him many months before that he flinched and looked away. "I'm not on the market."

"I thought you said you weren't married. Involved?"

"No."

"Then I'm harming no one by keeping you company." She squeezed his arm again. "Loosen up, darling. There's nothing worse than standing alone at midnight on Hogmanay."

"I'm not alone." Thane looked over at Robyn, Arro, and

Mac to see Lachlan had joined them. Where was Regan? He searched the crowd of guests and staff for her.

"Well, *I* am."

Angeline's forlorn tone brought his eyes back to her. She gave him a rueful, melancholy smirk. "I'm alone. I don't want to be alone at midnight."

As if on cue, the piper quietened the crowd with a blow of his mournful instrument. Then Lachlan's voice boomed into the night. "Ten! Nine! Eight …"

Everyone's voices joined him in the countdown, but Thane was too busy craning his neck in search of Regan. It was too shadowy to see much farther than a few feet, even with the lights along the side of the castle building offering reprieve from the darkness.

"Two! One! Happy New Year!"

Fireworks exploded into the sky above them right on time, illuminating everyone in pops and flashes of rainbow-hued light.

A hard yank on his waistcoat brought his head down, and Angeline slammed her mouth onto hers. Stunned into still-ness, the damn woman took advantage and wriggled her tongue past his lips to lick at him. At his lack of response, she released him abruptly, scowling. "Well, kiss me back! It's New Year's!" She jerked him toward her again, but Thane's gaze was drawn beyond her.

His heart stopped in his chest.

Illuminated beneath the raucous bangs of the fireworks, Regan stood in her uniform, staring at him and Angeline in absolute horror.

No!

Her eyes moved from the woman in his arms, the woman draped in his kilt jacket, to him.

And she looked at him with such hatred, Thane wanted to die.

404

"Regan."

She whirled, her ponytail whipping a guest in the face, and pushed through the crowd.

"Thane?" Angeline pulled at him.

He disentangled from her grip, shoving her aside as gently but as firmly as he could, before hurrying after Regan.

"Where are you going?" Angeline called petulantly at his back.

Thane could kill the woman!

And himself for being too much of a fucking gentleman to tell her to piss off!

A flash of copper-red hair beneath the lights of the fireworks caught his eye, and he saw Regan dash into the castle.

"Excuse me, excuse me," he muttered impatiently, his heart banging in his chest.

The deafening display in the night sky agitated his pulse even more.

There was no one in the reception hall when he finally made it inside. The sound of everyone breaking into "Auld Lang Syne," as was Scottish tradition after midnight, irritated Thane. Didn't they know not everyone was in a celebratory fucking mood now?

"Regan!" he shouted to be heard over them.

Desperation and fear shuddered through him.

Where would she go?

He knew the answer before he'd even finished the thought. Storming through the reception hall, Thane hurried to where he'd hidden for the past few hours before Angeline Potter found him and derailed his whole bloody evening.

Striding into the library, his pulse eased just a little as Regan spun from her spot near a bookshelf to face him. Her usually warm chestnut eyes were flat and dark.

"Why did you follow me?" She crossed her arms over her

chest. "Shouldn't you be out there enjoying the tongue gymnastics of a BAFTA Award–winning actor?"

He winced at the way her voice cracked with emotion. "That wasn't me." He approached her slowly and paused as she retreated. "Regan, *she* kissed *me*."

"Oh, really? I didn't see you pushing her off. It must have been such a hardship for you."

"It was, actually," he growled. *Her tongue was like a slug.*

"I'm sure she thought her kiss was welcome, what with you giving her your jacket to wear and letting her snuggle all over you." She spat *snuggle* like it was a dirty word, the flatness in her eyes replaced by angry fire.

Thane could deal with the fire. Fire was good. It was emotion. Flatness meant she no longer cared. And that, as fucked up as it was, he couldn't deal with. Staring at her, her chest heaving with agitation, her lips trembling with emotion ... God, he missed her. It had only been a week, and yet it felt like months since he'd held her.

"I gave her my jacket because she was cold. End of story." He moved toward her again, and although Regan didn't retreat, she eyed him warily.

"It's none of my business, I guess. You've made that clear. I just thought you'd have more class than to move on to someone else less than a week after we broke up. She's my age, you know."

"I'm not moving on to bloody Angeline Potter!" he yelled, beyond frustrated now.

"Like I said, none of my business. Just like I'm none of yours."

Yes, you bloody are. He stalked ever closer to her, eyeing the stupid cravat Lachlan made his staff wear, his fingers curling at the thought of ripping it off her throat so he could cover her skin in kisses and feel the throb of her pulse beneath his lips.

"You can kiss or sleep with whoever you want," Regan continued with a shrug. "Just like I can."

"You wouldn't," he bit out harshly.

Her eyes narrowed. "Oh, I would. Hell, Jared McCulloch has made it more than clear that he'd like me in his bed."

Jealousy and rage flared through him as if she'd just dropped a match on a pool of petrol at his feet. "That pup?" He closed the distance between them, forcing her to tilt her head to hold his gaze. The image of Regan naked beneath McCulloch's grandson nauseated him. "You'd only be doing it to fuck me out of your system, and you'd think of me the whole time."

Devastation leaked through Regan's defiance, cooling his anger. "True," she whispered. "I'd wish it were you instead of him ... but it wouldn't change the fact that it would be *him* inside me. His cock, his lips, his hands, his—"

Thane hauled her against him, swallowing the words he couldn't stand to hear. His kiss wasn't gentle or gentleman-like in the least. Holding her by the nape so she couldn't move, Thane kissed her like he wanted to fuck her. Hard, ravaging, deep. Pushing her toward the bookshelves, trapping her against them, pulling at her thigh to spread her so he could fall between her legs. The roles were reversed, he thought, a tickle of amusement softening his furious lust. He had easy access beneath his kilt, but Regan was in trousers.

Never leaving her mouth, barely giving her time to breathe, wanting her to be overwhelmed by him, Thane fumbled for the zipper on her uniform trousers.

He'd barely touched it when she pressed her hands against his chest. At first, he thought she was holding on to him.

But then a definite shove filtered through the fog of desire, and he released her quickly, stumbling away.

His chest heaved as he panted. His lips were as swollen as

Regan's looked. Curling his hands into fists, Thane had to force himself to stay still, to not fall on her like a starving man again.

That became easier when he realized she was crying.

"*Mo leannan*," he whispered hoarsely, reaching for her.

"Don't!" Regan pushed away his arm and rushed past.

"Regan!"

She whirled, looking so young and so … lost.

His heart thumped painfully.

"Do you know?" Regan asked, half yelling, half crying. "Do you know what it's like to love someone this much and have them only want this one thing from you?"

No, she couldn't think that. He shook his head to explain, but she cut him off as she continued, "And I was going to let you. I was going to let you screw me just so you could turn around and abandon me, again. Am I right? If we had sex right now, it didn't mean you were giving us a real shot, did it?"

Shame flooded him, making his skin too hot, too tight.

She laughed bitterly. "I didn't think so."

"Regan—" He had to clear his throat; her name came out like he had gravel in there. "I just don't want you to have any regrets about me."

"Too late," she bit out, backing away toward the door. "Because I already regret you. I regret every kiss I ever gave you, every piece of my heart … because as precious as every kiss and every piece of me is … you threw them away like I was nothing. And I'm the idiot who listened to everyone who said I should stay and fight for what I want. To show you I'm not going anywhere. But it will never matter, will it? I'll never matter to you like you matter to me."

Everything within him roared in outrage at her words, but it was like a raging fire bottled by fear. Before he could wrestle it open, Regan turned on her heel and fled.

Her last words rang in his ears, over and over and over. Thane stumbled back, hitting a wall, and he slid down it until he felt the floor beneath him. Drawing up his knees, burying his head in his hands, Thane fought back his frustration.

Why couldn't he just let the past go?

Regan wasn't Fran.

She was loyal to a fault.

And she loved Eilidh and Lewis. She would never hurt them.

"I'll never matter to you like you matter to me. I'll never matter to you like you matter to me. I'll never matter to you like you matter to me."

"You don't know how wrong you are," Thane whispered hoarsely.

Get up, then. Get up and go after her.

He wasn't sure how long he sat there debating before he heard his name.

Lifting his head, Thane found Lachlan towering over him. His big brother lowered to his haunches, his kilt kicking out over his knees with the movement.

"What's going on?" Lachlan's brow creased with concern.

"I'm a coward."

Lachlan sighed.

"I'm a selfish arsehole. Eilidh and Lewis ask for her every day. Eils cries at night before bed, wondering where she is."

"And you?"

"I feel like I'm missing a limb."

Lachlan sighed. "Then what's stopping you? She's yours as soon as you give her the right words. I'm frankly confused by it," his brother teased. "She can do so much better than you."

"Fuck off," Thane snapped, not in the mood.

Lachlan grinned. "Problem is, she's crazy about *you*. Any dafty can see it. She was watching you like a hawk all night.

Roman Bright was trying to get into her pants, and she was so busy searching the room for you, she didn't have a clue. It only made him try harder." His lips pursed. "I'll need to have a word with him. Remind him of club rules."

Thane's gut churned, not just at the thought of Bright pursuing Regan but of what she'd witnessed with Angeline. "I hurt her tonight."

His brother's amusement fled. "I know. But you can make it up to her. Christ, I had to fly all the way to Boston to grovel on my knees to get Robyn back. All you have to do is get up, get in the car with Jock, and follow the GPS tracker on Regan's SUV."

"She left?" He frowned.

Lachlan nodded. "She drove past my guests like a bat out of hell. Robyn made me tell security to open the gate for her."

Scowling at the thought of Regan driving around in the pitch-black while emotionally distraught, Thane got to his feet and admitted something he didn't want to. "I'm ... I'm afraid that one day she'll wake up and regret settling for me. For us. Because Eilidh and Lewis and I are a package deal. She takes on me, she becomes a mum to two young kids."

His brother gave him an understanding look. "She knows that, Thane. The rest is up to you. The fear doesn't go away. Every day I fight back the fear of losing Robyn. Some days it doesn't even cross my mind ... but there are other days it does, and it isn't easy, but I fight it back because you were right: life with her is worth that battle.

"Your concerns about Regan leaving you will eventually go away. But it might take years. You just have to decide to trust her, to trust that she's worth the risk. So if you're waiting for certainty, for that knot of dread in your gut to melt away, you'll be waiting forever if you don't go to her. The only certainty you can trust is how you feel. And you wouldn't be in this much turmoil, brother, if you weren't in love with her."

Thane let Lachlan's words sink in, and they did with such profundity, he glowered at him. "Why the fuck didn't you say that to me a week ago?" He pushed Lachlan roughly on the shoulder. "I need a car. Now."

His brother's lips twitched. "You can't. You've been drinking. Jock will take you."

"Now!" Thane demanded, already marching out of the room.

37

REGAN

The image of that odious woman smashing her lips over Thane's wouldn't leave my mind! It had to be Angeline Potter, of all people! The woman had just ratted on me hours before and then put her sweaty little paws all over Thane.

How dare she!

How dare he!

I'd never experienced jealousy like it, watching that woman kiss the man I love, wearing his freaking kilt jacket just to make the image oh so cozy. The jealousy when Thane went on the date with that woman from his office building had been bad, but nothing compared to this. It consumed me. Because I knew it was the future I had to look forward to if I stayed in Ardnoch. One day he'd meet someone "more appropriate," and I'd have to watch them kiss and watch her be affectionate with Eilidh and Lewis too. Watch them be a family together.

Tears blinded me and I forced them back, concentrating on the pitch-black road as I drove. Without even thinking about it, I found myself in Caelmore turning down the driveway toward home.

Except it wasn't my home anymore.

"I shouldn't be here," I whispered as the headlights bounced across the driveway. Lachlan and Robyn's home was in darkness, except for the outdoor floodlight. The hallway light was on upstairs in Thane's. While most of the windows faced out toward the sea, he'd designed one long, narrow floor-to-ceiling window on the upstairs landing that looked out toward the fields and driveway. The light above the front door was also switched on.

I shouldn't be here.

I slowed the SUV to a stop beside Eredine's tiny electric Smart car. She was so tall, I wondered how she fit in the thing. The kids would be asleep. It was wrong of me to come, but I just ... I just had nowhere else to run.

It was ironic and not at all funny that the one place I ran to, to get away from Thane, was the one place he'd find me.

"You're hopeless," I muttered, pushing open the door.

As I climbed the steps to the front door, I half expected Eredine to come out at the sound of my car. When she didn't, I fumbled in my purse for the keys I still had and should probably give back. Letting myself in, I breathed in the house's scent, and longing pierced my chest.

It smelled a little spicy, like cinnamon, but beneath the scent wafting gently from the kitchen was that indecipherable smell that was all Adair. It was on the kids' clothes and buried beneath the citrusy aroma of Thane's shower wash. I'd come to think of that scent as home.

Squeezing my eyes shut against the pain of loss, I took a breath and then opened my eyes when I realized how quiet it was. There wasn't even the murmur of a television.

Eredine must have fallen asleep.

Walking into the living area, it was the dirty plates smashed on the floor by the island that got the blood rushing in my ears first.

"Eredine," I whispered. I moved around the broken pieces, my gaze shooting toward the sitting room, looking for—

A limp hand peeked from behind the sectional.

"Ery!" I yelled, hurrying behind the large sofa to find my friend collapsed on the floor. "Oh my God, Ery." I fell beside her, brushing her curls from her face and wincing at the sight of the blood trickling down her temple.

She'd been knocked out.

Terror consumed me.

"Eilidh! Lewis!" I jumped to my feet, slipping on some kind of sauce off the plates and catching my fall on the stairs. Righted, I launched myself up them faster than I'd ever moved in my life. "Eilidh! Lewis!" I screamed as I reached the landing.

But when I burst into Eilidh's room, the duvet was thrown off her bed, and her new dollhouse was on its side like there had been a struggle. A sob burst out of me as I wrenched open her closet. "Eilidh!" I cried, pushing through the racks of clothing, hoping she was hiding.

Nothing.

Panic made my breath come in sharp, painful bursts, and I choked on my tears as I rushed from Eilidh's room into Lewis's.

"He isn't here," I gasped, trying to draw breath, trying to think.

His closet was empty too.

"Lewis!" I shrieked.

"Regan!" The voice cut through the blood pounding in my ears.

"Lewis?"

I turned around, following the voice.

"Regan!"

It wasn't Lewis. It was Ery.

414

Hurrying back downstairs, I found Eredine leaning against the island, pale, trembling as she touched her fingers tentatively to her temple. Crossing the room, I grabbed her elbow to steady her. "What happened? Are you okay? Where are Eilidh and Lewis?"

Tears rushed to her eyes and spilled over in an instant. "They're not upstairs?"

Fear clawed at my lungs. I shook my head.

"I was just … I was in the kitchen cleaning up. The kids were in bed. He came out of nowhere and I tried to get away," she sobbed, shaking so hard, I thought she might break. "He smashed me over the head with something. I'm so sorry."

"Who would take them?" I tried to stay calm, to not hyperventilate. They needed me. "Who would—" Realization dawned. "McClintock. Oh my God."

Where was my cell? I'd left my cell! "Where's your phone? We need to call Thane and the police. It's McClintock."

Eredine pushed off the island, frowning as she looked over at the dining table. "My cell *was* right there." She pointed to the table. "That's what I was rushing over for when he hit me." Her eyes came back to me. "Regan." Her gaze flew behind me and widened with horror. "Regan—"

Pain ricocheted across the back of my skull seconds before darkness descended.

38

THANE

He watched numbly as paramedics loaded Eredine into an ambulance despite her protests she was fine. She wasn't fine.

He and Jock had come home to find the SUV Regan had been driving in his driveway. His relief was short-lived when he discovered Eredine knocked out on his living room floor and his children and Regan missing.

Eredine had come to and told them what happened. She'd been knocked out twice, so there were no arguments about her going to the hospital.

The shared driveway was a mass of activity. Lachlan's security. The police. His family.

Thane watched from a distance, his emotions locked down so tight he couldn't feel anything.

Because if he let himself, he'd lose his goddamn mind.

Sean McClintock had kidnapped his children and Regan.

"We should never have taken security off them." He heard Mac growl at Arrochar. She tried to soothe him, but Mac paced up and down the driveway like a caged animal. The police wanted his team out of it while they tracked down McClintock, and Mac had not taken kindly to the order.

Thane hadn't either.

Walking toward Mac, he caught his eye and gestured for him to follow him down the side of the house toward the annex.

According to their calculations, Regan and his children had been missing for forty-five minutes. Time was passing too quickly. His family was getting farther and farther away. He stopped near the annex and turned to face Mac.

Checking over his shoulder to make sure the detective inspector in charge wasn't nearby, Thane waited a second and then said, "Fuck what they want. I want you out there, using whatever contacts you have to find this bastard."

Mac's expression hardened, and he nodded sharply. "Done."

"When you find them"—because Thane had no doubt Mac could—"no police. I want at him first before we hand him over."

Retribution raged in Mac's eyes. "That I can do."

Thane nodded, trying to keep a lid on the seething rage he'd bottled. He'd actually felt gutted for Sean, was determined to speak to the procurator fiscal on his behalf when the attempted kidnapping case went ahead because Thane knew grief did bizarre things to people.

And the bastard had come for his family again!

He had to keep calm, keep calm, keep calm. He moved to leave, but Mac's head suddenly snapped back, and he held up a palm toward him.

Thane froze. "What is it?"

Mac cocked his head. "Did you hear that?" he whispered.

His pulse leapt. "Hear what?"

"Shh." Mac strode past him and placed his ear to the

annex door. Thane cautiously followed him and strained to hear.

A dull thud sounded from inside.

"Fuck!" He lunged toward the door, but Mac held him back. He shook his head at Thane and reached slowly behind his back to pull out a gun he'd tucked into the waistband of his kilt.

"Behind me," he murmured to Thane. He reluctantly fell back.

Mac twisted the door handle, and it opened.

Thane frowned. That should have been locked.

Stepping quietly through the small entrance, his eyes fighting to adjust to the darkness, Thane stayed at Mac's back even though he was desperate to push ahead. Then Mac suddenly halted with a hoarse "Jesus Christ." And then, "Thane, get the light."

"Lights on," he called, but the annex didn't light up. The smart device must have been disconnected.

A muffled squeal from within the main room caused a score of renewed fear through his heart, and he lunged for the light switch at the door. Mac was already striding into the room, and Thane moved with him.

Fury and relief were all Thane felt at finding Eilidh and Lewis each tied to a garden chair. Lewis's chair was on its side, his son on the floor. Tears streamed down his children's faces, and their yells of relief were muffled by the duct tape over their mouths.

"Jesus Christ," Mac repeated in controlled rage as he hurried to Eilidh, tucking his gun back into his kilt and out of sight under his dress jacket.

Thane fell to the floor behind Lewis, struggling to untie the tightly knotted ropes binding his wrists behind the chair. "Knife!" he yelled at Mac.

"One second." Mac pulled a Swiss Army knife out of his sporran and proceeded to saw at Eilidh's bindings.

"It's okay, Eilidh-Bug," Thane promised, holding her teary gaze. "I'm here now." He turned to Lewis, embracing him over the chair. "Dad's here, bud. I'm going to take off the duct tape, okay?"

His son nodded frantically.

"It might hurt a bit, but I'll be quick."

Lewis nodded again.

Swallowing hard against the angry tears in his throat, Thane grasped a corner of the tape and yanked it off in one fast flick.

His son cried out in pain and then promptly burst into tears.

"It's okay, bud," Thane murmured through his own tears as he peppered his son's cheeks with relieved kisses. "I've got you, you're safe."

He strained to look from the corner of his eyes as Thane tried to untangle the ropes again. Lewis hiccupped. "I heard you outside. Tipped my chair."

Pride seared through him. "Good, that was good, Lew. I'm so proud of you." The fear he'd been trying to keep at bay clawed at him. "Where's Regan, Lew? Was she with you?"

Lewis stilled from his struggles to get free. "She wasn't here. The bad man took us out of our beds. He threatened to hurt Eilidh if I didn't go with him. I didn't want him to hurt her, so I went," Lewis cried.

Fuck.

Thane squeezed his eyes closed, wondering how on earth his kids would get through this latest trauma.

"You did the right thing, Lew. I'm so proud of you for looking after your sister."

"Daddy!" Eilidh shrieked as Mac removed the duct tape. She sobbed and then pushed off the loosened ropes to fly across the room. Thane caught her in his arms, probably holding her too tight, but nothing was better than feeling her warm and alive. Even as her tears soaked his shirt.

"Shh, my darling," he hushed, rocking her as she sobbed and hiccupped in his arms. "I've got you."

He nodded gratefully to Mac as he moved out of the way to the let his friend free Lewis.

"Was it the man who tried to take Eilidh last time, Lew?" Mac asked as he worked at the ropes.

"No, Uncle Mac." Lew's answer winded Thane.

He met Mac's eyes.

If it wasn't McClintock ...

"Who the hell has Regan?" Mac uttered the question that made Thane light-headed with renewed terror.

39

REGAN

Waves crashed.
They were so loud.

As it pulled me out of sleep, I wondered why the sea sounded closer, louder than usual. Had I left a window open? My head throbbed painfully.

What the hell?

Groaning as the headache became overwhelming, I pushed my eyes open, blinking into the dark of my bedroom. Why did my pillow feel weird?

Wait.

What?

I sat up slowly, my hands sinking into brittle winter grass. The moon streamed across the sky and the sea beyond. Harsh, icy wind buffeted through my hair and seared through my uniform.

I was sitting on a cliff top.

"I thought you would never wake up. It would have ruined everything."

That voice.

Suddenly, my night came back in a flash. Eredine's attack. The children missing.

It was him.

What had he done with Eilidh and Lewis?

Fear and wrath coexisted within, distracting me from the headache and consequent nausea. The bastard had knocked me out. Was I concussed? I felt concussed.

But I couldn't think about that. I had to find Eilidh and Lewis.

Turning slowly to face the man belonging to the voice, I searched frantically around him, but there was no sign of the children on the cliff with us. The waves were choppy tonight, crashing dramatically into the rocks below.

Austin Vale stood bathed in moonlight, fields stretching behind him and hopefully toward Ardnoch. I didn't know how long I'd been out and thus how far he'd taken me from my home.

"Where are they?" I glowered at the son of a bitch. "What did you do with Eilidh and Lewis?"

Bitter wind ripped across the cliff, and I shivered violently.

Austin lowered to his haunches several feet away from me, wearing a thick sweater with a jacket over it. Bastard.

"Eilidh and Lewis?" I demanded.

"They're fine, beautiful," he replied just loud enough to be heard above nature.

"Where are they? Why did you touch them?"

Oh my God, I'd put them in danger. Tears sprung to my eyes and I trembled harder.

"You make it sound sordid. It's not," he sighed heavily. "When I got here, you weren't staying in the house anymore. You were supposed to be in the house. Instead, you were stuck behind the security gates of that estate, and you never left. I got impatient."

I'd only been behind the gates for forty-eight hours. Which meant he'd not long arrived in Scotland.

"When I saw them leave the children behind with just that waif of a woman, I took the children to lure you out. Plus, I knew taking them would hurt you. And I want to hurt you a little, even though I love you so much."

I ignored the words that repulsed me and concentrated on the kids. How did he know what Eilidh and Lewis meant to me? "How do you know anything about me?"

"You think the occasional tail from your sister's cop friend was enough to stop me from finding you?" he scoffed. "I'm a determined man, Regan. I couldn't just sit back and let you think I didn't care. When a man loves his woman, he has to show it. No one would tell me where you went, so all I could think to do was keep running an image search. Nothing. You were like a ghost. I was low on cash for a while, which is a problem when it comes to resources, but I came into some money a few weeks ago, thanks to my brother. I hired a PI, and she did some digging for me. Found out about your sister and her engagement to that actor. From there, she found you. So I hired another PI here in Scotland. He emailed over photos and information about your life here. He couldn't get too close to the house because you had security on the kids, but he did his digging elsewhere and got what we needed.

"Last I checked, you had security on the kids for that attempted kidnapping." He tsked. "It's a good thing I'm here to end this, Regan, to take you from these people. Bad things keep happening around them."

I huffed in disbelief.

"By some twist of fate, when I got here, the kids weren't protected anymore. Not that I *planned* on using them, I swear. But the idea just fell into my lap when I couldn't get to you." He laughed. "And it needed to be tonight, beautiful. It's our one-year anniversary."

Horror and shame and self-reproach filled me.

Why had I let my guard down?

Why hadn't I realized that New Year's Eve was a night to stay alert?

Probably because you thought Autry or Dad would tell you if Austin tried to leave the States.

Why hadn't they?

"I was going to take them and leave a note for you to find me, but suddenly you were in the house. Like it was fate. There you were. It was easier to just stash the kids somewhere it might take your *boss*," he spat the word, "time to find them."

"Where?" I demanded, my heart pounding. "I swear to God, if you hurt them, I will fucking kill you."

His teeth flashed in the dark. "I love it when you're feisty."

I loathed him.

I loathed him with every part of my being.

"Don't worry. I didn't hurt them. I tied the kids up in the guest house. Everyone will be so busy trying to find them while they're right under their noses that we'll have time to do what we came here to do."

Eilidh and Lewis were physically okay. Traumatized, but alive. I took a deep breath.

"And what did you come here to do?" I dreaded knowing, but I was determined, despite the almost debilitating, pulsing ache in my head, that I wouldn't go down without a fight.

Tears suddenly thickened Austin's throat. "Die," he whispered hoarsely. "Tonight we're going to die together."

My breath came in harsh pants as terror tried to seize control of me. "Why? Why?"

"We're meant to be together, Regan. But you're too hard-headed to see that. I can't spend my life chasing you, trying to convince you of something I already know!" His voice got louder with his agitation. "And if I can't make you see it, then the only way for us to be eternal is to die together. We'll be together forever in death."

Oh my God, he'd lost it completely. "Austin, you're not thinking straight—"

"Don't tell me what I'm thinking!" he yelled, standing up to pace.

I scooted back a little, careful not to retreat too close to the cliff's edge.

"Do you know what it's like to believe something, to know something deep in your soul, and have everyone else call you a fucking psycho for it?" he spat.

"Austin—"

"It's like you're already dead!" he continued. "I've been grieving you for a year, and no one understands! And I can't take it anymore. I can't live like this anymore."

Hearing the loss in his voice, I shivered harder. He really believed that. His pain was real, even if his delusions about us were not. Needing time to think, time for someone to find us, I stalled. "What about your family? You mentioned a brother."

He'd never mentioned his brother while we'd been backpacking together. In fact, he'd definitively told me he was an only child.

Austin scoffed. "Like he gives a shit about anything beyond his addictions. He's an alcoholic and a gambler. Won big, though, a few weeks back. I took the money. I'm not sorry. He's weak. He doesn't deserve good things."

"What about your parents?" During our trip, he'd told us all about growing up in Oregon. His dad was a cattle rancher and his mom a schoolteacher. Austin's childhood sounded idyllic.

He gave a bark of bitter laughter. "What parents? Are you

referring to the mother who took her six- and eight-year-old sons in hand, told them they were going on a trip, and then abandoned them at a bus station? Or the father I never met?"

"But ..." I trailed off. He'd lied about his life. About everything.

"No one wants to hear that shit, Regan," he said, as if he'd read my mind. "They just want you to tell them you had a good life. That you and your brother weren't abused by a sick fuck of a foster father."

Renewed tears sprung to my eyes. "I'm sorry."

"Don't be. It made me a better person. Smarter. Harder worker. More intuitive. I mean, women came and went. Always giving me mixed signals. Always untrustworthy and making me work for it. But you ... the first moment you smiled at me with those incredible dimples, it was like being hit with a ray of sunshine. And I could tell you were lost. A lost angel who needed guidance." His voice hardened. "But you're so damn stubborn and such a typical *woman*. You don't even know your own mind. You can't be trusted with your own feelings."

Any sympathy or compassion I'd felt died. "You know"—I pushed up onto my knees, the world spinning a little—"I'm getting a little sick of people saying that to me." I wobbled as I stood up straight, but I forced myself to focus past the dizziness. "I know my mind. My heart. And while I'm very sorry that your life has been difficult, other people have gone through similar shit, and they don't resort to rape and kidnapping."

"I never raped you!" he shouted.

"You tried!"

"That wasn't rape." Austin tore his hands through his hair. "God, how could you think that, this whole time?"

"Because it's true! You held me down and you tried to have sex with me against my will. That's attempted rape,

Austin. Never mind the fact you continued to threaten to rape me in your emails."

"No, no, no." He started pacing frantically. "No, you're mixed up. You're remembering things wrong."

As he continued to rant, I glanced over my shoulder, and my head spun dangerously as I saw how high up we were.

Turning back to him as he paced and disagreed about what occurred between us last January, I knew there was no arguing with him. He saw things his way, and there was no showing him differently.

Austin stopped rambling and looked over at me, his expression feral in the moonlight. "I'll just have to show you. Remind you that for us, sex is about making love. Yeah." He strode toward me. "We should have that from each other before we go."

"No." I stumbled sideways and then tried to dart past him. We grappled, me pushing at his face, clawing at his neck, trying to escape. Yet he was so much stronger than I was, and I was so dizzy from the blow to my head.

Robyn's voice roared in my mind, instructing me, demanding I not let him get me on the ground, but my limbs wouldn't obey.

My foot slipped, hitting nothing but air, and I cried out in fright.

"Careful!" Austin gripped me to him. "We don't want you going over the edge just yet."

Suddenly, I knew why he'd brought me here.

He intended to send me over the edge with him tonight.

And I was not dying in the North Sea.

Tears of fury and desperation streaked my cheeks as he hauled me into his arms so tightly, I could barely breathe.

"God, I've missed you." Austin buried his face in my neck.

Every inch of me was repulsed by his hold.

"Please," I whispered, "don't do this to me."

He lifted his head to stare down into my eyes, and I saw nothing but belief in his.

I had no idea someone's faith could be so terrifying.

"This is how it's meant to be. You'll see that soon." He curled his foot around mine and I fell.

My back slammed into the ground, my head wound screaming with the impact.

And then Robyn's commanding voice was in my head again, reciting instructions as Austin fell to his knees and tried to grab at my hands.

Focusing on Robyn's voice, I forced my left knee into his gut to stop him from coming down on top of me as I wrapped my hand around his right wrist. Then I pulled back my right leg and planted my foot hard on his hip ... and I ripped at his hold on my arm and shoved him away from me with all my might, using the strength in my legs. He toppled backward as I rolled out from under him and scrambled to my feet. Eyes darting to him, I froze in shock as his arms windmilled at his sides.

And then he was falling out of sight.

His scream wrenched through the night air, chilling me to the bone.

Finally, I heard him crash into the waves below, just as they pounded against the rocks.

Nausea crawled up my belly as I tentatively walked over to the cliff's edge.

There was nothing but white froth in darkness under the moonlight.

No sign of Austin.

Shaking so hard my teeth rattled in my head, I stumbled back from the edge and sobbed. A sense of unreality descended over me.

Focus, Ree, I heard Robyn whisper. *Come back home.*

"Eilidh, Lewis," I murmured into the night. No one knew where they were. *They must be scared out of their minds.*

Rushing forward, pushing through what I was sure *was* a concussion, I ran from the edge and into fields sparse with winter grass. I had no idea where I was, how far from Ardnoch he'd taken us.

But as I followed the coast, I saw lights in the distance. Hurrying toward them, it took about ten minutes before a sense of overwhelming familiarity rushed over me.

I was near Gordon's trailer park at Ardnoch Beach.

Loud music thrummed from the park, and I could see shadowy figures outside the trailers, partying together.

Of course. It was still Hogmanay.

"Help!" I yelled hoarsely, running harder now. "Help!" The fields eventually gave way to a path carved by people trekking up onto the cliffs. The path sloped down toward the trailer park, and I stumbled on a large pebble, going over on my ankle. The jarring thud of hitting the ground on my hands and knees made black dots cover my eyes.

"No!" I shoved myself back onto my feet. I had to stay awake. I had to tell someone where Eilidh and Lewis were.

Rushing down onto the gravel, I saw two people sitting on the deck of their trailer watching everyone else dancing and drinking on the road that cut through the park.

"Help!" I yelled, trying to be heard over the music.

But I had to run right up to their deck before the older couple turned to me in surprise. I didn't know what I looked like, but the man broke out in a curse at the sight of me.

"Please, help!"

"What on earth?" the woman cried out, and they hurried down their deck steps to catch me as I swayed.

Focus, Regan, focus.

It all came out in a rush, and I got agitated as they made me repeat it. We drew attention from other people, and I was aware of the music fading out. Police were called, but I rambled off Thane's number, insisting they call him to tell him where Eilidh and Lewis were.

"The children are fine," the woman, Betty, said sometime later when I repeated the demand. "They've already found them. Your friend is on his way."

The news that Eilidh and Lewis were safe made me sob with relief. It was only when Betty said, "Your friend is here," that I became cognizant of the fact that I was inside their trailer with a blanket around me.

I didn't realize how much time had passed.

"Where is she?" I heard Thane demand loudly outside. He sounded frantic.

Launching myself off the trailer's couch, I pushed hands away that tried to stop me and hurried outside. Thane and Robyn stood by his SUV, glaring at two of the partygoers.

"Thane."

His head snapped toward me. Our eyes caught, his blazing with everything.

It took him less than two seconds to cross the distance between us and haul me into his arms. The feel of him, his scent, all of it overwhelmed me, and I melted like an ice cube by the fire.

"*Mo leannan.*" I felt his lips on my temple.

I smiled just as the black dots scattered across my vision.

"Regan?" Thane's voice turned sharp with concern. "Regan!"

I couldn't answer.

It was like the whole damn world switched off the lights.

40

THANE

Eilidh snuggled sleepily on his lap while Lewis slept beside Regan on the hospital bed. The nurse had not been amused when she'd discovered Lewis asleep on the bed, but Lachlan had made it clear no one was moving his nephew.

Thane had never been more thankful for his brother's imperiousness.

Robyn was curled up on the armchair opposite Thane's.

When Regan had collapsed in his arms, Thane almost had heart failure. However, to his everlasting relief, she'd gained consciousness only a minute later. She'd fainted from the shock of her ordeal.

Still, the doctors were concerned because Austin Vale had taken Lewis's baseball bat to the back of her head before dragging her out to that cliff. The same bat he'd hit Eredine with twice.

If the bastard weren't already fish food, Thane would have killed him.

Regan was being kept overnight for observation, as was Eredine. They'd both been warned they would mostly likely struggle with headaches for the next week or two. All that mattered, however, was there was no sign of brain injury. Miraculously, neither seemed to have issues with memory loss.

Arro was asleep in Ery's room.

Thane refused to leave his children or Regan, and the kids didn't want to be far from either of them. So they'd spent the rest of Hogmanay in the busy hospital in Inverness. Uncomfortable, but together.

He gazed through wearied vision at Lewis sleeping next to Regan, his small hand clasped in hers. Thane's chest ached.

The attack traumatized his children. He'd have to talk with someone. See if he should get Eilidh and Lewis counseling. This was something that could affect them for the rest of their lives, and Thane refused to allow that to happen.

Lewis's hand twitched in Regan's, and he pushed deeper into her side in his sleep. Thane's eyes drifted from his son to the woman he loved.

He'd almost lost her tonight.

But she was fierce. Determined to live.

Thank God for Robyn and those self-defense lessons.

The hospital door opened, and Lachlan gestured to him. Holding Eilidh close so as not to wake her, he stood slowly and made his way out of the room.

"News?" Thane whispered.

Lachlan reached out to stroke Eilidh's hair as he replied quietly, "Seth is distraught, as you can imagine. They didn't have the manpower or authority to keep someone on Austin at all times back in Boston. The last they saw him, he went into a property three days ago belonging to his brother. No one tailed him to the airport. Seth had an alert on his credit card, but he didn't use it to pay for a ticket. He didn't use any of his brother's credit cards either, so we assume he used cash."

"Regan mentioned a PI?"

Lachlan nodded. "Mac's still looking into that."

"Have they found Vale?"

His brother shook his head. "Search and rescue are still out looking."

Eilidh shifted in his arms, and he cuddled her closer. "When can Regan and Ery leave?"

"Not until later today," Lachlan sighed. "I know you want the kids with you, but we should really get them home."

"I don't want to leave them, which means leaving Regan." Neither thought appealed to him.

"Let me and Robyn take the kids," his brother offered. "You stay here with Regan."

"I can't."

"They'll be fine for a few hours with us," Lachlan insisted. "And you and Regan need some time alone to talk when she wakes up."

Thane's gut knotted. "I doubt she'll want to hear it."

"Brother." Lachlan leaned into him. "Before that bastard showed up ... Regan ran to the one place you'd find her."

It was true. Before they'd walked into the house and his world crashed down, he'd been beyond relieved to see Regan's borrowed SUV in his driveway.

"Eils and Lew need to eat. If they don't want to go to bed without you in the house, Robyn and I will camp out on the couch and watch movies with them until you return home."

Knowing Eilidh and Lewis would be content enough with that, Thane finally nodded. "Thanks."

Lachlan clamped him on the shoulder and gave him a comforting squeeze. "I'll go wake Robyn so you can tell her sister that you're in love with her."

Thane's lips trembled with tired laughter. "It's been a strange bloody twenty-four hours."

"It's been a strange bloody year," Lachlan countered before disappearing into Regan's hospital room.

REGAN

The beeping woke me up.

As the hospital room came into focus, so did the memories of the previous night.

And the last thing I remembered was Lewis falling asleep on the hospital bed beside me.

Where was he?

Panicked, I patted the space at my side.

"Hey, hey." A large, masculine hand took hold of mine. I followed it up a familiar arm clad in a white shirt. Still in his waistcoat and kilt, Thane sat by my bedside.

"Where are the children?" I croaked.

My tongue was like sandpaper, my mouth and throat dry as a desert.

Thane released my hand but only to get up to grab the cup of water from the small side table. Sliding an arm behind my back to help me sit up, he handed me the cup.

I drank thirstily, my eyes holding his. When I was done, I repeated, "Where are they?"

"At home," he said in that deep, reassuring voice of his. "Robyn and Lachlan are watching over them."

I waited as Thane took his seat again. "You stayed."

Something like despair flashed in his soulful eyes. "I don't think I can let you out of my sight for a while. As it was, Lachlan had to persuade me that letting the kids go home was best for them."

"You should have gone with them." I felt awful he'd had to choose. "I would have understood."

"We need to talk," he said bluntly.

Oh, no. Here it came.

The blame. The shame.

"I know!" I blurted out before he could continue. "I promised you my problems wouldn't bring trouble, and I got Eilidh and Lewis hurt. I'm so sorry, Thane. I can't ever make it up—"

"Hey, hey, hey." Thane moved to the bed, pulling me into his side, cuddling me close. "No, don't say that. Oh, *mo leannan*, you're breaking my fucking heart. Please don't blame yourself. This isn't your fault."

I sobbed at his kindness, because of course, it was my fault, and of course, he wouldn't see it that way. "I didn't see it ... I didn't see the dark in him, and I let him into my life and if I hadn't forced myself into your life—"

"I would be the same man I was a year ago," he cut me off, "existing for Eilidh and Lewis. Not unhappy, but not excited about life beyond them. I love my kids. I'm content to live for them. But I never imagined I'd wake up each morning feeling this much anticipation for what the day would bring. All because I have a woman I look forward to seeing every day, to talking with, to laughing with, to loving."

I pulled away from him just enough to look into his eyes.

My breath caught at what I saw shining in them.

"I found Eredine and the children so quickly last night because I was chasing after you."

"You were?"

Thane nodded, his eyes searching my face as if memorizing me. I didn't care that I probably looked like hell. He was looking at me like I was the most beautiful woman he'd ever seen.

"I never thought I'd be the kind of man to have insecurities," he said ruefully. "The Adair men are a cocky bunch."

I grinned at that.

He reached up to trace my smile with his thumb as his tone grew serious. "Fran's betrayal came out of nowhere. I couldn't have imagined that she would cheat on me. It shook me. It shook everything I believed in … Yet I also never thought it would stop me from moving on. While I hadn't searched for anything serious with someone new, I wasn't averse to it happening if the right person came along. I thought she'd be around my age, maybe have kids of her own, be settled in life."

He caressed my cheek, a dark hunger in his expression. "Then you showed up. I knew from your first day on the job, that morning in the kitchen, when I caught you looking at me and I teased you about my hands … I knew you were dangerous to me. Young, vibrant, beautiful, my brother's almost sister-in-law, with a bit of a reputation that I didn't know at the time wasn't earned."

My heart pounded so hard, it was a wonder he didn't feel it banging against him.

"But it was the way you were with Eilidh and Lewis that made me realize I was falling for you. The attraction got harder to ignore … and that first night I made to love you … I knew it then."

"Knew what?" I dared to ask.

"That I'm so in love with you, it scares me."

My breath caught as tears stung my nose.

He gave me that rueful smile again. "If it had just been about physical attraction, I could have controlled it, ignored it, never touched you, knowing how complicated the situation was. But I couldn't stay away from you."

"Me neither."

"And when you protected Eilidh … I was so far gone for

you. I kept telling myself to enjoy what I could, to remember you weren't staying here permanently."

"You didn't trust me," I whispered, the pain of his faithlessness still fresh.

"No ... I just couldn't get past my own damn insecurities." He turned into me, clasping my face in his hands. "Regan, to me, you are the most beautiful woman I've ever known. Inside and out. Sweet and hilarious and kind and smart. Sexy and uninhibited and loving. You could have anyone, go anywhere, do anything you put your mind to. You're extraordinary. I didn't trust in myself. I didn't trust that *I* was enough for *you*. That me and the children and Ardnoch are enough for you. I thought we were too ordinary."

His confession killed me. I wrapped my hands around his wrists. "Ordinary? You couldn't be ordinary if you tried. Don't you know you're everything to me? Only you can make my stomach flutter with just a smile. Only you can make my world perfect just by holding me in your arms. Only you can get me hot with just that look in your eye."

He grinned wickedly.

"Only you make me feel good about myself, make me feel wanted and at home in my own skin. When we're all together, you, me, and Eilidh and Lewis, it feels so right, it almost hurts with how wonderful it is."

He nodded, brushing my tears with his thumbs.

I tightened my grip on his wrists as I licked the salty tears off my lip. "I know with a certainty I've never had about anything before that I want to spend the rest of my life with you. I don't care if that scares you. I need to be honest and up-front, especially after last night, because life is too damn short, Thane. This isn't 'let's see how it goes and cool if it works out or cool if it doesn't.' I am madly, desperately, deeply in love with you, and I never want to be without you again," I sobbed.

He swallowed the cry with a hungry kiss that stole my breath. When he finally released me, it was to pepper kisses over my cheeks, his beard a familiar, delicious tickle across my skin. "I love you, I love you, I love you," he repeated between kisses. My heart felt like it might explode in my chest. "You're never leaving us again." He scattered kisses down my throat and continued to murmur, "I want you back in the house. My bed is your bed, living together out in the open. No more sneaking around. This is us."

He paused to look me deep in the eye. "You're my woman and I'm your man, and fuck what anyone else has to say about it."

I reached for him, pulling him back to my mouth, wanting to seal his promise with a kiss.

"Ahem!"

We broke apart, turning in each other's arms to find a nurse standing in the doorway. She gave Thane an amused but irritated look. "Do you mind detaching yourself from the patient while I check her over?"

Thane grinned before turning that boyish smile on me.

My belly fluttered.

"I just promised her I'm never letting her go," he said gruffly, "so I guess you'll have to do your checks with me right where I am. I'm not going anywhere."

41

THANE

T he sound of Lewis's light snoring woke him up.

Blinking his eyes open, he waited for them to adjust to the darkness so he could take in the sight before him.

A pain in his neck made itself known, but Thane didn't dare move. He was in an awkward half-sitting, half-reclined position against his headboard. Lewis was curled into him, his small head on Thane's chest, his little arm wrapped around Thane's waist. Thane's left arm rested down his son's warm back, while his free hand clasped the book they'd been reading.

His gaze drifted past his son to his daughter, her back pressed up against her brother's, but she snuggled into Regan, who held her close even in sleep.

A week had passed since Austin Vale's attack on Ery and the kids and his attempted rape and murder of Regan.

Sometimes, just saying the words in his head made Thane dizzy. It was surreal. Their family had been through so much in the past year.

439

SAMANTHA YOUNG

But they were here, with him in his bed, safe.

Regan still wasn't a hundred percent from her concussion, and Eilidh and Lewis didn't want to be far from her side since they'd seen her in that hospital bed. Her trauma seemed to have distracted them from their own, which told him just how much his children loved her.

Still, he'd spoken with a colleague at work whose wife was a child psychologist, and she'd suggested some family trauma counseling for them all. Their first appointment was next week.

They had to get Eils and Lew back into a routine, back into their own beds. As it was, Eilidh didn't even want to be in her own room. Thane considered redecorating the guest room and turning that into her bedroom, but he wanted to speak with the counselor first to discuss the best plan of action.

For now, they all slept together so Thane or Regan (or both) could be right there when either of the children woke from a nightmare. Tonight was the first night neither of them had one. That was progress.

It helped for them to know the monster who'd taken and tied them up was dead. Austin's body washed ashore a mile from Ardnoch Beach.

The danger to Thane's family was over.

Eredine was on the mend, though Lachlan and Robyn were done giving her space, worried that this latest assault would push her further away. She was ensconced in their guest room with no intention of letting her out of their sight until they were sure she was going to be okay.

Seth and Stacey wanted to fly over, but Regan videocalled to assure them she was all right and it wasn't worth the expense. Thane gathered they were hurt by this, but he couldn't help but be selfishly relieved they weren't returning to Scotland. Stacey was unpredictable, and he didn't like the way she treated Regan or twisted what was between them. They didn't need that kind of judgment in their lives right now.

Though, at some point, for Regan and Robyn's sake, bridges would have to be mended there.

"You're awake," Regan whispered, startling him.

"How did you know?"

"You sighed like the world was sitting on your shoulders." She reached out with her free arm, her palm resting upward on the pillow beside him. Thane took her hand in his, rubbing his thumb over her soft skin.

"I just want everyone to be okay," he whispered.

"We will be," she promised. "We'll all get through this together. Robyn's taking Eilidh shopping for her flower-girl dress tomorrow, so that will be a pleasant distraction."

"She'll love that."

"Maybe you and Lewis could do something with Lachlan, Mac, and Brodan?"

To Thane's shock and gratitude, Brodan had brought filming on his movie to a standstill to come home to check on them all. Unfortunately, he couldn't stay long, but they still had tomorrow with him. They'd kept the kids off school but tomorrow was Sunday, and they'd return on Monday. Back to their routine. "Maybe we should all do something together."

"We'll have dinner together at night," she reassured him. "We need to start doing things separately. Show them it's okay."

He knew she was right. And he loved how much she loved Eilidh and Lewis. "I adore you, Regan Demelza Penhaligon."

He could see her smile flash in the darkness. "I adore you, too, Thane Tavin Stuart Adair."

"Stop being mushy," Lewis yawned, "and go back to sleep."

Thane choked back a laugh as Regan snorted.

Yeah, they were going to be okay.

SAMANTHA YOUNG

EPILOGUE

REGAN

My back ached from sitting at the computer for the past two hours. But my essay was finished. Thank God.

Switching off the screen, I scooted out of the office chair that had now become mine as much as Thane's. Studying for a business degree while taking care of the kids wasn't easy, but I was determined to do it. Once I had my degree, I planned to apply for a business loan to open my own preschool. There was only one in Ardnoch, and after much investigation, I discovered it was a depressing little place where kids were monitored and kept safe but they weren't engaged or stimulated.

Preschool should be about fun. I was good with fun.

The Adairs owned a small plot of land in Caelmore that they were happy for me to build my preschool on—designed by Thane, of course. I was incredibly moved by Thane and his siblings' support, but I didn't want to launch myself into the venture through nepotism. I wanted to understand fully how to run a business. Hence the business degree.

Switching off the lights, I turned on the security and tiptoed upstairs to my family. Thane had gone to sleep not long after we put Eilidh and Lewis to bed, bemoaning my ability to function on five or six hours' sleep a night. I grinned, remembering his kiss on my neck and his warm, growly voice telling me not to work too hard.

Stopping at Eilidh's bedroom, I peeked inside to find her sprawled across her bed like usual. What a difference a couple years could make. With some counseling, the loving support of family, and the joy of me and their father being together, the trauma Austin left them with had mended. I worried it would come back to haunt them in later years, but all we could do was keep talking things through if we noticed them brooding. They hadn't brooded in a long time, though.

Smiling, I walked to Lewis's room and opened the door just a smidge. He laid with the covers kicked off, although it was winter. I moved to leave when I heard him whisper sleepily, "Mum?"

My heart wrenched in my chest as it always did when one of them called me that. Not even a few months after Thane and I became official, Eilidh started calling me *mum*. It was easier for her because she had no memories of Fran, only stories.

I'd thought I would always be Ree-Ree to Lewis, but he'd asked me on the day of my wedding to Thane if he could start calling me *mum* too.

It had filled me with so much joy, but later also a lot of guilt. I hadn't wanted Fran to feel like I was replacing her. Thane assured me I wasn't. We visited her grave together. The photos of her remained on the wall. Although not long after I'd moved in, Thane had replaced their wedding photo with one of me at Dunrobin Castle with the kids. When I saw that, I switched the photos back. Thane asked me why when he discovered what I'd done.

"Because Fran was a huge part of your life. You wouldn't be who you are today without her. The kids wouldn't be here. Your wedding photo deserves to stay on the wall, and it diminishes nothing between you and me."

Thane had never looked at me so tenderly. Well, until *our* wedding day.

Now our wedding photo hung on the wall too. The gallery had grown in the last few years.

"Sorry, sweetheart, I didn't mean to wake you," I whispered back.

Lewis grumbled something in his sleep and flipped onto his back, his light snores immediately filling his room. I doubt he'd even been awake when he'd called out to me.

Leaving them to sleep, I slipped into mine and Thane's bedroom, catching sight of him asleep on his side of the bed. Tiptoeing into the bathroom to change into my nightdress, I tried to be as quiet as possible.

Once in bed, I switched on my e-reader, the screen illuminating my face but not bright enough to wake my husband. I had to read before bed, especially after working. I needed business jargon and analysis out of my mind so I could relax enough to fall asleep.

Snuggling into my pillows, I delved into the latest historical romance from my favorite author. It wasn't long, however, before I hit a passionate scene that sparked the familiar, hot tingles between my legs. My breasts swelled against my nightdress and I squirmed a little, shooting Thane a look.

I'd been so busy these past few weeks, we hadn't had time for sex. I shouldn't wake him.

Then again … I doubt he'd complain.

Switching off my e-reader, I placed it on the nightstand and then slid across to push the duvet off my husband. He shifted, feeling the sudden breeze in his sleep. Smirking, my belly fluttering with anticipation, I climbed over him, straddling him. My lips found his in the darkness, his beard tickling my chin as I kissed him in his sleep.

He groaned but still didn't wake, so I lowered my weight onto his lap and undulated against him as I trailed kisses down his throat and stroked his stomach beneath his T-shirt.

Seconds later, I felt him harden and rise beneath me.

"Wha …" His eyes flew open in the dark, and I kissed him again. Harder. With a groan of realization, Thane's arm came around my back, and he returned my kiss.

Suddenly, I was flipped onto my back as he thrust between my thighs and kissed me like a starving man. When he finally let me up for air, he reached beneath my nightdress and pushed his fingers into my slick heat.

"Fuck," he muttered, his eyes flashing in the dark. "Hot book?" he guessed.

I grinned up at him. "Extremely."

"Thank Christ for romance novels. Remind me to buy you nothing but that for your birthday."

His kiss swallowed my laughter, his hands caressing and sculpting my body through the nightdress. When his mouth left mine to trail over my breasts, I stifled my moan. His lips closed around my nipple through the silk and he sucked, hard.

Fingers tightening in his hair, I rocked against him, needing him everywhere, over me, inside me, mouth, hands … Pushing his pajama pants down, I freed him, taking him tightly in my fist.

"Fuck." He pressed his forehead into my chest and thrust into my hand.

"Inside me," I whispered. "Inside, inside."

Thane chuckled as he tugged my underwear down. "Someone's impatient tonight. No foreplay, *mo leannan*?"

I shook my head as I ripped at his T-shirt.

His laughter was muffled behind his shirt as it got caught halfway off. With a tug and delicious flex of his biceps, it came off over his head and he threw it away. "What's gotten into you?"

"We haven't had sex in two weeks."

His lips twitched. "And that's a long time, is it?"

I frowned at him. "Yes."

"You might have a problem," he teased, and then made his rumbly, gruff sound of pleasure as he pushed inside me.

Stifling my cry of delight, I arched into him, loving his overwhelming thickness inside me. Clasping onto his face as he gently moved in me, I whispered back, "I do have a problem. I'm addicted to you. Shouldn't I be bored already?" I complained in jest. "Instead of wanting you more every day?"

Thane gave a sudden hard thrust into me, and I cried out.

"Shh," he admonished.

"I can't help it," I gasped, holding on to his back as he drove faster, harder.

"I'm taking an extended lunch tomorrow," Thane's chest rose and fell hard and fast as he grabbed hold of my wrists and pinned them above my head, "and coming home to fuck you so you can be as loud as you please."

He liked me loud.

I panted sharply as the tension spiraled tighter and tighter inside of me. I held back "the loud" so the kids wouldn't hear.

"What will you do to me?"

Thane's expression hardened with lust. "I'm going to spread you out on the kitchen table and eat my wife for lunch."

I bit my lip against a cry as he pushed me closer to the edge.

"Or maybe I'll have you wait in the annex, naked, and you can play naughty nanny for me." He grinned wickedly and then drove harder as the fantasy clearly got to him.

The sexy thought of playing out the early days of our affair coincided with one last push against the tension, and I clamped my lips tight and muffled my moan of release.

Thane kissed me as my hard, pulsing tugs of climax wrenched him, and he came with a groan, throbbing deliciously inside me. He released my wrists, and I wrapped my arms around him, not wanting him to pull out just yet. I kissed him, lazy, satisfied, wet kisses, and caressed his back, loving the feel of his skin, damp with perspiration.

He kissed along my jaw and nibbled at my ear.

"Tomorrow we play naughty nanny so I can scream that freaking annex down," I whispered.

"I'm looking forward to that." He peppered kisses down my throat.

"You must be exhausted. I wish I could say I was sorry I woke you."

He kissed my shoulder. "Wake me anytime for that."

"And if I just need you to make me oatmeal because no one makes oatmeal as good as you?" I half teased. His oatmeal was not like ordinary oatmeal. For a start, his was delicious.

"One: no, don't wake me for that unless you plan on thanking me with sexual favors," he cracked. "And two: you've lived in Scotland long enough, *mo leannan*. It's called porridge."

"If I keep speaking in Americanisms, will you spank me when we play naughty nanny?"

Thane threw his head back in a bark of laughter.

I hushed him and he shook his head, grinning. Then he

saw something in my eyes and raised an eyebrow. Squeezing me closer, he murmured against my lips, "Just when I think I have you figured out, you surprise me."

"Is that a good thing?"

"Oh, aye, *mo leannan*. You're the gift that keeps on giving."

My laughter filled our bedroom, and my husband had to quiet me with a kiss. As he lingered over my lips, tender, loving, I finally felt drowsy with sleep. "Up, before you fall asleep." Thane pulled me from the bed and helped me clean up in the bathroom.

When we returned to bed, he pulled my back into his chest and held me in his arms. "Happy here?" Thane asked gruffly.

It had become a ritual.

He'd ask me that two-word question.

I'd answer the same thing every time. And mean it from the tip of my toes to the depths of my soul.

"I'm happy wherever I am, as long as I'm there with you."

COMING SOON

ALWAYS YOU
AN ADAIR FAMILY NOVEL

OUT APRIL 28TH 2022

Arrochar Adair has loved her brother's ex-bodyguard and best friend, Mac Galbraith, for years. Once upon a time, she was too young for him, but now that she's a mature woman in her thirties, Arro can see no issue with their difference in age. But Mac is too loyal to her brother, Lachlan, to ever jeopardize their friendship by pursuing Arrochar despite his feelings for her.

For years Mac has found new and frustrating ways to keep Arro at a distance and finally he makes a decision that pushes her away for good.

Only problem is, just when everything seems to have settled down in Ardnoch, the Adair family face a new threat.

Mac will do anything to protect them. To protect her.

But with so much hurt between them will Arro let Mac close enough to let him ... before it's too late?

Official book description and cover coming soon!